Thomas Longueville

The Life of Sir Kenelm Digby

Thomas Longueville

The Life of Sir Kenelm Digby

ISBN/EAN: 9783743333451

Manufactured in Europe, USA, Canada, Australia, Japa

Cover: Foto ©Raphael Reischuk / pixelio.de

Manufactured and distributed by brebook publishing software
(www.brebook.com)

Thomas Longueville

The Life of Sir Kenelm Digby

Portrait of Sir Kenelm Digby.
by Vandyck.
From the Royal Collection at Windsor Castle.
By permission of Her Majesty the Queen.

THE LIFE OF

SIR KENELM DIGBY

BY ONE OF HIS DESCENDANTS

AUTHOR OF

"THE LIFE OF A CONSPIRATOR," "A LIFE OF ARCHBISHOP LAUD,"
"THE LIFE OF A PRIG," ETC., ETC.

WITH ILLUSTRATIONS

LONGMANS, GREEN, AND CO.

LONDON, NEW YORK, AND BOMBAY

1896

"He doth excel
In honour, courtesy, and all the parts
Court can call hers, or man could call his arts
He's prudent, valiant, just and temperate :
In him all virtue is beheld in state ;
And he is built like some imperial room
For that to dwell in, and be still at home.
His breast is a brave palace, a broad street,
Where all heroic ample thoughts do meet :
Where nature such a large survey hath ta'en,
As other souls to his, dwelt in a lane."

From *An Epigram to my muse, the Lady
Digby, on her husband, Sir Kenelm Digby.*
By Ben Jonson. Gifford's *Works of Ben
Jonson*, ed. by Col. Cunningham, 1875,
vol. ix., pp. 33, 34.

PREFACE.

LET me beg my readers to understand, at starting, that my own pretence in this book is very small. Having consulted and studied many volumes and documents in an endeavour to learn something of the life of a very distinct personage—Sir Kenelm Digby—I culled from them the matter which appeared to me the most interesting, and employed it in the making of a book, with intent to convey to others some idea of his character and career; but I neither read nor wrote about Sir Kenelm Digby with the object of bookmaking. I admit that, in dealing with the evidence relating to his proceedings, I have found it necessary to make a few deliberate omissions, and I can only hope that I may not have inadvertently fallen into the opposite extreme of sins of commission.

It is a curious fact that, even in these days of Lives and Memoirs, no thoroughly satisfactory Life of Sir Kenelm Digby should be in existence.

Of the shortcomings of my own I am but too conscious; and let me, in the words of Pope, make this earnest appeal to my critics and reviewers:—

The piece you think is incorrect : why, take it ;
I'm all submission; what you'd have it, make it.

For if a failure on my part should induce some able writer, languishing for want of a subject, to produce a really brilliant biography of Sir Kenelm Digby, my labours will not have been in vain.

T. L.

CONTENTS.

CHAPTER I.

An infant flirtation—Youth of Kenelm Digby—Family of Digby—Effects of Sir Everard's death on his son—Litigation about Gothurst—Venetia Anastasia Stanley—Ben Jonson's " Dedication of her Cradle " —Aubrey's description of her—Ben Jonson's—Her ancestry—Thomas, Earl of Northumberland—Wordsworth's " White Doe "—Venetia and her father—Was Kenelm Digby educated as a Protestant?—Act against recusants—Kenelm Digby under Laud—Kenelm Digby goes to Spain—He goes to Oxford—When did he become an Anglican?

CHAPTER II.

A Gentleman-Commoner at Gloucester Hall—His description of himself— Under Thomas Allen—The Mirandula of his age—Did Allen sell or bequeath his library to Digby?—Guarini—Venetia Stanley—Marriage of Princess Elizabeth—Venetia at a ball—Euphuism—Venetia's dancing—Her " Ancient Gentlewoman ".

CHAPTER III.

Venetia determines to communicate with Kenelm—Faustina offers to help—A rendezvous appointed—A coach and four—Attack on the coach—Kidnapped—A prisoner—The " deserving gentleman "— Supper—A walk in the garden—Escape—Attack by a wolf— Rescued by Sir Edward Sackville—Taken to the home of Lady Artesia—Matchmaking for Kenelm Digby—Kenelm Digby "backward ".

CHAPTER IV.

Kenelm Digby leaves Oxford—His portrait by Vandyck—His visit to Lady Artesia's—Acrostic on Venetia—A stratagem—A stag hunt—Flirtation in a thicket—Return of the truants—Kenelm to go abroad—Farewell tokens—Kenelm Digby goes to Paris—He goes to Angers—State of affairs in France.

CHAPTER XIII.

CHAPTER XIV.

CHAPTER XV.

CHAPTER XVI.

CHAPTER XXV.

CHAPTER XXVI.

CHAPTER XXVII.

CHAPTER XXVIII.

LIST OF ILLUSTRATIONS.

THE LIFE OF SIR KENELM DIGBY.

CHAPTER I.

YOUTH.

THE little love-makings of infant playmates, pretty and amusing as they may appear to their elders, are rarely long-lived, and even more rarely lead to any serious consequences. But there are exceptions.

Some time near the end of the first decade of the seventeenth century a boy and girl were frequently at play together. One of them in later years thus described their childish meetings : * "The very first time that ever they had sight of one another," they "grew so fond of each other's company that all that saw them said assuredly that something above their tender capacity breathed this sweet affection into their hearts. They would mingle serious kisses among their innocent sports : and whereas other children of like age did delight in fond plays and light toys these two would spend the day in looking upon each other's face, and in accompanying these looks with gentle sighs, which seemed to portend that much sorrow was laid up for their more understanding years ; and if at any time they happened to use such recreations as were sortable to their age, they demeaned themselves therein so prettily

---

* *Private Memoirs of Sir Kenelm Digby*, Written by Himself, p. 16. A life of Sir Kenelm Digby must almost necessarily be based upon this work, the original of which is in the Harleian Collection of the British Museum, No. 6758. The book was published, with a long Introduction by Sir Harris Nicolas, in 1827.

A

and so affectionately, that one would have said love was grown a child again and took delight to play with them."

The boy had some cause for being a grave child. He could scarcely remember the bright happy home-circle of his earliest years, years which had promised a brilliant future to the little lad, who was heir to large estates * and under the protection of a handsome and honoured father. But when he was not quite three years old his surroundings changed. Familiar faces, hitherto bright and joyous, suddenly became grave and sad. His father's voice and footsteps were heard no more; and his mother, who had been so playful and merry, could now only try to amuse him with obvious effort, and so generally with failure. By-and-by a winter's day came when all around him were in tears, and he was told that he would never see his father again. There were black clothes, discomforts, and cold journeys in a great carriage over rough roads. These incidents themselves were soon forgotten by so young a child; but a permanent gloom settled itself upon his home and undoubtedly darkened his early youth. Even the mirth and merriment of his games with his little brother must have been sorrowfully subdued when they took place in the presence of his broken-hearted mother.

By degrees he learned, possibly from servants or by means of eavesdropping, that his father had met his death on a public scaffold, as an alleged traitor.

These conditions and accidents affecting the infant life of Kenelm Digby probably did much to increase and emphasise the natural eccentricities of his character.

With the single exception of his father, Sir Everard, none of his ancestors had records other than honourable since his family had come over to England with William

---

* John Aubrey, in his *Letters*, vol. ii., Appendix, says he was " born to £3000 a year," which would then represent a very much larger sum than in these days.

the Conqueror.* Three Digbys, all brothers, had fallen on the field of Towton under the banner of the House of Lancaster; seven sons of the eldest of these three brothers had also fought for the Red Rose at the battle of Bosworth.

Part of the estates belonging to Kenelm Digby's father had been given to him from the forfeited properties of the supporters of the House of York. In a former work,† I have dealt with the tragedy of the life and death of Sir Everard Digby, and it will be sufficient to say here that very many of those who condemned his crime absolved him from unworthy motives, considered him more sinned against than sinning, and deeply deplored his fate.

Instead of dwelling upon the misfortunes and mis-doings of Sir Everard Digby, it is more to our present purpose to consider the probable effect upon a thoughtful, imaginative, and perhaps morbid boy, such as his eldest son, of knowing the circumstances of his father's death.

From whatever aspect the boy may have regarded his father's misfortunes, he must have felt himself to be in some sense, whether good or evil, a celebrity and a "personage". He must have known that he would be pointed out as the eldest son of the notorious Sir Everard Digby, who had given his life for what he had believed to be a noble cause. Young as Kenelm was, too, his affairs were the subject of litigation. Some of the most learned lawyers in the land were disputing the question‡ whether his

---

* In the Heraldic Visitation of 31st July, 1634, it is stated that there were seventeen quarterings in the windows of one room of Gothurst, the home of Sir Kenelm Digby, as well as four in the window of the great parlour. See Lipscombe's *Hist. and Antiq. of Bucks.*, vol. iv., p. 158.

† *The Life of a Conspirator*, by One of his Descendants.

‡ *An exact abridgment in English of the Eleven Books of Reports of the Learned Sir Edward Cook, Knt.*, p. 327. "Digbies Case, 7, Jacob fo. 165. A tenant of the king conveys his lands to the use of himself for life, the re-mainder to his son and heir in tail: and after is attainted of treason, the king shall have no wardship of any part of the land by 32 and 34 H. 8, because there is no heir, but the king shall have wardship in such a case before 20 H. 8, because there was an heir."

mother's estate, which had been settled upon her and her heirs at her marriage, was to be forfeited on account of her husband's treason, together with the husband's own properties, which had been seized on his arrest and taken possession of by the Crown on his execution.

And when, at last, the decision was given in his mother's and his own favour, he must have felt considerable elation at the victory of his mother's representatives over the king's lawyers, and some of the sensations of a conquering hero at returning with her to take possession of the beautiful house * at which he had spent his earliest infancy. He can scarcely have been unaware that he was a fine boy, a handsome boy, and a clever boy; and how far all this knowledge of himself, his antecedents, and his surroundings was conducive to a healthy condition of mind in early youth may, at the very least, remain doubtful.

If Kenelm Digby was a beautiful boy, what shall be said of his playfellow? The poets of the first quarter of the seventeenth century rivalled each other in extolling the charms of the Lady Venetia Anastasia Stanley.† Ben Jonson even composed a poem in "Dedication of her Cradle,"‡ so he may fairly claim to be heard first.

---

* Gothurst, a little more than two miles north-west from Newport Pagnell in Buckinghamshire. It had been built in the reign of Elizabeth by K. Digby's maternal grandfather, William Mulsho, to whom his mother was sole heiress. The house, which is in excellent preservation, now belongs to Mr. Carlile and is called Gayhurst.

† Venetia Stanley was often spoken and written of as "the lady Venetia"; but no title was thereby implied. It is true that she was co-heiress to a title in abeyance; but she was never actually more than a baronet's daughter and a knight's wife. Sometimes she was written of as "Mistress Venetia Stanley" or "Mrs. Venetia Stanley". Hence it is an error to speak of her as "Lady Venetia". "The Lady ——" was an expression which in the early part of the seventeenth century often meant no more than Mrs. or Miss would mean in our own days.

‡ *The Works of Ben Jonson.* By William Gifford. Edited by F. Cunningham, vol. iii., p. 357.

GOTHURST

The home of Sir Kenelm Digby: now called Gayhurst.

DEDICATION OF HER CRADLE.

Fair fame, who art ordained to crown
With evergreen and great renown,
Their heads that envy would hold down
        With her, in shade
Of death and darkness; and deprive
Their names of being kept alive,
By thee and Conscience, both who thrive
        By the just trade
Of goodness still: vouchsafe to take
This cradle and for goodness' sake,
A dedicated ensign make
        Thereof to Time;
That all posterity, as we,
Who read what the Crepundia be,
May something by that twilight see
        'Bove rattling rhyme.
For though that rattles, timbrels, toys,
Take little infants with their noise,
As properest gifts to girls and boys,
        Of light expense;
Their corals, whistles, and prime coats,
Their painted masks, their paper boats,
With sails of silk, as the first notes
        Surprise their sense.
Yet here are no such trifles brought,
No cobweb cauls, no surcoats wrought
With gold, or clasps, which might be bought
        On every stall:
But here's a song of her descent;
And call to the high parliament
Of heaven; where Seraphim take tent
        Of ordering all:
This uttered by an ancient bard,
Who claims, of reverence, to be heard,
As coming with his harp prepared
        To chant her 'gree
Is sung: as als' her getting up
By Jacob's ladder to the top
Of that eternal port, kept ope
        For such as she.

Venetia Stanley was three years older * than Kenelm Digby, and everybody knows how much more forward in many respects a girl is than a boy, even when they are of equal ages. Women, as Sir Henry Taylor had it, grow on the sunny side of the wall. Here is Aubrey's description of Venetia : † " She had the most lovely sweet-turned face, delicate dark browne haire ". " Her face, a short ovall ; darke browne eie-browe, about wch much sweetness, as also in the opening of her eie-lidds. The colour of her cheekes was just that of the Denmark Rose, which is neither too hot nor too pale. She was of a just stature, not very tall." I have said that Kenelm Digby was of good family ; but it was not better than that of many other English country gentlemen. His playmate's ancestry was much higher. She was the only daughter and sole heiress of Sir Edward Stanley, a younger son of Edward, third Earl of Derby. Her mother, who had died when she was only a few months old, had been the daughter and co-heiress of Thomas Percy, seventh Earl of Northumberland. Ben Jonson sang thus of her parentage :—

* Venetia Stanley was born in 1600; Kenelm Digby in 1603. Two poets, Ben Jonson, in his stanza, " Upon his birthday the eleventh of June," and Dr. Richard Farrar, " Born on the day he died, the eleventh of June," seemed to have no doubt about the date of his birth ; but Wood, in his *Athenæ Oxonienses*, ed. 1721, vol. ii., p. 357, declares it to have been on the 11th of July, and that Jonson only made it June " for Rhrimes sake ". His authority is a Book of Nativities collected by Dr. Richard Napier of Buckinghamshire: " K. Digby's Own County MS. in the hands of Elias Ashmole, Esq.". Mr. Bruce in his Preface to K. Digby's *Voyage into the Mediterranean* states that "the Rev. W. D. Macray of the Bodleian Library" affirmed that the particular paper in question was written in Sir Kenelm Digby's own handwriting.

† Aubrey's *Letters*, written by eminent persons in the seventeenth and eighteenth centuries, and *Lives of Eminent Men*. Longman, 1813, vol. ii., Appendix.

* I sing the just and uncontrolled descent
Of Dame Venetia Digby, styled the fair :
For mind and body the most excellent
That ever nature, or the later air,
Gave two such houses as Northumberland
And Stanley, to the which she was co-heir.

*　*　*　*　*

And tell thou Alde-legh, none can tell more true
Thy niece's line, than thou that gav'st thy name
Into thy kindred, whence thy Adam drew
Meschines honour, with the Cestrian fame
Of the first Lupus, to the family
　　By Ranulph —— †

She was in fact the grandchild and co-heiress of the
Earl of Northumberland, who was beheaded on account
of his share in the rebellion of 1569, and of whom, together
with his friend the Earl of Westmoreland, Wordsworth
wrote :— ‡

> Two Earls fast leagued in discontent,
> Who gave their wishes open vent
> And boldly urged a general plea,
> The rites of ancient piety
> To be triumphantly restored,
> By the dread justice of the sword.

Her father, who, although "a negligent husband "§ during
his wife's lifetime, had been heart-broken on her death,
had ‖ "retired himself to a private and recollected life,
where without the troubles that attend upon great fortunes
he might give free scope to his melancholic fantasies ;
which to enjoy more fully in the way that he desired,
he judged it expedient by removing his daughter from
him to take away such cumbers as might disturb his
course, since it was requisite for the education due to her

---

* " Song of her Descent." *Works of Ben Jonson.* By W. Gifford.
Ed. F. Cunningham, vol. iii., p. 358.
　† The rest of this poem has been lost.
　‡ " The White Doe of Rylstone," canto ii.
　§ *Private Memoirs*, K. D., p. 14.
　‖ *Ib.,* p. 15 *seq.*

high birth to have many about her, that would ill agree
with his affected solitariness ".   Accordingly he sent
Venetia Anastasia " to a kinsman of his whose wife, being
a grave and virtuous lady, had given him assurance that
no care or diligence should be wanting on her part to
cultivate those rare natural endowments which did already
shine through her tender age.   Their house * in the
country was near to that " in which Lady Digby lived with
her two little boys, " which gave occasion to frequent
interchanging of visits between " the two families.

The " first innocent years " † of the little boy and girl
had scarcely passed, " whiles fortune seemed to conspire
to unite their hearts," " when she turned about her inconstant wheel in such sort that, if their fates had not been
written above in eternal characters, even then their affections had been by a long winter of absence nipped and
destroyed in their budding spring ".   For while Venetia,
although by three years the elder of the little pair, was
still " of such age that with her tender hand she could
scarcely reach to gather the lowest fruit of the loaden
boughs : her father, that yielded daily more and more to
his discontents, and fainting under the burden of them
which age made to seem heavier, sent for her back to his
own house ".

Her boy-admirer was also removed from the scenes of
their youthful flirtations.   He was scarcely in his teens
before he was taken out of the hands of his Catholic
mother to be brought up by preceptors professing the
religion of the State.   Although both his parents had been
Catholics, he was not to be educated in their faith.

" An Act " ‡ had been passed " to prevent and avoid

* It was Euston Abbey in Oxfordshire.   Aubrey's *Letters*, vol. ii., p.
330.   And it was about thirty miles from Gothurst.   Introduction to
Private Memoirs of K. D., p. 13.

† *Private Memoirs*, K. D., p. 18.

‡ Stat. 3, Jac. l. c. 5.

dangers which may grow by Popish Recusants," and Section XXII. of this law laid down that "because recusants convict are not thought meet to be executors or administrators to any person or persons whatsoever, nor to have the education of their own children, much less of the children of any other of the king's subjects . . . be it therefore enacted, by the authority aforesaid, that such recusants . . . shall be disabled to be executor or administrator . . . nor shall have the custody of any child, . . . but shall be adjudged disabled to have any such wardship or custody of any such child," etc. Section XXIII. began : "And that, for the better education of the said children, and of their estates, the next of kin to any such child or children, to whom the said lands, tenements, or hereditaments of such child or children cannot lawfully descend, who shall usually resort to some church or chapel, and there hear divine service, and receive the Holy Sacrament of the Lord's Supper thrice in the year next before, according to the laws of this realm, shall have the custody and education of the same child," etc.

Therefore, when Kenelm Digby was about thirteen, or nearly fourteen, he was sent to a Protestant tutor ; and the tutor chosen for this purpose was Laud, afterwards Archbishop of Canterbury, but at that time very lately made Dean of Gloucester.* Laud, who was then about forty-three, had just become established in the favouritism of James I., and had entered into residence at his deanery for the first time on his return from Scotland with the king. It must be admitted that his attitude towards the Scottish clergy had not been considered judicious by James ; but he was nevertheless on a firm footing at Court, and he had ample opportunities of saying a good word there for his pupil.

It might be thought that Laud would make a stern and

* Introduction to *Private Memoirs*, K. D., p. 8. Also Lipscombe's *Hist. and Antiq. of Buckinghamshire*, vol. iv., p. 149.

severe tutor ; the man, however, had a kind, a gentle and a friendly side to his character, as all who have studied it impartially must be aware ; and a friendship sprang up between the preceptor and the pupil which lasted throughout their lifetimes. Laud must have found the intelligent though peculiar boy an amusing companion, and the lad's oddities and precocious remarks may have distracted Laud's thoughts from the very disagreeable correspondence with his bishop which took place soon after he went to Gloucester. This correspondence concerned the removal of the communion-table from the "middest of the quire" and the placing of it "altarwise" against the east wall.

Kenelm Digby had scarcely been a year at the house of Dean Laud when he was sent abroad. He crossed the sea and travelled among "foreign nations" for "seven or eight months".* To Mr. Gardiner is due the credit of discovering whither and wherefore he made this expedition. " A kind and fortunate suggestion of Mr. Gardiner," says Mr. Bruce, in his additional notes † to the *Voyage into the Mediterranean*, "that Digby might have accompanied his relative Sir John Digby, the future Earl of Bristol, on his extraordinary mission to Spain to open negotiations for the marriage of Prince Charles and the future Infanta, has led to the clear establishment that such was the fact. In a list of gentlemen who were to accompany Sir John Digby, prepared by Sir John himself, the tenth name is that of ' Mr. Kenelme Digby '" (*State Papers*, Spain, 1618, fol. 20). " They sailed from Plymouth on or about the 28th August, 1617, and quitted Santander on their return to England on the 27th April in the year following" (*State Papers*, Spain, 22nd August, 1617, and 12th May, 1618).

On his return, Kenelm Digby was sent to Oxford, as a gentleman commoner, at Gloucester Hall, which is now

* *Ashmole MS.* 174, folio 77.   Also Pref. to *Voyage*, p. 17.
† P. 95.

Worcester College. This was "about 1618," * when he was of the age of fifteen. Wood states that this was "after he had been trained up in the Protestant religion". Several other authorities make very similar statements. On the other hand, Mr. Bruce, in his excellent Preface to Sir Kenelm Digby's *Voyage into the Mediterranean*, gives what has the colour of strong evidence in favour of the theory that he did not become a Protestant until he was between the ages of twenty and thirty, or was even older still.

How are these apparently contradictory statements to be reconciled ? For the present it may be sufficient to say that, while rival historians are quarrelling as to whether, at a certain time, he was a Catholic or an Anglican, there exists a third possibility, namely that, strictly speaking, he was neither. We know that Sir Kenelm Digby was brought up, partly under Catholic, partly under Protestant influences, at the former time in his mother's very Popish home at Gothurst, at the latter in Laud's very Anglican deanery at Gloucester. If, therefore, the boy was somewhat disingenuous, he may have been tempted to go to Mass at Gothurst and to assure his mother that he had not joined the Anglican Church, and yet to go to the cathedral when at the deanery of Gloucester and to tell Laud that he no longer went to communion at a Catholic altar, thus inducing each to believe that, if the boy were not pestered, in good time all would be well.

* Wood's *Ath. Oxon.*, ed. 1721, vol. ii., p. 351.

CHAPTER II.

THE new gentleman commoner at Gloucester Hall was no ordinary undergraduate. He was of noble bearing, tall and handsome, charming in manner, and well expressed in his attire. He was notorious as the son of a man who had suffered for high treason ; he had been to Spain, and that not in the character of an ordinary traveller, but in the suite of an ambassador entrusted with a mission of the utmost delicacy and importance. He was the heir to a beautiful house and a good estate, he was clever, and he was in love with a lady of great beauty and high degree ; and yet he was only fifteen !

Nor was he ignorant of his own good points. Some years afterwards he wrote the following description of himself as a youth ; it is put into the mouth of another person, but as the words are his own and he did not pretend to have heard them spoken, they prove that he was not troubled by false modesty : * " Although the great strength and well framing of his body make him apt for any corporal exercises, yet he pleaseth himself most in the entertainments of the mind, so that having applied himself to the study of philosophy and other deepest sciences," "he is already grown so eminent that I have heard them say who have insight that way, that if a lazy desire of ease or ambition of public appointments, or some other disturbance, do not interrupt him in this course, he is like to attain to great perfection : at least I can discern thus much, that he hath such a temper of complexion and wit that his friends

* *Private Memoirs*, p. 59 *seq.*

(12)

have reason to pray God that he may take a right way, for it cannot keep itself in mediocrity, but will infallibly fall into some extreme ".

Kenelm Digby's future line of study was a good deal influenced by his being placed under the charge of the celebrated Thomas Allen. Allen, or Alleyn, a Staffordshire man of very fair family, whom Wood calls* "the Father of all learning and virtuous Industry, an unfeigned lover and furtherer of all good Arts and Sciences," was a philosopher, not only of remarkable ability, but, like his pupil, of a peculiar and somewhat eccentric disposition. He had been a scholar of Trinity,† " but being much inclined to lead a retired life, and averse from taking Holy Orders, he left the College and his fellowship about 1570, and receded to Gloucester Hall ". Even the promise of a Bishopric from Leicester ‡ did not avail to tempt him to become a clergyman and enter public life ; nor did offers of honours and dignities from Henry, Earl of Northumberland, " Albertus L'askie, Count or Prince of Sirade in Poland," and other " Princes and Nobles " induce him to emerge from his retirement.

Allen was about seventy-six when Kenelm Digby went to Gloucester Hall, and he did not actually conduct Digby's tuition, though he superintended and directed it. As he " was accomplished with various sorts of learning," § but

* *Athen. Ox.*, vol. i., p. 574.

† *Ib.*

‡ *Ib.*, p. 575.

§ A rather well-known story told of Allen may show the superstitious awe then entertained by the common people towards men of science : " In his day pocket watches were little known in remote districts. Visiting at the Scudamores in Herefordshire, Allen left his timepiece under his pillow. The chamber-maids finding the thing, and hearing it cry tick! tick! concluded it was Mr. Allen's familiar spirit. They determined to drown the infernal spirit, and canted it with the tongs out of the window into the moat : unfortunately for their good intentions the string by which it was suspended caught in an alder and so," writes Aubrey, " the good old gentleman got his watch again." Mr. Bruce's Preface to K. D.'s *Voyage into the Mediterranean*, p. xix., footnote.

before all things " an eminent antiquary, philosopher and
mathematician," "as one saith," " the very soul and sun of all
the mathematicians of his time," he naturally turned Kenelm
Digby's mind in the direction of the sciences which he
himself loved best, and he succeeded in making his pupil,
at least after a fashion, an antiquary and a philosopher.
It is likely, also, that he may have discussed political and
diplomatic affairs to some extent with his young charge
and interested him in such things ; for Wood says that,
during Leicester's period of power, "few matters of State
passed but he (Allen) had knowledge of them ".   Allen
took a great fancy to his pupil and held a very high
opinion of his abilities.   He called him * "the Mirandula †
of his Age ".   As the author of the *Biographia Britannica* ‡
says, he "quickly discerned the natural strength of his
faculties, and that spirit of penetration which is so seldom
met with in persons of his age," *i.e.*, fifteen to sixteen.
" He took pains, therefore, to show him the right method
of applying his wonderful capacity."   The same authority §
states that Allen eventually " bestowed by his Will upon
Sir Kenelm Digby " his " excellent library of manuscripts,
as well as printed books ".

Aubrey ‖ tells us that, when he was at Oxford, Kenelm
Digby " did not weare a gowne there, as I heard my cosen
Whitney say ".   There are several complaints, written
about that time, of undergraduates not wearing their gowns,
and it may be that the tradition which prevails, or at any
rate did prevail in my time, at Christ Church, of never
wearing them in the streets, is of ancient date.

Besides philosophy and his other academical studies,

---

* *Athen. Ox.*, vol. ii., p. 351.

† Giovanni Pica Della Mirandola, Count and Prince of Concordia
(1463—1494).   Remarkable for his memory as a child.   He became a
philosopher, theologian and linguist.

‡ Edition 1750, vol. iii., p. 1701.

§ *Ib.*, p. 1703.

‖ *Letters*, vol. ii., Appendix.

Kenelm Digby dabbled in poetry, both as a composer and as a translator. He was a great admirer· of the Italian poet Guarini, who had died only about six years before Digby went to Oxford. The works of that poet had attained great popularity in this country, and were probably the fashion among the undergraduates at Oxford when Kenelm Digby was at College. He made a translation of Guarini's *Il Pastor Fido*, of which the following fragment may serve as a specimen. I have somewhat modernised the spelling.

> * They lying in the shade
> Of some green myrtle grove they favour
> Do freely speak and court each other ;
> Nor any flames of love she feels
> That from his knowledge she conceals ;
> Nor sooner she discovers them but he
> Those flames doth feel as well as she.
>
> Thus they a perfect happy life enjoy
> And know not what death means before they die.

We must now take leave of our undergraduate for a time, and look back at what had happened to the subject of the juvenile flirtations recorded in the previous chapter.

It would appear that Sir Edward and his daughter spent some years in London, or chiefly in London.

Venetia was taken into society as soon as she was old enough ; and, so far as can be inferred, her father considered that a girl was very soon old enough to mix in society. An exceptionally beautiful girl, in the charge of a father who seems to have had very lax ideas of the responsibilities of a parent, at the balls and other entertainments of the Court of James I. was placed in a very dangerous position. At her first regular ball, " a principal nobleman of the Court," " whose heart was set on fire with the radiant beams that sparkled from her eyes," said to

* *Poems from Sir Kenelm Digby's Papers*, Roxburgh Club, pp. 4 and 5.

Venetia, as he sat next to her, without any previous introduction :— *

"Fair lady, I shall begin to endear myself to your knowledge by taxing you with that which I am confident you cannot excuse yourself of: for if by the exterior lineaments of your face, and by the habitude of the body, we may conjecture the frame and temper of the mind, certainly yours must be endowed with such perfections, that it is the greatest injustice and ingratitude that may be, for you to imprison your thoughts in silence, and to deny the happiness of your conversation to those whose very souls depend upon every motion that you make".

If the reader should lose patience at this long and ridiculous rodomontade, he should remember that the strange fashion of "Euphuism," if already moribund, was not yet defunct. † Venetia was astonished at being spoken to at all by a man whom she only knew by name, and still more so at being addressed in such a tone by a stranger. Annoyed as she was, she replied to him in civil language

---

* *Private Memoirs* of Sir K. Digby, p. 23.   The remainder of the account of her experiences about this time is taken mainly from these *Memoirs.*

† See *The Monastery*, by Sir W. Scott.   Edinburgh ed., p. 7.   "After the acknowledgment of the Queen's (Eliz.) matchless perfections, the same devotion was extended to beauty as it existed among the lesser stars in her Court, who sparkled, as it was the mode to say, by her reflected lustre," p. 155.   "John Lylly . . . wrote that singularly coxcomical work, called *Euphues and his England* . . . all the Court ladies were his scholars, and to *parler* Euphuisme was as necessary a qualification to a courtly gallant, as those of understanding how to use his rapier, or to dance a measure," p. 8. "In England, the humour does not seem to have long survived the accession of James I."   If we are to judge from Sir Kenelm Digby's *Private Memoirs*, however, "the humour" survived a few years later.   Perhaps the best caricature of Euphuism is Shakespeare's in "Love's Labour's Lost".   The artificial style bearing that name was not confined to the polite speeches of gallants.   It even reached to the books of devotion of the period; and the modern Jesuit, Father Thurston, calls *Mary Magdalene's Funeral Tears*, a book written by a Jesuit, who was martyred at the end of the sixteenth century, "a piece of undiluted Euphuism," *The Month*, No. 368, p. 236.

but in somewhat the same pedantic style, declaring that if nature had bestowed any exterior attractions upon her, of which she was quite unaware, she was so conscious of counterbalancing defects that she felt obliged to undeceive her admirer by speaking to him, "whereby," said she, "through my rudeness I am sure you will gather more arguments to make you ashamed of what you say you have conceived of me, than to confirm you in it".

Quite ignoring the courteous retort contained in her last sentence, he made her another long and flowery speech, ending by begging "that you will give me leave to love and adore you, and not be displeased that one of so small merit as I am, should be so ambitious as to style himself your humble servant". Fortunately at that moment one of the maskers * "came to take" Venetia "by the hand, beseeching her to follow him in a 'corrente'".† So, giving her tormentor "a disdainful look," she went away with her partner to dance.

The principal nobleman was not the only man in the ballroom attracted by the beautiful new comer; many other young courtiers admired her; "which was the cause that when they had seen how skilfully she kept time with her feet to the music's sound, she was suffered no more to return to her former seat: for it addeth much to the grace of good dancers to have their lady observe due distances, and to move themselves, as it were, by consent, in just proportion; every one in their turn beseeched the like favour of her that she had done to their companion, before he could lead her back unto her place": "yet in this they deceived themselves; for her excellency, that would brook no partner, engrossed to herself all the commendations, while they had scarce any notice taken of them". Poor Venetia "was wearied with her much exercise, before the beholders could be satisfied with delight"; and it was an intense relief to

---

* *Private Memoirs*, K. D., p. 26 *seq.*, for the remainder of this chapter.
† According to Shakespearian spelling, this would be " coranto ".

her when, some time after the crowing of "the watchful cock," the king adjourned "the assembly and the continuance of these recreations to the next night".

When she had returned to her lodging and was undressing, she "related to the gentlewoman that waited upon her in nature of a governess, what had passed at court, and what language" the nobleman who had so greatly annoyed her had addressed to her. Unfortunately this nobleman had already "won Faustina"—"for that was the ancient gentlewoman's name"—"to assure him of assistance in his pursuit"; for he had admired Venetia for some time, and had formed his own private plans concerning her; although "he had been so unhappy that until this night" he had never had an opportunity of speaking to her. Meanwhile he had bribed "the ancient," but easily corruptible, "gentlewoman ".*

When Faustina had listened to Venetia's account of her experiences, she expressed her regret that she had given "so cold an entertainment to the respects of so noble and deserving a gentleman". This "deserving gentleman"— a name by which I shall call him for the future, instead of using the classical pseudonym of "Ursatius" given him by Digby—was, she said, well known to be "the discreetest, the most courteous, and the most generous among all the noblemen in this kingdom," and, she added, he "excelleth them as much in completeness of good parts and the graces of nature, as he doth in the gifts of fortune, and greatness of estate". But what mattered this to Venetia, who already loved so devotedly the boy-playmate of her childhood?

"Dost thou then, Faustina," she exclaimed, "think that any of these considerations can make me false to that affection, that in respect of me had no beginning, for my memory reacheth not to that time, and which I am resolved shall die with me?"

* The likeness of the conduct of Faustina to that of the nurse in " Romeo and Juliet " is interesting.

SIR EVERARD DIGBY

From a portrait belonging to W. R. M. Wynne, Esq. of Peniarth, Merioneth.

Faustina then praised Venetia's usual discretion ; but after begging pardon for her boldness she suggested that it was not displayed to advantage in the present instance. She advised her young mistress not to let "passion blind" her altogether, but rather to consider "what an advantageous change" she would make by forgetting Kenelm Digby and "embracing" the "deserving gentleman," who, said she, in "the splendour of nobility, abundance of riches, and favour with his prince, is eminent above all others" ; whereas Kenelm "hath hardly escaped, by his mother's extreme industry, with the scant relics of a shipwrecked estate, and from his father hath inherited nothing but a foul stain in his blood for attempting to make a fatal revolution in this state".

Without losing her temper, Venetia, wearied out as she was, then spoke very firmly to her "gentlewoman". " Methinks, Faustina," she began, "you speak in his prejudice with more passion than you can accuse me of in loving him." It was true, she continued, that it was the custom of the times to visit the sins of fathers upon their children ; but Faustina had no business to upbraid Kenelm "with another man's offence". " Besides," "to speak a little in his father's behalf, all men know that it was no malicious intent or ambitious desires that brought him (Sir Everard Digby) into that conspiracy (the Gunpowder Plot) ; but his too inviolable faith to his friend (Robert Catesby), that had trusted him with so dangerous a secret, and his zeal to his country's ancient liberty ; which, being misled by those upon whose advice he relied, was the cause of overthrowing the most generous, discreet, worthy and hopeful gentleman that ever this country brought forth". " And as for his estate, although it were much less than it is, yet it would be plentiful enough for one that loveth him for his better part, which is his mind ; besides that I am so much beholden to fortune, that I am myself mistress of so much as may satisfy a heart that can content itself with con-

veniency, more than which is excess and superfluity ; which
is too abject and mean a thing to enter into the lowest
thoughts of one that is acquainted with the divine light of
a noble and heroical love, as mine is.   Therefore I am resolved I will no longer be a patient martyr ; but will
speedily use some means that he may hear from me, and I
have news of him."

   " Faustina perceiving her lady to grow more passionate
by contradiction, and the guiltiness of her conscience
making her doubt that " Venetia " saw too far into her
heart, thought it most expedient for the present to give
way to her vehemence ".   Therefore she promised " her
best and faithful service to procure her content, now that
she perceived clearly which way it was resolutely bent ".

   As soon as Venetia had " laid down in bed, and the
curtains " were " drawn, wishing her good rest and joyful
dreams, with a low curtesy she took her leave and went
into her own chamber ".

CHAPTER III.

A PLOT.

THE ancient gentlewoman made no reference to Venetia's love affairs for some days, and then, taking an opportunity when she perceived * "the sun of her beauty shining through the clouds of sadness," she "seeming to bear a part with her in her sorrow, towards whom she proposed to have a natural tenderness, as having been under her charge and care from her infancy, she promised her faith and secrecy in whatever might conduce to her content. Wherewith" Venetia, " being much joyed gave her many thanks, and, after long debate what was fittest to be done, they concluded that Faustina should inquire after" Kenelm, "and when she had fully informed herself concerning him, that she should send a discreet messenger to him, with a letter".

Faustina went out soon afterwards, and did not return till night, when she came " to her lady with a cheerful countenance, the messenger of good news," and " told her how gracious heaven was to her desires: for, having heard how " Kenelm "was come the night before to the city, she had sent a messenger to him, who took so fit an opportunity of accosting him, that he had large and private discourse with him ; wherein he had concluded that the same servant should come the next day about sunset, to be his guide to the park,† that is three miles out of the city, if" Venetia "could have conveniency to come then to meet him there".

* *Priv. Mem.*, K. D., pp. 41 to 65, contain most of the events and conversations in this chapter.

† Very possibly what is now called Hyde Park. If Lady Venetia were living a little to the east of the then very fashionable Strand, or in Hol-

"How," replied Venetia, "should he put that in doubt? I hope he measureth not my flames by his own, when he maketh such a question; for no sea between, nor hell itself, should hinder me from running into those wished arms."

Faustina recommended that, "for less notice sake," instead of using her own carriage for the expedition, she should commission her faithful old governess to hire one for her, and that it should be in waiting a short time before sunset at "the back door of the garden". Venetia, who does not appear to have disturbed her mind much about social convention, agreed to this arrangement, and as she wished to see her beloved Kenelm alone, she decided to leave the ancient gentlewoman at home. Her anxiety was so great and her anticipation so eager that she passed the "night and part of the next day with much unquietness". At last "the declining sun, that was ready to plunge himself into his lover's bosom, summoned her to begin her journey to hers," and, with the help of Faustina, she dressed herself as becomingly as she was able for her expedition. Punctual to its appointment, a hired coach with four horses was waiting for her at "the back door of the garden"; Venetia entered it and started towards the trysting place.

If the first setting out in the sombre hired vehicle was somewhat dreary, the drive was not the less destined to be an eventful one. "She was scarce gone half-way to the appointed place, when five or six horsemen well mounted, overtook the coach." They summoned the driver to stop, an order which he obeyed with suspicious alacrity. Then two of the horsemen "alighting, came into the coach," "and drawing their poignards, threatened her with death if she cried out or made any noise; assuring her withal, that from them she should receive no violence if she would sit quietly; and therewithal drew the curtains

born, it would be about three miles to a distant and retired part of Hyde Park, suitable for such a clandestine meeting.

that none might see who was in the coach as they passed by ".

The carriage then moved on, and a terrible journey it must have been for the poor lonely girl, with two armed men sitting with her in the darkened coach, and threatening to murder her if she uttered a sound. To add to her terrors the sun had now set, and the natural darkness rendered the curtains needless. Even when night had fairly settled down, the great coach did not stop ; on and on it went throughout all the dreary hours of gloom.

Venetia, in "an abyss of sorrow, and fearing the worst that might happen to an undefended maid that was fallen into rude hands," had begun to think that that awful night would never end, when she fancied she perceived a faint glimmer of dawn. Just then they came to a house and drew up at the door. Venetia was helped out of the carriage with great show of civility, and, on entering the house, was received in the hall by an old housekeeper, who, "entertaining her with comfortable speeches, and the assurance of all service intended to her, which she should quickly perceive to be true, brought her into a very handsome room, remarking that after so tedious and troublesome a night as of necessity she must have passed," it would be better to leave her for a little time to herself.

Wondering where she was and what was about to befall her, she at first listened anxiously for the slightest sound ; but, by degrees, nature began to assert itself after her sleepless night, a heavy drowsiness came over her, she fell asleep in her chair, and slept for many hours. The afternoon was far spent when she awakened with a start, at hearing some one make a false step on entering the room. It was almost dark, as the curtains, which had been drawn when she entered, had not yet been disturbed. Thoroughly alarmed, she sprang up, and to her horror, "by the glimmering of the light that stole in between the chinks of the drawn curtains," she distinguished the most unwelcome

features of the "deserving gentleman" who had made
himself so odious to her at the ball. He drew nearer. She
was afraid to move. When he had reached her side he
knelt down. During an awful and apparently lengthy
pause he was silent. Suddenly he began :—

"Before I came into your presence, fairest" Venetia, " I
had proposed to myself many things that I would say to
you, to excuse my deceiving you in getting you hither ;
but that divinity that is about you doth so astonish me,
that I forget all studied eloquence, and am forced to betake
myself to the naked and simple expression of a faltering
tongue, that speaketh but the overboilings of a passionate
heart. What error I have committed is caused by love ;
he was my guide, and hath brought me to that pass that,
without it be requited by yours, I cannot live."

"Alas !" replied Venetia, "how ill your deeds and words
consort together. You mention love, but perform the
effects of extreme hatred. You sue to me for life, and in
a treacherous manner have brought mine into your power ;
but, howsoever, at least I have this content remaining "—
and then she assured him that any ill-treatment on his part
would cause her to commit suicide, adding : " my injured
ghost shall be a perpetual terror to your guilty soul, which
I will so pursue, that I will make you fly to hell to save you
from my more tormenting vengeance ". And the eyes of
Venetia Stanley, more beautiful than ever in her anger and
her despair, glared at him in a manner betokening the
sincerity of her words.

Her treacherous wooer " was so amazed, that he was
long in replying to her resolute answer ; but, at length,
like one new coming out of a trance, he called his spirits
together, and strived what he could to lessen the error he
had committed, laying much of the fault upon Faustina's
negotiations, and telling her how she had been the plotter
of all, and that, for his part, his intent was never to have
used violence ; but that he gave way to his action, seeing

how negligent her father was of her, that left her so young and in the tuition of so false a servant, to live by herself in a dissolute age ". Therefore, having observed from her coldness towards him at the ball, that she was unlikely to come to his house voluntarily, he had determined to get her there by stratagem, and thus afford her a haven of refuge from the wicked gallants of the Court. He hoped that, when she had had sufficient proof of his devotion to her, she would consent to marry him ; meanwhile, "he besought her to consider herself mistress of all that he had, for, in effect, she should find it so, and assured her that all the means he would use to attain his desires should be love and service ".

Venetia had little doubt that these gentle words were " but a cunning invention of his to try first if he could win her consent by fair means ". Nevertheless, she felt helpless in his hands ; so she "thought it her best course not to overthrow his hopes altogether, but so to suspend them that she might gain time, wherein only consisted the possibility of her safety ". Accordingly, she replied that his actions had been so ill-suited to his fair words that "she could not believe that he intended really what he said ; but when, by experience, she should find him to love her as worthily as he professed, that might be an inducement to her to think better of him than she did ".

Doubtless, the deserving gentleman reflected that a woman who once hesitates gives consent, and felt quite satisfied with the course things were taking. The old housekeeper, "none else being suffered to attend them," now came into the room, bringing supper, of which Venetia must have been in sore need. When it was over, her host, taking her "by the hand, led her down the stairs into a garden that her chamber window looked into, all the several parts of which she narrowly observed.

" At length, the sun setting and a gummy dew beginning to fall," he "asked her if she was not tired with walking, which intimation of retiring she taking hold of, they returned again " to the house. Venetia now professed herself exceedingly weary and expressed a wish to return to her room for the night and go to sleep as soon as possible ; so the host " took his leave and wished her a quiet and happy night, commanding the old woman to attend diligently upon her ".   " This confidential servant then helped her to bed," and " retired herself into an inner chamber ".

The first thing Venetia did, when she found herself alone, was " to have a good cry," as is said in these days, or, as Sir Kenelm Digby expressed it, " she gave liberty to her sighs and tears ".   Very soon, however, she began to consider what she could do to escape ; for she felt no confidence whatever in the plausible professions of her captor.

When out walking with him, she " had observed how, in one corner of the garden, there was an arbour seated upon a mount which overlooked the wall, and by that place she deemed that she might most fitly take her flight.   Wherefore, when by her loud snoring she perceived that her guardian was fast asleep, she rose with as little noise as she could, and, tying her sheets together, made one of them fast to a bar in the window, and by that let herself down so gently that she came to touch ground without any hurt, and then going straight to the arbour, she got down the wall by making use of her garters, as before she had done of her sheets ; and then finding herself at liberty in the park, she directed her course one certain way until she came to the pales, which with some difficulty she climbed over ; and then she wandered about large fields and horrid woods, without meeting any highway or sign of habitation."

On and on she walked, she knew not whither, all through the long night, until, as the morning was beginning to break, thinking herself far enough from the house of her late captor, she sat down to take some rest.   It was a desolate spot, but she was wearied out, and felt as if she could no longer either walk or keep her eyes open.   Just as she was on the point of dropping off to sleep, " a hungry wolf* came rushing out of a wood that was close by, and perceiving her by the increasing twilight, ran at her with open mouth ". Venetia ran away ; the wolf ran after her. Naturally the wolf ran the faster and soon seized hold of her dress and pulled her down.

Fortunately her screams were heard by a young sportsman who had been out all night endeavouring to harbour a stag in the wood. Running in the direction of the sounds of distress he caught sight of her almost immediately after she had fallen ; whereupon he blew his horn and the wolf, being frightened, ran off, though too late to save his life, as the young hunter's servants came up with " strong and swift dogs," which caught the wolf and " quickly made an end of the unhappy beast ".

The youth and his servants lifted the girl from the ground and found her " almost dead with fear " ; " from the wolf's merciless teeth " she " had received some wounds in several places about her, the pain of which, and loss of blood, and her wearisome journey made her almost faint, so that, resting " herself " upon a green bank, she told her deliverer who she was," and part of the adventures which had befallen her ; " and he having requited her with informing her of his name and quality, stood as one amazed, sucking into his veins the fire of love, which was kindled at that beauty, that yet shined with admirable majesty through her bleeding wounds ".

He was still gazing at her, silent in admiration, when she distracted him by inquiring " what palace that was which they saw close by them, and could discern the rising sun gilding the tops of the highest turrets and pinnacles about it ? "

He answered her " that an old lady, famous for her virtue and zeal in religion, dwelt there, whose name was Artesia ".†

---

* See Appendix A. † I give the pseudonym.

"What!" exclaimed Venetia, after asking one or two questions as to the old lady's identity. "Then, I see that amidst my miseries, Heaven hath not abandoned all care of me; for this is the place that, of all others, I should have wished to be in," Lady "Artesia being my kins-woman, and one that I am sure will compassionate my late disasters. Therefore, sir, I shall not be ashamed, since fortune hath made me owe my life unto you, to beg the favour of you to conduct me thither."

Sir Edward Sackville, for he it was *—a brother of the Earl of Dorset—answered :—

"Fairest lady, I must lament my evil fortune that will not permit me to attend you thither; for there is some private cause that makes it very unfit for me to come to that house, but my servants shall wait upon you, and see you safe there; and I hope, in some other place, I shall have the happiness to express the much respect I bear unto you; and, in the meantime, from this hour forwards, I vow myself unto you in the strictest ties of an humble and affectionate servant". "I do not wonder," said Venetia, "that you use this language to me, when I consider it is the custom of generous souls to oblige themselves more by conferring benefits than by receiving them; but, howsoever, it belongeth to me to acknowledge upon all occasions that I am more your debtor than it is in my power to requite."

Sir Edward then took his leave and ordered two of his servants to conduct her to Lady Artesia's house.

Venetia was received by her relative with as much kindness as astonishment, and Lady Artesia insisted that, for the present, Venetia should regard the house as her home. The wounds inflicted by the wolf were gradually healed, although "some light scars" remained, and Venetia

---

* My reasons for identifying "Mardontius" as Sir Edward Sackville will be found in the Appendix B.

by-and-by recovered from the anxiety, fatigue, and exposure to which she had been subjected.

None of her misfortunes or adventures had distracted her mind from the one great object in which it was concentrated, that object being Kenelm Digby. To obtain news of him was her chief wish, and it was plain that Faustina had not in reality communicated with him in London. As good luck would have it, Venetia's present position was propitious to an inquiry, as she was aware that Lady Artesia was a great friend of Lady Digby.

" One evening as they were walking in the garden," Venetia summoned up courage to speak to her hostess about Lady Digby, and Lady Artesia " gladly falling upon the subject, it being the nature of most persons to let the tongue go willingly where the heart draweth it, spoke much in commendation of that lady ; extolling with what an admirable wit and understanding she was endued, and how, being left a widow in the flower of her youth, accompanied with a flourishing beauty and a plentiful estate, yet she was so much wedded to her dear husband's love, that she neglected all the advantageous offers of earnest and great suitors, that she might with the more liberty perform the part of a careful mother to the dear pledges of their virgin affections ".

Lady Artesia described Lady Digby's two boys in glowing terms, dwelling upon the charms and the virtues of each, but especially of Kenelm. All this was very pleasant hearing to Venetia ; but presently Lady Artesia said that which " shot her heart through " as it were with an arrow from the black quiver of death itself. " Their mother is ever dear to me," she observed, " and if I can effect what I have affectionately endeavoured and solicited, we shall be able to leave our posterity the inheritance of our affections as well as of our estates ; for I have laboured long, and " Lady Digby " hath not been wanting on her

part, to join in marriage her eldest son and my grandchild
that you see here ; who, if partiality deceive me not, besides
that she shall inherit a great estate of her father's, is so
much beholden to nature that she may show her face
among the fairest—when you are away, I mean ".

Venetia almost fainted on hearing this speech ; but a
desire " to know the worst " revived her a little, and she
inquired " what it was that hindered the effecting of it,
since you two, that are the guiders of it, are equally affected
with the desire of it ? "   " It is," answered Lady Artesia,
" the backwardness of " Kenelm, " of which his mother, one
day complaining to me, told me what an answer he had
made to her a little before, as she had solicited him to
condescend to her just desire, it being so much to his advantage.   ' Madam,' quoth he, ' marriage cannot well be
performed by attorney.   Besides, to have it complete in
all respects, the first motives of it should not be sordid
wealth or other convenience, but a divine affection.   And
I must confess that, although I know this gentlewoman do
every way deserve better fortune than I can bring her, I
feel not yet this flame in me towards her, which is indeed
only a gift of heaven.'   ' Therefore as long as the weakness
of our estate obligeth you not to sell me to repair that, I
beseech you give me leave to look a little while about me,
and to please myself awhile with flying abroad before I be
put into the mewe.' "

Lady Artesia went on to bemoan this condition of
mind ; for, said she, " by this speech of his, and knowing
his mother's indulgence to give way to his desire, I doubt
much whether what I have so much longed for will ever
come to pass ".   Still, she was determined " to leave
nothing unattempted," and she intended to try whether
her grand-daughter's " silent beauty " could " persuade him
to what yet he had ever been averse ".   And then to
Venetia's intense joy she announced that she had invited
Lady Digby to bring Kenelm on a visit to her house, and

that she expected them "within three days". Her last words to Venetia were " like a gentle gale of wind, that in a burning day creepeth over sweet and flowery meads, and breathes upon the languishing face of the faint traveller that is almost dead with heat ".

CHAPTER IV.

THE CHASE.

KENELM DIGBY only stayed about two years at Oxford. It may be doubted whether the line of study into which he was directed by Allen was according to the usual course.* " Upon his leaving the University " " in order to travel, he was considered a very extraordinary person, and such high expectations of him raised as he lived afterwards to fulfil ".

He was a very smart and gay looking young man when he arrived with his mother at Lady Artesia's stately home. Vandyck's picture of him in his youth represents him with plentiful curly black locks, a soft and silky moustache, daintily turned up at the corners, bright eyes, a large and splendid lace collar and a magnificent embroidered doublet. His immense size must have added greatly to the effect of his presence, and the reputation of his ability to the respect with which he was received.

Venetia took care "to disguise her affections " for Kenelm in the presence of his mother, who anxiously " observed all passages between " them. For the first " two days that they were together they could have no conveniency of free discourse ; whilst their fire increasing by presence and each other's sight, the keeping of it in too narrow a room without any vent almost smothered their hearts ".

The young philosopher, if somewhat in awe of his mother, was none the less determined to make love to his

* *Biog. Brit.*, ed. 1750, vol. iii., p. 1702.

old playfellow, who was now one of the most beautiful and attractive women in England. An acrostic in verse, in his own possession, but by some other hand, may have expressed his own feelings about her :—

* TO THE MOST FAIRE AND VERTUOUS GENTLEWOMAN,
MRS. V. S.

V	nmach't for beauty, chaster than the ayre
E	ven by the Gods themselves belou'd for faire
N	ature haveing made A worke soe excellent
E	nvide she had soe much perfection lent.
T	elling the world at yoʳ auspicious Birth
I	oue would desend from Heaven to rob the Earth
A	s thinking nature had delt much vneven,
S	uch beuty to giue men was fitt for Heaven
T	riumphant Phebus sittinge on his carr,
A	dmires yoʳ luster thinks you brighter arr,
N	or can he guide his coach when he Aspies
L	ooke he soe much doth on yoʳ radiant Eyes.
E	ach other God now loues (and haue in graven
Y	oʳ name ith starrie firmament of Heaven).

In the presence of his mother he took no special notice of the one object of his affections ; but in order to enjoy her society and declare his love to her, he had resort to stratagem.

†"One day as she had by accident let her glove fall, he took it up, and having a letter written in his hand, which he had written a day before and awaited an opportunity of delivering it, did thrust it into the glove, and kissing it, gave her, who putting her hand into it to pull it on, felt a paper there, which conceiving how it came in, she kept safe till night." When she had "retired to her chamber," was in bed, and had dismissed her servants, she "read it by the help of the watch-light which stood burning by her : and being thereby instructed how she should govern

* *Poems from Sir Kenelm Digby's Papers*, Rox. Club, p. 12.
† *Priv. Mem.*, K. D., pp. 67 to 80.

C

herself when the occasion was presented to procure a fit and secure meeting, sleep stole upon her as she was entertaining her pleased thoughts with the hope of that blessed hour ".

The very next day " that blessed hour " arrived, for Lady " Artesia and her son, and all the company that was at her house, were invited to hunt a stag in the forest that was near adjoining ; when being in the midst of the chase, and every one attentive to the sport," Venetia, " staying to be among the hindmost, turned her horse down a " ride " that led another way than where the hounds had gone, which she did in such a manner as those that were near her might conceive " her to be " weary with a long chase," and taken by her horse, which was " hot and impatient of the bit," in a different direction from her intention (as ladies sometimes are taken by their horses even in modern times) when she tried to pull him up.

Kenelm Digby, who had also been " staying to be among the hindmost," worked his way, unnoticed, in the same direction ; and thus they rode on " till being so far got from the rest of the company, who in such a wild place could not find them out, they alighted and led their horses into a thicket, where " the pair of lovers sat down together, while their horses " grazed by them ".

It was not the mouth of the valiant young philosopher, but " the coral lips " of Venetia that opened the conversation when they had seated themselves, side by side, in the thicket. She began :—

" The confidence that I have of your respect, my dearest Kenelm, in thus exposing my honour into your hands, is, without any other, a sufficient testimony of the love I bear you ".

Kenelm replied with a burst of euphuistic eloquence. " Angels and souls," he exclaimed, " love where they discern greatest perfections, and I were too blind if I did not discern yours." He could not, however, resist the temptation of putting in a good word for himself, by adding, "in me, where knowledge and understanding is the ground of a noble and spiritual love, other obligations are scarcely considerable".

When he had gone on for some time in this strain, Venetia spoke again :—

" I must yield, in the manner of expression, to you that have the knowledge of wit and learning to clothe your conceptions in the gracefullest attire ; but in reality of love I will never yield to you ; for I take Heaven to witness, I have tasted no joy in this long night of absence, but what the thoughts of you have brought me ".

"Oh, think not," began Kenelm in return, "that when the heart speaks upon so serious and high a theme, wit or study can have any share in the contexture of what one saith ; lovers can speak as effectually in silence as by the help of weak words." He dared not contend with her as to "who loveth most," for he knew that, as she surpassed him, "in all excellent faculties of a worthy soul, so she excelled him in the perfection of love". And he concluded a long and passionate harangue in this manner: " I, by soaring up to perfections above me, do daily refine myself, whilst you are fain to let yourself down, unless it be when your contemplations, rolling like the heavens about their centre, do make yourself their object ".

" Fie, fie," said Venetia, " stop that mouth, which, were it any other but whose it is, I would call it a sacrilegious mouth, that thus blasphemeth against the saint that I adore." And then, dropping compliments, she gave him a history of her late misfortunes and adventures.

Kenelm also forsook his flowery adulation to give her a matter-of-fact account of his mother's "earnest and daily solicitations" that he should marry Lady Artesia's granddaughter. He told Venetia that in order to escape from this projected alliance, he had persuaded his mother to allow him " to travel into foreign parts for two or three years ". By that time he would be old enough to be his own master, and then, said he, " shall I come home free from those fears that now hold my soul in continual anguish, and enjoying your favour, shall in one short hour recompense all the torments that I have already suffered, and till then shall suffer, for your sake ". Nevertheless, said he, something within him whispered that he should take heed how he built the hopes of his " future joy and bliss upon the continuance of a woman's affection during a long absence ".

That whisper, replied Venetia, was from " some wicked fiend sent" by "the invidious enemy of mankind". " Confidently pluck him out from thence," " for that sun that is now declining to the west, shall alter his course, and rise where soon he will set, and his beams, which are now the author of life and vegetation, shall dart cold poison and destruction upon the world, before I suffer my clear flame to burn dim, or the heat that is in my breast to grow faint ; but who, alas! can ascertain me that the delights which you are going into, and the variety of great actions which will daily take up your thoughts, and the rare beauty of accomplished and ingenious ladies which you shall see, may not in time make you forget your love, your faith, to a poor maid that had nothing to plead for her, but her infinite love to you ? "

Then " her declining lids did let fall some drops of crystal upon her modest crimson cheeks, which showed like the morning dew upon a bed of roses that seem to weep because the sun maketh no more haste to display their beauty ". Kenelm, " drying " them " with his lips, was some time before he could frame " an answer, which, when it came, was of very great length, and ended : " Neither time, nor distance, nor other beauties, nor all the con- spiracies of hell can make me other than what I am : which is, and in that title I most glorify myself, your devoted slave ".

" With these and other pleasing discourses of like

nature," they passed a very happy afternoon, until un-
mistakable signs of sunset reminded them of the existence
of other people, especially such as Lady Digby and Lady
Artesia. Therefore they sprang up and mounted their
horses. It was even later than they had supposed, and, to
make matters worse, they had forgotten their way "in the
wild forest"; the consequence was that they "wandered
up and down as in a labyrinth, till by chance they met a
keeper that put them in a right path".

Over the scene which followed when the belated pair
entered the dread presence of Lady Artesia and Lady
Digby, Sir Kenelm prudently draws a veil. And this
much only are we informed, that Lady Digby, who before
had discouraged Kenelm's wishes to go abroad, now "used
all diligence she could to haste her son's intended journey";
while Lady Artesia "demeaned herself with such coldness
from thenceforward towards" Venetia, that Venetia "con-
jecturing the cause of it, did shortly take a fair occasion of
leaving her, having first made her a noble present of a
jewel that would manifoldly countervail her expenses in
entertaining her; and from thence went to 'London,'
where she might hope best to receive news of her" Kenelm,
"and to have means to convey hers unto him".

It was arranged that Kenelm Digby was to go to Paris
and to remain for some time at its University. Before
starting, he had the good fortune to obtain one more interview with Venetia, "when they both renewed the protesta-
tions of their affections and vows of constancy". Then
Kenelm took from his finger a diamond ring which he had
always worn and gave it to her, "entreating her, whensoever she did cast her eyes upon it, to conceive that it told
her in his behalf, that his heart would prove as hard as
that stone in the admittance of any new affection".

Venetia had no jewel or other present at hand to give
him as a love token in return; so she let down her
splendid hair, and cutting off a long lock, which "seemed

as though a stream of the sun's beams had been gathered together and converted into a solid substance," she desired him to wear it for her sake. Uncovering his arm, Kenelm gallantly bound "this precious relic" round it, and bade his lady-love farewell. Before leaving England he wrote this quoted letter, which, although of no great intrinsic interest, may be worth giving as a specimen of his letter-writing at the age of seventeen. It is of import as regards the contention that Kenelm Digby became a Protestant in his youth ; for, as will be seen, he asks the " Parson of Great Linford "—a place only two and a half miles distant from his home at Gothurst—to pray for him. Considering that, if he had still been a Catholic, the Parson would probably have prayed for his becoming a Protestant, this piece of evidence is not to be disregarded :—*

"Good Mr. Sandie,

"Once againe before my going I have resolved to salute you with a few lines and to lett you know that I have now dispatched all my businesse and am to begin my iorney tomorrow. I have sent you a manuscript of elections of divers good authors which I wish may be of good use to you, if not I pray you let it lie safe in your trunke till my returne, where I would it were of the propertie of leven to draw more to it, but I hope Sir the affection I beare you will find acceptance in your opinion, and my desire of deserving of you be a sufficient motive for you to repose confidence in me. The newes here is little, onely that the match with Spaine goeth well on, and the voluntaries for Bohemia are now putt off for a moneth, so that I thinke that businesse will come to nothing. The Prince tilted on Friday in great pompe, the King went in state conducted by the lord Maior on Sunday to Paules Church where the Bishopp of London made a sermon to exhort

* *Ashmole MS.* 240, fol. 131 (Article 54).

him and the People to repaire that church that is much
out of order. This Sir is all I heare and I am now forced
to leave in hast, recommending my selfe to your prayres
and I pray you Sir during my absence retaine some
memorie of your

> " faithfull and loving servant
> " Ken. Digby.

" London in great hast this 30 of March 1620."

Endorsement: * " To my verie Loving friend Mr.
Sandie, Parson of great Linford att his house there, in
Buckinghamshire these, with a packett, with speede ".

Arrived in Paris in April, 1620,† Kenelm Digby found,
in the attractions of that city and in his studies at its
University, some distraction and pleasure; although no
place, from which Venetia was absent, could at that time
afford him any real " content ". When he had been there
for some length of time the heat became very trying,‡
" and the plague raging in that populous city, so that all
those that had any possibility of subsistence in another
place left it, he retired to a little city called " Angers,
" inferior to none in all the country for wholesomeness of
air, beauty of buildings, pleasure of situation, abundance of
provisions, and courtesy of persons that inhabit there. He
had not been long here " when " the warlike sounds of
horrid arms, of neighing horses, and of loud trumpets,
proclaiming civil dissensions, were heard there to fright
away the sweet tranquillity which reigned in this till then
happy place; the occasion whereof will not be displeasing
to relate from the first beginning ".

He then proceeds to describe the assassination of Henry
IV. of France, and to tell of the young prince (Louis XIII.)
who was " immediately proclaimed and crowned king, but
being under age, the power and management of affairs re-

---

* Fol. 134.   † *Ashmole MS.* 174, fol. 77.
‡ *Priv. Mem.*, K. D., p. 81.

mained with his mother, who, being a woman of great judgment and strong parts, carried business with a high hand". The quarrels between the queen-mother, Marie de Medici, and the princes and nobles who, as Digby says, "being of turbulent spirits, seemed to disdain her sex and the rule of a stranger, she being daughter to the Prince of Florence," or rather of Francis II., Grand Duke of Tuscany, are too well known to be insisted on here.

Details are then given of the queen-mother's fondness to the Marquis de Concini, "a gentleman of her country," who "grew so insolent that the peers of" France "could not brook his greatness," of the young king's "deep apprehension of his mother's dishonour," and of how "he caused the marquis to be slain without any form of process, and confined his mother to a little town (Blois) two or three days from the court, with a strong guard upon her. But what cannot fury do in a woman's breast?" It is a matter of history that the queen-mother * escaped by a ladder from her bedroom window at night and that she was soon afterwards joined by Richelieu and other supporters; that Lugnes, at the king's wish, entered into negotiations with her, one of the conditions being that she should abandon the Duc d'Epernon, which she refused to do, whereupon Lugnes sent troops against him; that Richelieu brought about a meeting between the king and his mother at Tours, and that after this meeting, the queen-mother retired to Angers.

At Angers, Digby tells us, she raised forces, as she "gave out," to "remove some evil councillors that were about the king her son, for pretences of justice and holiness are never wanting to any undertaking, be it never so undue, wicked, and unjust". Whilst she was waiting, at Angers, "in expectance of her other troops, she entertained herself with masques, feasts, musics, and such other recreations

---

* Bush's *Queens of France*, vol. ii., pp. 96-7.

as might make time slide more pleasingly by her ". To a gay youth the " masques, feasts and musics" would be great attractions, and Kenelm says that he enjoyed " the greatest content that any place could afford him " in his still love-sick condition.

In the meantime, although the queen and her party imagined the difficulties of the king to be so great, and their own security so confirmed at Angers, a " place which was compassed in with rivers, and inaccessible when the bridges were broken down and the passages guarded," the young king was preparing to attack them. But of this more presently.

While Kenelm Digby was well amused, poor Venetia, in London, was " labouring with an impatient desire of hearing of him who was the only object of her loving thoughts ". It was just as well that she was ignorant of a very remarkable adventure which befell him " within * the flinty ribs of this contemptuous town ".

* _King John_, act ii., scene v.

CHAPTER V.

A LADY-IN-WAITING.

AT one of the balls at the Court of the queen-mother, Kenelm Digby was introduced to a lady-in-waiting, Lady Leriana,* with whom he danced and enjoyed pleasant converse. There was nothing approaching to a flirtation between them, but she was very courteous and friendly to the young Englishman.

He had been long enough in France to observe that French manners and customs differed in many ways from English; yet he was rather surprised when, the next day, a messenger came to him in Lady " Leriana's name" asking him to go back with him to his young mistress's suite of apartments at the house which the queen was for the time using as a palace. When they reached it, he was less astonished at being conducted to the rooms of a lady of the Court by a " back way"; † yet it did not seem a very

---

* I use the pseudonym given in the *Private Memoirs*.

† Unpublished portions of Sir K. Digby's *Private Memoirs*. Their Introduction runs as follows: " Although the following sheets could not, with propriety, be retained in a volume destined for general circulation, they are far too curious to be allowed to remain in manuscript; and as the memoir to which they belong is not complete without them, a few have been printed for the use of those who may wish to render their copies perfect. It will be seen that these pages are equally remarkable for that eloquence for which every other part of Sir Kenelm Digby's extraordinary work is distinguished; and which must be considered, even by the most fastidious, amply to redeem the warmth of colouring that caused them to be omitted." Nothing could redeem their grossness; but lest alarm should be felt at my making any use of them, I may say at once that, although the facts and conversations of the first half of this chapter are taken from them, I will guarantee that the most fastidious shall find nothing in it that shall offend them.

dignified or complimentary arrangement for his reception. Lady Leriana was waiting for him and gave him a most "courteous salutation," and then she did what somewhat astonished him : "she first went to shut the door fast, and to see all about that none else were within hearing ".

Oh, memories of the divine Venetia! was this pretty Frenchwoman going to make love to Kenelm? Judging from her first words, it looked like it !

"Courteous" Monsieur Digby, she began, "if you have ever been acquainted with love's power (the knowledge of which makes the gentle minds indulgent to others smart), you will give but an easy censure of the office I now perform, wherein I become the applier of the sovereign and only remedy to a friend's wounded heart. The rest of what I have to say is but short ; I shall only give you the first knowledge of your happiness," "Sit you down then, and thank your stars". Having said this she rose, and lifting a portiere curtain left the room, looking back to tell him that she would send to him the charming and noble lady who had fallen so deeply in love with him.

Kenelm "was so amazed with her unexpected discourse, that he could not of a sudden recollect himself to frame an answer, neither would her hasty departure from him have permitted it, although he had been provided with a premeditated one ". The moment he was alone he wondered who the young lady of the Court might be who was so anxious to marry him, and why she should wish to declare her love to him under such unusual circumstances.

He had scarcely called "his thoughts together" when "he saw the hanging," beneath which Lady Leriana had left the room, suddenly raised and a lady entering. Imagine his feelings when he beheld his blushing would-be bride ! * "She was in the prime of middle life," in fact she was forty-seven, while Kenelm Digby was about

---

* *Old Court Life in France*, by Frances Elliot, vol. i., p. 331.

eighteen ; she had "grown stout and unwieldy, her delicate complexion had become red and coarse, and her voice was loud and harsh ; but her height, and the long habit of almost absolute command, gave her still an imposing presence".

This corpulent lady who had come to offer her hand and her heart to the English boy was none other than the widowed queen of the late Henry IV. of France!

She was alone. " Taking him by the hand, with an unsteady and trembling pace she led him to that part of the chamber which was most in shadow," and her "faint and wavering voice uttered these words out of her panting bosom " : " Wonder not," Monsieur Digby, "that I seek the obscurest place I can to hide those blushes, which discover too plain the state of my afflicted soul ". " Reason hath in me given eyes to love, and teacheth me that I was never truly happy till the hour that I first saw you, and even then I made you master of my heart, and of all my affections, for then methought I felt an angel tell me that you were worthy of it."

In any case such a speech from a woman, old enough to be his grandmother, would have been disconcerting to such a stripling, but, coming as it did from a queen, it was infinitely more embarrassing. He " remained in such confusion at her unlooked-for language that all he could frame himself unto for the present was to kneel down and kiss her hand, hoping by this act of civility to waive a further reply ".

But he was not to get off so lightly as this, for " the queen soon took away that subterfuge from him ".

" Do not my words deserve an answer?" she asked. " You remain as one amazed : have my words struck you dumb? or hath the affectionate expression of a loving woman, which should give vigour and life to the senses, bereaved you of yours?"

Of a truth, this grandmotherly love-making was a very

serious business !   Horrible visions of a morganatic marriage with the middle-aged queen must have flashed before
his imagination, as still kneeling he replied :—

"Madam, my own guiltiness of the little worth that is
in me, in no measure correspondent to the great favour that
you are pleased to do me, doth so abash me that I know
not with what words to make a condign acknowledgment
to you ; and the posture that I remain in is but due for me,
so mean a vassal of yours, to so great a princess ; therefore
be pleased to deliver your commands to me, if in anything
I may be able or worthy to do you a service whilst I remain upon my knees to receive them".

"Nature," said the queen, "made us all equal."   And
then, oh, horror of horrors ! the vast-presenced lady "cast
her arms about his neck ".

At this he quickly rose to his feet and said : "Alas,
madam !"   "You cast away your affection upon one that can
neither deserve nor requite it."   "My heart is not mine own,
nay, it is so long that it hath lived in another breast (and
beyond my memory) that I cannot tell whether it were
born with me or no ; and for a greater obligation of her
plighted faith, hers who hath mine liveth in me, and
keepeth me alive, to whom when I prove false may my
own hand send my guilty soul from this accursed light,
and my affrighted conscience pass the horrid sentence of
damnation upon it.   Now, then, that I have said thus
much, I doubt not but you will, if not hate, at least scorn
me as much as before you loved me."

This must have made it clear to the queen that he was
in no mood to marry her.

"Ah ! foolish young man," she replied, "what fond
chimeras possess thy deluded brain which suffer thee not
to see and know thine own happiness?"   "In a cursed hour
my eyes first saw thee."   "No woman certainly was thy
mother," "but nature, gathering all her seeds of horror into
one sum, sent thee a dire prodigy into the world ".   "Go

thy way, thou shalt not long glory in the trophies of my despised affections, but dearly thou shalt buy the knowledge of the fury of a living queen justly incensed at thy scorn."

Having said this "she flung from him in a violent manner, leaving him not so much in fear of the effects of her rage as he was perplexed with her love. Her back was no sooner turned than" "he hasted to the door that he came in at".

"On his way back to his lodging he reflected upon what had passed, and was contriving with himself how to behave himself for the future, when of a sudden a confused noise, that seemed to be of men oppressed with some violent fear, drew his senses another way."

Its origin was soon apparent. "The hasty running of many disordered troops of soldiers towards the queen's palace, with the countenance of death stamped on their faces," betokened a defeat of the queen's army. The truth was that the king, her son, had suddenly swooped upon her soldiers, "although their number exceeded his twenty-fold; yet the sacred presence of their sovereign struck such awe and terror into them, that they forsook the field, and left there all their ensigns, and many of their lives. The next day the queen sued for peace, and withal made her lamentations of her past injuries in such effectual manner to her son, that, together with the authority of a parent, it moved his heart to so much tenderness that he confessed that one tear of a mother could wash away greater wrongs than she had done him."

The rout and truce above described followed the well-known battle of Pont de Cé, and they must have come in very opportunely to distract the queen-mother from her disappointment in love. Eager and anxious conferences with Cardinal Richelieu on State business would serve as a salutary check upon her somewhat untimed cravings for the affections of a mere boy.

The queen "gave orders for the disbanding of her troops,

most of which remained behind at Angers. At which time they
grew very discontented," " so that in conclusion, when they
were no longer restrained by the authority of their commanders, from whose jurisdiction they were now absolved,
before they went out of it they saccaged the town, and
committed many murders, but they made more pillage
of wine (that boiled in their blood and fumed in their
brain) than of any other goods ".

Here Kenelm Digby perceived his opportunity, for, he
continues, " in the number of which so slain," he " caused
his servants to give out that he was one, himself lying
concealed in the meantime in a friend's house, he hoping
by this means to free himself from the trouble of the
queen's love, and from the danger of her fury ; which he
so handsomely carried, and sorrow for the loss of their
master so well personated by his servants, that the news of
it was soon divulged, and believed by all men, and among
the first it came to the queen's ears ".

It was well that he had resort to this deception, for, in
spite of her anxieties about the defeat of her troops and
the making of a truce with her son, she had given " scope
again," he tells us, " to her loving passions, and had sent to
inquire after him, intending to leave no industry and
means unattempted either of gifts, prayers, or threats, that
might induce to " " bring him to her feet ".

Believing that, if he remained in France, the queen-
mother would sooner or later hear that he was alive, he
secretly went in a southerly direction, crossed over by sea
into Italy and established himself at Florence,* " intending
to spend some time in that pleasant climate, where the sun
seemed to cast more propitious beams than upon any
other place," and where " noble minds apply themselves
to contemplative and academic studies, wherein their
spirits working upon themselves, they are so refined, that

---

* *Priv. Mem.*, K. D., p. 88.

for matters of wit, civility, and gentleness, these parts may be the level for the rest of the world to aim at ".

Kenelm Digby had the good fortune to pay his first visit to Florence in a time of peace. The Medici were in full power, and Cosmo II. was grand duke. The city had already attained its highest reputation as the home of literature, science, and art.

In the world of science, which was much more attractive than that of art to Kenelm Digby, the attention of Italy, nay, the attention of Europe, was at that time concentrated upon one famous mathematician and astronomer who lived at Florence, namely Galileo. Six years earlier he had been summoned to Rome, and ordered not to promulgate certain theories ; but he was again at Florence, preparing his *Dialogues on the Ptolemaic and Copernician Systems of the World;* and it was not until twelve years later that he was again summoned to Rome, before the Inquisition, and condemned to a quasi-imprisonment.*

The lately issued treatises of two northern philosophers were occupying the attention of learned men at the time of our young Englishman's arrival at Florence almost as much as the theories of Galileo : these were the " Laws " of the German astronomer Kepler (the third of which preceded that arrival by but three years) and the *Novum Organum* of Bacon, which perhaps may not have reached Florence until some months after Digby's arrival.

In regard to the philosophy of the last-named author,[†] Lodge writes of Kenelm Digby :—

" With respect to his philosophy, it would be difficult to say whether his succeeding so immediately as he did

---

* Of that imprisonment Galileo himself wrote : " I have as a prison the delightful palace of Trinita di Monte ". Of his second jailer again he wrote : " My best friend, the Archbishop of Siena, at whose house I have always enjoyed the most delightful tranquillity ". His third and last prison was his own villa near Florence.

† *Portraits of Illustrious Personages*, vol. v., p. 147.

to the illustrious Bacon might be deemed more fortunate or disadvantageous to him, since in profiting largely by the discoveries of that sage he lost through the carelessness of some, and the malignity of others, the credit of originality ". Lodge, however, maintains that he "gave form and birth to many of Bacon's mighty conceptions ".

Be this as it may, Kenelm Digby had the advantage, if advantage it were, of studying philosophy at different schools, under philosophers of various nationalities, first at Oxford, secondly at Paris, and thirdly at Florence. Possibly, three courses of but moderate length under separate professors, or sets of professors—not, perhaps, of the same school of philosophy—may have been more conducive to a curious, showy, and broad-minded scholarship than to securing a solid, profound, masterly, and permanent knowledge of the subject ; nor can it be fairly denied that this was more or less the result in the case of Kenelm Digby.

There is strong reason for supposing that Digby acquired the secret of the "Sympathetic Powder," with which his name is so much associated, during this stay at Florence. He seems to have made use of the powder within the next two or three years, and he says that he [*] " had the secret " from " a religious Carmelite, who came from the Indies and Persia to Florence," where he refused the urgent request of " the Great Duke of Tuscany " for initiation into its mysteries ; he, nevertheless, imparted to Kenelm Digby in return for " an important courtesy " which that young Englishman had rendered to the said Friar.

As to the compound itself, in Dr. Napier's recipes among the Ashmolean MSS. is one, which Mr. Black in his catalogue says " is apparently the original of Sir

---

[*] *Sir Kenelm Digby's Discourse upon the Sympathetic Powder.* I quote from a footnote to the *Biog. Brit.*, ed. 1750, p. 1702.

Kenelm Digby's celebrated 'powder of sympathy'". Its
virtues far exceeded Orfius'

> Strange Hermetic powder,
> That wounds nine miles point blanck would solder.
>
> *Hudibras*, part i., cant. i.

The following is the full text from the Ashmole MS. :—

"ASHMOLE MS. 1488, II. 73*a*.

"To make a salve y^t healeth though a man be thirty miles of.

"Take mosse of a ded mans hed 2 onc., mans greace 2 onc., mum-
mia mans blood of each half an onc., linseed oyle 2z, oyle of roses
bolearminick of each an onc., bet them together in a mortar till it be
fine leeke (?) an oyntment, keepe it in a box; and when any occasion
is to use it, take the weapon wherwth a man is wounded, or for want
thereof take an other iron or peece of wood and put into the wound,
and so far as it is bloody anoynt it wth y^t salfe and each morning
lay a cleene linen cloath uppon the wound wet in the patientes ——"

Perhaps I may have quoted enough.

It does not appear to have been exactly what some
modern chemists call in their advertisements " an elegant
preparation ". Of the use Digby made of it I shall have
something to say later on.*

His ardour in studying the arts and sciences in no way
lessened his devotion to the beautiful girl in England to
whom he was so much attached, nor did it weaken his
recollections of her ; on the contrary, one of his very first
acts on arriving at Florence was to write letters to Venetia †
" to advertise her of his health and to prevent the rumour
of his death, which happily might come to her ears ".
As time went on, his interest in his studies as well as his
" content of noble and learned conversation " in the City
of Flowers was much interfered with by his intense mortification at receiving no replies to these letters. " His
doubtful fears, and yet he knew not what to doubt or
fear, plunged him into a deep melancholy, from which he
daily upon occasions interpreted to himself many sad
passages of near ensuing disasters."

* In his *Discourse* at Montpelier, Sir Kenelm admitted that Vitriol was
the only essential ingredient in the Sympathetic Powder. (Page 137.)

† *Private Mem.*, K. D., p. 90.

CHAPTER VI.

THE reason of Venetia's silence was that she had not received a single letter from Kenelm. "The first," * he tells us, "miscarried, and the rest were industriously intercepted and suppressed by his mother, who was jealous of his affections." From all that can be learned of the character of Lady Digby, I think that he must have been mistaken in imagining that she would stoop to so mean an action as intercepting letters ; but, whatever the cause, Venetia certainly did not receive Kenelm's letters. And something even more unfortunate happened : † the false news of his death was borne upon the wings of fame with such speed that in a few days after the loss of the battle of Pont de Cé it was known in London, "where it found" Venetia "labouring with an impatient desire of hearing of him who was the only object of her loving thoughts ".

On learning the fatal news, Venetia was paralysed with grief ; " it locked up all her senses as in a dull lethargy ". She remained in this condition for some time, and then " she seemed to waken out of a dream " and give vent to such pitiful lamentations, " as, to have heard them, would have converted the most savage beast into a flood of tears ".

She implored death, which had robbed her of her " dearest jewel," to level at her his " leaden dart ". She

* *Private Mem.*, K. D., p. 102.
† *Ib.*, pp. 90 to 102.

(51)

accused herself of having only a weak love for Kenelm, since
she could not "call sorrow enough" to break her heart.
If death would come to her in no other manner, her hand,
"so often made happy with his burning kisses," should
perform "the glorious act" of self-destruction.   Then
the thought struck her that "the gates which lead souls
into the region of bliss are shut against them that lay
violent hands upon themselves"; therefore, as Kenelm was
"doubtless enthroned in happiness among the blessed
angels that in this life he resembled," suicide seemed
hardly fitted to her desire.

During her days of deepest woe, she refused to receive
any visitors, "pretending indisposition of health," but with
one exception, and that was the man who had saved her
life—Sir Edward Sackville.   This youth "at the first sight
of her drank into his bowels the secret flames of a deep
affection"; and although, owing to not being on visiting
terms with Lady Artesia, he could not see Venetia while
she was under her roof, "he had immediate notice" when
she went from Artesia's house to "London.   Thither he
followed her, with all speed," and declared his love.   At
"the very beginning of his passionate discourse," she interrupted him and told him never to use such language to her
again; yet, in consideration of his having saved her life,
and the "knowledge of the much that, for her sake, he endured," she "allotted to him so much of her goodwill as a
sister may bear to a brother," and confided to him the news
that her affection "was wholly and only vowed" to Kenelm
Digby.

Sir Edward was sufficiently a man of the world to be
aware "that women's passions are not perpetual, but that
by how much more violent they are, so much less durance
they have to use"; and he was prudent enough not "to
venture the loss of all by striving to make too sudden a
gain of all".

When Venetia had mourned Kenelm for some time

and "the stormy violence of grief was a little over," Sir Edward, "like one cunning in the nature and qualities of passions, would not bluntly oppose her sorrow" or "unreasonably distract her thoughts to contrary objects," but he first appeared "to bear a part with her in her grief, till he had got so much credit with her, and insensibly won such an inclination in her to like what he said and did, that, at length"—well, at length, many long lines go on to break the fact to us "that she took delight in his company," although "she desired him to content himself, and to seek no further from her, for that, ever since" Kenelm's "death, her heart was also dead to all passionate affections".

All these brotherly and sisterly delights and contents, however, were destined to be fraught with evil consequences. When Venetia's acquaintances, who had been refused admittance on the ground that she was suffering from "indisposition of health," learned that Sir Edward Sackville was the constant companion of her convalescence, "that monster which was begot of some fiend in hell, and feedeth itself upon the infected breaths of the base multitude, Fame! made a false construction of her actions, and did spread abroad a scandalous rumour of the familiarity of Sir Edward" with her; which, peradventure, "the latter increased by speaking more lavishly of her favours than he had real ground for, thinking to do himself honour".

Unhappily, when once this rumour was "on foot, it was too late for her, that was so young, so beautiful, and at liberty in the world, to suppress it". Yet Digby solemnly declares that Venetia's "soul was as white and free from a spot as virtue is," although he admits that her grief at his own supposed death, and the consolation which she obtained from talking about it to Sir Edward, "made her so much forget her wonted discretion, as through too much indulgency to admit" him "to a nearer familiarity than in terms of rigour was fit for her, or than her affection did really call him unto".

On hearing that she was the subject of an atrocious scandal, she was covered with confusion.   When she lamented it to Sir Edward, he implored her to put an end to the base rumour by withdrawing " her former resolution of solitariness and marrying him ".   " The nearest of her friends that had a quick sense of her good importuned her to accept this good offer, both because it was in secular respects such a fortune to her as she had no reason to refuse "—Sir Edward was heir apparent to his brother the Earl of Dorset—" but most of all they represented to her that she had inconsiderately brought herself so much upon the stage, and submitted herself to the world's censure " for Sir Edward's " sake, that she could not now retire from him without much dishonour ".

The last argument had its effect upon her, and although neither love for Sir Edward, nor his merits, nor his wealth, nor any other motive could prevail upon her to accept his hand, " the sense of her honour " instigated her, a year or more after Kenelm's supposed death, to give " a cold and half-constrained consent to condescend to " Sir Edward's suit.   After all, he was not an unattractive wooer.   His handsome features, as portrayed by Vandyck, are well known, and Clarendon * writes of " his Person Beautiful, and graceful, and vigorous ; his wit pleasant, sparkling, and sublime ; and his other parts of learning and language, of that lustre that he could not miscarry in the world ".

He began to " provide † with much splendour and magnificence, all things necessary to give an honourable solemnity to their nuptials," and he " obtained leave from " Venetia to " have her picture drawn by an excellent workman ; which, afterwards, he used to show as a glorious trophy of her conquered affections".   As this picture eventually led to much ill-feeling and annoyance, and even threatened at one time to involve fatal consequences, it

---

* *Hist. of the Reb.*, vol. i., pp. 59-60.

† *Priv. Mem.*, K. D., p. 102.

may be worth quoting Ben Jonson's verses to the " picture" of Venetia's " Bodie," which may have been called into existence by the noise afterwards made about the very portrait in question. I have not copied them from any printed edition of Ben Jonson's poems; but from a MS. among my own inherited Digby papers, which were formerly in Sir Kenelm's possession. It is in a remarkably clear but unknown hand. The water-mark on the paper is of the time in which Kenelm Digby lived. It will be observed that Jonson's name is spelt " Johnson ".

A PICTURE OF THE BODIE OF THE LADIE VENETIA DIGBY.

BY BEN JOHNSON.

Sitting and readie to be drawne,
What make these velvetts silkes and lawne,
Embroideries, feathers, fringes, lace
Where everie limme takes like a face.

Send these suspected, helpes to ayde
Some forme defective, or decay'de ;
This beautie without falsehood faire,
Needes nought to cloathe it but the aire.

Yet something to the Painters viewe
Were fitly interpos'd, so new ;
He shall if he can understand,
Worke with my fancie, his owne hand.

Drawe first a cloud all save her necke.
And out of that make day to break,
Till like her face it doe appeare,
And men may thinke all light rose there.

Then let the beames of that disperse
The cloud, and shew the universe,
But at such distance, as the eye
Maie rather yet adore than spye.

The heaven design'd, Drawe next a spring,
With all that it or youth can bring,
Four rivers braunching forthe like seas,
And Paradise confining these.

Last Drawe the circle of this globe,
And let there be a starry robe
Of constellations 'bout it hurl'd,
And thou hast painted beauties world.

But Painter, see thou do not sell
A copie of this peece, nor tell
Whose 'tis, but if it favour finde,
Next sitting wee will drawe her minde.

A few verses may be sufficient from the very long poem
which accompanies it :—

THE PICTURE OF THE MINDE OF THE LADYE VENETIA DIGBY.

BY BEN JOHNSON.

Painter you are come but may be gone,
Now I have better thought thereon,
This work I can performe alone,
And give you reasons more than one.

Not that your art I do refuse
But here I may, no colours use,
Besides, your hand will never hitt
To draw the thing that cannot sitt.

.   .   .   .

No! to express this minde to sense,
Would aske a heavens intelligence;
Since nothing can report her flame
But what's akinne to whence it came.

.   .   .   .

The voice so sweet the wordes so faire
As some soft charme had stroakt the aier
And though the sound were parted thence
Still left an Echo in the sence.

.   .   .   .

Thrice happie house that hast receipt
For this so loftie forme ; so straight,
So polisht, perfect round and eaven,
As it slidd moulded off from heaven.

.   .   .   .

In action winged like the winde,
In rest like spirits left behinde
Upon a banke or field of flowers,
Begotten by that winde and showers.

In thee faire mansion lett it rest,
Yet knowe with what thou art possest,
Thou entertayning in thy brest
But such a minde, maks't God thy guest.

We must now return to Kenelm Digby. He had sent letter after letter to her whom he loved so dearly, imploring her to write to him, yet no answer came. He was getting into a feverish state of anxiety; even philosophy did not avail to distract his mind from the one subject of its care. Presently a young Englishman came direct from London to Florence. Kenelm hoped that perhaps by judicious management of the discourse he might by degrees learn something from the traveller about Venetia. When they first met, however, he thought well only to ask the latest news from London. Well, said the new-comer, thinking to entertain him, the latest piece of gossip was that that pretty girl, Venetia Stanley, old Sir Edward's daughter, had—and then he gave the worst construction of the scandal relating to Venetia's intimacy with Sir Edward Sackville. Indeed he endeavoured to amuse his listener by a richly embroidered account of the whole affair, which he "delivered" * "with such circumstances as went much to the prejudice of her honour".

Now the ordinary temper of Kenelm Digby's mind was "noble"—it must be understood that I am giving his own description of it—"being by nature composed of an excellent mixture," and it was "so richly cultivated with continual study and philosophical precepts"—these again are his own words—that formerly it stood "in defiance of fortune; but now he was so overborne with passion, that he might serve for a clear example to all who may promise most of themselves, that none can be so perfect in this life"—not even Kenelm Digby—but that "he may be humbled and put in mind, at his own cost, of the frailty of human nature".

* *Priv. Mem.,* K. D., pp. 103 to 108.

" Sinking " under the " insupportable weight " of his anger and sorrow " he became equal with the lowest natures ; but he differed from them in the manner of expressing it, for, whereas they for the most part yield to tenderness, and bemoan themselves," he " broke out into a torrent of fury, cursing all womankind for " Venetia's sake.

" Injurious stars ! " he cried, " why gave you so fair and beautiful an outside to so foul and deformed a mind ? " And much more to the same effect. " She," exclaimed the philosopher, " deserveth now nothing but dire execrations from my afflicted and restless soul ; which yet my melting heart, whensoever I think on her, will not permit me to utter, but smothereth my just curses ; yet, thus much will I swear, and call heaven to witness, that, for the future, I will have irreconcilable wars with that perfidious sex ; and so blaze through the world their unworthiness and falsehood, that I hope their turn will come to sue men for their love, and, being denied, despair and die."

Then in his fury he " tore from his arm the bracelet of her hair," and thus apostrophised it : " Thou, once dear pledge of my lady's virgin affections, but now the magic filtre of her enchanting and siren-like beauty, thou canst witness how I have, day and night, ever since I wore thee, sighed her name ; be now her forerunner into the fire, that will one day torment her traitorous soul ; and as thou consumest there like a sacrifice to the infernal furies, and that thy grosser elements turneth into ashes, may thy lighter and airy parts mingle itself (*sic*) with the mind, and tell her, from me, that when rage and despair have severed my injured soul from my cold limbs, my ghostly shadow shall be everywhere present to her, and so affright her guilty conscience, that she shall gladly run to death to shelter her from my greater plaguing power ".

He threw her lock of hair " into the fire that was in his chamber ; when that glorious relic, burning, showed by the blue and wan colour of the flame that it had sense, and took his words unkindly on her behalf". But he was so exhausted by his trials and his temper as no longer to be able to "frame his voice into an articulate sound"; and "casting himself upon his bed," he lay there sighing "out the deep anguishes of his tormented soul all that day and night, and the next".

In England in the meantime things were not going quite smoothly in connection with the projected marriage between Venetia Stanley and Sir Edward Sackville.

Sir Edward was "a young man * of an unstayed spirit, though his much wit could disguise that and many other of his imperfections".

Clarendon says : † "The vices he had were of the age, which he was not stubborn enough to contemn or resist ; he gave them full scope without restraint, and indulged to his appetite all the Pleasures, that season of his life (the fullest of jollity and riot of any that preceded or succeeded) could tempt, or suggest to him". Yet, wild and unstable as he was, he cannot have been without a considerable share of ability and tact, for Bacon ‡ included his name among the half dozen which he submitted to Buckingham, out of which that royal favourite was "to pick one" to act as an intermediary between the two great men when a reconciliation was to be attempted after their estrangement.

Sackville's desire to marry Venetia Stanley, says Kenelm Digby in his *Memoirs*, " proceeded much from the supposed difficulty of the task "; and, when she had consented, " he soon grew cold ". Still he continued to make the necessary arrangements for the wedding and its "utmost ceremonious performance"; but being for some time absent at his country house providing for its reception of

* *Priv. Mem.*, K. D., pp. 109 to 111.
† *History of the Rebellion*, vol. i., p. 60.
‡ Spedding's *Letters and Life of Francis Bacon*, vol. vii., p. 320.

his beautiful bride, " his eyes were, during that absence, inveigled with a new rural beauty," "whose favour he solicited with as much fervour as ever he had done his late mistress ".

It was now Venetia's turn, instead of being the subject of a scandal, to hear of one. The attentions paid by her betrothed to the " new rural beauty " were described to her by a friend, whereupon a " generous disdain enflamed her heart which made her despise" Sir Edward, and she determined " to sequester herself from the conversation of men," forming for herself in England much the same opinion of mankind that Kenelm Digby had formed for himself of womankind in Florence.

From this resolution of self-sequestering " no persuasion of her friends nor humble and self-accusing repentance of Sir Edward's could draw her ". For, as soon as he had discovered that she would have nothing more to do with him, his wish to marry her revived, and he "did apply himself in the most affectionate manner that he could to regain her favour " ; thus proving " that in sensual minds love is armed, and, as it were, spurred on by difficulties ; and groweth fat and languisheth when it walketh in an easy path ". All his " industry " was nevertheless in vain. At most, Venetia had merely liked Sir Edward ; but now she " armed herself with hatred against him and answered all his visits and courtesies with harsh affronts ". At last he became so weary of being snubbed " as to be glad to intermit " his attempts at a reconciliation, and he contented himself with hoping that time might " mollify her heart".

And now that Venetia Stanley is safely " sequestered " and Sir Edward Sackville has become at least " intermittent " in his attentions, we must take a rather lengthy leave of her in order to follow the fortunes of Kenelm Digby.

CHAPTER VII.

WHILE the love affairs of Kenelm Digby, Sir Edward Sackville, and Venetia Anastasia were causing such private excitement, negotiations for a marriage of great public importance were in progress. King James I. had been informed through the Duke of Lerma * that his royal master was prepared to give his daughter Donna Maria, the Infanta of Spain, in marriage to Prince Charles of England.

Even at the first whisper of such a marriage being considered possible a very strong adverse feeling was expressed by a very large number of his subjects in England. The Puritans were furious at the very idea of an English prince being wedded to a Roman Catholic. Archbishop Abbot was scarcely less opposed to it ; but Laud, who hated Abbot, was more tolerant in the matter.

There were other, and very different, ecclesiastics whose objection to the proposal of such a marriage was almost as strong as that of either Abbot or the Puritans. The Pope and the authorities at Rome were indignant at the notion of the marriage of a great Catholic princess to a Protestant, whose father was persecuting and making martyrs of his own Catholic subjects. It seemed doubtful whether a dispensation would be granted, until it was represented that conditions might be laid down obliging King James no longer to allow priests to be put to death for their religion, or lay-Catholics to be persecuted, within his realm.

* Lingard's *Hist.*, vol. vii., chap. iii.

It was important that a diplomatist of the greatest skill should represent the English king at the Court of Spain. For this purpose, so early as the year 1617, James selected Sir John Digby and sent him to Madrid to pave the way for future negotiations. On that occasion, as we have seen, Sir John had taken with him his young relative, Kenelm Digby.

Sir John Digby was a younger brother of Sir Robert Digby of Coleshill, ancestor of the present Lord Digby. Sir John gained credit early in life by his conduct when he was despatched by Lord Harrington * to apprise the king of the intention of the conspirators in the Gunpowder Plot (one of whom was his own relative Sir Everard Digby, the father of Kenelm) to seize the Princess Elizabeth. He held high situations at Court † before he was accredited with the mission to Spain. On his return from that mission, he was created a peer in 1618, as Baron Digby of Sherborne.

Just as everything, after months and even years of tedious delay, seemed to be on the very verge of a final settlement, Philip III. of Spain died. Both James and Charles thereupon wrote to the new king of Spain, as well as to his favourite Olivarez ; Gondomar was persuaded to return to his master and urge the suit, and Lord Digby was made Earl of Bristol and sent to Madrid as English ambassador.

Lord Bristol had heard the rumour of his young kinsman's death with great regret, and when the news that Kenelm was still alive and well at Florence reached him in Spain, he very kindly wrote to invite Kenelm to come at once and join him at the English embassy at Madrid.

All places seemed the same to Kenelm Digby in his despondency ; yet, as he modestly writes in his *Memoirs*, ‡

* *Voyage into the Mediterranean*, Preface, p. vi.

† Burke's *Extinct Peerage*, p. 171.

‡ *Priv. Mem.*, K. D., pp. 118 to 153, is the authority for the remainder of this chapter.

"his generous heart represented to him, that it would be meanness in him not to employ for others' profit those talents which God and his better nature had bestowed upon him". In reality he no doubt longed for change of scene and action ; so he accepted the invitation and started on his journey, "going the first part of it by land and the rest by sea ".

Among his fellow-travellers he found a " Brachman of India ". This " Brachman " "exceeded most of his time " in "sanctity and deep knowledge of the most hidden mysteries of theology and of nature ".*

In spite of his love-sickness and mortified pride, Kenelm "entered into much familiarity" with the Brahman, who "one day as they rid together behind the rest of the company," with many apologies for his presumption, proceeded to tell Digby that he was troubled at observing "so much sadness and deep conceived grief to sit upon" his brow, and offered to place his "advice or endeavours" at his disposal ; or at the least, even if he should be unable to help him, he begged to be permitted to condole with him in his misfortunes.

" Reverend sir," replied Digby, "anything concerning me is not worthy your thoughts, which are always employed in divine and high speculations, but since you descend so low as to take notice of the outward apparel of my afflicted mind, I will give you thus much satisfaction herein, as to tell you that my misfortunes are such as it is not in the power of any man to remedy them."

" But," answered the Brahman, "if you will not acquaint me with the particular, give me leave to tell you in general, that no accident can be so bad in this life, but that the

* We need not trouble readers with the question whether a Brahman would not lose his caste by travelling in Europe. Probably the man may have been a Buddhist. Sir Kenelm would have been likely to have dabbled in "Esoteric Buddhism," had he lived during the last quarter of the nineteenth century.

celestial bodies have power to turn it to good; and
when men bear their adversities with temperate and constant minds, it doth in a manner challenge of justice that
they reward his patience with that blessing."

Kenelm Digby then professed the heterodox and
pessimist opinion that "it is blind chance that governeth
the world, which mingleth and shuffleth men's good and
bad actions, and their condign retributions, in fatal darkness, and then distributeth them with promiscuous error".

What a doctrine from a friend of Bishop Laud and
"the Parson of Great Linford"!

"You cannot be a competent judge in your own cause,"
rejoined the Brahman; "therefore, if you will let me know
what it is that thus afflicteth you, I doubt not but to
make you evidently see the error of what you now said,
and confess that not chance, but the heavens and stars
govern this world, which are the only books of fate;
whose secret characters and influence, but few, divinely
inspired, can read in the true sense that their Creator
gave them."

Digby said that he would welcome "any diversion to
draw" his "thoughts from the corrosive object that day
and night they" were feeding upon, but he begged the
Brahman to "mention no more that which he would be
happy to forget," and for his distraction and instruction to
give him leave to "oppose" him in his theory that "the
stars are the books of fate," since it appeared to overthrow "the liberty of the will which certainly is the only
pre-eminence that man can glory in, and that we are
taught to believe, and see evidently to be true".

They then entered on a long discussion upon such
matters as "elemented agents," "the humours of man's
body," and "things, consentaneous unto reason". Kenelm
Digby propounded a further heresy in denying "that
upon some occasions angels and devils do interpose themselves in our actions".

So polite was the Brahman in controversy, that Digby said to him : " I perceive that courteous language is not confined to princes' palaces, since you, who have ever studied things and not words, are so complete a master therein ". But he attacked the spiritualistic theories put forward by the Brahman.

Then said the Brahman : " It is in my power, as I said to you before, to show you by lively and undeniable experience that what you impugn is true," "therefore I will boldly do for you, whom I have reason to affect so much, what to another I would not acknowledge to be in my power ; so that do but tell me what you desire to be informed of, be it never so remote, or in what form you would have a spirit appear unto you, and your wish shall be undoubtedly accomplished ".

Digby, who felt horror at " the thought to have any communication, though at never so great a distance, with infernal spirits," told the Brahman that he considered it best for both of them to rest satisfied with " credence," especially as " such an experiment" would require " many troublesome preparations, and be dangerous in the effecting it, through the rebellious contumacy of the infernal spirits, which only " he conceived " to be at men's command, if any be ".

The Brahman replied : " These excuses shall not make me waive the satisfying your curiosity ". "When after much patience, and by abstracting my thoughts from sensual objects and raising my spirit up to that height that I could make right use of those powerful names which this art teacheth, I got a real and obedient apparition as I desired ; then, by virtue of the same names, I bound the spirit that I had called into a hallowed book which I had prepared of purpose, and always carry about with me ; and that I no sooner open and call him by his name, which is well known to me, but he presently obeyeth whatsoever I command, and thus without any unlawful part or wicked

E

means, a man cometh to have him his slave and servant, who of his own nature is his chiefest enemy. Therefore now I have told you what I can do, there remaineth but that you express your will and I will see it fulfilled."

Digby replied that he could not find words to express his gratitude for so generous an offer, adding: "But you may judge what a deep sense I have of it, since that alone shall draw from me the confession of what formerly your much urging me could not, and which nothing but my solitary pillow, continually wet with my tears, or some sequestered desert place, have heard me tell". Then he gave the Indian a full account of Venetia's supposed perfidy, ending by saying: "It is but a wild and imperfect relation that hath yet come to me, but such as did at the instant almost strike me dead, and hath made me ever since hate my life. Now my desire is, since you do not confine me within any bounds, that I may be particularly informed of all passages concerning her since I last saw her; so that I may either from the truth, which yet may be disguised or overshadowed to me, draw some ground of comfort, at least of less sorrow, or else have a perfecter knowledge of her unworthiness and my misery, since suspended and uncertain thoughts is (*sic*) the greatest anguish that can happen to the mind. This then is the cause of my sorrow, and the sum of what I desire."

As soon as he had finished speaking, the Brahman "drew out of his bosom" a little book encased in lead. Opening it, he showed it to Digby, who saw that its leaves were of very thin parchment, "inscribed with various figures, and pentacles and sigils of sundry colours". "Now," said he, "I will confirm what I have spoken, and give you complete satisfaction in what you request, whereunto all circumstances are propitious, the day being clear and serene"—the Indian magician required no darkened room, or dim religious light, for his wonder-working—"the sun having got the victory of all the obscure clouds that this morning would have darkened his beams, and the place where we chance now to be in so opportune, that we cannot wish a better."

He then dismounted from his horse and asked Digby to do the same. They had been riding through a wood, and the Indian left the path and led the way into a thick grove. He kept his eyes fixed upon the magical characters in his book and " murmured to himself words of a strange sound ".

Although unwilling to interrupt the incantation, Digby, on seeing a lady sitting upon the broken trunk of a dead tree, a little way in front of them, touched the Brahman with one hand and pointed to her with the other. She was sitting " in a pensive posture, so that but part of her face " was visible to them. " Her radiant hair hung dishevelled upon her white shoulders, and together with them was covered with a thin veil that from the crown of her head reached to the ground." A gentle breeze which was stirring occasionally lifted part of the veil and " played with her long golden locks."

She was supporting her head with her hand, and her uncovered and beautifully modelled arm rested upon her knee. From the glimpse that could be caught of the lashes of one of her eyes, it could be seen that there was a tear hanging from them.

Kenelm Digby stood entranced " at this unexpected and fair sight "; but the magician paced slowly on, and the lady, apparently disturbed by the sound of his footsteps, turned her head and then rose from her seat.

Immediately Kenelm recognised " the face of his once beloved " Venetia, " which seemed to be over-clouded with grief, but so that sorrow there looked more lovely than joy could do in any other place ".

" A strange conflict " " between love and disdain " raged within him; but love soon got the mastery, and, " not being able any longer to contain himself, he ran towards her, and kneeling down, offered to take her snowy hand, and was beginning to speak, when a greater wonder drew him to silent admiration ; for when he thought he had taken her by the hand, he found that he grasped nothing but air, which discourteously fled from his embraces ; as also three several times that he strived to take hold of the hem of her garment, so many times he found himself deceived ".

Then the Brahman raised him up and informed him that what he saw was "nothing but a vision procured by his art, and that that spirit should answer him to whatsoever he demanded ; and that he chose this form to make him appear in, to the end that he might judge by the true resemblance of her countenance and posture, the quality and temper of her mind ". It was disconcerting to find that what he had mistaken for the divine Venetia was in reality an evil spirit, which had assumed her form. Nevertheless, with his usual courtesy, Kenelm Digby had a compliment to pay to the devil.

" I now believe," he cried out, "that infernal spirits can transform themselves into the appearance of angels of light ; and since you would take upon you the shape of such a one, you have done discreetly to choose hers that is the perfectest work that God hath created."

Then he asked the spirit a number of questions, and received as answers much what has been given, in the preceding pages, concerning Venetia Stanley's experiences and adventures since he had last seen her, "all which he as greedily listened unto, as the poor prisoner at the bar doth to an unexpected sentence of absolution that the judge favourably pronounces in his cause ; for he evidently saw that she could not be accused of an unworthy mind, or of a depraved will or of inconstant affection ; but that it was the unjustness of fortune, or, at the worst, a little indulgency of a gentle nature which sprung from some indiscretion, or rather want of experience, that made her liable to censure ".

Kenelm was overjoyed at being assured "that her soul was pure and her mind the same he ever believed it to be ". Yet " the edge of his joy was taken off, when he considered who it was that gave him this relation ". If Venetia had fallen, as he had been informed at Florence, and had yielded to the temptations of evil spirits, what more likely than that an infernal messenger should endeavour to deceive him as to her innocence?

The spirit itself seemed to divine his thoughts; for, while he was standing, silent and irresolute, it spoke again.

" I now read in thy fantasy," it said, "and know thy doubts and fears as well as thyself. It might satisfy thee to know that those powerful exorcisms that have bound me where I am, do also bind me to obedience and truth; but thou shalt have a more material testimony to witness for me that I know and speak truth, and that within a few days; therefore, when thou shalt find thyself in the midst of a troop of armed men, and having no other weapon but thy sword, shall wound most of them, and save thy own life by killing two, the principal of them : then remember what I have foretold thee of it, and believe what I have said of Venetia Stanley's integrity, and that in despite of all oppositions and both your strongest resolutions, you two must be joined in one sacred knot; for none can change, though awhile they may struggle with fate."

Perceiving that Digby made no reply and asked no further questions, the Brahman, once more muttering some mysterious words, closed his book; and, exactly at that moment, the apparition disappeared.

CHAPTER VIII.

A BATTLE.

KENELM DIGBY had sent "a servant * one day before him to provide a convenient house near the ambassador's, and other necessaries" at Madrid, so, on arriving at that city, "he found everything in readiness for his reception and comfort".

The "first thing he did was to go to kiss the hand of his kinsman," the Earl of Bristol, "who received him with all the demonstration of joy and honour that might be, and caused him to stay supper with him".

He had arrived at Madrid at a very critical time. His relative, the English ambassador, had been at immense pains to further the Spanish match; but Buckingham, as Kenelm Digby says, feared that if Bristol "alone had the honour of it, he should gain thereby so much strength that he might in time be able to contest greatness with" himself, "who had ever a jealous eye of his rising". For this reason he had determined to take "that business out of the hands of" Bristol and to "attribute to himself the honour of effecting it".

As every reader of English history is aware, Buckingham had persuaded King James to despatch Charles, Prince of Wales, with himself, under the names of John and Thomas Smith, secretly to Spain, and he had intended thus to gain the credit of the marriage if it should actually take place.

Among a bundle of papers that belonged to Sir Kenelm

* *Priv. Mem.*, K. D., p. 154 *seq.*

Digby, formerly in the possession of my cousin, the late
Henry Bright, and published by the Roxburghe Club, is a
manuscript copy of the poem supposed to have been composed by King James on the expedition of Prince Charles
and Buckingham to Spain— "Jack his Sonne and Tom
his Man," as he calls them.   One verse may be sufficient
to show its style : —*

> The Springe neglectes his course to keepe
> The Ayre contynuall stormes do weepe :
> The pretty Birdes disdaine to singe
> The Maides to smile the woods to springe
> The Mountaines droppe the valleys morne
> Till Jack and Tom do safe returne.

Buckingham had hoped to reach Madrid before Bristol
heard anything about the expedition ; but, in a conversation with Gondomar, Bristol had gathered enough to infer
that such a journey was contemplated, and he had even
sent a messenger to try to prevent it.   This messenger,
however, was sent off too late, and the prince and Buckingham passed him near Bayonne.†

At the date of Kenelm Digby's arrival at Madrid, Bristol
was in a state of great anxiety with regard to the possible
visit of his jealous rival with Prince Charles, hoping that
his despatches to the king might be in time to prevent it,
yet at the same time fearing that the unwelcome guests
might possibly arrive at any moment.

As will appear in due course, Bristol was on very confidential terms with his young kinsman, and Kenelm Digby
would probably hear much that was interesting, in a private
conversation, either before or after supper, on this first
evening of his visit.   Kenelm himself says that, ‡ "at their
first encounter, they had much greediness of enjoying each
other".

* *Poems from Sir K. Digby's Papers*, p. 43.
† Lingard, *Hist. Eng.*, vol. vii., chap. iii.
‡ *Priv. Mem.*, K. D., pp. 154-165.

When it became time for Kenelm to return to his
lodgings for the night, Lord Bristol told "his son "* with
many of his servants and torches to accompany him".
The ambassador and his young relative had been so interested in their conversation that "the night had slided
insensibly away," and the streets were quite "quiet and no
living creature stirring in them".   It was a most lovely
moonlight night, so much so that "the coolness and solitude" were almost the only signs "that it was not day".

It seemed absurd to be accompanied by servants bearing
torches "which could serve but for vain magnificence " when
it was as light as noon ; so Kenelm Digby begged that
they might be sent back to the British embassy, and
ordered his own servants to hurry on to his lodgings.

Kenelm, therefore, Lord Bristol's son, and a friend who
had come with them, strolled on alone, " softly," " sucking in
the fresh air and pleasing themselves in the coolness of the
night which succeeded a hot day, it being then in the
beginning of summer".   The three young men were enjoying their walk in the beautiful night, and were " entertaining themselves in some gentle discourse," when their
attention was arrested by " a rare voice, accompanied with
a sweet instrument ".   They presently saw whence the
sounds came.   " A gentlewoman in a loose night habit "
" stood in an open window, supported like a gallery with
bars of iron, with a lute in her hand, which with excellent
skill she made to keep time with her divine voice, and that
issued out of as fair a body by what they could judge at
that light, only there seemed to sit so much sadness upon
her beautiful face that one might judge she herself took
little pleasure in her own soul-ravishing harmony ".

* In the introduction to the *Private Memoirs*, K. D., it is said that this
was probably the son of the Countess of Bristol by her first husband, Sir
John Dive of Bromham, County Bedford; but there are several difficulties
in the way of this conjecture. As Kenelm Digby simply says "his son," I
have been content to use the same expression.

The three Englishmen stood entranced by "this fair sight and sweet music". Lord Bristol's son, who knew who the lady was, had advanced a few steps nearer the window, when fifteen men suddenly rushed out, with drawn swords in their hands, and the moonbeams glistening on their figures showed that they were wearing coats of mail.

Lord Bristol's son instantly drew his sword and gave the foremost of his assailants a smart blow on the head that would have killed him if he "had not been armed with a good cap of steel". As it was he reeled backwards and staggered as if about to fall.

Unfortunately the wielder of the sword fared the worst; for his weapon " broke in many pieces, so that nothing but the hilt remained in " "his hand "; considering, therefore, that discretion was the better part of valour, he resolved "to live to fight another day," and, to the best of his powers, ran away towards his father's house.

Curiously enough, his friend's sword served him in the same manner, but, unlike himself, his friend stood " still in the place where his sword broke, defending his enemies' blows with the piece that remained in his hand". His adversaries, however, seeing that he was disarmed, turned upon Kenelm Digby.

Finding himself beset by so many opponents, Kenelm " retired to a narrow place of the street that he might keep all his assailants in front of him ". " There he found himself in a difficulty," because the overhanging balconies " took away the light of the moon," while his enemies had little lamps on their shields, which only threw a light in front of them; so poor Kenelm had anything but what Sir Lucius O'Trigger called a " pretty light for sword-play," as his foes " had not only the advantage of seeing him when he could not see them," but also "dazzled and offended his eyes with the many near lights ". Still, he had only to deal with one antagonist at a time, and did very fairly, as he stood at bay in his narrow passage; and he was able " to tell by the feel " (if I may be permitted to use that expressive, if ungrammatical phrase) that his weapon several times entered human flesh, while he himself was thus far untouched.

The idea did just flash through his mind that by turning sharply round and running through the narrow passage he " might seek the saving of his life rather by the swiftness of his legs than by an obstinate defence " ; but he determined to fight to the last.   Presently it occurred to him that, as he had given no offence, he was probably mistaken for some one else ; accordingly he spoke, as best he could in Spanish, " a tongue that he was not well master of," and asked " what moved them to use him so discourteously that was a stranger there, and was not guilty of having injured any of them ".

Then one of the men, who had been fighting with him, came forward.   A " cassock embroidered with gold which he wore over his jacket of mail " betokened that he was " of the best quality among them ".   In a furious tone he exclaimed : " Villain, thou liest, thou has done me wrong which cannot be satisfied with less than thy life ; and by thy example let the rest of thy lascivious countrymen learn to shun those gentlewomen where other men have interest, as they would do houses infected with the plague, or the thunder that executeth God's vengeance ".

These words roused the British Lion, and Kenelm " now dispensed his blows rather with fury than art ; but his hand was so exercised in the perfectest rules of true art, that without his endeavours or taking notice, it never failed of making exactly regulated motions, which had such force imparted to them by just anger, that few of them were made in vain ".

Finding their enemy a very dangerous man in single combat, some of the party " made a circuit," entered the narrow passage further on, " and came to assault " Kenelm Digby " from behind " ; but the first to do so struck him so lightly as only to give him a timely warning.   Perceiving the desperate condition in which he was how placed, Kenelm "made a quick thrust at him that was nearest before him," and " the other's jack not giving way," " with the whole weight of his body "—be it remembered that he was a great heavy fellow—he knocked the man down, and, forcing a passage through the others, he beat an orderly retreat through the narrow street, towards the ambassador's house, walking backwards and fencing off his adversaries as they followed him.

Suddenly one of the fellows " pressed so eagerly and unwarily upon him," and "lifted up his sword to make a blow at " him so unexpectedly, that Kenelm had to make a duck, or jump to escape it—" he avoided it with a gentle motion of his body " is his own account of the movement ; but he gave the man " such a strong reverse * upon the head that, finding it disarmed, for he had lost his iron cap with much stirring in the scuffle, it divided into two parts, and his brains flew into his neighbour's face ".

The unpleasant bespattering which this man thus received either blinded him, for the moment, or grievously disconcerted him ; so Kenelm, observing the opportunity, stepped upon the fellow's sword with his left foot, and with his own sword " did run him into the belly under his jack, so that he fell down, witnessing with a deep groan that his life was at her last minute ".

Now it so happened that the second of these two men whom Kenelm slew, one after the other, was the " master, for whose quarrel only they all fought," none other, in short, than the gentleman in the cassock embroidered with gold ; and "the whole band at once rushed to succour their wounded lord ; but all too late, for without ever speaking he gave up his ghost in their arms ". After this they took no further notice of Kenelm Digby, who "had time to walk leisurely to the ambassador's house ". When he was half way

* " Ah, the immortal *passado*, the *punto reverso*," *Romeo and Juliet*, scene iv.

there, he met Bristol's son leading a party of armed men
to his rescue, the reason of his being so late in coming
having been that, on his return, it had been long before he
" could get the gates open," " though he knocked and
called loud," " for all in the house were gone to take their
rest ".

The next day the reason of the attack was ascertained.
It appeared that a Spanish " nobleman," the nobleman in
the embroidered cassock, " having an interest in a gentlewoman that lived not far from " the British embassy, was
jealous of Bristol's son, " who had carried his affections
too publicly ". He had therefore " forced her to sing in
the window where " his rival " saw her, hoping by that
means to entice him to come near to her, while he lay in
ambush, as you have heard, to take his life from him ".

When Kenelm had time to think the matter quietly
over he recollected the prophecy of the Brahman's familiar
spirit, which had been fulfilled to the very letter; and, to
his intense joy, he was now able to believe in the assurances
of his dear Venetia's purity and integrity, which had been
given him by the same unearthly and uncanny being.

Of course the encounter was the principal piece of
gossip the next day in Madrid, and Kenelm woke to find
himself famous in that city. In course of time, too, the
news reached London ; and in London it reached Venetia
Stanley. This was the first intimation she received that
Kenelm was still in the land of the living.

" If before she lamented the loss of him," * Venetia
" had now as much reason to renew the lamentations of her
own misfortunes, which, she feared, would make her eter-
nally to lose him, though his other friends had found him
again, and thus, in the midst of all their joys, she alone
remained in clouds of sorrow ".

One effect of her sorrow was to make her hate Sir

* *Priv. Mem.*, K. D., p. 165.

Edward Sackville, * " with as much bitterness as so sweet a soul could entertain, as being the cause of all her misfortunes ; who, being inflamed by her disdains, did now again renew his suit to her with more violence than ever he had done before, and cursed himself for throwing away, like a prodigal wretch, the jewel which he would now sell himself to buy ".

If Kenelm Digby was the hero of the hour on the day after the midnight brawl in which he had so greatly distinguished himself, his exploit was soon eclipsed by an event of much greater moment.

The very next evening,† at about eight o'clock,‡ Prince Charles and Buckingham, who (on mules §) had outridden their companions, presented themselves at the door of Bristol's house in Madrid, and asked admittance.

Kenelm Digby's host had now to endure many mortifications. On the first meeting of the king and the English prince, Bristol was merely used as an interpreter. The dispute between the two representatives of England became more and more acute. Buckingham, says Kenelm Digby,‖ accused Bristol " for having given undue advertisements in his letters home, making the matter (of the prospects of the marriage) better than in effect he found it to be," while Bristol showed him documents signed by Philip to prove the contrary, and attributed the new difficulties only to Buckingham's " precipitate journey and his rash bringing the prince along with him ".

Knowing that religion formed the chief obstacle to the royal match, Bristol endeavoured to mollify ¶ " the chief

---

* *Priv. Mem.*, K. D., p. 169.

† *Ib.*, p. 168.

‡ Ellis's *Letters*, cclxxxi.

§ *Ib.*

‖ *Priv. Mem.*, K. D., pp. 170 to 182.

¶ The Archbishop of Toledo is the person suggested by Sir Harris Nicolas as being probably meant by the " Mufti of Egypt " in the *Private Memoirs*. It may have been De Massini, the Papal Nuncio.

man in ecclesiastical affairs," by sending Kenelm Digby to converse with him on the subject, partly because he knew intimately some "of his nearest kinsmen" in Italy and had brought to him letters of introduction from them,[*] "but principally because their religion was the same, which was but rare, and therefore by him the more esteemed among the English".

As this is Kenelm Digby's own account, he appears to have professed to be a Catholic when in Spain, whether he then actually was one or not.

As I have already said, the question of his religion at different periods of his early life is a very difficult one. It may be that as a boy and a youth he was nominally a Catholic, but of an exceedingly lax and unpractical kind; or that he either called himself a Catholic and went to mass, or allowed it to be inferred that he was an Anglican and went to Protestant churches, according to his locality, his surroundings, his convenience, and his interests.

The prince and his attendants endeavoured to show the similarity between the rituals of the Anglican and the Catholic churches; but displayed no inclination to embrace the religion of the infanta.

The prince's servants and chaplains, wrote Chamberlain to Carleton,[†] were to follow him with chapel furniture, Latin prayer books, etc., the service was to be performed in Latin, and the Communion was to be celebrated with wafers and wine mixed with water.

Whatever line Kenelm Digby may have been ordered by his great relative to pursue with the "chief man in ecclesiastical affairs," after one of his interviews with him, Bristol applauded[‡] "much the well carriage of it". "It is a very great comfort to me, my much loved cousin," said Bristol, that you are endowed with "such excellent

---

[*] *Priv. Mem.*, K. D., p. 672 *seq.*
[†] *S. P. Dom. James I.*, vol. cxlii., No. 38.
[‡] *Priv. Mem.*, K. D., p. 172 *seq.*

abilities of the mind " ; " so that I do not know wherein any man may justly say that you are short. I will only accuse fortune that hath given your education * in a religion that is contrary to what now reigneth in " Great Britain ; and he expressed a hope that Kenelm would formally join the established Church ; for, if he would only do so, he added, " I do not think any man is likely to go beyond you in having honourable and great employments from your prince, whereby you may win yourself much honour, and illustrate our whole family, if that only consideration (of religion) do not prove an impediment ".

This shows how much progress Bristol believed Kenelm to have made in Prince Charles's favour.

The youth replied that " the gentler muses " were more to his taste than courts, but that he would none the less be glad to serve his God, his king, or his country. As to religion he took up an apologetic line. People were " not likely to err if " they would but look into their " own hearts, which are the temples " the " general and omnipotent cause of all causes " " delighteth most in, and then worship that author of nature according as " they " found written there ". God's mercies would " supply for their other defects of ignorance ".

After he had finished his remarks on the subject of religion, Kenelm rejoiced that he had been able to bring himself " upon even terms with the world, considering the misfortunes " which " had accompanied him from his very cradle " ; and also that Lord Bristol by his " virtuous and heroic actions " had brought to the family of Digby " much honour and splendour ".

In reply, Bristol " persuaded his kinsman to apply himself industriously to the service of the prince, of whom he gave " a splendid character, shrewdly ending, however,

---

* He must have meant an education from his mother. As we have seen Kenelm Digby was sent at the age of thirteen to be educated by Laud, and at fifteen to Oxford.

by saying it "was of such an excellent mixture, that it was not to be doubted but he would be a glorious prince, if the goodness of his nature did not incline him to be won upon, through affection, by bad counsellors".

Bristol's testimony to the virtues of Prince Charles, " and the daily seeing him do all princely exercises with singular grace, and his affableness and benignity to all men, made " Kenelm Digby " in a short time not only dedicate his ordinary attendance to him, but also his heart and all the faculties of his soul ".

CHAPTER IX.

AT MADRID.

DURING his sojourn in Spain, Prince Charles exhibited his weakness, his obstinacy, and his insincerity. In spite of these deficiencies in his character and his physical infirmity of stammering, there was a personal charm about him which few could withstand. Kenelm Digby became much attached to him, and it is needless to say that it was greatly to his interest to be so. Charles also on his side must have taken a strong personal fancy to Bristol's young relative to notice him at all; for it would be in the face of the opposition of Buckingham, who would surely do nothing to encourage him in favouring one of the family of his hated rival.

There was one person at Madrid upon whom Prince Charles's attractions were powerless. The infanta, the object of his expedition, with whom he really seems to have been in love, never cared about him. She became very melancholy on his arrival, and vowed she would never marry him unless he became a Catholic. Gondomar was under the impression that Prince Charles was willing to become one, were it not for his fear of Bristol; accordingly he urged Bristol not to prevent the prince's conversion, assuring him that Buckingham would throw no obstacles in the way of it.*

We have already seen, by his conversation with

* Gardiner's *Hist. Eng.*, vol. v., p. 17.

Kenelm Digby, that Bristol had no personal inclinations towards the Catholic Church ; but he went to the prince and asked him with what object he had come to Spain.

"You know as well as I," replied Charles rather curtly.

"Sir," said Bristol, "servants can never serve their masters industriously unless they know their meanings fully. Give me leave, therefore, to tell you what they say in the town is the cause of your coming : That you mean to change your religion and to declare it here. I do not speak this that I will persuade you to do it, or that I will promise you to follow your example, though you will do it. But, as your faithful servant, if you will trust me with so great a secret, I will endeavour to carry it the discreetest way I can."

At this Charles showed signs of considerable annoyance. "I wonder," he said indignantly, "what you have ever found in me that you should conceive I shall be so base and unworthy as for a wife to change my religion."

Bristol apologised, but gave Charles some good advice which, like most other good advice, displeased the person to whom it was tendered. The prince disliked the straightforward honesty of Bristol, greatly preferring the deceitfulness of Buckingham, who genuflected whenever he passed the altar of the Blessed Sacrament in a church,* consented to listen for hours to the religious opinions of friars, as if inclined to join the Catholic Church, and never attended the Protestant services at the English embassy.

It must have been a relief to all concerned when the prince and Buckingham left Bristol's house for apartments which had been allotted to them in the royal palace ; but, from that time, Bristol was little consulted about the negotiations for the royal match, and was placed in a most anomalous and invidious position. Under such conditions

* Gardiner's *Hist. Eng.*, vol. v., p. 28.

it must have been a convenience to him to have his young relation, Kenelm Digby, in constant attendance on Prince Charles, for through him he was enabled to ascertain what was going forward.

At first, there were great rejoicings in Madrid. The people in the streets sang the song of Lope de Vega :—

> Carlos Estuardo soy
> Que, siendo amor mi guia,
> Al cielo d'Espāna voy
> Por ver mi estrella Maria.*

Among Sir Kenelm Digby's papers is a copy of a letter,† headed "From the Lord Marques Buckingham to his Lady from Spaine," describing the rejoicings. How Kenelm Digby happened to get it is a mystery, especially when we consider his patron's relations to the writer. It runs : "We are all well pleased and the brauest enter-tayned that ever were men. The Prince is now Lodged in the Kinges pallace : so that his M^{tie} and he Lye vnder one roofe. He was brought thither wth the greatest pompe that ever was, cominge through all the Towne on the Kinges right hand vnder a Canopie, and wth the same respecte that they do the Kinge of Castile. All the Councell came to kiss his hand, wth order, to do no favour nor bestowe any office duringe his abode here wthout his directions. The Prisons were all set open wherein there were above án 100 prisoners and xx^{ty} of them condemned to dye, six for coyning fals money. For 8 daies they make Bonefires and fireworkes throughout all the Towne, and I never saw People more ioyed in all my daies.

---

* " Charles Stuart I am
    Whom love has guided afar ;
    To the heaven of Spain I come,
    To see Maria my star "

is the translation given in D'Israeli's *Life and Reign of Charles I.*, vol. i., p. 66.

† Printed with *Poems from Sir K. D.'s Papers*, p. 41.

There are three Grandees appointed every day to waite
contynually in his Privie chamber and he is served for his
Carwer Cupbearer and Server wth none but Marquesses
and Earls."

Even the infanta, though she was very frigid to the
English prince at their first meeting, consented to his suit
after a time, on being assured that her marriage would
probably lead to the conversion of the English nation.

To Buckingham all appeared to be progressing smoothly
towards the accomplishment of the royal marriage ; but
Bristol, who knew Olivarez far better than he did, was
not so confident, and his misgivings were well founded,
for hitches soon occurred. Kenelm Digby was now
placed in a peculiar position. He was a great favourite of his relative, the Earl of Bristol ; he was rapidly becoming a great favourite of Prince Charles, with whom
Bristol himself was somewhat out of favour ; he was often
thrown into the company of Buckingham, who was the
sworn enemy of Bristol and the chief friend and adviser of
the prince.

This, with the exception of his undesired interview with
the queen-mother of France, was his first experience of
courts. Whether it was a wholesome beginning is more
than doubtful. He found himself in a very hot-bed of
intrigue and deceit. The great Spanish minister, Olivarez,
was, as Mr. Gardiner very truly says,* only "a liar of" "a
different stamp from Charles". Buckingham was plotting
solely for his own personal interests and for the destruction
of his enemies. The Spanish Council, says Lingard,† "had
ministered ample cause of offence" by their vexatious
delays, and their attempts to take advantage of "the presence of the British prince," and Mr. Gardiner, like many
other English historians, seems to think that Philip III.
did not act straightforwardly. To make matters worse,

* Vol. v., p. 104.
† Lingard's *Hist. Eng.*, vol. vii., chap. iii.

Buckingham,* by "the publicity of his amours, and his unbecoming familiarity with the prince, daily shocked the gravity of the Spaniards".

Here was a pretty school for a young courtier or a young diplomatist! Probably the most honourable man concerned was Kenelm Digby's own relative and patron, the Earl of Bristol; and, on the whole, the young cavalier was fortunate in being thrown under his influence. Clarendon thus writes of Bristol's virtues and failings :—†

"The Earl of Bristol was a man of grave aspect, of a presence that drew respect, and of long experience in Affairs of great Importance. He had been by the extraordinary favour of King James to his Person (for he was a very handsome man) and his parts, which were naturally great, and had been improv'd by good education at home and abroad, sent Embassadour into Spain, before he was thirty years of Age, and afterwards in several other Embassies, and at last, again into Spain." "Though he was a Man of great parts and a Wise Man, yet he had been for the most part single, and by himself in business—which he managed with good sufficiency—and had liv'd little in consort, so that in Council he was passionate and supercilious, and did not bear contradiction without much passion, and was too voluminous to discourse."

Another of his contemporaries, David Lloyd, speaks of his ‡ "Coming to Court with an Annuity of Fifty pounds a year, besides a good Address and choice Abilities both for Ceremonies and business. He kenned the Ambassador's craft as well as any man living in his time." "The *Spanish* Match managed by him from 1616 to 1623 was his masterpiece," etc.

In May, when Charles had been two months at Madrid, he perceived that his popularity was on the wane in that

* Lingard, *Hist. Eng.*, vol. vii., chap. iii.
† *Hist. of the Reb.*, vol. ii., pp. 201-2.
‡ *Memoirs of Excellent Persons that Suffered*, pp. 579-80.

city ; and, as his rooms in the royal palace were few and
small,* he wrote to stop some of his retinue, including two
chaplains, who were on their way to Spain. D'Israeli †
considered the suite of Prince Charles " mostly ill-chosen.
Some of them were the hare-brained parvenus of Buckingham." Nevertheless, as I have already shown, there were
men of more or less note among them. Yet " Most ‡ of our
company," says one of them, " did nothing else but play
at cards ; for, to say the truth, there was nothing to be
done else ".

Kenelm Digby found other pleasures than gambling.
He mentions having § interested himself very much in a
" Noble man of great quality, that " he " knew in Spaine,
the younger brother of the Constable of Castile," who was
" born deafe, so deafe that if a gun were shot off close by
his eare hee could not heare it ; and consequently he was
dumbe ". But he " could heare by his eyes (if that expression may be permitted me) " ; for a certain priest, " after
strange patience, constancy and paines," by teaching him
to observe the movements of people's lips, " brought the
young lord to speake as distinctly as any man whosoever,"
which shows that the teaching of the deaf and dumb to
converse by this method is no new thing.

Kenelm Digby was greatly taken by the unfortunate
youth ; for " the lovelinesse of his face, and especially the
exceeding life and spiritfulnesse of his eyes, and the comeli-
nesse of his person and whole composure of his body
throughout, were pregnant signs of a well-tempered mind
within ". The Prince of Wales, too, " was very curious to
observe and inquire into the utmost of it ". " I doubt not
but his Majesty remembreth all I have said of him and
much more." " It is true, one great misbecomingnesse he

---

* Gardiner, *Hist. Eng.*, vol. v., p. 43.

† *Life of Charles I.*, vol. i., p. 70.

‡ *Ib.*, p. 71.

§ *The Nature of Bodies*, by Sir Kenelm Digby, p. 307, ed. 1665.

was apt to fall into whiles he spoke, which was an uncertainty in the tone of his voyce ; for not hearing the sound he made when he spoke he could not steddily govern the pitch of his voice, but it would be sometimes higher, sometimes lower, though for the most part what he delivered together he ended in the same key as he begun it." " He would repeat after any body any hard word whatsoever, which the prince tried often, not only in English, but by making some Welchmen "—Sir Richard Wynne and his servants, in all probability—" that served his Highnesse, speake words of their language. Which he so perfectly echoed that I confesse I wondered more at that than at all the rest." This he gives as a marvellous instance of the generosity of nature in increasing " the sharpnesse " of other senses when one is lost ; for this Spaniard was endowed with " an ability and sagacity " to pronounce difficult words " beyond any other man that had his hearing ". " His so exact imitation of the Welch pronunciation " was the more extraordinary because " that tongue (like the Hebrew) employeth much the guttural letters, and the motions of that part which frameth them cannot be seene nor judged by the eye ".

Buckingham was pressing Charles to return to England, and the prince at one time consented, " wherein," says Kenelm Digby, " he showed that his affection to his friend prevailed above his own judgment, and above his love to his mistress, for he sticked not to express to some that were about him that he saw no other reason for his sudden departure, more than " Buckingham's " earnest solicitation ; and that he discerned so much sweetness, and so many perfections, accompanied with excellent beauty, in the king's sister, that he conceived no lady in the world was so worthy of his affections as she was ".

Bristol wrote * to King James: " The truth is, that this

* *Hardwicke*, S. P., l. 476.   I quote from Gardiner's *Hist. Eng.*, vol. v., p. 115.

king (Philip of Spain) and his ministers are grown to have so high a dislike against my lord Duke of Buckingham, and on the one side to judge him to have so much power with your Majesty and the Prince, and, on the other side, to be so ill affected to them and their affairs, that if your Majesty shall not be pleased in your wisdom either to find some means of conciliation, or else to let them see and be assured that it shall in no way be in my Lord Duke of Buckingham's power to make the Infanta's life less happy unto her, or any way to cross and embroil the affairs betwixt your Majesties and your kingdoms, I am afraid your majesty will see the effects which you have just cause to expect from this alliance to follow but slowly, and all the great businesses now in treaty prosper but ill ".

Occasionally, though rarely, during the many months spent in Spain, the Prince of Wales personally appealed to Bristol for assistance, while Buckingham held aloof; * but not with happy results so far as Bristol was concerned; and Charles felt the gravest dissatisfaction with that minister for admitting that there was something to be said for the Spanish view of affairs in the Palatinate; † for the prince had come to Spain determined to make the offer of his hand to the infanta the price of the restoration of his brother-in-law to the Electorate. With his patron in semi-disgrace, if nothing worse, Kenelm Digby must have exercised considerable tact in continuing to ingratiate himself with the prince. At any rate he showed plenty of energy. ‡ " He did set himself forward in the noblest manner that he could, and was inferior to none in magnificent expenses, whereby he might make the prince take notice how desirous he was to do him honour there, and to gain his favour; and for his diligence about his person he soon got the style of a careful servant."

* *Hardwicke*, S. P., l. 476. I quote from Gardiner's *Hist. Eng.*, vol. v. pp. 52, 53, 59.

† *Ib.*, p. 108.

‡ *Priv. Mem.*, K. D., p. 182.

CHAPTER X

THE GAME OF LOVE.

THERE were some adventures on his own account await-ing Kenelm Digby before leaving Spain.

He was on very familiar terms with Lord Kensington, who was * " Captain of the King" of England's "guard, and a complete courtier, and noted for applying himself very affectionately to the service of ladies ".

This nobleman regarded Kenelm as a mere boy—he was only twenty—and a student, and when he considered his fine figure, his handsome countenance, and the neces-sity of a reputation for gallantry for a young courtier, he thought he would do him a service by giving him a little friendly advice. With this intention he took an opportu-nity of saying : " When I look upon you," Digby, "methinks I see enough that telleth me your abilities might win you the affection of any lady ; but when I consider how you daily pass by the fairest faces without seeming to have any sense of the divine beams of beauty that shine there, I begin to doubt that the fault proceedeth from your mind, which, I understand, hath been trained up in scholastical speculations, and hath always conversed with books at such times as you have not exercised your body in the use of arms and managing of horses and such other disciplines as become a gentleman and a soldier ; so that I see there may be excess in the best and most commendable things, for these, that in a moderation may be esteemed chief ornaments, do beget either a dull stupidity or a rude bar-

* *Priv. Mem.*, K. D., pp. 183-191.

barousness in those that adore them too affectionately;
and I doubt much that from one of these two causes doth
proceed your having no special object of admiration here
among the ladies, where so much beauty reigneth : but I
shall fail much of my aim, if before we go from hence, I do
not wean you from your learned modesty, or civilise your
martial wildness, one of which certainly it is that maketh
your heart so rebellious against the power of fair eyes ".

This fatherly and edifying lecture was delivered with
smiles and courtesy, which encouraged Kenelm to apologise
for his fault with some candour.   " You should not censure
me," he replied, " before you are certain that I have no "
lady-love " and feel not in my breast the heat of love's
flames ".   If he had one, he said he owed " this blessing to
the sacred muses," and " the soul-ravishing delight which
they feed them withal that retire themselves into their
sanctuary ".   But he promised that, like " the famous
Syracusan mathematician (who was long before he could
be drawn to let down his knowledge, which soared high in
spiritual speculations abstracted from gross matter," " so
low as to employ it in making mechanical instruments,"
and then without any difficulty did " such admirable things
as seemed miracles to the ignorant vulgars "), he, Kenelm
Digby, would " make truce with higher contemplations and
let down " " his judgment to make love to a " lady in
order to " reduce " Lord Kensington " out of " his " error ".
And, added the bumptious boy, " I will apply myself to
the service of that great and fair lady for whom you continually sigh, because you receive from her so small encouragement to continue that hitherto unlucky affection
of yours ".   " I am nothing at all deterred with the consideration that she is the greatest lady of " Spain " and the
richest, and of the noblest family, and in highest favour
with the queen ; and, hitherto, an enemy to all intimations
of love.   But, because my conquest may be the more
glorious by having a worthy rival, I will engage you to

continue your suit, lest, when you see me to have got the
start of you, you may give over your course, pretending the
change of your affection, when, indeed, it is the barrenness
of your hopes; therefore name what wager you will venture
upon the success of our loves, which the most fortunate
man therein shall win, and the prince shall be our judge."

Instead of making him angry, which it well might have
done, " this overture " " pleased the earl very well, who
ordered the quality of the wager should be at the loser's
discretion ". He was absolutely certain of his own success,
" since his passion was real and the other's but feigned ;
besides that, in every respect for the mysteries of the court
and of winning ladies' affections, wherein he had long
experience with happy success, he preferred himself much
before" Kenelm Digby, " who was yet scarce entered into
his apprentisage there ".

Our young hero lost no time in paying his attentions
to the lady, whom he calls Mauricana.* " Whenever she
went abroad, he was the next to attend her chair ; if she
went to any place of devotion, he went too, but behaved
himself so there as if she were the only saint that he came
in pilgrimage unto; if she were a spectator to any public
entertainment, as of tilting or the like, he would make there
himself known for her servant by wearing the livery of her
colours, clothing his servants correspondently ; and at any
comedy or masque at the court where she was present, he
would teach his eyes in their dumb language to beg her
favours so effectually, that many times in public conferring
them upon him, she did exceed that reservedness which is
practised among the ladies of those parts ; so that she
was not a little censured by many that knew no more of
her but by the outward face of her actions."

In short, his " continued industry " supplied for his

* " Uncertain, but the first lady of the bedchamber to the Queen of
Spain," says Sir Harry Nicolas in his *Private Key to the Memoir of Sir
Kenelm Digby*.

" want of love," and the Lady Mauricana fell violently in
love with him. This was soon so apparent that Lord
Kensington acknowledged himself beaten and paid his
wager.

The fame of Kenelm Digby's "dearness with this so
great lady, the first of the bedchamber to the queen, and
of vast wealth," was carried as a piece of entertaining
gossip from Spain by some of the prince's couriers who
went to England with letters to the king, and there it
reached the ears of Venetia Stanley. It had been bad
enough when she supposed him to be dead ; it was worse
to learn that he was alive, but that his heart was dead to
her and given to another.

Meanwhile " the discreetest of those that loved him "
" daily solicited him to delay no time " in asking the Lady
Mauricana to marry him, which "they understood she
much desired " ; but his old love for Venetia was as great
as ever, and he was determined either to win her again, or
to forswear the whole female sex for ever.

The Prince of Wales had been at Madrid between five
and six months, and it was near the end of August when,
after several threats to leave Spain, he actually showed
signs of taking his departure.   " Those * who watched
him closely," says Mr. Gardiner, "doubted whether he
would not have lingered on, if Philip, who was by this
time thoroughly tired of his guest, had not taken him at
his word, and assured him that his presence with his father
would be the best means of facilitating those arrangements which were the necessary conditions of the infanta's
journey in the spring."

" Among † the rest that provided to attend the prince
in his return," Kenelm Digby was one ; "which was no
sooner known by Mauricana but she sent for him, and
there used all the powerful means to divert his intention

* *Hist. Eng.*, vol. v., p. 113.
† *Priv. Mem.*, K. D., p. 194.

that an interesting beauty is mistress of; sometimes endearing her own extreme affection to him, which she
would raise in value by recounting the scornful disdains
wherewith she had paid great princes' loves; then by
taxing him with falsehood and treachery, in inveigling
away her heart to make it serve only for a trophy of his
inhuman cruelty; then by representing the advantages
which his match with her would bring him; but most of
all she relied upon the force of her fair eyes and charming
looks ".

It was a repetition of the case mentioned in the old
days :—*

> Will you hear a Spanish lady,
> How she woo'd an Englishman ?
> Garments gay as rich as may be,
> Decked with jewels, had she on:
> Of a comely countenance and grace was she,
> Both by birth and parentage of high degree.

Finding all other means of vanquishing him unavailing,
"she sought at least to win time for the present, hoping
that when the prince was gone, she might the more easily
work his heart to her desires, and therefore only sued him
to stay while the stormy season made it unsafe to pass the
seas";—one can imagine her describing the horrors of the
Bay of Biscay—"that in that while she might, by little and
little, teach her soul how to bear future misery, and not be
plunged into it unkindly all at once".

The young Englishman began to regret that he had
trifled with the affections of this beautiful and hot-blooded
Spaniard. His "very bowels were then even torn in pieces
between a sad constancy and tender pity ". He tried "all
he could to sweeten her passions, and to excuse the expression of his affections, which he said he perceived she
mistook, for that he never made approaches otherwise than

---

* "The Spanish Lady's Love," by Thomas Deloney. Published before
1596. *Antient Songs and Ballads*, ed. 1877, p. 240.

in a courtly manner, as desiring to be called her knight, which title he would still maintain by all the real service that it might challenge from him, and should attend mindful with singular delight of the great favour she had done him".

On the utter unscrupulousness and infamy of Digby's conduct in deliberately breaking this poor girl's heart, and in sacrificing it to his own reputation as a lady-killer, it is needless that I should moralise. One of the worst features of the whole business is that, in describing it, he was evidently intensely proud of the performance.

The Lady Mauricana can scarcely have failed to perceive the insincerity of Digby's fine phrases, but worse was to follow; for he next proceeded to inform her, not only that he did not love her, but also that he loved another. " His affections had once been, though unfortunately, engaged elsewhere with too great force to place them upon any other object."

Besides, to cut the matter short, " for the present he was obliged to attend to the prince his master, into whose service, in an honourable place, he was now received ".

His vain and heartless verbal remedies did no more to " cure her mind " than the words of " ignorant standers-by do to bring health to one that lieth burning in a violent fever ". The unhappy girl " remained wedded to sorrow and despair," and not long after their author, Kenelm Digby, had departed from Spain, " seeing she could not have him whom only she thought worthy of her, she left the world that afforded her but a constant succession of continual torments, and consecrated the rest of her days to a worthier spouse, among other vestal virgins of noble quality ".

Kenelm was very fortunate in being in attendance on Prince Charles on his journey from Madrid to the coast.*

* Probably, too, he had his share in the "fifty" thousand ducats in jewels, "which the King of Spain distributed amongst the English gentrie" of the Court. See old tract in Nichols' *Progresses*, vol. iii., p. 910.

Two whole days were spent at the Escurial, where a great festival was held.

The journey of the prince and his retinue to the coast was like a royal progress. A number of officials were sent by Philip to accompany them throughout the long ride of more than 200 miles to Santander, where Charles was to embark in Rutland's ship, the *Prince*, in which a most gorgeous cabin had been decked out in preparation for the voyage of the infanta to England.

Digby states * "That the winds and seas seemed to rejoice in the prince's return," for they had an excellent passage. On 5th October Charles landed at Portsmouth, and, hurrying off to London, reached York House soon after daybreak on the following morning, when there were uproarious rejoicings, the public pleasure being increased by the knowledge that the young Prince of Wales had returned without the unwished-for Spanish bride.

Unfortunately Kenelm Digby was unable to "be a witness of the joyful acclamations that accompanied him to the Court ; for he had no sooner set his feet upon the shore, but that a great indisposition took him, which hindered his journey thither and his attendance on his lord for some days ".

As soon as he was well enough to travel, he went home to see his mother at Gothurst.† This must have been a wearying journey for an invalid, for the distance cannot have been much less than eighty or ninety miles. Lady Digby would be delighted to see her son and to hear of the favour shown him by the Prince of Wales. She had besides another matter to discuss with him. As we have seen, she had long been averse to his flirtations with Venetia Stanley, and now she could, as she thought, tell him certain things about Venetia which were calculated to put a final stop to any desire on his part to marry her.

As Mr. Bruce puts it : ‡ "The world was busy with

* *Priv. Mem.*, K. D., p. 197.
† Preface to *The Voyage*, etc., pp. xxii., xxiv.
‡ *Ib.*, p. xxiv.-v.

the lady's reputation.   She lived in London apart from her father and her other relations, a life of dangerous independence, and was one of the attractions of the gayer part of what would now be termed ' society '."   Clarendon states that she had "acquired * for herself a reputation no less extraordinary than her beauty," and some very ugly stories were in circulation respecting her relations to Sir Edward Sackville.   It is only necessary to refer to the second volume of Aubrey's *Letters* † to see what free use was made of her name, and what ill-natured scandal was talked about her.   Lady Digby would scarcely have been a woman if she had not repeated some of this gossip to the son whose affections she was so anxious to divert from the girl.

Sir Kenelm had been to a great extent reassured by the statements of the spirit which had been raised by the "Brachman of India," statements which had been supported by the fulfilments of the spirit's prophecy that he should be attacked, and that he should kill two of his adversaries ; but he may have reflected that spiritual manifestations are, at best, visionary and unsubstantial things, in which the imagination may play a larger part than their subjects suppose.   It must be remembered, too, that even the spirit, while guaranteeing her purity, admitted her indiscretion, and Digby might pardonably reflect that, after all, a demon's notion of purity would possibly fall somewhat short of that of the Mrs. Grundy of the period.

Although to go to Gothurst was to go far from London, it was not in the young courtier's case to go far from the Court, for the king was staying with Sir Oliver Cromwell,‡ an uncle of the future protector, at Hinchinbrooke, a place

* Preface to *The Voyage*, etc., pp. xxiv.-v.

† *Letters*, vol. ii., Appendix, p. 331.

‡ Wood's *Ath. Ox.*, vol. ii., p. 351.   Lodge, however, in his *Portraits*, ed. 1850, vol. v., p. 149, says that the following event took place "at the house of Lord Montague at Hinchinbrooke ".

near Huntingdon which had formerly been a Benedictine convent, and had been given by Thomas Cromwell at the dissolution of the monasteries, in the reign of Henry VIII., to a kinsman. Although Hinchinbrooke was only an easy day's ride from Gothurst, Kenelm Digby may have found it a fatiguing one, for he started with "more haste than his indisposition would well give way unto". But he would naturally be anxious, now that he was in the service of the Prince of Wales, to be presented to the king.

On the 23rd October, eighteen days after reaching England, Digby presented himself at Hinchinbrooke and obtained an audience from the king, who must have heard something about him from the Prince of Wales. James first complimented him upon his learning, and then having asked for a sword, he proceeded to knight him with it ; but so clumsy was he that, instead of touching him upon the shoulder with the blade, he very nearly poked the point into one of his eyes, and, curiously enough, the chief enemy of the Digby family, Buckingham himself, prevented the threatened catastrophe and guided the king's hand to perform the ceremony properly.* Honours rarely come singly, and Sir Kenelm was at about the same time appointed a gentleman of the privy chamber to the Prince of Wales.

Chamberlain wrote † in December, probably to Carleton, that Buckingham hated the name of Digby ; but that the king had nevertheless knighted one who bore it.

---

* Digby's *Discourse on the Powder of Sympathy*, p. 105. Preface to *The Voyage*, etc., p. xxiv. Very probably James's clumsiness was owing to gout. See *S. P. Dom. James I.*, vol. cliv., No 17. "The court would not come hitherward at Hallowtide by reason it was beset with waters at Hinchinbrooke by Huntingdon, and withal the king overtaken with the gout or pain in his arms so that he could not remove." (Chamberlain to Carleton.)

† *S. P. Dom. James I.*, vol. clv., No. 21.

CHAPTER XI.

THE COURSE OF TRUE LOVE.

It was towards the end of December, 1623,* that Sir Kenelm Digby went to London, nearly two months after he had first met King James at Hinchinbrooke. He was still more or less in a condition of " indisposition ".† The day of his arrival was fine and the sun "shined out more comfortable and glorious"—oh, fearful and wonderful combination, "comfortable and glorious"!—"more comfortable and glorious beams than it had done of many days before, which was the reason that many persons of quality came out into the fields to refresh their spirits, with sucking in the free and warm air ".

Just as he was entering in at the gates of the city, and meeting carriage after carriage, Sir Kenelm recognised in one of them the beautiful features of his beloved Venetia Stanley. He felt "like one come suddenly from a dark prison to too great a light ". " After so long absence, her beauty seemed brighter to him than when he left her." She was sitting pensively in one side of the coach by herself, and her carriage had passed and gone before he had time to recover from his first emotion at seeing her again, after so long an interval.

No sooner had Sir Kenelm alighted at his lodgings than he sent a servant to find out Venetia's abode, and to ask her leave to call upon her at any hour she might please on the following day. His object in visiting Venetia

* Preface to *The Voyage*, etc., p. xxv.
† *Priv. Mem.*, K. D., p. 201 *seq.*

(98)

was " only to please himself in so fair a sight, deeming her unworthy of his more serious affection, whom he conceived had so soon forgot her vows made to him at his going out of" England, let the truth or falsehood of the grave scandal be what it might. He would appear to have lost faith in the " Brahman " and the manifestations of his familiar by this time.

To his great delight his servant returned with Venetia's address and a gracious invitation to her rooms.*

" It is too great for me to describe the motives of their hearts and souls at their first meeting ; nor can it be conceived by any but such as have loved in a divine manner and have had their affections suspended by misfortunes and mistakes."

The reunion was by no means a matter of rushing into each other's arms and vowing never to part again. On the contrary, " the subject of their discourse " " was the challenging each other of much unkindness ".

Venetia began the attack by upbraiding Kenelm for never having written to her. " A timely advertisement of his health," she said, " would have prevented the inconveniences grown by his rumoured death." It was obviously all his fault.

On his own part Kenelm declared that he had written letter upon letter to her without receiving any answer, and he reproached her " for giving too sudden credit " to the report of his death, " and so soon bestowing her affections upon another " ; therefore the fault was entirely hers.

" Both of them used their best endeavours to discharge themselves and fasten the blame upon the other ; but in conclusion they both saw that there was more of misfortune in it than of fault on either side," and a peace of some sort was patched up before they separated. Sir Kenelm offered to call upon her again very soon, received leave to do so,

* *Priv. Mem.*, K. D., p. 203 *seq.*

and freely availed himself of it.   His visits became very frequent, and she " willingly received them ".

" Her excessive beauty and gracefulness " fairly over-powered him, in spite of his resolution " not to engage his affections too far," because of " the doubtful rumour that Sir Edward Sackville " had once had much interest in her affections.   Love was restored, but not confidence.

It may have been about this time that Sir Kenelm sent to the Lady Venetia a letter, enclosing a translation which he had made at sea, probably on his voyage from Spain, of Amyntas.   This is the only love-letter which passed between them that I am able to lay before my readers :—

" To the fairest and most generous lady Mrs. V. S., most noble lady and mistress.*

" To obey you (that have all power over me) I send you this rugged translation, which oweth you more of his being than unto me ; for the liking that I discovered in you to such compositions was my first motive to make Amyntas into English ; and since your commands have made him see light, without which I should never have cast my eyes a second time upon the loose and scattered papers that contained his passions, knowing how unproportionable it was that so sickly a birth as they had should aspire to a long life ; for they were begotten upon the sea, when during the tedious expectation of a favourable wind all things, even my very thoughts (unless they were such as came accompanied with your worth and virtues), were trouble-some unto me.   And now that I have made this shepherd ready for your view, methinks he suffereth more in this dis-guise than ever he did by his mistress's disdain, seeing how much singular grace he hath lost by his change of habit. All that I can, or will, say in my own behalf is this, that surely the gross and drowsy vapours of the dull and misty clime from whence I came remained still clogging of my

---

* *Poems from Sir Kenelm Digby's papers*, Rox. Soc., p. 1.

brain when I undertook this piece, which when it shall
please you (through your goodness) to disperse and overcome with the powerful beams of your grace and favour, I
will confidently set upon some nobler task whereby I may
with more industry and better expression make it appear
how much I desire to serve you. And in the meantime I
kiss your fairest hands, and with all the power of my soul
do rest

" Wholly at your devotion."

(The signature and date are torn off.)

[Endorsed :—

" The dedication of Amyntas ".]

Whether to find out the truth of the scandal which had
been rife concerning her, or thinking that a young lady,
who had been living in what we should call " such a fast
set " would not be very prudish, I am not aware, but, on
one occasion he spoke to her in a style which would have
been considered unbecoming in such a strict house as his
mother's. Instead of being entertained, Venetia instantly
stopped him. " Her heart swelling with a noble anger
and disdain, she banished him from her presence, and it
was long before he could (induce her to) take off that hard
sentence, though he daily offered up to her much sorrow
and unfeigned signs of repentance."

I am quite aware that I am exposing myself to the
danger of severe criticism for writing of Venetia Stanley
as if she had been a paragon of virtue. Aubrey's gossip
about her has been very generally believed and Sir
Kenelm's tribute to her purity has been much discredited.
I admit that there may be two sides to this question ; but
I am bold enough to maintain that that which I present
may be defended, and, for my own part, I would rather
champion a lady's honour than impeach it, whether she be
living or whether she be dead.

Sir Kenelm is not the only witness in her favour.

It may appear ghastly while treating of her love affairs to produce an elegy written after her death ; yet in describing the wooings of those who have been dead more than a couple of centuries, why should I hesitate to do so? Ben Jonson, in the course of his very long elegy, entitled " Her *ΑΠΟΘΕΩΣΙΣ*, or Relation to the Saints," * writes of her as if, instead of being unchaste, she were pure and holy.   He says :—

> She had a mind as calm as she was fair,
> Nor tost or troubled with light lady air
> But kept an even gait, as some straight tree
> Moved by the wind, so comely moved she.
> A tender mother, a discreeter wife,
> A solemn mistress, and so good a friend,
> So charitable to religious end
> In all her petite actions, so devote
> As her whole life was now become one note
> Of piety and private holiness.
> She spent more time in tears herself to dress
> For her devotions, and those sad essays
> Of sorrow, than all pomp of gaudy days ;
> And came forth ever cheered with the rod
> Of divine comfort, when she had talked with God,
> Her broken sighs did never miss whole sense ;
> Nor can the bruised heart want eloquence,
> For prayer is the incense most perfumes
> The holy altars, when it best presumes.
> And hers was all humility ! they beat
> The door of grace, and found the mercy-seat
> In frequent speaking by the pious psalms,
> Her solemn hours she spent, or giving alms,
> Or doing other deeds of charity,
> To clothe the naked, feed the hungry.   She
> Would sit in an infirmary whole days
> Poring as on a map, to find the ways
> To that eternal rest, where now she hath place,
> By sure election and predestined grace !

* *Works by Ben Jonson.*   By William Gifford.

Surely this is a description of a good, and not of a bad, woman!

Among the many admirers of the lovely Mistress Stanley was a Mr. Clerk, one of the gentlemen of the bed-chamber of the Prince of Wales, and consequently well known to Sir Kenelm Digby, the more so as he had been in Spain with the prince. This young gentleman * "was so hard to please in the choice of a wife, that of many advantageous overtures which had been made to him he would accept of none"; it was the more curious that he should be so sought after and so fastidious because he had only one hand,† "but declared himself that until he did meet with such a woman as both for mind and body he could wish nothing to be mended in her, he would live a single life". For this he was justly punished; for he fell over head and ears in love with Venetia, asked her to marry him, and got refused for his pains.

Finding that "by himself he could not prevail" with Venetia, "he discovered the violence of his passions to" Kenelm Digby, "there being much entireness between them, begotten by their daily conversation in their both serving the same master".

Clerk ‡ was under the impression that Digby "sued not to her (Venetia) for himself, but that withal he had an interest in her in an honourable way"; therefore "he beseeched him, with the greatest adjurations that might be, to endeavour himself in his behalf".§

* *Priv. Mem.*, K. D., p. 206.

† "King James was wont pleasantly to say that Stenny (the Duke of Buckingham) had given him two very proper servants: a secretary who could neither write nor read, and a groom of his bedchamber who could not trim his points," Mr. Clerk having but one hand. Clarendon's *Hist. of the Reb.*, vol. i., p. 64. Mr. Howel, again, wrote from Madrid of "Mr. Clerk (with the lame arm)," Nichols' *Progresses*, vol. iii., p. 934.

‡ "He was trusted by the Duke (of Buckingham) as his agent in affairs of questionable propriety," Gardiner's *Hist. Eng.*, vol. v., p. 415.

§ *Priv. Mem.*, K. D., p. 107 *seq.*

"Here," says the modest and humble Sir Kenelm, "one may perceive what a divine thing the obligation of friendship is in a generous and gentle heart; for" he himself, "that would rather have consented to the loss of his life than to see her in another man's possession, his flames daily increasing, became himself a mediator for his friend, to gain him that content that would cause himself eternal sorrow; which he did not in a cold manner, as only to acquit himself of his promise, but used and urged all the arguments that he could to win Venetia" to this match "so much to her advantage in temporal respects".

This was carrying honour to an extreme point; but zealous as Kenelm seems to have considered himself in his friend's service, one can hardly believe that that friend would have been quite so anxious to have him as an advocate if he had been aware of Kenelm's own devotion to Mistress Venetia.

All Sir Kenelm could get from Venetia, in return for his importunities on behalf of his friend, was "a flat denial". Her misfortunes, she told him, "had broken and deadened her heart," and her best affections towards any man for the future would be only platonic. At hearing this Sir Kenelm manifested "much impatience because it concerned him so nearly," and perceiving this, Venetia regretted the days when it had been "much otherwise" "and they had lived so happily and joyed only in each other". Then she taxed him with his changeableness, since he was now actually proposing to her on behalf of another man. This however, she confessed, did not prevent her from feeling more "good-will to him by infinite degrees to any one else"; and at this Sir Kenelm "rested much contented," and apologising for his "importunity for his friend" he took his leave.

A few days later, having occasion to make a journey into the country, he came to say good-bye to her. When he entered her rooms she happened to be taking a siesta, and, begging the servant not to disturb her, he determined to wait patiently until she should awake.*

"The closing of her eyes made the beauties of her face shine with a greater glory, like the starry firmament when the sun is set. He remained awhile like one in a trance, admiring that heaven of perfection, and accusing his fortune that made" it seem so improbable that, after their many misunderstandings, she should ever become his wife.†

And then he made a fatal mistake! Looking at "her coral lips" he resolved to "steal what she had often refused him," and gave her a kiss.

Venetia awoke. "Ashamed and angry," she immediately employed herself "in reprehending him". "She spoke in such a grave and settled manner that it was evident it was no affected nicety, or seeming to be displeased with what she liked, but that her words were the true interpreters of her thoughts"; and "she continued chiding him as angrily as so angelic and sweet a creature could ".

With a blush of indignation and horror, she imagined that the shameful scandals, which had been spread about concerning her fame, had reached Sir Kenelm's ears and emboldened him to take the liberty of kissing her. She reflected that she had been living alone and receiving her men friends with less ceremony than some of her most prudish relatives approved. Who could blame him, therefore, if he had misjudged her position and her character? And as to the liberty—the kiss—did she not still love the old playmate of her childhood from her inmost heart—him and no other? Had they not often kissed each other as children? Why should their past misunderstandings keep them any longer apart?

* See Appendix D.

† A detailed account of this scene is given in the unpublished portions of the *Private Memoirs*, p. 31 *seq.*

Her first impulse had been to load him with abuse and to drive him from her presence for his impertinence. Then came a revulsion of feeling; and it struck her that she ought rather to disabuse him of the calumnies which had probably led him to imagine that she would tolerate the liberty which he had taken, than to upbraid him for taking it.

Changing her tone, therefore, she frankly told him that she feared she could not but too easily divine his reasons for believing it possible thus to insult her with impunity. Doubtless, he had heard and credited the lies which had been current about her. Waiving the question whether a true friend would have listened to them for a moment, she would now defend her own honour in his presence, since, alas! it appeared to require defence, even before the man who, of all the world, she had hoped, would have been the most eager to defend it; and she considered that she could best justify herself by boldly declaring that "she cared for no other witness of her honour than the innocency of her own conscience," and by giving him the candid, if humiliating, assurance that she would " never be constrained in, or nice in acknowledging her affection to him as long as he made virtue the companion of his, howsoever the malice of the world might censure her actions ".

Sir Kenelm besought her to put away from her mind the very recollection of the scandals and the scandal-mongers ; but he felt " as one quite deprived of all sense," and, as a distraction, he asked her to sing something for him.

" She needed not to be twice entreated," " wherefore, after she had tried, with soft relishes to herself, how far her voice would reach, that she might take the song in a fit tone, her sweet and charming breath gave life to these following words," which at the same time proclaimed that a man who loved her ought never to have doubted her honour, and practically admitted her love for Digby :—*

* Unpublished portion of *Private Memoirs*, K. D., pp. 3-8.

Begone, proud tyrant Honour, and remove
Thy throne out of their hearts that love :
Thy ceremonious laws restrain
The freedom of their joys in vain.
They know thou hast no real essence
Nor canst affect the mind or sense
With any true delight or joy;
And only those weak souls that weigh
Their happiness by the false scale
Of opinion, value thee at all;
Who in the end too late do find
That vulgar breath is like the wind,
Which only on such empty things doth seize,
As want stolidity themselves to peize.
But when Love's purer flames do set on fire
Two hearts with mutual desire,
Each is the other's happiness,
And in themselves they do possess
The greatest blessings that this life
Can give ; and their full joys no strife
Of various passions can molest,
Nor anxious thoughts disturb their rest ;
And their free minds are curbed in
By virtue from committing sin ;
And not by hope of praise and fame,
Or servile fear of public blame ;
Such only when th' are seen refraine from ill ;
But these, their conscience always guides their will.
Then whilst my spotless thoughts from vice are free
In spite of this chimera I'll happy be.

The moment she had finished singing, the thought
occurred to her that her old friend's kiss had been given
with the purest intentions and had been meant to be a
manifestation of honest love. Why should she not recip-
rocate that love? His conduct might have been indiscreet,
but he was not the first man who had lost control over
himself in the passion of the moment. Therefore, having
avowed her own perfect innocence, she would let him see
how she loved him ; and, going up to him, she gave him
"a burning kiss".

Yet this kiss was an even greater mistake than his had been! It was misunderstood! Although his "soul was ravished," and he was astounded at her "miraculous perfections," he took "a short leave" and left her presence to ponder in solitude over this exciting interview and his position towards this enchanting woman. He had not long to wait for another proof of her affection.

Buckingham,[*] "having by sinister means broken the peace and alliance with" Spain, "sought to provide likewise so for the future that he might be secure they would not piece again, whereunto he knew the old king to be much inclined"; therefore he sought to bring about a marriage between Prince Charles and the sister of the King of France—Spain's mortal enemy—and he obtained his master's leave to go to Paris to negotiate the matter.

Among those appointed to accompany him (curiously enough, considering how Buckingham [†] "hated the name of Digby") was Sir Kenelm; but his friends expressed their fears that he would not be able to provide at short notice the funds necessary for so expensive an expedition. [‡]

Happily this came to Venetia's ears, and "she greatly rejoiced that she had so apt an occasion to make expression of the much that she would do for Kenelm Digby" "were it in her power, and presently" she "took up money upon the best jewels and plate that she had, and engaged such lands as were hers, either in present or in reversion"—*i.e.*, she pawned her trinkets and mortgaged her land—"and having gathered together a large sum she sent it to" Sir Kenelm, "entreating him to make use of it without encum-

---

[*] *Priv. Mem.*, K. D., p. 207 *seq.*

[†] *S. P. Dom. James I.*, vol. clv., No. 21.

[‡] Buckingham would have expected his attendants to be richly appointed. When he eventually made his expedition to Paris he took for himself twenty-nine suits of clothes, on one of which the jewels were worth £20,000, and those on another £80,000. *Ellis's Letters*, No. cccvi.

bering his estate, which consisting of settled rents would soon quit the greater debt, and thus she made him at once master of all she had or could hope for ".

Now before Venetia performed this generous act Kenelm Digby's mind had been " so equally balanced as one could not guess which way it would incline ". In one scale were " the consideration of her worth and perfections," and his love for her ; in the other were " the dissuasions of some of his friends, particularly of his mother ". Her munificent offer " was like the throwing in of a great weight into " the scale which held the " worth and perfections ".

I regret that after so much romance the scale should have been turned by anything so sordid, but truth compels me to own that thus it was ; for, says Sir Kenelm of himself, " his heart yielded, and he resolved to get her for his wife ". Before he was "to get her for his wife," however, he was to have a certain amount of trouble, as will be seen presently.

CHAPTER XII.

MARRIAGE.

BUCKINGHAM'S proposed expedition to France did not take place at the time intended, so Kenelm Digby had no occasion for availing himself of Venetia Stanley's generosity, and he remained in England to pay court to her. To his intense astonishment, when he offered to bestow himself upon her, instead of throwing herself into his arms, she gave him "a flat refusal, pronounced with much settledness and a constant gravity" ; and, with many tears, she lamented that she could not without dishonour accept the " suit of him that she loved above her own life ".

This was her reason. As, " she acknowledged ingenuously," she had once promised to marry Sir Edward Sackville, and had given him leave to have her picture,* which

---

* Which picture this was, or where it now is, is very doubtful. Pennant in his *Journey from Chester to London*, published in 1811, when describing Gothurst, says: " In the long room upstairs is the picture of his (Sir K. Digby's) beloved wife, Venetia Anastasia Stanley, in a Roman habit, with curled locks. In one hand is a serpent, the other rests on a pair of white doves. . . . The doves show her innocency ; the serpent, which she handles with impunity, shows her triumph over the envenomed tongues of the times. In the same picture is a genius about to place a wreath on her head. Beneath her is Cupid prostrate ; and behind him is Calumny, with two faces, flung down and bound, a beautiful compliment on her victory over malevolence. Her hair in this picture is light and different in colour from that in the other " (the portrait of her at Windsor). Aubrey, in the Appendix to vol. iii. of his *Letters of Eminent Persons*, says : " Sir Edm. Wyld had her picture . . . which picture is now at Droitwich, in Worcestershire, at the inne, where now the towne keepe their meetings. Also at Mr. Rose's, a jeweller in Henriette Street, in Covent Garden, is an excellent piece of her, drawne after she was newly dead. Sir Kenelm had several pictures of her by Vandycke." Her portrait, still hanging at Windsor Castle, is well known.

(110)

Portrait of Lady Digby.
by Vandyck.
From the Royal Collection at Windsor Castle.
By permission of Her Majesty the Queen.

he still kept upon "the assurance" of their engagement, "and therefore she would never suffer that one man should possess her so long as" another man held "such a gage of her former, though half-constrained, affection".

Sir Kenelm did all he could to convince her of her "wrong judgment" on the matter, pointing out that, since Sir Edward had been the first to violate the engagement, she was free from it ; and that, as to the picture, she could not punish him better than by telling him to keep it to look at ; but when he "perceived that all he said could not move her fixed mind" "he ceased to solicit her".

Then he sent a friend to Sir Edward Sackville to convey a challenge "to fight with him in mortal duel till one of them was deprived of their life (*sic*), for that the earth could not bear them both at once". Sir Edward readily consented to the duel, a time and a place was appointed, and both combatants appeared on the ground.

The stringent etiquette, which in later years forbade the principals in a duel to speak to each other until it was over, was not yet in force ; and, when Sir Kenelm met Sir Edward on the field,* "he declared at large the cause of his enmity with him, taking upon him to be the revenger of the wrong he had done to" Venetia Stanley, "and by sending him out of the world, to make a way to himself of gaining her". He also told him Venetia's feelings with regard to the picture.

Sir Edward, on learning the cause for which he was challenged, refused to fight in such a quarrel. The Lady Venetia herself, said he, had already punished him "too rigorously" by "rejecting him after his repentance," thereby making "him the only sufferer" ; and his life could not possibly stand in the way of Sir Kenelm's marrying her, as he had by this time lost all interest in the woman, although he admitted that he had formerly "loved her

---

* *Priv. Mem.*, K. D., pp. 2-6.

equal with his own soul". As for the picture, if she wanted to have it, she was welcome to it, and he would be happy to send it to her by Sir Kenelm, together with a written declaration of what he had already said, adding to it " that his tongue spoke false if ever he uttered anything to her dishonour, and a disclaiming of ever having had any interest in her, beyond what the laws of modesty and honour would permit her ".

With this Sir Kenelm was satisfied.

I venture to regard Sir Edward Sackville's statement as very strong evidence of Venetia Stanley's purity, for, although Kenelm Digby calls him " too unworthy to be his enemy," and writes about " the meanness of" his spirit, Sir Edward was no coward ; on the contrary, he was a courageous combatant, for he afterwards fought a desperate duel with Lord Bruce under the walls of Antwerp,* killing Lord Bruce and very nearly dying of his own wounds, having been run through the body and severely pierced in the arm, besides having a finger cut off.

Nor was Sir Edward Sackville the only gay cavalier who ever refused to fight a duel, as the following extract † will show :—

" It is reported that Sir Kenelm Digby (a person very famous for valour and other great parts) did receive a challenge from a certain young courtier, whose reputation in that kind was yet in question and his person (by lowness of stature) a little contemptible. But this challenge was flatly refused by Sir Kenelm, and when the young spark complained that he had blemished his honour and therefore did not deal like a gentleman to deny him a way to clear it, Sir Kenelm replied that he would give it to him under his hand that Sir Kenelm Digby had refused to fight a duel with Mr. A. B. So confidently may a known and

---

* Lodge's *Portraits*, ed. 1850, vol. v., p. 38 *seq.*
† *Crosby Records, A Cavalier's Note-book*, p. 151.

valiant spirit slight all the rash contempts of an inferior person."

Sir Kenelm returned to Venetia after meeting Sir Edward in the field in excellent spirits, believing that he had now overcome every obstacle to their union ; * "but her heart was so settled by being long fixed upon her melancholy resolutions of living for the future a solitary life that, although now the principal causes of them ceased, yet, like water that being made to boil will not go suddenly cool though the fire be taken from it, she could not so soon relent or slacken her rigour, that he might from thence draw to himself any ground of hopes".

After "much solicitation and not prevailing," he fell into despair, comparing his fate, in being for the future without the happiness of living with Venetia, to that of "the unfortunate and wretched souls in the last day," whose greatest suffering "shall be their perpetual banishment from the blessed sight of God".

Then, "he made a vow that, after he had taken his leave now of her, he would never see her more "—a curious contradiction to his preceding lament—nor England " for her sake, but would wander like a lost man through the rest of the world," for, if he were to remain where he might occasionally get a glimpse of her, "the sight of her would be but like the punishment of Tantalus, to increase in him the desire of what he must never enjoy ".

When he had said this, and much more in the same strain, Venetia cleared "her face with gentle smiles," and began :—

"Certainly," Kenelm, "if you love me as much as you would have me believe, your stars are no less cross in teaching you how to express it, than mine are in making me take the resolution of ending my days in a single and retired life ". And presently she proceeded to indulge in

---

* *Priv. Mem.*, K. D., p. 218 *seq.*

H

what, according to modern slang, might be termed a little gentle chaff :—

" I think you cannot give me the example of any man, that though the abundance of their (*sic*) love to any lady who loved them as you know that I do you, which I take God to witness is as much as ever sister did a brother "— how venerable is this familiar arrow in lovers' quarrels !— " did take a resolution and confirm it with a vow of never seeing her more ". But Venetia had a yet sharper and a more poisoned dart in her quiver.

" Peradventure," "you are so well acquainted with foreign parts that all places are alike to you to afford content, and those best liked of you, where you shall not be in danger to have my true zeal to check your loose delights, and tax you of inconstancy and ingratitude". If he had " grown weary of loving " her, he need not, she said, have broken it to her so suddenly as this. " It is unkindly done, to make my love the cause of your inconstancy, and to cast off into an ocean of sorrow the near-sinking vessel of my fortune and content, which held but by one anchor, and now must needs suffer shipwreck for your sake."

Then came a " flood of tears, true witnesses of her bleeding heart ". Wherefore Sir Kenelm, " who thought no sorrow could have exceeded his, was now fain to mitigate hers ; but his bowels were so shut up and, as it were, congealed with grief, that it was a long time before he could frame to himself any distinct conceptions, and then before he could apparel those in fit words ; during which profound silence on both sides, interrupted only with some sighs and tears, their hearts did melt with tenderness, like a heap of snow opposed to the sunbeams, and then, being endued with love's magnetical virtue," " each of them resolved to themselves (*sic*) to admit of no motions but such as were conformable to the other's desires ".

And so this foolish and illogical lovers' wrangle ended. " Of a sudden a most bright and glorious day of joy rose out of the lap of their late dusky and clouded night of sorrow ; and as the sunbeams illuminate the whole hemisphere at one instant, so this mutual consent of their wills banished immediately all dark and uncouth shadows of discontent, and made all things, even their own tears, smile upon them."

In short, Kenelm Digby proposed to Venetia Anastasia Stanley and she accepted him.

" Then to crown their joys with that ceremony which might make them permanent and holy, the minister of those rites joined their hands in that sacred knot which had long before knit their affections, and was now equally welcome on both sides."

It may be inferred that their marriage was a very private one, if not absolutely clandestine, or what follows would have been unmeaning and useless. Sir Kenelm, "being thereunto moved by sundry weighty respects, desired " Venetia, "and the rest that were then present, to conceal it for some time, which she did for his sake, and for the importance of the reasons readily consented unto, although till it were discovered it might reflect upon her honour for admitting him to greater familiarity than belonged to any but a husband ".

Herein Sir Kenelm would seem to have acted selfishly and unfairly to his bride. If the wedding had need be kept a secret, this should have been mutually agreed upon beforehand. To appeal to her feelings immediately after it, was to place her in a very difficult position. It might be to his interest with his mother, and to his advancement at Court, to conceal his marriage ; on the other hand, considering the scandals which had been current about his wife, a clandestine wedding was pretty certain to make the tongues of the gossip-mongers more active about her than ever. If Digby had been marrying a woman much beneath him in position, there might have been some grounds for privacy on the part of the young courtier ;

but, far from this being the case, Venetia Stanley was of much higher lineage than himself.

Another person's affairs gave Kenelm Digby much to occupy his mind just at this time. His benefactor and relative, Lord Bristol, the man to whom he owed his start in life, was in trouble and making use of his services.

When Bristol was recalled from Spain, it was notorious that he was to come home in disgrace. On hearing of this, Olivarez promised if he would remain in Spain to give him his choice of an office or estate,* but Bristol declined, preferring, as he said, even to be beheaded in England to living in luxury abroad.

On reaching Calais he lingered for some little time, although the wind was favourable for crossing to England,† the reason probably being a fear lest he might be arrested on landing in his own country. Sir Kenelm Digby being anxious to cross over to Calais to report to Bristol how matters stood with the king, he went to Dover ‡ and there applied to Lord Zouch for a pass, which was refused unless Sir Kenelm could produce a license from one of the king's secretaries. Either Sir Kenelm,§ or Simon Digby who was with him, then tried to bribe the searcher to let them cross without a license, but in vain ; and it ended in their having to await the arrival of their distinguished kinsman on the English coast.

Buckingham on his part was determined to prevent an interview between Bristol and the king ; and he consulted with Pembroke and Hamilton as to the advisability of having Bristol sent to the Tower ; but eventually all that was done was to procure an order from the king that Bristol should consider himself a prisoner in his own house.

* S. P. Dom. James I., vol. clxi., No. 36. Letter of Nethersole to Carleton.

† Ib., vol. clxiv., No. 1. Chesterman to Conway.

‡ Ib., vol. clxiii., No. 75.

§ Ib., vol. clxiv., No. 1.

Bristol asked for a trial, but this was refused ; and it was suggested that if he would surrender his Vice-Chamberlainship and promise to live in seclusion at Sherborne, no further proceedings should be taken against him. This he indignantly refused to do. If he had done wrong, he was willing to be tried and punished ; if not, why should he be exiled from Court and from office ?

He was next given to understand that all should be forgiven him if he would sign a paper acknowledging himself to have been guilty of mismanagement in the negotiations for a marriage between the Prince of Wales and the infanta, at the Court of Spain. This offer he also respectfully, but very decidedly, refused.

As he was not permitted to approach the king to defend himself, he employed Sir Kenelm Digby to represent his case both to the king and to Buckingham. In reply to a letter from Sir Kenelm on the subject, Bristol wrote to him as follows :—*

" Good Cosen,

" I give you thankes for your paynes in my businesse, in which, whatsoever the success shall bee, my obligation to you shall be the same." Then he said that a letter received from Kenelm had led him to hope that a mere reply on certain points connected with the prince's expedition to Spain was all that would be required of him ; but that the Duke of Buckingham had written to him demanding his signature to the formal acknowledgment mentioned above ; and informing him that, if he came to London, he must consider himself under arrest. " My present request," said he, " I hope shall bee but modest, which is only that I may know clearly what his Majestie's pleasure is, to the end I may not fall into error, and I shall most willingly and readily obey it whatsoever it shall bee,

---

* Bristol to Sir K. Digby, 16th March, 1625. *S. P. Dom. James I.,* clxxx., v., 59.

no way doubting but his Majestie in his own deue time will afford me a gratious and an equall hearing." He had sent his replies to the propositions to Kenelm, and he requested him to present them "unto his Majestie and to his Grace," trusting that the king would not "have it injoyned to a gentleman to acknowledge faults hee is no way guilty of". He wished Kenelm, who had "allready taken much paynes in this businesse," to tell the duke that he was most anxious to be reconciled to him, to regain his good opinion and friendship, and to be in a position "trewly and hartely to love and serve him"; and so, he concluded, "desiring to heare from you with all convenient speed, I recommend you to God, and rest

"Your affectionate Cosen, to doe your service,

"Bristol."

"Sherborne, the 16th of March, 1624."

Accompanying this letter was one to Buckingham himself, beginning :—

"May it please your Grace, Hopinge that your noblenes and equitye wilbe such as a trew and cleare answere wilbe more acceptable to your Grace than an unjust acknowledgement, I have entreated Sir Kenelham Digby to deliver unto your Grace my answer unto the proposition which he brought unto me from you," etc.

Within eleven days of the date of this letter, James I. was dead. A couple of months later, Bristol's great enemy had gone to France to make terms for the marriage of the Princesse Henrietta Maria with the new King of England. During his absence, Sir Kenelm took the opportunity of obtaining an audience from Charles and pleading the cause of his relative. The following is a letter which he wrote to Bristol, giving an account of the interview :—*

* 27th May, 1625. Add. MSS., 9806, fol. 1.

"May it please your Lordship. As soone as I came to the towne I went to my Lord Chamberlaine, and saide unto him what your Lordship bade me. He expressed much feeling of your Lordship's sickness, and made a seriouse profession of his faith and friendship to your Lordship, and that, if God should please to call you, he would continue it to your sonne. The next morninge (to-day) he brought me to the King, who gave me a gratious and full audience, and I delivered to his Majestie the message that you gave me as effectually as I could, to draw from him some testimony of his affection towards your Lordship. And truely, my Lord, he did receive the newes of your ill state with much tenderness and asked me many particulars how you were, and bade me hasten to lett your Lordship know he was very sorry for your sickness, and protested in the deepest manner that might be that he hadd no personall displeasure or grudge—These were his words—against your Lordship; but that he held yow to be an honest and sufficient man, and one that loved him, and had endeavoured his service really, and should be gladd of any good that arrived to yow. And in the other point concerninge your business, he would not have your Lordship conceive that he thinketh you to be a delinquent, and to have offended in any matter of honesty, or not performance of what was commanded you; for if that had beene, then this course that hath been should not have been used with you, but you should have been committed to the Tower, and brought to a publique tryall :— but the true cause why your Lordship's thus in suspense and removed from the Court is because your Lordship in the treaty of the Spanish match (he thinketh) was so desireous of it and soe passionate for it (as he confesseth himself was alas after he hadd seene the lady) that you trusted more to the Spanish Ministers and theire promises than was fitting in discretion; and, although your Lordship, on the other side, carried it soe judiciously that yow can be

taxed for nothing in publique Court, but can justifie yourself and make the Spaniard appeare dishonest, and soe
free yourself, yet between him and you he doubteth not
but your Lordship will acknowledge you were too forward
and confident in it, which if your Lordship doe lyve and
doe make acknowledgement of unto him, you shall then,
without more adoe, kiss his hands and lyve in peace with
honour, and, in the meanetyme he would have your Lordship believe he hath a good opinion of you, and loveth you,
and will be glad to heare of your recovery.   Then, of himself he sayde that peradventure your Lordship might sus-
pect that your freeness with him might prejudice you ; for
he sayde, you had been as free with him as ever any man
had been, but he protested uppon his death and salvation
that he never communicated to any body anything that
your Lordship ever spoke to him in that way of freeness
and privacye.   And, for what concerned himself, he was
soe far from taking it in evill part, that, were it for nothing
else, he were obliged to love you for your honesty, and he
ever dealed plainly and truly with your Lordship.   Therefore, whatsoever be at any tyme saide unto you, you may
be confident was from his heart, and he approved of all
you ever saide to him, but onely once, which he never had
told to any one but to me then, and you would remember
it by these tokens.   Your Lordship showed him a little
before going out of Spayne a letter, wherein you writt of
the Duke of Buckingham, which he misliked, and told your
Lordship you expressed much spleen against the Duke,
and therefore would have you alter it.   The letter you sent
away, without first showing it unto him, but when he
returned to England he saw it, and found you had altered
it much after the manner he had baid you—His Majestie
alsoe told me that, though you much desired the match,
yet he thinketh you did not labour soe effectually as you
might have done to effect what he so extremely desired,
which was to have the Infanta then along with him ; and

whilst the Duke and Conde de Olivares were good friends, and that you were fallen out with the Conde, which he sayd was indeed for being an honest man to him, you were very cold in soliciting that particular; but that, as soone as the Conde and Duke were fallen out, which was not personall betwixt them, but caused by the business of the quarrell, or receiving satisfaction for the wrong he had done you; wherein, his Majestie sayth, he discovered much yll will in you to the Duke, and an aptness in you to be over confident in the Spaniards, when theire promises concurred with your desires.

"The sum and conclusion of his Majestie's discourse was that, personally, he hath a very good affection to your Lordship, and the error which he conceiveth to be committed by you is such that the least acknowledgement shal expiate it, and then you shall have his favour againe as before. I hope this relation will bring much content unto your Lordship, espetially I telling you that the King seemed to me to speake it very affectionately and much resenting your sickness, which I pray God soone to free you of, that you may in due time take notice to his Majestie of what I write to your Lordship as you shall thinke fitt. And soe, with remembrance of my humble service to your Lordship, I rest

"Your Lordship's most faithfull servant,

"Kenelhme Digby.

"London, 27th May, 1625."

Nothing would induce Bristol to yield. On the other hand, Charles was not to be persuaded to take him back into his favour. Only two days before Henrietta Maria landed at Dover, a time at which he must have had many other things to think about, he wrote to Bristol :—*

"Our pleasure is that you remayne under the same restraint and confinement as you were ordered to by our

---

* Charles to Bristol, 10th June, 1625. *S. P. Charles I.*, xviii., 34, I.

late deare Father, untill wee shall give further direction. And wee doe by these our letters excuse your not coming to our Parliament," etc.

For the next six months Bristol remained at Sherborne, but, when the time approached for Charles's coronation, he wrote to the king asking for his liberty.   The king's reply was to accuse him of having endeavoured to persuade him to become a Catholic at Madrid.   Bristol then petitioned the Lords that he might either be brought to trial or be allowed his rights as a peer.   The king compromised the matter by sending him a writ to attend the House of Lords, and with it a letter, written in the king's name by the Lord Keeper, telling him that he did not wish him to avail himself of it.

Bristol, to the horror of Charles and Buckingham, appeared in London in April, saying that as the writ was under the king's great seal, while the letter was only from the Lord Keeper, he was bound to obey the writ and not the letter.   Shortly afterwards, in the House of Lords, Bristol and Buckingham mutually impeached each other.

In June, 1626, Bristol was sent to the Tower,* and I will anticipate by saying that in March, 1628, he was restored to his seat in Parliament at the instance of the Lords.†

---

* Gardiner's *Hist. Eng.*, vol. vi., p. 123.
† *Ib.*, p. 231.

CHAPTER XIII.

SYMPATHETIC POWDER.

If I anticipated at the end of the last chapter, I must now do the exact contrary, and go back to a time a little before King James's death. Any curiosity connected with science interested that learned fool, and the young courtier, Sir Kenelm Digby, was fortunate enough to be possessed of something well calculated to entertain him.

There are people, perhaps not a few, whose sole idea of Sir Kenelm Digby is that he was "the man with the Sympathetic Powder". In an earlier chapter * mention has already been made of this concoction; and its supposed constituents were there given. What the superstitious mess was really made of is a matter of comparatively little moment; but Sir Kenelm's own account of the use to which he put it has at least the merit of curiosity. He says :—

"Mr. James Howell,† well known for his publick works and particularly for his *Dendrologies*, endeavouring to part two of his friends engaged in a duel," had seized their swords in his hands, when "one of them, roughly drawing the blade of his sword, cut to the very bone the nerves and muscles of Mr. Howell's hand; and then the other, disengaging his hilt, gave a cross blow on his adversary's head, which glented towards" Mr. Howell, "who heaving up his fore-hand to save the blow, he was wounded on the

* Chapter v.

† *Biog. Brit.*, ed. 1750, vol. iii., p. 1702. The address from which this is taken was delivered in French before a meeting at Montpelier, in France, in the year 1657.

(123)

back of his hand, as he had been before within. The two combatants, seeing Mr. Howell's" condition, stopped fighting, took him home, and sent for a surgeon, " but this being heard at court, the King sent one of his own Surgeons, for his Majesty much affected the said Mr. Howell ".

Sir Kenelm happened to be lodging very near, and four or five days afterwards Mr. Howell came to him and asked him to try to cure his wounds by means of the famous sympathetic powder ; adding that his surgeons feared mortification and intended amputation. " In effect his countenance discovered that he was in much pain, which he said was insupportable, in regard to the extreme inflammation. I asked him then for anything that had the blood upon it, so he presently sent for his garter wherewith his hand was first bound, and having called for a basin of water, as if I would wash my hands, I took a handful of powder of vitriol which I had in my study and presently dissolved it. As soon as the bloody garter was brought me, I put it within the basin, observing in the meanwhile what Mr. Howell did, who stood talking with a gentleman in a corner of my chamber, not regarding at all what I was doing ; but he started suddenly, as if he had found some strange alteration in himself. I asked him what he ailed ? I know not what ails me, he replied, but I find that I feel no more pain ; methinks that a pleasing kind of freshness, as if a wet cold napkin did spread over my hand, has taken away the inflammation that tormented me before. I answered, since you feel already so good an effect of my medicament, I advise you to cast away all your plaisters, only keep the wound clean, and in a moderate temper betwixt heat and cold. This was presently reported to the Duke of Buckingham and a little after to the King, who were both very curious to know the circumstance of the business, which was, that after dinner I took the garter out of the water, and put it to dry before a great fire. It was·

scarce dry but Mr. Howell's servant came running, that
his master felt as much burning as ever he had done, if not
more, for the heat was such, as if his hand were betwixt
coals of fire; I answered, that though that had happened
at present, yet he should find ease in a short time, for I
knew the reason of his accident, and I would provide
accordingly, for his master should be free from that inflammation, it may be before he could possibly return unto
him, but in case he found no ease, I wished him to come
presently back again; if not, he might forbear coming.
Thereupon he went, and at the instant I did put again the
garter into the water, he found his master without any
pain at all."

"King James, who had received a punctual information
of what had happened, would fain know how it was done.
I readily told him what the author, of whom I had the
secret, said to the Great Duke of Tuscany on the like
occasion: it was a religious Carmelite, who came from
the Indies and Persia to Florence; he had also been in
China, and having done many strange cures with his
powder, after his arrival in Tuscany, the Duke said he
would be very glad to learn it of him. The Carmelite
answered, that it was a secret he had learnt in the Oriental
parts, and he thought there was not any person in Europe
who knew it but himself, and that it deserved not to be
divulged, which could not be done if his Highness meddled
with the practice of it, because he was not likely to do it
with his own hand, but must trust a surgeon, or some
other servant, so that in a short time divers others would
come to know of it as well as himself. But a few months
after, I had an opportunity to do an important curtesy
to the said Fryar, which induced him to discover unto me
his secret, and the same year he returned to Persia, so
that now there is no other knows this secret in Europe
but myself. The King replied, that I need not be ap-
prehensive that he would discover anything, for he would

not trust anybody in the world to make experiment of his
secret, but that he would do it with his own hands, and
therefore desired some of the powder, which I delivered,
whereupon his Majesty made sundry proofs, whence he
received singular satisfaction."

I have quoted from the *Biographia Britannica*, which
says that Sir Kenelm, in his *Discourse upon the Sympathetic
Powder*, states that all this was "registered among the
observations of the great Chancellor Bacon, to add, by
way of appendix, to his Natural History". This appendix
was never published; so no notice of Sir Kenelm's powder
appears in Bacon's works; though that great writer
describes something of a very similar kind, in a receipt for
making a "weapon salve"; and he declares that, when
he was in Paris at the age of sixteen, he had very many
warts on his hands, and that the ambassador's wife had
them rubbed with a piece of bacon, with the rind on, a
remedy which produced a cure, not by the direct action
of the bacon on the warts but in consequence of the bacon
having been afterwards nailed to the post of a bedroom
window that looked in a southerly direction.

In his preface to the *Voyage*,* Mr. Bruce says that
Sir Kenelm's own account, given above, was not written
until thirty years after the occurrence of the events which
it describes, and to this interval he attributes "some of its
more obvious touches of the marvellous," and he remarks
upon the noteworthy fact that Mr. Howell, the author of
the celebrated and gossiping *Familiar Letters*, although the
subject of the cure, never so much as mentions it. This
is the more observable because "he writes of Sir Kenelm
with extraordinary deference, and refers to him always
with the greatest respect, as to a person his superior in
station and acquirements, but there is never any allusion
to the Powder of Sympathy". And then Mr. Bruce

* *Voyage into the Mediterranean*, p. xxix.

accounts for the cure, if cure there were, in a very sensible manner. The King's surgeon, says he, according to Sir Kenelm's own account, had put plaisters on Mr. Howell's wound, which irritated it and interfered with the natural process of healing; when, therefore, in accordance with Sir Kenelm's directions, Mr. Howell had "cast away all" his "plaisters," and kept "the wound clean," the relief was instantaneous and the cure only a matter of time. But "King James probably thought it a wonder upon a par with the virtues of his own royal touch, and the world at large looked upon Sir Kenelm with a kind of awe".

This powder of sympathy is noticed by Sir Walter Scott. In his note, "W" (Appendix), to his lines—*

> She drew the splinter from the wound
> And with a charm she staunch'd the blood;
> She bade the gash be cleansed and bound:
> No longer by his couch she stood;
> But she has ta'en the broken lance,
> And washed it from the clotted gore,
> And salved the splinter o'er and o'er—

he quotes the greater part of a rendering of Sir Kenelm Digby's *Discourse upon the Cure by Sympathy* which slightly varies verbally, here and there, from the translation given in the *Biographia Britannica*, though not in fact.

"Let not," says Sir Walter, "the age of animal magnetism and metallic tractors smile at the sympathetic powder of Sir Kenelm Digby." Reginald Scot mentions the same mode of cure in these terms: "And that which is more strange . . . they can remedie anie stranger with that verie sword wherewith they are wounded". And presently Sir Walter adds concerning this sort of cure:—

"It is introduced by Dryden in the *Enchanted Island*, a (very unnecessary) alteration of the *Tempest* :—

"*Ariel.*—Anoint the sword which pierced him with this

---

* *Lay of the Last Minstrel*, Canto the third, No. XXIII.

weapon-salve, and wrap it close from air, till I have time to visit him again " * (Act v., scene 2).

In his Notes to the *Biographia Britannica*, Kippis † says of Sir Kenelm's account of his cure of Mr. Howell : " It is not easy to give credit to all which he relates concerning his Sympathetic Powder ".   And it may be that the incredulous may incline to go further, and say that, if Sir Kenelm wrote that which was untrue about this powder, he may have written equally untruly about other matters. Yet when we consider how implicitly some people believe in their favourite quack medicines, and what wonderful cures they declare to have resulted from their use, until they suddenly repudiate them altogether for some other panaceas equally impotent, if nothing worse, we may surely absolve him from any graver dishonesty than self-deception in this particular.

The sympathetic powder was by no means the only chemical nostrum treasured by Sir Kenelm Digby.

Among the Ashmolean manuscripts are mentioned several others, to say nothing of decoctions half way between cookery and medicine in *The Closet of the Eminently Learned Sir Kenelm Digbe K^{nt} Opened.*

---

* According to Wood (*Ath. Ox.*, vol. ii., p. 354), there were several editions of Sir Kenelm Digby's discourse on the cure of wounds by " the Powder of Sympathy ". Lond., 1658, Oct. " Spoken in French in a solemn assembly at Montpelier in France, 1657, and translated by Rich. White, Lond., 1660." " Reprinted at Lond., with the *Treatise of Bodies*, in 1669 [it is not in my own edition (1665) of that work], and translated into Lat. by Laur. Stransius of Dormstad in Hassia. It is also printed in the Book entit. *Theatrum Sympatheticum* published by Job. Andreas Endter at Norimberg, 1662, in qu., and is also printed in the German language. This is the so much approved sympathetic Powder said to be prepared by Promethean Fire, curing all green Wounds that come within the compass of a Remedy in a short time, and likewise, the Tooth-ach infallibly."

Whether the sympathetic powder was to be applied to the tooth itself, or to something belonging to the patient elsewhere, does not appear ; and this is the first we hear of its preparation by " Promethean Fire ".

† *Biog. Brit.*, Kippis's edition, vol. v., 9, 197.

In the former * is a recipe "written by the hand of Sir Kenelm Digbie Aug 28. 1625". This would probably be of much the same date as that at which he learned about the sympathetic powder. Then there is a prescription for "S(ir) K(enelm) D(igby's) pils for the head". †

In the same collection is a paper showing that Sir Kenelm ‡ communicated to Dr. Napier sundry recipes in August, 1624, that is, when he was of the age of nineteen, and that he wrote from Gothurst for some of the same pills with which he had already "experimented". Among these precious concoctions was that "of my Lord Duke of Northumberland," § viz., "the dosis of his graces powder to be taken by everie one". Another ‖ was "to prepare ladanum etc. etc. which etc. stoppeth etc. inward bleeding".

A letter ¶ signed "Ruthven" mentions "two receipts" sent to Sir Kenelm, which Dr. Napier wished for, "the one (here is a certain chemical mark), the other the oyle of gold".

A prescription for "oatmeal pap" ** is rather for the nurse than the doctor; and in Sir Kenelm's *The Closet, etc., Opened*, those who tend invalids may learn how to make it. A little oatmeal should be boiled in milk, then the milk should be strained, some butter and yelk of eggs should be beaten up with it, and, as a flavouring, a little orange-flower water and "amber-grease" should be added.

Nurses will be interested, again, in the section "about water gruel". †† This gruel ought to be boiled till it rises " in great ebullition, in great galloping waters". When the upper surface "hath no gross visible oatmeal in it," it should be skimmed off, and it will be found very much better " than the part which remaineth below with the body

* 1388, iv., 10, 147.
† *Catalogue of the Ashm. MSS.*, by W. Black, p. 135.
‡ Ashm. MS., 1730, f. 166a.　　　§ *Ib.*, f. 167a.
‖ *Ib.*, f. 167ab.　　　¶ Ashm. MS., 1458, 110b.
** *The Closet, etc., Opened*, p. 159.　　†† *Ib.*, p. 163.

I

of the oatmeal". Yet—and mark this!—even "that will make good water gruel for the servants". It is difficult to realise the times when servants could be fed upon water gruel, especially second-rate water gruel. But we must continue the prescription. Nutmeg, an egg, some butter and some sugar are to be added to it, and as a finishing touch a little "red-rose water".

Another prescription for invalids from the same book is interesting, as it proves the use of meat juice for consumptive and other patients to be no novelty. The stuff is denominated "Pressis Nourissant".* Only very slightly roast half a leg of mutton, a piece of veal, and a capon, and while they are still partially raw "squeeze all their juice in a press with screws"; add the juice of an orange, and warm enough to take the chill off but no more. The book informs us that this juice has cured people suffering from consumption.

Here is another semi-medicinal food. It was obtained from a "Jesuite that came from China,"† who said that the Chinese "sometimes use in this manner". They beat up the yelks of two eggs with fine sugar and then poured a pint of tea upon them, stirring them up well. This preparation "presently discusseth and satisfieth all rawness and indigence of the stomach, flyeth suddenly over the whole body into the veins, and strengtheneth exceedingly". I have never tried this recipe as it stands, but I can answer for its excellence when coffee is substituted for tea.

The same "Jesuite" taught Sir Kenelm how to make tea. "In these parts, saith he, we let the hot water remain too long soaking upon the tea, which extracteth into itself the earthy parts of the herb." The water ought to "remain upon it no longer than you can say the Miserere Psalm very leisurely. Then pour it upon the sugar" in the cups.

* *The Closet, etc., Opened*, p. 165.   † *Ib.*, p. 155.

Three hundred years ago, and much later for that matter, when people were a little ailing, the universal remedy was a caudle. Sir Kenelm recommends "Flommery Caudle," * which he describes as "a pleasant and wholesome Caudle". To make good "Wheaten Flommery," † you must soak the best wheaten bran in water for three or four days, and then "strain out the milky water from it, and boil it up to a gelly," seasoning it with sugar and orange-flower water. Now mix "ale and wine" and put into the mixture a few spoonfuls of the cold flommery. After stirring it all up, "there will be found remaining in the caudle some lumps of the congealed flommery, which are not ungrateful".

It is unnecessary that I should quote at length a valuable prescription given to Sir Kenelm by "My Lady Stuart," consisting of the "Metheglin for the Collick and Stone of the same Lady"; ‡ but it may be worth observing that his friend Sir Thomas Gower used to make a pleasant and wholesome drink by pouring five gallons of honey into forty gallons of "small ale," when the latter was "still warm," and "stirring it exceedingly well with a clean arm till they be perfectly incorporated". This preparation was made "about Michaelmas for Lent".

If some of these directions may appear neither palatable nor wholesome for invalids, no exception can fairly be taken to Sir Kenelm's directions for making "Vuova Lattate," § which consisted of eight eggs beaten up with nutmeg and sugar in a quart of "fine broth".

In this chapter I hope I have succeeded in demonstrating the interest taken by Sir Kenelm Digby in the sick and wounded, and the pains to which he put himself to study remedies for their relief; from the powder of sympathy for the latter, to "pils" and water gruel for the former.

* *The Closet, etc., Opened*, p. 286. † *Ib.*, p. 158.
‡ *Ib.*, p. 108. § *Ib.*, p. 196.

CHAPTER XIV.

A SECRET MARRIAGE.

THE secrecy which Kenelm Digby had enjoined concerning his marriage led to some rather inconvenient complications. If few people were aware that the pair were married, many knew that they lived together, and "many mouths were filled with various discourses of their familiarity". *

Among those who looked with disfavour upon the unaccountable intimacy between Kenelm and Venetia was Robert Digby, son of the elder brother of the Earl of Bristol, and the ancestor of the present Lord Digby. Between this Robert Digby and his cousin, Kenelm, "was contracted a very strait friendship," and, on the strength of it, Robert ventured to talk to Kenelm in a brotherly, if not a fatherly, tone, respecting the very peculiar footing upon which he appeared to stand towards the rather too renowned Venetia.

He opened the subject in these respectful terms: " I am so bold, dear cousin, upon the friendship which hath linked our hearts together, that I dare adventure, without being asked my advice, to deliver you my opinion in what I believe most men else would shun the very mentioning thereof to you".

As well they might, unless they were prepared to cross swords with the somewhat bellicose Sir Kenelm !

" I must give this testimony of you without adulation, that in all qualities belonging to a generous and worthy

* *Priv. Mem.*, K. D., p. 224 *seq.*

(132)

gentleman, you may be a pattern to all those that I have ever known, were it not only for continuance in one action, which doth, I will not say eclipse, but much alloy, in my opinion, the splendour of the rest."

Kenelm's error would not be "imputed to a crime" in less worthy persons; but, he exclaimed, "it fareth with you as with the richest jewels, wherein a small blemish falleth much of their value; and with the fairest colours, in which a little stain is soon perceived".

Without mentioning Venetia's name, he told him that he must be aware of the subject at which he was hinting, "the assaults of a woman's beauty". And he besought him not to "suffer shipwreck in the ruinous ocean of sense and pleasure, which at the best is ever accompanied with satiety and repentance".

Sir Kenelm would now have been placed in a rather awkward predicament if his cousin had not gone on to enforce his good counsel by declaring love to be "the weakest of all the passions," and its "least evil" to be "to abastardise the mind, to make it effeminate, unfit for any worthy action, and so wholly and anxiously employed in low desires that it can think of nothing else as long as it is possessed with this fever".

Here was Kenelm's opportunity! Instead of defending his relations with Venetia, he defended love in the abstract from the charges brought against that passion by his cousin, and, after a preamble as long, and quite as polite and as pompous, as Robert Digby's, he said: "Hear then my defence of love, and then let slander grow dumb and swell till it burst with its own venom".

Accordingly, the well-meaning Robert Digby, instead of convincing his cousin of what he believed to be his sin, was compelled to listen to a very lengthy and impassioned panegyric on the virtues of the "joy and content of lovers".

Whether he "were satisfied or no with this discourse"

Robert Digby "did not at all express by any words ; but
after a long and profound silence on both sides," he did
not argue the question, "not thinking it good manners to
oppose farther what he saw had taken so deep root in his
friend's heart".

Sir Kenelm's ambiguous position led to a much more
serious dispute with two other friends, George (possibly
Kirke),* groom of the bedchamber to Charles I., and a man
named Nugent,† between whom and Sir Kenelm there had
"been heretofore great friendship and familiarity".

It seems that Sir Kenelm had sometimes "sighed out "‡
his "affectionate flames" in respect to his lady-love in the
presence of Nugent, who, on such occasions, invariably
strove to win him from his "devotions, or at least, by
bitter invectives and taunts," to make him "ashamed of the
condition of a loving martyr," in which he had placed
himself.   Friendly as they were, however, Sir Kenelm
did not let Nugent know that he was married.

One fine summer's evening, Sir Kenelm and Nugent
"were entertaining" themselves "for their pleasure upon
the river," when they met a boat in which were the former's
good wife, Lady Digby, and her bosom friend, a girl
called in the *Private Memoirs* Babilinda.   They were
"listening to a song accompanied with excellent music
that they had brought out with them, having allotted this
pleasant and calm evening to their recreation in this kind ".
Babilinda, by a "certain scornful and disorderly pulling off
of her veil," suddenly "displayed the lightenings of" her
splendid eyes, which completely dazzled Nugent's "and
wounded him to the very soul".   He "grew like one

* In his notes to Mr. Bright's *Poems and Papers of Sir Kenelm Digby,*
Mr. Warner thinks it very possible that this may have been the real name
of "Famelicus"; therefore I use it, although the identity remains doubtful.

† Sir Kenelm calls him Nugentius.   I merely give the Anglicised
version of the same name.

‡ *Private Memoirs,* K. D., p. 244 *seq.*

amazed ". " It was a long time before he could frame
any word, and at last he only gave evidence of his passions
by his deep sighs." In a moment he learned the cruel
lesson " that love is begotten at first sight, and that some
light or disdainful action of a conquering beauty is able
to subdue and tame the sternest and wildest heart ".

The fact was, Sir Kenelm tells us, that " the little God,"
Cupid, was offended with Nugent for sneering at his
friend's affection for Venetia ; and in revenge for " this
blasphemy of his," he " kindled such a fire in his breast
that he soon felt all the tormenting passions that most
lovers do but weakly feign ".

Digby rowed up to the boat in which his wife and
Babilinda were sitting, and introduced Nugent ; and this
was the beginning of " a long suit " from the latter to the
beautiful Babilinda.

Nugent's advances were most frigidly received by their
object, with the consequence that his affection for her
became all the more desperate and uncontrollable ; and
the most humiliating part of it was " that he sucked in
this furious heat, and drunk this bitter poison, in the
presence of him whom he had so often taxed with loving ".
Babilinda had no special affection for Nugent. Her
heart, thus far " unacquainted with the very colour of
passionate affection, could yet take pleasure to see the
effects of her fair eyes upon others' yielding ones ".
Moreover, Nugent's " fretting disposition" made him " unapt
to purchase and win love " ; consequently " his suit and
company became tedious and troublesome to Babilinda ".

When he " found that he could not warm the cold
and frozen heart of her that he so much loved, a foul
passion crept into his bosom," and made him intensely
jealous of his friend Sir Kenelm, whom he made the
mistake of imagining to be Babilinda's true love.

He was well aware that Kenelm Digby's own heart was
given to Venetia, but, so long as Digby continued paying

court to her, he believed that Babilinda would see him and love him, as she was constantly with Venetia. He, therefore, conceived the dastardly desire of endeavouring to bring about an estrangement between what he supposed to be the pair of lovers, Kenelm Digby and Venetia Stanley, not knowing them to be man and wife.

Among the many young men who had been over head and ears in love with the famous beauty, the Lady Venetia, was Kenelm Digby's brother groom of the bedchamber, George ——.* He indeed loved her " violently, and making some indiscreet expression of it, had received from her a public and weighty affront, which made him convert all his affections into rage and desire of revenge ".

How great had been George's admiration for Venetia Stanley may be inferred from the following limping lines,† signed " G. K.," and believed to be by him. They are taken from an effusion entitled :—

A BREEFE AND MYSTICAL DESCRIPTION OF THE FAYRE
AND STATELYE VENETIA.

> Though faire Venetia Stand-ley by the shoare,
> Where none can come, but by sayle or oare.
>
> .   .   .   .
> Such, in love as be not chast,
> Must not their anker on Venetia cast.
>
> .   , ...
> Whose storme-stedde here arrives, shall ne'er repent
> This shoare is sure to, stayyan ill event.
> Let men then goe from Britaine great to Grecia
> What can they see, that lookes like our Venetia

---

* Once again, I admit that there is a certain amount of assumption in fathering " Famelicus " upon George Kirke.

† *Poems from Sir K. D.'s Papers,* p. 14.

S. P. Dom. *Charles I.,* vol. cciii., No. 61, gives a proclamation forbidding any to trade with Guinea and Binney except George Kirke, Sir Kenelm Digby and others, to whom a patent had been granted. Another State paper, see *Cal. Sta. P. Dom.,* 1665-6, p. 365, contains a petition from George Kirke stating that he is in prision about a matter of £4000 which had been spent on robes and wearing apparel for Charles I.

The Lady of the Sea, life of our land.
O happie he whome she shall take by hand.
For hee with ioye, enjoye for ever shall,
This citie, sea, wreathe, anker, Crowne and all.
Faire, rare Venetia Stand-ley still, still flourishe
All valiant hartes, and vertuous hopes to nourishe.
                VENETIA STANLEY,
                Stay an il event.

Endorsed : " G. K. to V. S.".

Of George's former love and present hatred of Venetia,
Nugent was well aware, so he and another friend, who
also hated the Lady Venetia and was anxious to do her
an injury, went to George and persuaded him to make a
scandalous statement about his relations to her, "assuring
him that they would govern the business so that he should
never be questioned for what he said, and that they knew "
Kenelm Digby " to be of such a hot spirit and so violent
in things that concerned his " honour, "that upon this
rumour, which they would cunningly insinuate to" him,
he would be certain, without further inquiry, to "cast off
her friendship" and have nothing more to do with her,
which George "desired as much as they, knowing that
above all other things this would most afflict" Venetia,
" against whom he was now grown rancourously spiteful ".

Accordingly George agreed to the plot, and Kenelm
Digby was informed of his statements concerning the
Lady Venetia by Nugent and his fellow-conspirator.
Happily Sir Kenelm discerned "their malice afar off" and
behaved himself "in such sort that they doubted not but
that " he believed the story and was deeply impressed by
it. This he did, fearing that otherwise they might " spin
a farther web to embroil" him more.

" As soon as " he "had quitted himself of their troublesome company, without giving time to " George " to avail
himself of any new subtleties by delays," he sent to challenge him to prove the truth of his assertions at the point
of the sword in mortal combat.

Sir Kenelm knew well enough that all George had said
against his wife was false; and that "she ever despised
him," but he writes: * "I judged this way of proceeding
was requisite both to right her and myself, because that
knowledge would not be sufficient to lead other men's
beliefs, unless with his own mouth I made him give himself
the lie".

The challenge to a duel was not at all to George's taste.
"When he saw his life at stake," he most frankly and
ingenuously confessed that "he had no ground of truth, or
for suspicions in all that he had said; but that his own
hatred to her had first suggested to him to injure her in
the deepest manner that he could, and then the malice
of" Nugent and his friend had "blowed the coals in his
breast, till it broke into this unworthy and false slander;
which, he averred, and said he would maintain with his
life, was wholly their plot; and then related all the
particularities which I have told you, whereby himself
hath got the repute of an indiscreet, rash and dishonest
coward; and the other two, the esteem of malicious, unworthy, and cankered wretches".

Not long after this episode, his first domestic trouble
befell Sir Kenelm. He was in London; but his wife had
gone to the country to pay a visit to her father, who was
still ignorant of her marriage. Sir Edward Stanley desired
her one day to go out riding with him, which for certain
important reasons, just at that particular period, was a
very undesirable and indiscreet thing for her to do; yet,
rather than disobey her husband or bring trouble upon
him, she would not tell her father of her marriage and
she risked the danger of the ride.

The next day, news reached Sir Kenelm that his wife
had had a fall from her horse, by which " she had received
some bruises," and had been " brought speechless home

* *Private Memoirs*, K. D., p. 252 *seq.*

to her chamber "; and that she was very dangerously ill. He started off at once to go to her. On his arrival, he asked to be allowed to see her and was admitted, although her father was not even now aware that he was her husband.

The sight of him "brought new strength and vigour to" his wife's "dismayed senses," while he was astonished to find himself the father of "a fair son". Both father and mother agreed that not even Sir Edward Stanley should be informed of the birth of the baby; and, "by providing discreetly for the due carriage of all things," which was "no easy task, they both behaved themselves in such sort, that she soon recovered her perfect health and strength, and the cause of her sickness was not so much as suspected".

This clever concealment was chiefly owing to the skill and care of "one fearful and inexperienced maid," who "was privy to what was between" Kenelm and Venetia. Yet Sir Kenelm admits that "what was done would seem impossible, and not to be believed by any that did not know it was done".

As soon as Lady Digby was perfectly re-established in her health, her husband left her and returned to London. For some time gossip had been very busy with their names; and it was now bruited about that they had been staying in the same house together in the country; that the Lady Venetia had had an accident, and that Sir Kenelm Digby had been nursing her.

This rumour reached the ears of his relative and patron, Lord Bristol, who had long been uneasy about the reported infatuation of his protégé for the renowned beauty. If the attempt of Robert Digby to cure his cousin of his love-fever took the form of a friendly remonstrance, that of John Digby, Earl of Bristol, assumed the shape of a reproof. He began "in a grave and friendly manner" to compliment him on his usual judgment and prudence, and then went on to remark upon the change which he had lately observed in him.

"I entreat you," he said,* "to look a little into yourself, and then you cannot but acknowledge how you now scarcely cast an eye upon the studies which, heretofore, you applied yourself unto with much eagerness and no less benefit ; that your endeavours to increase upon your master's (the King's) favour and grace are mainly slackened, which if you had made right use of, in all probability your rank and fortunes might, by this time, have been ranked with the foremost ; and that you do not
* put yourself forward into great and honourable actions with that zeal and vigour that you have done. All which effects of a weakened and decayed mind, I can attribute to no other cause but your having entertained into your breast a servile affection, which, wheresoever it entereth, is a clog to generous spirits, and freezeth all heroic thoughts in their very births, and overthroweth the worthiest resolutions ; and will cause any men to sink in the value of the world ; begetting, if not contempt, at least a mean esteem, especially when it is conferred upon one (*i.e.*, Venetia) that hath been known in hers to have been formerly engaged to another, and hath lived altogether at liberty under her own conduct in the world."

Then he urged him "not to sit still in idleness, but to aim at worthy fortunes" which might "raise" his house.

A marriage with Venetia Stanley, said he, "will not only not increase, but lessen your estate, since in your mother's disposal is a great part of what shall be yours if you displease her not, and you know that she is mainly averse to" the match for which you are yourself so anxious. "Yield to reason, and let not the world say that all your understanding, your knowledge, your learning, the vigour of your mind, and the well training of it up in virtuous actions, cannot defend you from the snares of beauty."

These words "with others of a like nature" were

spoken " with much authority and seriousness," yet through them all "shined much affection". They "did pierce" Sir Kenelm "to the very soul, who was distracted and torn asunder between his love and obligations to her that he loved better than himself, and his reverence to him that he loved and respected as a father, and that had, above all men else, given him solid demonstrations of a worthy friendship". Lord Bristol had kept so straight to the point that Kenelm had no opportunity of escaping on any side issue, such as the defence of love and passion, of which he had availed himself when remonstrated with by his cousin Robert.

With "deep and amazed sorrow" he said: "My honoured Lord," " the affectionate reverence that I bear unto you, doth so waken my sense and wound it so deeply when you pass the condemning sentence of dislike upon my actions, that, considering it is not in my power to alter the tender of them," " I do wish myself out of the world, to the end that I might take away the occasion of your censure, and yet not be false to that affection, which, next to my faith in God, is above all things else, deepest rooted in my soul".

His defence was very long; it is needless that I should notice more than a few portions of it.

" For being cold in thrusting myself into great actions," said he, " I hoped I shall be pardoned at least by those that know how happy a thing it is to live to one's self; for certainly, no exterior thing in this world is worthy the exchanging of one's leisure for it."

Lord Bristol had reminded him of his mother's wishes. Reverting to these, he exclaimed :—

" I wish that I may perish in that hour that I make light account of the filial duty that I owe her, but parents would do very well" "to examine thoroughly how far their jurisdiction reacheth before they stretch it to extremities. Howsoever she may dispose of her estate, I shall not be

moved therewith." Finally, respecting the base scandals
which had been rife with regard to Venetia's fair name, he
cried enthusiastically : " I am confident that her life will
belie any rumour that may have been spread abroad to her
disadvantage by malicious persons, and believed by others
that take up their opinions upon trust ".

Just as Lord Bristol " was beginning to frame a reply,"
his " solicitor " most opportunely entered to discuss some
very disagreeable business, "which for the present took
away " his lordship's " memory " from " the former theme,"
and Sir Kenelm, " being glad of any occasion of diversion,
and of keeping him from returning to it," changed the
conversation to a subject which Lord Bristol " was never
weary to discourse of," namely, his ill-treatment by the
king and Buckingham, which I dealt with in a former
chapter.

CHAPTER XV.

A GREAT UNDERTAKING.

As we saw in the last chaper, Sir Kenelm had come to the philosophical conclusion that peaceful leisure was a happier condition than that of a fawning courtier or a feverish place-hunter, and it may have been some time during this period of his life that he gave vent to his feelings on the subject in a poem of very moderate merit, beginning :—*

> My thoughts and holy meditations
> Shall henceforth be my recreations;
> As for the world's applause or Princes' grace,
> Youthful delights, or hope of higher place,
> Since these are things which others only lend
> My happiness on them shall not depend;

and ending :—

> Therefore so long as I from vice live free
> In spite of world or king I'll happy be.

Happy as he had been in his retirement, with one of the most beautiful and charming women in England for a wife, he took Lord Bristol's lecture very seriously to heart. †"Being retired into his chamber, after many discourses in his understanding, he concluded that it was necessary for him to employ himself in some generous action that might give testimony to the world how his affections had nothing impaired the nobleness of his mind, nor abated the edge of his active and vigorous spirit, nor that any private engagement should in him be a warrant to idleness.

* *Poems from Sir Kenelm Digby's Papers*, Rox. Club, p. 6.
† *Private Memoirs*, K. D., p. 301.

Whereupon he resolved to undertake something that might tend to the king's service and gain himself honour and experience."

Probably at the instigation of Buckingham, the proceedings of Kenelm Digby were watched with suspicion. On the 11th June, 1626, Secretary Conway wrote to the Mayor of Dover "to make stay of" * Sir Kenelm Digby and others, "if they shall embark themselves".

Happily for his interests, in 1627 Buckingham started on his ill-fated expedition to the Isle of Rhé. Here was Sir Kenelm's opportunity. "When the cat is away, the mice will play"; and he explained his wishes to the king himself.

In his preface † to Sir Kenelm's *Voyage*, Mr. Bruce thus summarises them : " The design was that of a general privateering voyage, similar to one which had lately been carried out by the Earl of Warwick ; but with an ultimate, although concealed, intention to capture the French ships which were usually to be found in the Venetian harbour of Scanderoon. Buckingham had very much disliked Warwick's expedition, as emanating from the royal authority, and not from himself as Lord Admiral, but the power and public position of the Earl of Warwick had sufficed to carry him through in spite of Buckingham's antagonism."

Under these circumstances, Sir Kenelm was a brave man to run the risk of Buckingham's anger by asking the king's permission to embark upon a very similar undertaking.   Charles received his request very graciously, gave him leave of absence, as one of his Gentlemen of the Bedchamber, and promised him a commission under the Great Seal, which should be as ample as " any gentleman of his quality " had ever had.

On obtaining this promise, Sir Kenelm at once began

* *Cal. Sta. Pa. Dom.*, 1625-6, p. 352.
† P. xxxi.

to make his preparations ; Secretary Coke drew up the commission, and the king signed it.

It is worth pausing here to consider why, as Kenelm Digby was so popular at Court, he should first withdraw himself in a great measure from it in order to lead a very private domestic life under a secret marriage, and secondly why, when he resolved to try to distinguish himself, he should choose a field of labour which would take him for a long time far away, not only from the wife to whom he was so devotedly attached, but also from the society in which he was so brilliant an ornament.

That he was a brilliant ornament to the Court is obvious from abundant evidence. Much was said and written in his praise, and, as a specimen of the latter, I may quote a few verses from the following poem * (or piece of doggrel, as the reader may please to call it) addressed to Sir Kenelm Digby by Henry Gower :—

TO THE RIGHT HON. AND TRULY NOBLE Sᴿ KELLAN DIGBY KNIGHT.†

Thie courtly eare bend to my Rustique straine
Brave Digbey, for a Prince did not disdaine
To heare Apollo sing cloathed like a swaine.

Though hee was from the harmonious sphere confin'd
For being to his fatall sum to kinde
He did on earth a Royall Patron finde.

. . . .

Herein thie vertue doth brave knight excell
Whose sailes no prosprous gales of chance doth swell
Nor to strike them tumultous blasts compell.

---

* In the *Poems from Sir K. D.'s Papers*, Mr. Warner says that these lines must have been written as late as the year 1623, because K. D. is called " Sir " and " Knight " in them ; but not later than 1627, because they contain no mention of his successes in the Mediterranean, which would certainly have been made much of in a panegyric had they taken place when it was written.

† *Poems from Sir Kenelm Digby's Papers*, Rox. Club, p. 37.

K

In different fortunes thou an equall minde
Dost ever beare, whether the various winde,
Be rough or milde, the same wee thee doe finde.

Thee noble Digby, whose renowned praise
Should it be crowned with the deserved baise
Unblinded fortune should t' honor raise.

.   .   .   .

The Florentines who doe amazement count
The birth of ignorance amaz'd recount
How bravely thou thie armed steed didst mount.

How like Alcides, or the God of fight,
Or like Dianæs lustre shining bright
Thou dist all others with thie glorious light.

O maist thou up to highest honour rise
And shyning brightly from the starry skies
Exiled Hermes sweetly patronise.

May Jove thie name during the starrs enrowle
To the Carowsing his Ambrosium bowle
No honour is condigne, a worthier soule.

And wee who are by Mydas heires opprest
When thou to Jove shalt be a constant guest
Upon thie sweetest influence will feast.

The affectionate Admirer
of your Vertues,
HENRY GOWER.

There are also plenty of tributes in prose to his attractions and virtues.

His contemporary, Anthony Wood, writes of him : [*] "His person was handsome and gigantic, and nothing was wanting to make him a complete chevalier. He had so graceful elocution and noble address that, had he been dropt out of the clouds in any part of the world, he would have made himself respected."

Lodge says of him : [†]   "Exquisite parts, with a most

---

[*] *Ath. Oxon.*, vol. ii., p. 351.
[†] *Portraits of Illustrious Personages*, Bohn, MDCCCL., vol. v., p. 147 *seq.*

happy temper, produced in him their usual result, a perfect politeness ". " On the accession of Charles I.," " Sir Kenelm Digby became one of the chief ornaments of Whitehall. Charles, who did not love gaiety, highly esteemed him for his admirable talents ; but to the queen, who before her misfortunes had a very lively disposition, he rendered himself infinitely agreeable, and she seems to have conceived a friendship for him which lasted through life. He was a party in all the royal diversions, which indeed he frequently planned and directed, and such were the volatility of his spirits, and the careless grace of his manners, that it should have seemed that he had been bred from his infancy in a court."

The author of the *Biographia Britannica* * says that he made "a great figure in" the Court of Charles I., "though he was not remarkable for paying his homage to the great favourite" (Buckingham). "He became, notwithstanding, a Gentleman of the Bedchamber, a Commissioner of the Navy, and a Governor of Trinity House, which employments, if they added but little to the weight of his purse, served however to heighten his reputation."

To return again to contemporary testimony, Lloyd, in his *Memoirs of Persons that Suffered*, calls him † "a gentleman of a strong body and brain," his soul being one of those few souls that understand themselves, and a man "of a fluent invention and discourse," and "of a great faculty in Negotiations ".

But much more important is the testimony of Lord Clarendon, who says of him : ‡ " He was a man of a very extraordinary person and presence, which drew the eyes of all men upon him, which were more fixed by a wonderful graceful behaviour, a flowing courtesy and civility, and such a volubility of language as surprised and delighted ;

* Ed. MDCCL., vol. iii., p. 1703.
† Pp. 580-1.
‡ I am quoting from Chalmers' *Biog. Dict.*, 1813, vol. xi., p. 77.

and though in another man it might have appeared to
have somewhat of affectation, it was marvellous graceful in
him, and seemed natural to his size, and mould of his
person, to the gravity of his motion, and the tune of his
voice and delivery ".

Why then should such a man have turned his back
upon the scenes in which he was so much welcomed and
honoured?   Was it because he feared that when his
marriage with Venetia Stanley should become known he
would lose popularity, if not court-favour?   I think not,
and I am confirmed in this opinion by the words * of
Clarendon, who says that his " great confidence and
presentness of mind buoyed him up against all those
prejudices and disadvantages (as the attainder and execution of his father for a crime of the highest nature ; his
own marriage with a lady, though of extraordinary beauty,
of as extraordinary a fame, etc., etc.) " " which would have
suppressed and sunk any other man, but never clouded or
eclipsed him from appearing in the best places, and the
best company, and with the best estimation and satisfaction ".

I am rather inclined to attribute his decision to seek
fame in foreign adventure, partly to a hope of obtaining
the honours of a hero, and partly to an impression that he
could have no hopes of distinction at home so long as the
all-powerful hatred of Buckingham overshadowed the
fortunes of the Digbys.

But before he started, many obstacles were to be
encountered.

Nor did all the opposition proceed from his enemies.
When he unfolded his plans to his wife, she burst into
tears and begged him to give up all idea of the expedition.

" Is it possible," † she asked him, " that the day can
come wherein my sight doth offend your eyes, or that you

* Chalmers' *Biog. Dict.*, 1813, vol. xi., p. 77.
† *Private Memoirs*, K. D., p. 303 *seq.*

shall find such amiableness in dangers and tempests, as for the gaining of them to hate my presence? What sin have I committed to alienate me from your affection, or rather, what have I not done to win and preserve it?" "If not for my sake, yet let this innocent part of you," and she pointed to her child, "persuade you not to leave him a distressed orphan, and me a desolate widow, to lament your long or peradventure perpetual absence. Consider that although heretofore it was in your single power to dispose of yourself, yet now I have an interest in you, which I will never be so cruel to myself as to relinquish; and without my consent, you infringe the eternal laws of justice to undertake such an action, and therefore have reason to expect from above rather heavy judgments than blessings to accompany it." She said much more to the same effect, and her heart was "deeply wounded with affection and grief".

Her husband was placed in a most painful position. He was convinced by what Lord Bristol had said to him that his duty lay in endeavouring to gain distinction, and he had already committed himself to the expedition by word of mouth to the king; yet he was very sensible to " the enchanting effects of a beautiful and beloved woman's tears, and had his soul almost fettered in the golden chain that came from her fair lips".

It was a struggle, and a hard one; "but the sense of his honour came to his thoughts, and banished all weak tenderness out of his heart, so that he remained immovable in his resolutions, although he could not choose but grieve extremely at her sorrow, whom he loved above all temporal respects," and "he made use of all the arguments of which" he could bethink himself to induce her to endure his short absence with patience, "assuring her that it would be the cause of both their complete happiness"; for that, when it should be over, he "was resolved to retire himself to a private life, where, removed from the cumbersome distractions of the Court or city, he might without any interruption enjoy the quiet blessings of her sweet conversation, and would then attend to nothing but to love, to ease, and to tranquillity: but that if he should do it abruptly and of a sudden, it could not be without the impeachment of his honour and worldly dignity, and that therefore he chose this way to make a leisurely, secure and honourable retreat, and as it were with displayed ensigns, which after such an action that would give testimony of his courage and resolution, all men would say to be made through judgment and highness of a mind despising what the vulgar holdeth most dear and in greatest admiration, and not through a weak, shameful, lazy, or uxorious humour: and therefore he desired her that she would not with her sorrow give him the sad presage of some great ensuing disaster".

By degrees Lady Digby yielded; and although she could not "suddenly wean her heart from the sense of passionate grief, yet the discretion taught her to contain the expression of it". She thus showed herself an excellent wife, and that "her will depended wholly upon" her husband's, "howsoever her desires and affections might be repugnant to it when she considered any danger he might incur".

From another quarter came opposition which was far less easily overcome.

As soon as the king's commission became known at the Admiralty, Nicholas, Buckingham's secretary, interfered. It was, said he, an infringement of his master's jurisdiction. He sent a copy of it to Sir Henry Marten, the Judge of the Admiralty, asking his opinion, and declaring it to be derogatory to the duke's office of Lord High Admiral.* Buckingham, he said, would think those whom he trusted very remiss when he heard that such a grant had been made to Sir Kenelm.

* S. P. Dom. Charles I., vol. lxxx., No. 76, Oct. 9, 1627.

Marten appears to have agreed in objecting to the grant of the commission to Sir Kenelm and to have given his reasons in writing ; for, rather more than a fortnight later, Nicholas again wrote * to him saying that the king had not only commanded the Lord Keeper to stay the commission, but ordered Marten's objections to be forwarded to the Attorney-General, with instructions to prepare a new one. Nicholas added that he had urged the king not to give Sir Kenelm a commission at all, but only letters of marque ; and that he was trying to use the power of all Buckingham's friends to get the commission totally annulled. At the same time he spoke highly of Sir Kenelm personally, and thought him worthy of encouragement, provided it were not at the duke's cost.

In another fortnight a new commission † was signed by the king. It empowered Sir Kenelm to make a voyage and to take prizes of Spanish or French ships, or those of the archduchess, or any other princess or prince not in league or amity with England ; but it omitted the permission, given in the earlier commission, of executing martial law.

The very next day Nichloas lodged objections ‡ to this commission also, as an infringement of the rights of the Lord High Admiral, and a reply,§ on behalf of Sir Kenelm, was entered against them.

The Lord Keeper, Coventry, was then consulted, and at his advice a third commission ‖ was drawn up and signed a week later. This is only one of the many instances of the manner in which Charles I. would withdraw promises and play fast and loose not only with agreements, but with such serious matters as the royal sign manual and the Great Seal itself.

---

* *S. P. Dom. Charles I.*, vol. lxxxii., No. 86, Oct. 25, 1627.
† *Ib.*, vol. lxxxiv., No. 36, Nov. 7, 1627.
‡ *Ib.*, No. 43, Nov. 7.　　　　　　　§ *Ib.*, No. 44.
‖ *Ib.*, No. 72, Nov. 14, 1627.

* " The king's approbation of the intended voyage, and
any sanction of Sir Kenelm's designs beyond mere license,
was struck out.   The expedition was carefully deprived
of everything like a public character."   The grant, as it
now stood, was little more than permission † to a gentleman who sought adventures to embark upon a voyage
for the increase of his knowledge, whereby he should be
better able thereafter to do service to the king and his
realm.   "The crew were to be in obedience to the commanders under pain of such punishment as " Sir Kenelm
should "see cause" to be inflicted, without saying by
whom, and a proportion of any prizes which might be
taken was to be divided among the co-adventurers.

Three days before the signing of this third and last
commission, Buckingham landed at Plymouth ‡ from his
expedition to the Isle of Rhé; but he had not returned to
London when the king put his hand to the instrument.   On
the very day of that event, Nicholas § wrote to the duke,
longing for the honour of kissing his hands, and telling
him that all things were at a stand awaiting his arrival to
give them life and direction.   Apparently Buckingham
had written to him in terms of reproof; for Nicholas remarked that when the duke returned to London he would
find out who was to blame for having been remiss.

The day after the king had signed the commission to
Sir Kenelm, he issued another letter to him, ‖ in which
he mentioned the dues which would have to be given, out
of every prize taken, to the Lord High Admiral.

When Buckingham reached London and heard of what
had taken place with regard to Sir Kenelm Digby, he
had the whole matter reopened.¶   He insisted that

---

* Mr. Bruce's Preface to the *Voyage, etc.*, pp. xxxii.-iii.
† *Ib.*
‡ Gardiner's *Hist. Eng.*, vol. vi., p. 201.
§ *S. P. Dom. Charles I.*, vol. lxxxiv., No. 74, Nov. 14.
‖ *Ib.*, No. 79, Nov. 15.
¶ Mr. Bruce's Preface to the *Voyage, etc.*, p. xxxiii.

Digby should take out letters of marque from himself, in addition to the commission which he had received from the king, and that he should give bonds for the performance of the stipulations contained in them. The matter was finally settled in an interview between the duke and Sir Kenelm in person.

During these long months of negotiations and delay, Sir Kenelm had been busily preparing for his expedition. As to men and officers, his difficulty was, not * "to win into their company," but "to defend himself from their importunity," and many of those who implored to be allowed to join him were "persons of quality". His principal officers were Milborne and Sir Edward Stradling of St. Donat's in Glamorganshire, a man, like Sir Kenelm, of literary tastes.

His chief ships were the *Eagle*, of 400 tons, and the *George and Elizabeth*, of 250 tons. Of the rest of his "fleete and men of warre," as he calls them, we have no complete list, and the *Eagle* and the *George and Elizabeth*, both "of London," are the only ships mentioned in the Warrants † for Issuing Letters of Marque, etc.

Everything was now ready, the last farewell was taken of his beautiful wife and his infant son, and Sir Kenelm prepared to start for the coast.

---

* *Private Memoirs*, K. D., p. 302.
† *Cal. Sta. Pa. Dom.*, 1628-29, p. 303.

CHAPTER XVI

EMBARKATION.

FAREWELL had been said by Sir Kenelm to all his friends save one. John Digby, Earl of Bristol, the friend and relative who had given the son of an attainted and executed traitor a glorious start in life, stood by him as he was about to enter the coach which was to convey him to his " shippes which lay att anchor in the Doynes by Deale ".*

Indeed he had ordered it to meet him at Lord Bristol's house, as he wished his last visit, before leaving England, to be paid to his benefactor.

Lord Bristol told him that he had a final word to say : Let Kenelm put him " free from suspense," and tell him " whether he were married or no ". " His great familiarity with" the famous beauty "and her entertaining of it did make most men believe he was, and yet his not public avowing it did make him doubt it ".

Then Kenelm acknowledged " ingenuously that he was " married to Venetia, and he gave his reasons for having kept the matter a secret. Bristol appeared to understand the feelings which had prompted him to secrecy, and " told him that the same friendly affection which had formerly moved him to dissuade him from the match did now call upon him to co-operate with his ends and to do him service as much as he could ; therefore he bade him rest confident that in the time of his absence he would pay to his wife the same respect that he had ever done to him, and

---

* Sir K. D.'s *Voyage into the Mediterranean*, p. 1. My account of the expedition is taken almost entirely from this book.

would employ his best talents to justify his action and to make others approve it ".

If ever man had a generous and loyal friend, Kenelm Digby had one in his distant cousin, the Earl of Bristol.

Well might he render "him condign thanks, and at his parting from him" entreat "him to believe that he would behave himself in such sort in this voyage that, howsoever fortune might deal with him, he would be sure to win himself honour, without a good share of which he would never return ; and that, although she should do her worst to him, he would triumph over it all with a glorious death. After which being spoken, he went into his coach to go to the port where his ships stayed in readiness for him, and wanted only his presence and a fair wind to set sail."

It was not until a fortnight after he had left London that " the fair wind " for which not only his own captains, but those of " many other vessels that had been a long time wind-bound there," were hoping, came to his assistance.

As he was in the very act of embarking, a messenger galloped up in haste with the important news " of his wife's safe delivery of a second and hopeful son ". By way of a thank-offering and a parting present, he sent her the happy news that she was " to conceal their marriage no longer".

I may as well say here, as elsewhere, that the Digbys had, in all, four sons, including one who died very young ; to the remaining three Ben Jonson wrote the following prose and poetry :—

* But for you growing gentlemen, the happy branches of two so illustrious houses as these, wherefrom your honoured mother is in both lines descended; let me leave you this last legacy of counsel; which, so soon as you arrive at years of mature understanding, open you, sir, that are the eldest, and read it to your brethren, for it will concern you all alike. Vowed by a faithful servant and client of your family, with his latest breath expiring it.

BEN JONSON.

* *Jonson's Poems*, by W. Gifford, ed. P. Cunningham, vol. iii., p. 330.

TO KENELM, JOHN, GEORGE.

Boast not these titles of your ancestors,
Brave youths, they're their possessions, none of yours
When your own virtues equalled have their names,
'Twill be but fair to lean upon their fames;
For they are strong supporters: but, till then,
The greatest are but growing gentlemen.
It is a wretched thing to trust to reeds,
Which all men do, that urge not their own deeds
Up to their ancestors; the river's side
By which you are planted shows your fruit shall bide.
Hang all your rooms with one large pedigree;
'Tis virtue alone is true nobility:
Which virtue from your father, ripe, will fall;
Study illustrious him, and you have all.

When we think of that thorough landsman, Kenelm
Digby, who had never had anything to do with ships,
except in the character of a passenger, taking command of
a fleet, we may feel inclined to smile; but it may be well
to remember that such a proceeding had had a comparatively recent precedent, when Philip of Spain ordered the
Duke of Medina to prepare himself to take command of
the great Armada: for that admiral-against-his-will pleaded
that, in the first place, he knew nothing whatever about a
ship, and that, in the second place, he was invariably sick
whenever he sailed in one.

On Sunday, the 6th of January, 1628, the wind veered
from the south-west to the north-east; and "about 2
of the clocke afternoone," Sir Kenelm "sett sayle in the
Eagle, and Sir Edward Stradling," his Vice-Admiral, "in
the *Elizabeth and George*, the rest of the straightest fleete
and men of warre being gone 4 houres before" them, "and
then out of sight when they sett sayle".

On the 9th they stopped a Flemish ship, but found
that it had been licensed a few hours earlier by an English
man-of-war that had "rummiged his hold and opened his
letters, and suffered his mariners injuriously to make

pillage of much that he had"; so it was allowed to proceed. On the 10th they chased "a small Frenchman"; but, although they "did fetch upon him," he "gott of," and on the 11th, they had a "stirne chase" after five Dutch vesséls with a similar result. That night, says Sir Kenelm, "wee sprung a leeke" in the "powder roome". During the three succeeding days and nights there was a storm, which on the fourth subsided to a "steedie fresh gale att northeast". On the 16th, a ship, which they thought looked like 500 tons, "brought her spritsaile yard alongst shippes, and in warrelike manner fitted herself for fight". "In like manner wee fitted ourselves for fight, which wee had no sooner done but shee made all the sail shee could to get from us, and succeeded in doing so."

On the 17th day they were off the south coast of Portugal, and reached the latitude of Cape St. Vincent in stormy weather; but on the 19th the wind fell, and in an almost calm sea they came in sight of "the high land on the Barbarie coast" on one side, and the land on the Spanish coast on the other. They stood out to sea "till 4 of the clocke," when the wind "coming att west north-west," they made for the "entrance of the gutt," under all the sail they could carry, in order "to gett the narrow of the straightes that night, so to avoide being discovered by the shippes at Gibraltar."

They got through "the narrow of the straightes" by about 11 of the clocke," and, keeping "close along the Spanish shore," they were off Marbella by daybreak. About two o'clock in the afternoon,* seeing a ship flying "Hamburg colors," Sir Kenelm "made in towards her". As he drew near, "shee made a shott from me wardes". Several shots were then exchanged from Sir Kenelm's ship and his Vice-Admiral's on the one side, and the Hamburg ship and the "castle under whose shott shee

* Jan. 20, 1628.

rode at anchor" on the other; and then, Sir Kenelm perceiving that "there was no fitt proportion betweene the damage" he might receive and the good he might "gett," as the latter, at best, would be "but wine and fruites," while the former might be "an unfortunate shott among" his "mastes," calculated to overthrow his "future designe," he steered from the shore; in short, he ran away, and the wind rising he "was soon out of shotte either of the castle or the shippe".

On the 27th a very serious thing happened. "My men," says Sir Kenelm, "begun to sicken apace, for sixteen fell downe this afternoone."

The next day he "descryed a sayle," and making for her perceived that she was about "to fitt herselfe for fight"; but on nearer acquaintance she turned out to be an English-man, à *propos* of which, says Sir Kenelm, "this observation is worthy noting, that, whereas all other shippes did runne from us * as fast and as long as they could, I yett never mett with any English, were they never so little or contemptible vessels, but they steyed for us and made readie for fight".

There was great excitement on the 31st. At midday Sir Kenelm began to chase "2 sayles" and before dark "fetched them up". They were Flemish ships of about 250 tons each and "they had made ready for fight, and (as their manner is upon such an occasion) their men were all drunke, so that they were verie unruly and quarrelsome with my men that I sent abord him, which made me send more, to the number of 40, to master them, but my men were very disorderly in pillaging their mariners' chestes and clothes, which upon their complaintes I made be restored, and my people that were faultie to be brought to punishment".

---

* But was the Hamburg ship under the castle, above-mentioned, an instance of this? Who "did runne" on that occasion?

The next morning,* however, he searched the ships that he had taken, and finding their " billes of lading " " agreable to their goodes," he licensed them, although, says he, " in my private opinion I believe they were faultie if I could have proved it " ; for they were observed to throw " many letters " overboard. But he had by no means done with " faultie " ships for the day. That very evening about five o'clock he found himself near " 7 sayles coming along the Spanish shore ". As it grew dark he lost sight of them, but, " having sett them by the compass," he suddenly discovered that he was close upon them at, or about, seven.

" Their Admirall," which looked about 400 tons, " shott a peece " at Sir Kenelm, which " grazed close by " his " stirne " and made off. Sir Kenelm then had two of his " fore-peeces " shott among them, to see if they would strike ; but instead of doing this they returned " their broade sides ". Sir Kenelm singled out their admiral, " att which," says he, " I shott not till I was within pistoll reach, then I gave him my gunnes as fast as we could discharge them, he doing the like with me, and all the while my Vice-Admirall entertained some of the rest in the same manner ".

This was the first regular action in which Digby was engaged, and it was a sharp one. At last the enemy's admiral hailed him, whereupon he " did the like to him " and caused his " great shott in the meane time to cease ". The foreign admiral said his name was Horne, " and I bad him amaine for the King of England ; whereto he bad me to come abord him, and att the instant shott 2 great shott, both which raked through my shippe. I then gave over all other discourse but of my great gunnes, which we played so well that by nine of the clocke hee begun to fall off from us with his consortes " and " wee heard them make lamentable cryes ".

* Feb. 1.

"I had not men enough abord me," he says, "to use
our great gunnes and to trimme our sails"; "I had neere
50 men sicke abord me," "so that I had not 30 good seamen in my shippe, and I was fain to distribute my gentlemen to the service of the ordnance, and I had not then
men enough to loade and putt out the gunnes, so that after
2 hours' fight, having given them between 60 and 80 shottes,
wee lett them goe".

Probably they were very glad to be rid of them.
Four shots had gone through the hull of Digby's ship,
one of them entering his own private cabin. Other shots
did some mischief among the sails, one passing close to
Sir Kenelm's head, and, says he, "wee had one man's arme
shotte off and another's eare," but he adds with evident
satisfaction, "I imagine we did the enemyes much hurt
and spoyled many of their men".   It was just as well to
think so ; but, short-handed as he was, it is probable that
he could not have gone on much longer if the enemy had
persevered.   The battle was, at best, a drawn one, and there
can be little doubt that on this occasion the expedition
was on the very brink of ruin.

Even as it was, things were not now looking very
cheerful.   The battle had been exceedingly unsatisfactory,
and the epidemic on board the ships was increasing with
alarming rapidity.

Of the 3rd February he writes: "Hourely my men
sickened more of an infectious disease that tooke them with
great paine in the head, stomake, and veines, and putrified
the whole masse of the blood, and caused much vomiting,
yet they dyed not suddainely of it, but lingered on with
paine and extreme weaknesse".   There is a sad account
of this outbreak in the *Private Memoirs*.*   "It came to
pass that in a very short time almost all were possessed
with it, by reason of the great number of men enclosed

* *Private Memoirs*, K. D., p. 311.

in a small room." "If natural affection to his friend or charity moved any one to be so tender as to do to another the offices belonging to a sick man, many times with a sudden death he prevented the other's languishing one; and by this means it happened often that dead bodies lay many days in their cabins and hamacas." "But sometimes there were mean fellows that would come to steal what they found about the bodies of those that were of better quality, and then by their own sudden death in the same place they would betray their theft."

This seems in direct contradiction to his statement that they "dyed not suddainely".

"But that which of all others seemed to cause most compassion was the furious madness of most of those who were near their end, the sickness then taking their brain; and these were in so great abundance that there were scarce men enough to keep them from running overboard, or from creeping out of the ports, the extreme heat of their disease being such that they desired all refreshings, and their depraved fantasy made them believe the sea to be a spacious and pleasant green meadow."

The sickness and mortality grew to such a point that "all the principal officers* of the fleet" came to Sir Kenelm and "advised and besought him to bear up the helm and return home"; but he represented to them that, now they were at such a distance from England, no good would be gained by such a course. To make matters worse a dead calm set in.† Sir Kenelm says: "I was in such a distresse with the sicknesse of my men, that it was all that both the watches could do together to tacke about the sailes". Then followed ten miserable days. The epidemic steadily increased; when there was any wind at all, it blew in the wrong direction, and on one occasion there was "a furious and cruell storme," with "gustes of raine, snow, and haile".

* P. 313.   † Feb. 4.

L

At last they managed to reach Algiers, and only just in time. "If," says Sir Kenelm, "I had stayed out forty-eight hours longer, I had not had men enough to saile my shippe." There was a delay in the permission to land, owing to some "combustion" among the officials; but the question of admitting people from the fever-stricken vessels seems to have presented no difficulties.

It must have been a great relief to Digby when, on the night of the 17th of February, he went "ashore to the English Consul's house, Mr. Friswell".

The next day he was received by "the King" and was treated with much courtesy. He remained at Algiers for more than five weeks, and during that time he had plenty to do in making a treaty with the Government.

"The King" began by hoping that the King of England would redress the injuries done by the English to his unfortunate people. Upon inquiry, however, Sir Kenelm found that there was another side to the question. Six weeks before his arrival, the British Consul had been "brought out to be burned and hardely scaped," and it was thought likely that he "would be againe," after Sir Kenelm's departure, if he "left not thinges settled". Another little matter was that there were about forty or fifty Englishmen in captivity at Algiers; and yet one more was that "the French upon verie lowe conditions treated a peace with the Algire men (Algerians) with intention to joyne with them to overthrow the English trade in the straightes".

It should be remembered that, only about five years before Digby's visit to Algiers, this and the other States of Barbary had thrown off their dependence on the Porte,* and that they had immediately become neither more nor less than a nation of pirates.

The Porte at that time had been so much embarrassed in its war with Persia as to be unable to subdue the pre-

* *Ency. Brit.*, vol. ii., p. 570, eighth ed.

tensions of the Algerians or to put down their piratical practices. All it could do was to send them a severe reprimand, to which they replied that they were the "only bulwark against the Christian powers"; and when Digby landed at Algiers their abominable piracy was in full vigour. He appears to have made a treaty in the name of the King of England with the King of Algiers, as if he had authority for so doing; and possibly he may have been empowered thus to deal with him.

The principal points on which he insisted were that whenever the Algerians should receive "losse by oures att sea," they should not come for satisfaction upon our merchants who might have put themselves into their power by having entered their ports; but that they should "in a legall manner informe our King of it, and ask justice of him"; that they should allow our merchantmen to come into and go from their ports without seizing their sails, which it would seem they were in the habit of doing; that English "shippes of warre," *i.e.* semi-privateering expeditions like Sir Kenelm's, might go freely to Algiers with their prizes "and pay nothing but such dues as belong to the State for what they sell by way of merchandise"; and that Sir Kenelm should be allowed to take away with him the English captives. In return he not only promised justice from the King of England, but held out brilliant hopes that his "example" in going to Algiers "would bring many English thither, and be the cause of a neerer correspondence for the future betweene the two nationes".

After many interviews with the "Bassa, Muftis, Cadis, and Duana," he obtained from the Algerians an agreement to the terms, and they "promised to pay (and settled it in a way) a great summe of money that the last Bassha before had taken from Mr. Frizel, and to restore 3 prizes taken by some captives of theirs from some of my lord of Warwikes".

Sir Kenelm, however, paid what they had "cost unto

their patrones" for the captives, and considering the loss of
men which he had sustained by the terrible epidemic, he
may have not been altogether without consolation, when
performing this most virtuous action, especially as they
were "the best and usefullest men," "gunners, carpenters,
and pilots".

He paid £1650, or about £33 apiece, for them, and,
as we shall see later on, it was not until thirty years later, in
the reign of Charles II., that he was repaid ; not that this
delay was owing to any want of perpetual asking on his part.*

Considering the length at which Sir Kenelm describes
the terms of his treaty with the Algerians, it is curious
that little, if any, mention is made of it in any history. Sir
Dudley Carleton had suggested † "a Truce with the Pirates
of Algiers," in January, 1625 ; but this truce does not appear
to have been made. In September, 1628, the Council
wrote to Lord Conway ‡ asking for a copy of the Treaty
with the Algerians ; and Conway wrote in reply § that
"his memory does not charge him with any copy of the
capitulations with Algiers, save one from the merchants".
In October, a Proclamation ‖ was made to forbear hostility
towards the people of Algiers ; and it is just possible that
this may have been in consequence of the receipt of the
treaty made with that country by Sir Kenelm Digby in
the preceding February ; but, if the treaty had proved of
any value, we should probably find more records of it,
and his own unwillingness to "come without extreme
necessity" to Algiers, on his return journey, expressed in a
much later portion of his diary,¶ looks as if he himself did
not consider the treaty very effective.

* S. P. Dom. Charles II., vol. xlv., No. 19.
† History of Algiers, J. Morgan, ed. 1731, p. 660.
‡ S. P. Dom. Charles I., vol. cxvi., No. 32.
§ Cal. Sta. Pa. Dom., 1628-9, p. 322.
‖ S. P. Dom. Charles I., vol. cxix., No. 8.
¶ P. 63.

In the middle of his visit he learned of a design of " some of the men in " his " Viceadmirall " to steal a ship. Having discovered the ringleader he " layed him in chaines for future punishment, and after a publike reprehension and admonition pardoned the rest ".

While at Algiers, Sir Kenelm, who delighted in curiosities, even when they took the unpleasant form of monstrosities, found something to his taste. He says,* " I saw when I was at Algiers . . . a woman having two thumbs upon the left hand, four daughters " " had all resembled her in the same accident, and so did a little girl, a child of her daughter's, but none of her sons ".

On the 25th of March, he went on board his ship and " despatched away Mr. Vernon for England with the Bassha and Duanas letters to the King, giving also by him particular account to Sir John Cooke, Secretarie of State, of what had passed here ". If, therefore, Vernon returned to England in March or April with the " Basshas and Duanas " treaty, it is very curious that, in the following September, Conway should have said, when the Council asked for a copy of the treaty with the Algerians, that his memory did " not charge him with it ". Nevertheless, the fact of the Council asking for it shows that its existence was asserted.

On the 27th Sir Kenelm weighed anchor and set sail " with a faire westerly wind," having arranged with his Vice-Admiral to visit the east side of Majorca, to go from thence to Minorca, and then on to the Hyéres, in search of " a sattie, the want of which " he " apprehended verie much ".

---

* *A Treatise of Bodies,* ed. 1669, p. 226.

CHAPTER XVII

THE VOYAGE.

As the little fleet was sailing round the north-east coast of Majorca, in the large bay of Alcudia, which looks towards Minorca, on the 30th of March, they "descryed a shippe riding att anchor". They "were upon her so of a suddaine that she could not weigh anchor, but cutt her cables and loosed her sailes to be gone from" them, but they "plyed" their "great shott and small shott" to such effect as to cut her "toppesaille halliardes" and to make her crew afraid of coming on deck to mend them.

Then Sir Kenelm went up to her and "borded" her with sixty men, when her own men tried to set fire to her "powder chestes that were on the deckes"; but fortunately "they would not take". Yet the crew did Sir Kenelm some damage; for, from below, "they shott four great ordinance that raked through the fore part of" his "shippe and did some hurt".

By that time, the Englishmen had cut open the hatches, and the foreigners, who were Frenchmen, yielded. In the course of the battle, Sir Kenelm very "neerly" sent a "great shott" into his own Vice-Admiral, which had clumsily got on the opposite side of the Frenchman.

He spent the next day in mending the ship that he had taken. It was of 250 tons; and, after keeping and distributing a dozen of her thirty sailors among the crews of his own fleet, he put the rest, with their captain, into a small boat of their own, gave them "victuals for a day or two, and £5," which was all the coin he had left after redeeming

(166)

the English captives at Algiers, and sent them ashore, " verie well satisfyed ". Then he put some forty or fifty men into the French ship, gave her into the command of Henry Stradling, the brother of Sir Edward, made her his " Rereadmirall," and named her the *Hopewell.*

Very squally weather followed during the next few days ; and, instead of going as he had intended to the Islands of Hyéres, he was driven towards the South of Sardinia.

After several vain attempts to capture a " sattia," he " visited the Bay of Cagliari," where he saw five ships at anchor ; but as he heard that " there lay 12 Brass peeces besides much ordinance in the castle " above, he thought it more prudent to " attempt nothing in that place ".

As he sailed on, after he had rounded Cape Carbonara, " in the beginning of the night," he sent one of his boats, well-manned, near the shore.

There its crew found " a fisher boate with six men asleepe in her ; with the noice of their bording her they awaked, and 5 leaped overbord, thinking our men had bin Turkes ; the other we tooke, and he gave us notice of severall vessels in the bay, but that they rid under watch towers, the least of which had 3 brasse gunnes in them ". So they put the man ashore, stole his boat, and made off.

At six o'clock the next morning Sir Kenelm determined to make an attack upon these ships in defiance of the watch towers and the brass guns. One of his ships attacked a " fregate " that had " neer 20 tonnes of wine in her," and " towed her off," while another did the same to a sattia, which " rid att anchor," " loaden ". Sir Kenelm himself went on board his new ship, the *Hopeful*, because she " drew but little water," and sailed " close in under the fort neere within musket shott," in pursuit of a " great and faire sattia," which he captured. All this time the forts kept firing upon them ; two men were killed and six or seven wounded on board the *Hopeful* alone, and the fighting

was " verie hot," both with " brasse guns " and " musketts ".
Having got what he wanted, Sir Kenelm sailed away.

Just when everything seemed prospering, a fresh trouble
came.   Such a storm arose as they had not yet encountered.   Sir Kenelm lost a boat " with a man and a
brasse faucon in it," and afterwards the "great and faire
sattia," which " was certainly verie rich," sank also.   They
were now somewhere off the south-west coast of Sicily ; but
" knew not the ground," which by their " lead " " appeared
foule and rockie ".   Fortunately their anchors " took hold,"
or nothing could have saved them.

On the 9th April the weather improved a little and the
ship again weighed anchor ; but what a change had taken
place in the fortunes of Sir Kenelm in two days !   On the
Sunday night, after making his captures, he " had a fleete
of 7 sayles, and had taken so much as " " would have
payed " all the expenses of the expedition and left a good
balance beyond it, and now he had only " one shippe "
and had barely escaped with his life.

In moody spirits he sailed along the coast of Sicily,
rounded Cape Passaro, the extreme south point, and then
went in a northerly direction towards Italy and the
Straits of Messina.   As he approached them, he " descryed a shippe plying to gett into them ".   He " stood
with her, and shee as boldly to " him, and both prepared
for action.   Sir Kenelm hailed her captain and asked him
to come on board and show his commission and bills of
lading.   He refused ; whereupon Sir Kenelm warned
him that he " would shoote at him," and shortly afterwards
gave him a broadside, when he immediately " strooke his
toppesailes ".   He said that he " would have fought, but
that his men forced him to yield ".   His ship was of 300
tons, carried thirteen good guns, and was laden with corn.

After taking this prize, Sir Kenelm sailed in an easterly
direction, until reaching Cape Spartivento, one of the
most southern points of Italy.   There he waited for four

and twenty hours in the hope of getting some news of his fleet, but none came. He then set sail for the island of Zante, off the coast of Greece, intending there to sell the corn in his prize, which, by the way, was so "leakie" as to be a "great cumber" to him.

The next day, 13th April, was Easter Sunday, and on the 14th, to his intense joy, he found his "Viceadmirall and Rereadmirall" both making for Zante. Like unsuccessful fishermen, they had wonderful stories to tell him about the prizes which they had "almost caught," and of their size and quality. One suspicious excuse given by the Vice-Admiral for missing a capture was that his ship had been "much out of trimme, by reason of wines they had taken in the day before that were not then well stored". Perhaps he might better have said "not wisely but too well".

On the 17th they met two English ships, the captain of one of which, "Captain Frenchfield," brought Sir Kenelm the excellent news that his "prizes were both safe att Zante". As he also stated that he had just sold a quantity of corn there, which he also had take in a prize, Sir Kenelm very sensibly thought he would get a better market elsewhere; so he judged "fitt to putt in first at Cephalonia".

Both Cephalonia and Zante were at that period under the Venetian Republic.

If the authorities and the inhabitants were civil and obliging to Sir Kenelm, it was more than could be said of his own crew, some of whom "tooke occasion to sowe mutinous discourses," the burden of which was that they ought immediately to have "their partes and share of the money" obtained for the plunder. "He gave his men such dayly worke as might make them forget the shore;" and, when that did not serve as a thorough remedy, he called a general assembly on board his own ship, dilated on the powers conferred upon him by his commission from King Charles, asked his men what they wanted, and, "in con-

clusion," " flatly refused all they desired," assuring them
that " if any man did use any more such seditious
speeches," he " would send him into England with a
complaint to the court of the admiraltie, there to be
punished for his misdemeanour". Having thus asserted
his authority and reduced them to submission, he gave
them, the next day, " the strongest assurance" that everything would be arranged " evenly and to their best advantage". This was so unexpected that it " wonne
much upon them". Such, he moralised, " is the effect of
gentlenesse and fair wordes after rigour upon a just
ground, with the vulgar ".

There were two dangerous men, however, still to be
dealt with. One was none other than a captain against
whom aspersions had been " loged " to the effect that " he
had imbezilled away much of the goods" entrusted to
him. Before a general council of the commanders,
nothing could be definitely proved against him ; but, for
all that, Sir Kenelm " could not free him from much
faultinesse," and, as the man asked for permission to go
home to England, he gladly gave it to him. The other
delinquent was the quarter-master of Digby's own ship,
who had been " the maine cause of all the disorder " ;
and he " putt " him in chains. Then he was judicious
enough to redistribute his crew among the different ships.

Within a fortnight of the settlement of this disturbance,
another man gave trouble. This was the skipper of the
" corne prize " which Sir Kenelm had taken. He was " a
factious and seditious man," and " he did maliciously goe
to informe, first the Generall of the Gallies, then the
Proueditore,* that " Sir Kenelm had " treated him in a
verie ignoble manner, and was but a pirate ". Therefore,
he begged them to arrest Sir Kenelm's ships and restore
his goods and his ship to him. Sir Kenelm was able to

* This, like many other words in Kenelm's writings, is spelt differently
in different places.

show his commission from the King of England, and the authorities gave him power to deal with the skipper on shore as fully as if he had him on board ship; but the skipper slipped off in a bark which he hired for a night with money that had been entrusted to him by Sir Kenelm for another purpose, and, worse still, he persuaded some of Sir Kenelm's crew to desertion.

On the 20th of May Sir Kenelm set sail and reached Zante in six hours. The Provvidatore of that island was soon tired of his new visitor, who began to "descry sayles," "to plye about," and to "fetch up" vessels after his favourite fashion. Accordingly the Provvidatore sent a syndic to him, representing the "interressess of state which it was necessary to looke into," "and he forbade him to invade any shippes that came thither, which (if permitted) would interrupt the scale of their trade; therefore, he desired" him, "in a faire and respective manner, to make what hast" he "could to be gone from thence".

Sir Kenelm made some excuses, and remarked upon the ships coming in and out of the harbour which he could fairly and easily have captured, if he had not refrained out of consideration for the feelings of the Provvidatore; but it ended in his taking himself off and all his ships, in four or five days, after he had spent a good deal of money in the island in purchasing provisions.

He then (on the 19th) sailed in a southerly direction, and as he passed the island of Cerigo, at the foot of Greece, "the castle made several shottes" at him, but fortunately without doing him any injury.

On the 6th of June he passed along the coast of Asia Minor near Phineka, where he was told that "a great fresh river disimbogues into the sea, and is excellent watering".

There he "fetched up" several ships; but none belonging to nations with which he could pretend to be "at war". The first actual "take" that he made off the coast of Asia Minor was a boat in which "were two men that had bin

long dead "; and, curiously enough, the second was of one
("a sattia ") with no men at all in her, either living or dead.
She had "all things fitting but never a man in her, the
sails fitted, and the rudder made fast amidships". " We
moored," says Sir Kenelm, "the new found boat att our
sterne ".

Sir Kenelm had reason for believing that he might find
plunder in the Gulph of Iskanderum, or Scanderoon, or
Alexandretta. If any reader should be ignorant of its
exact locality, it may be unscientifically described as the
corner of the sea made by the meeting of the coasts of
Syria and Asia Minor. Only about a year before Sir
Kenelm's visit, an Algerian fleet had entered the Gulph of
Scanderoon,* seized a Dutch ship and a smaller boat, and
then landed. The Turkish Aga and all the inhabitants
had deserted the town on their approach; and the Algerians first plundered the warehouses and afterwards set
them on fire. The loss of the English and Dutch merchants alone was computed at 40,000 dollars.

Sir Kenelm "had intelligence" "that there was great
force of galliones and galligrosses in the road that might
oppose" him. On the 10th of June, towards evening, he
came so near the headland to the south-west of the Gulph,
as to think that his ships might be seen from the shore; so
he "tooke in all" his "sailes and lay a hull till night," and
then "stood in for the shore to anchor within a point
about four leagues from Scanderoon, where for the land
they could not descrye" them, "from thence intending
to goe in in the morning with the brize"; for he tells us
that the wind, "as of custom," freshened every day at
about 10 A.M.

He then summoned all the "captaines and masters"
from his other ships and held a "councell". They made
"the exactest preparations" they "could for a fight, and

---

* *History of Algiers*, J. Morgan, 1831, p. 662. The date given is 1527,
but this is evidently a misprint for 1627.

to fire powerfull enemies". It was "exceeding hott when it was calme, and a thick viscuous dew fell after sunsett". Fortunately, most of the men "had their health well," so they were in readiness to fight their ships to the best advantage in spite of the intense heat.

During the night a boat was sent into the Gulph to reconnoitre "the roade (unseen)" and to bring back "word early in the morning". The boat's return was awaited with the keenest anxiety ; but many of the morning hours passed without its appearance, and it was not until eleven in the forenoon that it reached Sir Kenelm's ship.

The boat's crew reported that there were, in the roads, two English ships, two Venetian "galliegrosses," two Venetian "galliones," and four French ships, one of which "was come in but a day before, and had still a hundred thousand reals of eight abord her".

The French vessels were the only prey which Sir Kenelm could pretend to have the right of seizing, as the Venetians were supposed to be on friendly terms with the English ; but these Frenchmen he was determined to take.

He "first made a short speech to encourage" his men, and then he "stood in with the roade as fast as" he could. Fearing that, if the Venetians should understand his object in time, they would give him notice not to attack any ships in the roads, and would thus delay his undertaking, with the result of allowing his prey to escape, he tried a ruse. Having written a formal letter to "the general," or admiral, as we should call him, of the Venetian ships, informing him of what he was about to do, he took care that it should not be placed in his hands until too late to frustrate his own designs. He says he "contrived it so that my letter should be delivered even as I came within shott".

Signor Antonio Capello, the "commander of most fame and reputation for valour among the Venetians," was very irate at this palpable artifice, and was most unwilling to receive such a visitor, especially as there was a treaty between his nation and the French. He received Sir Kenelm's messenger roughly, and sent him word that, if he did not leave the road immediately, he would sink his ships.

Sir Kenelm, nothing daunted, pursued his course, but a shot at his flag presently showed that the Venetian meant to be as good as his word; yet Sir Kenelm hoped that the other was only trying to frighten him, and not only did not return his shot, but even fired a salute. When he "had endured 8 shotte from him patiently," however, he thought it time to proceed to business, and he "then fell upon his vessels with all" his might.

The Venetians and Sir Kenelm Digby's ships did the best they could to destroy each other. About 500 shots were fired from both fleets. "It continued a cruell fight for about 3 hours. It was most part calme," says Sir Kenelm, "else I had offended him much more."

In a philosophical work,* Sir Kenelm gives a curious account of some of the indirect effects of this battle. He says it "was a very hot one for the time, and a scarce credible number of pieces of ordnance were shot from my fleet". The report of our guns had, "during all the time of the fight, shaken the drinking glasses that stood upon shelves in" the English consul's house in the town of Scanderoon; "and had split the paper windows all about; and had spoiled and cracked all the egges that his pigeons were then sitting upon; which loss he lamented exceedingly, for they were of that kind which commonly is called *Carriers*, and serve them daily in their commerce between that place and Aleppo".

The alarm of the inhabitants would necessarily be intense, and, when they recollected the devastations of the Algerians in the previous year, they must have reflected that their lot was indeed cast in evil places.

* *A Treatise of Bodies*, ed. 1665, p. 304.

Towards the end of three hours' cannonade, Sir Kenelm felt certain that he was getting the best of it, and, the wind freshening in his favour, he "prepared to bord the gallioones, and so meaned to stemme the galeazzes, for" he "could gett the wind of them, having much maimed their oares, and they being so frighted (as it appeared by their working and the issue) that they lost all their advantages".

Then the "Generall" sent to Sir Kenelm "beseeching peace and acknowledging his error in a verie direct manner, having hoised his yarde strippe to be gone out of the roade in case" of refusal. Just at this time the English vice-consul came on board Sir Kenelm's ship, and entreated him to grant the Venetian's request, which he did on con-dition that the French vessels should be abandoned to his discretion.

Sir Kenelm's ships seized all the French except one, which had run aground; but, during the engagement between his own ships and the Venetians, the Frenchmen had wisely taken the opportunity of carrying all their goods on shore; so he in reality obtained very little plunder by this desperate battle. He "sent to take the gunnes and anything of value" that remained in the French vessels, and was on the point of setting fire to them when the English vice-consul implored him not to do so; for that, if he did, English merchants might be made to pay a heavy impost for the damage done; for this reason, there-fore, although he considered that he had fairly taken them, he acceded to the vice-consul's request. He "onely tooke away their flagges and some brasse bases for" his "boates heads, and sent for" his "men off them, and the next day rendered them to their owners".

During the battle Sir Kenelm "lost noe men, but killed 49, and hurt many of the Venetians". It was the greatest success of his whole expedition to the Mediterranean, and perhaps the greatest of his life. He fought and overcame, he tells us, the "best vessels by much, as well galleazzes as galliones," of the Venetians.

A more impartial authority, Lord Clarendon, says that "in that drowsy and inactive time," Sir Kenelm Digby's victory at Scanderoon "was looked upon with general estimation ".

CHAPTER XVIII

PRIVATEERING.

THE vice-consul was not far wrong in his expectations. Sir Kenelm was still resting after his victory at Scanderoon when news arrived that the Venetians had sent word of his proceedings to Aleppo, and that, in retribution, all the English " marchants were putt in prison " there. These unfortunate merchants, however, obtained leave to send three other English merchants to the Gulph of Scanderoon to ascertain what Sir Kenelm had really done. This was not the only batch of English merchants who suffered on account of his raids, and his name, in consequence, became almost as unpopular among his fellow-countrymen on the coast of the Mediterranean as among his enemies. A petition,* dated the same month, is among the State Papers, from the merchants trading to the Levant, to the council, setting forth measures which they begged might be taken to restrain the proceedings of Sir Kenelm Digby and his partners. They complained bitterly of losses thus suffered.

While he remained in the roads of Scanderoon, the Venetians gave Sir Kenelm " the signiority "; but, for all his honours, he had not altogether a happy time there. " The weather was extreme hott "; there were " fogges " which made " the place exceedingly unwholesome "; when the " brize " blew from the shore, it brought with it " much corruption and stinkes," and his " men were verie sensible of the badnesse of the air, and generally all broke out in their bodies to a sharpe itch ".

* S. P. Dom. Charles I., vol. ccxxi., No. 103.

On the 16th June,* Sir Kenelm's fleet sailed out of the Gulph of Scanderoon and all the Venetians saluted it; but it did not go very far away, as there was "certaine intelligence of 2 verie rich vessels loaden with money from Marseilles" which our pirate—I beg his pardon, I mean our Admiral of the British Fleet—was anxious to seize and appropriate.

Polite as the Venetians had appeared when saluting Sir Kenelm on his departure, they evidently feared him more than they loved him ; for, when he was at anchor "in a sandie bay, about seven leagues from Scanderoon," and he sent ashore for wood and water, the inhabitants promised him "in the morning a store of fresh provisions, but before night they were commanded from Scanderoon, upon paine of death, to furnish" him with none.

On the 22nd he was "advertised of a disgust"—that is to say, he learned that there was a quarrel—between Captain Stradling, his rear-admiral, and Mr. Herris, a gentleman of his own ship. Hearing that they had both been landed, he suspected a duel, therefore he went ashore also, and "so seasonably" "that he came betweene them in their first assault with their swords. They resigned their weapons to" him, and he "tooke order for the safe custodie of them both that night". The next day he inquired into the whole affair, and " finding nothing to lye heavie upon the honors of either of them," he "was a meanes to accommodate the businesse," after giving them both a severe lecture.

While he was still in the "sandie bay" "watching for the vessels loaden with money," his friend, the "English vice-consul att Scanderone," came to him "desiring" him "to be gone". He told him "how it cost the English marchants att Aleppo much money in bribes about" his " coming into the roade "—and still more about what he did

when he got there, he might have added ! But the vice-
consul admitted some difference of opinion to exist among
the Venetians on the subject, some " condemning the
Generall of their Galleazzes for beginning with" him ;
others condemning Sir Kenelm for not performing
" ceremonies of dutie" which they said were due to him,
" being lord of the port of these seas ".

It may be worth a passing notice that the vice-consul
did not go on board Sir Kenelm's ship, but asked him to
go ashore to speak to him. " The wind and sea," says
Sir Kenelm, "were verie high, so that my boate was
billaged and all of us tumbled into the sea, likewise two
other of my shippes boates were sunke." Perhaps his
ducking may have disturbed his temper ; for he does not
seem to have yielded to the vice-consul's entreaties. At
any rate, a couple of days later, the vice-consul came to
him again "with letters from the consul and all the
marchants att Aleppo, expressing their hard condition in
verie pittiful manner, and earnestly desiring me to depart
from their coast". And once more on " the last day of
June the vice-consul sent to me," he says, " from Scanderone to desire me againe to depart out of this gulfe, for
that our nation att Allepo fared much the worse for my
abode here ".

At last he came to the conclusion that he would " loose
no more time in these partes," so, cheered with the news
that the " Venetians att Scanderone had, since " his "coming
from thence, buried 45 men more that had dyed of the
hurtes they had received in their fight with " him, "and
that they still dyed dayly," he determined to be off.

Before starting, he accepted an invitation from the
natives to go ashore for a day * to hunt the wild boar.
" I tooke with me," he says, " 100 small shott and pikes,
and went 3 or 4 miles up into the countrie." What sport

* 3rd July, 1628.

he had he does not tell us; and we may infer that he had none, or he would have told us of his success. In the evening the sea was too rough to allow of his returning to his ship. "Wherefore I gave a Turke some money (he leaving his bow and quiver of arrowes in pawne for his honesty) to provide us some victuals; who went to one that I had treated well abord me, and he brought downe goates, sheepe, hens, milke, egges, mellons and bread baked as thinne as paper. Wee made great fires in a grove by the seaside, and roasted the flesh upon the ends of pikes, and passed the night verie well."

It was calmer the next morning, and he went on board his ship. He was just on the point of weighing anchor to make a start, when he "perceived some men on the shore waving to" him; so he sent a boat to find out who they were and what they wanted. It turned out to be only the eternal "vice-consul of Scanderone," who had once more come "to renew his solicitations for" Sir Kenelm's departure.

For the next three days he cruised about, working his way slowly and reluctantly from Scanderoon. As he was short of provisions, Captain Stradling went ashore to get "fresh victuals," and sent a man carrying a white flag of truce a little distance in front of him. Some horseman kidnapped this standard and its bearer before Captain Stradling and his men could come to the rescue; and when the captain followed and begged to be allowed to ransom the man, the native horseman not only refused, but "layed ambushes to gett more" of his crew. In revenge for this, Sir Kenelm contemplated landing "100 men or 2," at night, to surprise "their villages by the shore," and to burn "their countrie (which was full of grapes and corne)"; but on consideration he refrained, because, as he says, "I was almost assured our marchantes must answere the hurt I did".

For a fortnight, from the 3rd of July, he sailed westward, to the island of Crete, where he exchanged some "courtesies" with the Greeks, and obtained provisions for his ships. He spent the next fortnight in lying in wait for French ships on their way to the East, but nothing of consequence happened, with the exception of a storm, which made even their "ancientest seamen" "sea sicke".

A month after * they had seen the last of the "Vice-consull of Scanderone," they were cruising about twenty-three leagues from Crete when they "descryed a sayle," and very shortly "fetcht her up". Whereupon she "first putt out English colours"; but when the captain of Sir Kenelm's ships ("Captain Beaumond") flew French colours, a proceeding which was obviously unjustifiable, "shee also putt out French colours," and "shee said shee was of St Mauro, but had no commission nor formall instrument to testifie of whence they were". Sir Kenelm gives the following curious description of what then passed : "Captaine Beaumond told me that one of them confessed to him (in Italian by interpreter) that they had 20,000 dollars in readie money. When I sent for him he denyed it, and would not acknowledge that he could speake or understand Italian, whereupon I sent him abord my owne shippe to threaten him with tormentes to make him confesse, but they could get nothing out of him but that if he said any such thing it was in iest."

Surely, when our admiral of the fleet took on board his own ship the officer of a foreign vessel and threatened him with torture if he would not confess that he had a great deal of money with him, he somewhat forgot the English officer in imitating the English pirate.

Sir Kenelm had the ship searched ; but the 20,000 dollars were not to be found, so he let her go, after he had taken from her a topmast, a "cocke boate," and a couple of barrels of wine, of which, he says, "wee had never a

---

* 5th August, 1628.

droppe, nor of bevurage in all our fleete, but all dranke water "—and that "stunke".

On the 8th of August they came in for "a maine storme and a furious pelting wind," which did them some damage, and three of his ships disappeared altogether.   When it subsided another trouble followed.   Sir Kenelm's ships began to be in serious want of water, so they sailed in a northerly direction and put in at the port of the Island of Milo. Sir Kenelm was much struck with this "land locked" and "brave port".   "The consull there for strangers" immediately "came abord him," and the Turkish governor or caya received him with "much courtesie".   Sir Kenelm "feasted the Turkes, who were very barbarous and bestiale in" comparison with others that he had seen. Here he "putt the master of the Rereadmirall out of his place for dis-orders on shore and disrespects to his Captaine," but as the "Captaine became a solicitor for him," he restored him to his charge.

While Sir Kenelm was at Milo one of the most im-portant events happened in his whole life, so far as his biographers are concerned ; for it was there that he began, and wrote the greater part of, the *Private Memoirs*, from which I have quoted so freely in the earlier part of my work.   In the storm lately mentioned, he had been sepa-rated from some of his fleet, and it was necessary "to mend the defects" occasioned by it to his own ship.   "I was courteously invited," he says,[*] "ashore by a person of quality of that place ; whereunto when I had settled my important business in a good train, I willingly condescended, being very confident of the friendliness of that people, but more in the strength that I had there, which was such that they had more reason to beware doing me any displeasure than I to fear any attempt of theirs ; and hoping that, through the pleasantness of that place and the conveniences of the

* *Priv. Mem.*, K. D., p. 322 *seq.*

shore, I might somewhat refresh myself, who was then much distempered in body and suffered great affliction in my mind."

Through the mistake of his servant, his books were not brought on shore, so he had little wherewith to amuse himself. His "courteous host was much troubled" at this, and among other means of diverting him he made him "a liberal offer to interest" him "in the good graces of several of the most noted beauties of that place, who," he says, "in all ages have been known to be no niggards of their favours, which might peradventure have been welcomely accepted by another that had like me had youth, strength, and a long time at sea to excuse him if he had yielded to such a temptation. But I, that had fresh in my soul the idea of so divine and virtuous a beauty (as Venetia) that others' in balance with hers did but serve to show the weakness and misery of their sex, thought it no mastery to overcome it ; but yet was in some perplexity how to refuse my friend's courtesy without seeming uncivil." *N.B.*—He was writing this diary chiefly for his wife's reading !

After some consideration, he came to the conclusion that his best plan would be "to pretend some serious business, which of necessity did call upon" him "to write many despatches, and into several places ; and thus, without his" host's "offence or suspicion," he "might enjoy solitude and liberty". His "pretence was not altogether feigned, but" he "soon made an end of what concerned business," and then he took it into his head to write his autobiography, deeming "it both good diversion for the present, and pains that would hereafter administer" him "much content". Accordingly, "having pen, ink and paper," he wrote his "wandering fantasies as they presented themselves," "suddenly in loose sheets of borrowed paper, and that in not so full a manner as might be intelligible to any other," and with fictitious names. Indeed, without some extraneous knowledge of the people concerned, it would be difficult to make much of his *Private Memoirs*. He wrote them, he says, only "to please myself in looking back upon my past and sweet errors," and not with any "desire that my follies may after me remain on record".

After sailing from Milo,* he came across his three ships which he had lost, and was pleased to find that they had captured "2 French sattias" during their absence.

He was almost becalmed among the islands of the Archipelago, but he soon learned that even in these placid waters the sea is not invariably still; † for one night was "the foulest for raine, for vehemence of thunder and lightening, for extreme darknesse and violent snatches of winde that ever" he saw.

Sir Kenelm next anchored at Delos, with which he was enchanted. "There," says he, "are brave marble stones heaped up in the great ruines of Apollo's temple, and within the circuit of it is a huge statue, but broken in two peeces about the wast." Though somewhat weather-worn, "the yieldinges of the flesh and the muscular parts are visible, so that it is still a brave noble piece, and hath by divers bin attempted to be carried away, but they have all failed in it".

He determined, he says, "to avayle myselfe of the convenuencie of carrying away some antiquities there". And he had a double object in doing this; for, not only did he want to take home the "antiquities," but also to find work for his sailors; "because idlenesse should not fix their mindes upon any untoward fansies (as is usuall among seamen)," "I busied them in rolling of stones down to the seaside," including "one stone, the greatest and fairest of all, containing 4 statues". Hard indeed must work of that sort have been for the sailors, "it was now so hott ‡ that swimming a nightes I found the water warmer than att any time in England ".

As usual when he stayed for a few days at any place, after putting in at another island, his men became troublesome, and he "punished by ducking and other wayes a dozen or sixteen of" his "men that had been disorderly on shore, and that" he "had much difficultie to gett abord againe". This ducking must have been conducted with considerable vigour for, "with the much and violent motion of the roape the blocke did take fire ".*

Certain rumours which reached his ears now made him begin to fear lest an attempt should be made to "surprise" him "and fire" his ships. He observed too that boats, sent, it was said, by the Sicilians and Neapolitans, came "to spye what he did ; and he was told that some twenty-eight galleys were tracing his steps to surprise" him "att some advantage". He put in, therefore, at "a fitt port" "over against Ithaca," the best that he "ever saw," and there he "kept all the day sentinels upon the hilles, and in the night boates to watch at sea " ; so that he "might be advertized" if any fleet should come to attack him ; and he had "alwayes above 50 peeces of ordinance" ready for his defence. The thought that he himself might be "descryed" and "fetcht up " was not to be endured for an instant.

---

* Possibly this may have been very similar to the "keel hauling" practised within Captain Marryat's memory.

CHAPTER XIX.

RETURN TO ENGLAND.

THE threatened attack never came off, and Sir Kenelm was able peacefully to sell to the inhabitants a quantity of " rise," which " began to be full of wormes ". He spent some days in repairing his ships, and then went to the Bay of Patras.

Of course, while he was at anchor here to provision his ships there was bad behaviour among his men. Besides a quarrel,* he found that his steward had stolen some sugar and rice ; so, as a punishment, he says, " I made him to be first ducked (with a gunne shott off) and then towed att my boats sterne to every one of my shippers, expressing his fault to them ".

The next day Sir Kenelm went very near to getting into a great scrape. He had gone on shore to the consul's house, when some servants of the caya's came there, turned him out with great violence, beat several of his followers " in outrageous maner," " carried them away prisoners," and tried to seize Sir Kenelm himself also ; but he " subtilely gott out of their handes ".

Sir Kenelm's " victuall was verie short, therefore patience and temporizing with their furies " were his " best remedies in these perplexities with this people, that is unresistable and uncouncellable in the violence of their motions ". It was absolutely necessary for him to lay in a very large stock of provisions before starting on his homeward journey ; for he was interdicted from every

* 8th October, 1628.
(186)

place under Venetian dominion, and he had reasons for being anxious to avoid both Algiers and Tunis.

In his necessity, he was forced to part with a large quantity of goods "at an inferior value"; and he sold his sattia, "partly because shee was an auncient vessell and could not brooke the winter season," and partly because he "wanted money to buy victuals and necessaries for" his voyage home. Throughout his stay of eighteen days at Patras he "had continual vexation and trouble through the injustice and tyrannie of the Turkes". Even the consul there failed him "in many thinges of honesty and humanitye, and cheated Sir Edward Stradling with a false diamond, selling it to him upon his word for a true one".

Sir Kenelm says that the "soyle" in these regions "produceth excellent tobacco". Perhaps he did not smoke; for he says "they of my companie that smoke of it told me that some would be worth 20s. a lb. in England, which they bought for 1s.". Finest cut Turkish tobacco is worth about a guinea a pound in England at the present day; but I doubt whether any tobacco would now be worth the value of a sovereign of the year 1628 per pound.

Sir Kenelm was glad to sail away from the lands of "the unspeakable Turk," as he has been called in our times; but his pleasure in doing so was destined to be chilled by a very disagreeable incident. As he anchored off Cephalonia, near a fleet of eight English and five Dutch currant ships, homeward bound, on the 28th of October, a French sattia was seen, and when Sir Kenelm "shott at her" she "yielded"; whereupon the captains of two of the English ships, who previously had not meddled with her, also "shott att her". As soon as Sir Kenelm's men boarded her, so also did theirs; and, as they sent more men than he had sent, they overcame his people, broke open the hold, "committed great disorder," carried away several "bagges of money," and "with a hawser made her fast to one of their shippes".

This Sir Kenelm could not and would not stand; so he went on board her himself with a strong following, cut the hawser, " put off all their men "—it must have been very pretty fighting between the rival Englishmen— anchored her near one of his own ships, and "streight nailed up the hatches of the hold ".

While at anchor at Cephalonia one of his ships joined him from Lepanto, where, for a wonder, the authorities had treated his men well, making a proclamation that no Turk should injure them upon pain of death, " which was fleaing [flaying] and roasting alive ". Here he heard first of the death of the great enemy of his family, the Duke of Buck-ingham. On leaving Cephalonia, he examined some of his " English beefe " that was still left and " found it to be verie bad ". " Att first the flesh was excellent good," and he attributed its decay to the fact that the merchant's men " drew not the bloodie pickle from it ".

He then went to Zante, where the Provvidatore, who had not been friendly on a former occasion, made an ex-cuse to proclaim that no Englishman should go on shore on pain of death, or any native supply an Englishman with provisions, although Sir Kenelm had already sent money on shore in prepayment for various provisions. A party of foreign merchants in the town went to the Provvidatore to intercede for Sir Kenelm; but he threatened to throw some of them over the castle walls and to send the re-mainder to the galleys ; and he said that Sir Kenelm and his captains were " *ladroni e corsari*". There is many a true word spoken in jest!

" Vnderstanding how peremptory he was, that day being the 11 of November," * Sir Kenelm shaped his " course homewards". Three days later he " mett with " his

* 1628.

"shippes again," and his fleet made the best of its way westward, constantly chasing ships which usually turned out to belong to friendly nations and consequently to be ineligible for prey.

When within sight of Sardinia he came up with his other ships again, and the day * after they had rejoined each other they caught three sattias, laden with wheat, peas, and cheese. This took place close to the diminutive island of Serpentara, off the south-eastern extremity of Sardinia. As he "came under the castles," which had peppered at him on his way out, he says, "they shott at me, and I likewise att them".

He was not very lucky with the three captured sattias. One went to pieces on some rocks just after they took it, and another, "worth about £1000" including her cargo, was wrecked in a storm two days afterwards, and "sunke all att once directly downe under" Sir Kenelm's own "stemme, so that nothing appeared afterwards of her but some pieces of broken bordes".

On the 10th of December, when cruising near the island of S. Pietro, off the south-west of Sardinia, he and his fleet attacked two ships, one of 500 tons with "24 pieces of ordinance" and the other of 400 tons with "14 pieces". One carried prohibited goods from Sardinia to Spain, the other was a "Ragusa shippe". They showed considerable fight, and when the captain of the largest of them was bade "Amaine for the King of England," he "spoke wordes of high disrespect to the King, and waiving him with a bright sword called to the gunner to give fire, which by and by he did, and shott 7 pieces att" Sir Kenelm's "pinnace, all which hatt (*sic*) her, and one shott down her mizen mast, and others cutting her rigging". The stranger might have held her own had not one of Sir Kenelm's other ships come up to his assistance, "and

* 29th November, 1628.

never putt out gunne till she was within pistole shott, but then did it with great soddainenesse, and with as much dexterity ".

The captain of the strange ship then "stroke his flag thrice and hoisted it att last aloft and so lett it stand ". Sir Kenelm's captain spoke tó him, to which he replied " in a muttering manner " ; and " of a soddaine " his men were observed to be on the point of firing a broadside ; so the English captain instantly ordered his own men to deliver " one broadside and 2 volies of small shott," which they did with such effect that the enemy "strooke his toppe-sailes ".

Leaving his defeated foe in the custody of his other ships, he went in pursuit of the remaining enemy and " soone fetched her up ; and after 5 shott shee lay by the lee ". When Sir Kenelm examined his prizes the next day he found them " loaden with the peculiar proper goods of some Genua marchantes ". The captain of the larger prize begged to be " lett goe for Italie," " because he was sicke"; and Sir Kenelm sent him off with 50 sacks of wheat, and he gave the other captain 260 sacks and liberated him also. All the Greeks and all the Italians whom Sir Kenelm had taken on board as sailors, with only two ex-ceptions, also asked to be put on shore, "because they heard of great preparations to be made in Spaine to fight " Sir Kenelm's fleet as it returned through the Straits of Gibral-tar. Since they seemed so nervous and disinclined for battle, he granted their request.

Before leaving, the captain of the larger prize told Sir Kenelm that his late ship, which was called the *Jonas*, was so leaky that she would never reach England. Sir Kenelm fancied that he " dissembled," and only said it to put him " out of love with her " ; but it turned out to be quite true that she was " verie extremely leakie," and the men " grew to pumpe continually, and could not free her with both pumpes ". It was, none the less, worth while to spend a

great deal of labour in trying to save her and bring her
safe to England; for she was a very "rich shippe, esteemed
worth above two hundred thousand crownes," being the
most valuable prize that he had captured during the whole
of his voyage.

The wind was very favourable for a run from Sardinia
to Gibraltar and through its straits, so Sir Kenelm made
the most of it. It blew too much rather than too little,
and he came in for several storms, though happily they
carried him in the right direction. He caught sight of
"Gibraltar hill about 12 leagues off to the eastward, and
the north side of it is so steepe upright that the toppe
hangeth over the foot of it".

On 1st January, 1629, about eight days after leaving
Sardinia, Sir Kenelm was opposite Gibraltar. There were
no signs of the preparations which it had been said were
made in Spain to attack him as he should pass through the
Straits. Even if any such attack had ever been contemplated, he may have escaped notice owing to the bad weather,
for he "passed the straights with many stormy gustes of
wind". Four o'clock on a January morning, again, was a
time at which ships might best hope to pass unnoticed.
Sir Kenelm got safely through the Straits with all his fleet,
and was soon sailing securely in the Atlantic Ocean.

Off the coast of Lisbon, he spoke with an English man-
of-war and learned that there were "verie many English"
ships upon the coast, so he came to the conclusion that he
had "little reason to stay longer hereabouts than for a faire
winde". His fleet would have made a much more rapid
voyage homewards but for the "ill-going of the *Jonas*, for
whom yet" Sir Kenelm "was faine to stay often times".
The constant pumping necessary to keep her afloat was a
great strain on the crew, and he had to keep sending a
"fresh spell of men" every now and then to her, and "to
increase their allowance of victualles because of their hard
labors". The Bay of Biscay is not invariably calm in

January, and Sir Kenelm came in for "a rolling easterne sea," "a stiffe gale and a growne sea," "gustes of misling raine and snow," and a "storme".

Three weeks after passing through the Straits of Gibraltar, he reached the mouth of the English Channel, and received an agreeable assurance that he was approaching his native clime in the shape of "a thigge fogge, which dimmed the sunnes light, and soone resolved itselfe into misling droppes". Further up the channel, the weather changed, and he encountered "the cruellest storme that ever" he "was in".

On the 26th of January he saw the cliffs of the Isle of Wight. Here he chased a ship, but without success. This was the last ship hunt he ever had, and it must have been mortifying not to "fetch her up". On the 27th he passed Dover, but owing to "foule" weather, ships running aground, and various mishaps, it was not until February 2nd * that he "came to an anchor by Woolwidge," and on the 3rd his relation and benefactor, the Earl of Bristol, "and much other Company came aboard" Sir Kenelm's ship, and he "went ashore and received gratious entertainment from the King and a happy welcome from all" his "frends". Sir Kenelm must have been almost as much relieved as his great relative at the disappearance of the Duke of Buckingham. Bristol had been restored to royal favour a short time before the death of Buckingham, so now everything seemed in favour of Sir Kenelm's advancement, especially as he had returned a hero.

He had come back to England, however, at a time when there was plenty to distract the attention of the king and the court from his own adventures. While he had been sailing up the English Channel, Parliament had met, and Selden had risen to charge the Government with breaking the Petition of Right.† He had exposed the

* 1629.

† Gardiner's *Hist. Eng.*, vol. vi., p. 13 *seq.*

harsh dealings in the Star Chamber, and the country was in a ferment. There had been violent debates upon tonnage and poundage, as well as upon the very different subject of religion. Pym and Eliot had been declaiming at the very time of Sir Kenelm's landing at Woolwich. On the very day that Digby had received " gratious entertainment" from the king, the king * had with difficulty restrained his vexation in the House at the opposition of the Commons, and had spoken there with irritation, and the following day an uproar arose among the Commons at the appointment by Charles of Montague as a bishop.

Amidst all this political excitement Sir Kenelm must have found his own achievements regarded as a mere welcome distraction from more serious matters rather than as the most important news of the day, and in the political turmoil people were too busy for petty hero-worship. In short, he returned at rather an unfortunate moment for his own celebrity, and he may have been glad to seek the privacy of his home to take into his arms his beautiful and affectionate wife, to receive the welcome of his eldest boy, and to see for the first time the babe that had been born as he was on the point of embarking upon the voyage from which he had just returned in safety and with renown.

* Gardiner's *Hist. Eng.*, vol. vi., p. 42 *seq.*

CHAPTER XX.

SHIPS AND CHURCHES.

AFTER his return from his voyage, Sir Kenelm Digby posed as a victorious British admiral, who had performed brilliant services for his country; but he soon had to appear, under quite another character, to give an account of his proceedings before the Court of Exchequer in various lawsuits * respecting the prizes which he had taken. A good many foreigners put themselves to great trouble and expense to come and claim them. A man named Spinola appears to have protested that his goods ought to have been exempted because he was an Italian subject; but the judge, Sir H. Martin, disallowed this claim on the ground that, in the bills of lading, Spinola was "stiled" "of Madrid," that he was "a Vezino † of Spain," "an especiall officer of great trust in the King of Spain's Court, and a Cavallero of the Order of St. Jago". Other appeals were disallowed to Italians on the ground that they likewise had become naturalised in Spain.

Certain claims against Sir Kenelm, on the contrary, were admitted. For instance, he was made to restore "three Barrells of Cocheneal" to a Venetian; certain goods out of the *Jonas* to some Genoese; "133 Sernes of Bariglia" to a Venetian; to another Venetian "90 great sacks of wool, and 270 Sernes of Bariglia"; to another pair of Genoese "45 baggs of wool"; to a Venetian "37 baggs

* S. P. Dom. Charles I., vol. cxlvii., No. 30.
† A naturalised subject.

(194)

of wool"; to three others 32 sacks of wool; and to various Genoese and Venetians other parcels of goods.

Possibly it may have been as an investment for some of their prize money that Sir Kenelm Digby and his vice-admiral, Sir Edward Stradling,* petitioned the king for leave to build houses for themselves with stables and coach-houses, in Old Witch Close, bought of Richard Holford, lying on the east side of Drury Lane towards Lincoln's Inn.

Sir Kenelm also endeavoured to obtain estates in the country.† The sheriff of Hampshire had had a suit in the Star Chamber with one Thomas Taylor, the owner of Bradley Manor in that county, and claimed his estate. Sir Kenelm Digby agreed to invest in it, " as his Majesty's farmer thereof ". When the sheriff went to take possession, Mr. Taylor and his wife and sixteen children refused to leave. They "resisted with firearms," ‡ and "the sheriff's party answered with ordnance, and made approaches up to the door of the house, but were ultimately obliged to retreat ". Taylor then petitioned the king, complaining that he was being "stripped out of his estate by the oppression of Sir Kenelm Digby ". Sir Kenelm also petitioned, stating that Taylor had had with him " a tumultuous body of sailors under the command of a captain, who defended the house in a warlike manner for six or seven hours, and killed one of the sheriff's men with a poisoned bullet ". I have not succeeded in tracing the result of this dispute.

Sir Kenelm also tried to obtain from the Crown the estate of Sawton,§ in Cheshire, which had been escheated through its owner, John Calvely, dying without heir. This, as well as estates in Lancaster, Denbighshire and Hun-

* S. P. Dom. Charles I., vol. clxiii., No. 51.
† Ib., vol. clix., No. 10. Also No. 53.
‡ Cal. Sta. Pa. Dom., 1629, xxxi., p. 172. Also p. 179.
§ S. P. Dom. Charles I., vol. clix., No. 25.

tingdonshire, which had also belonged to the Calvely family, were granted to Sir Kenelm, the tenure to be socage, with a rent of £5 for ever. In this case, again, a petition was presented to the Crown against Sir Kenelm's tenure ; but the matter ended in his favour. Sir Kenelm's successes under the English flag at sea were rewarded by his appointment as a commissioner for the navy.* Coke wrote to Nicholas that his appointment seemed a wise one, though some were displeased at it.†

There was a report,‡ wrote Rowland Woodward to Francis Windebank, that a fleet of fifteen ships was to be commissioned to prevent the Dutch from fishing on the English coast, and that it was to be commanded by Sir Kenelm Digby. Woodward expressed serious misgivings as to the consequences if it were to be under such a commander, which shows that Sir Kenelm's proceedings in the Mediterranean had not met with universal approval in London. Nothing, however, came of the proposition against the Dutch fishermen, so far as Sir Kenelm was concerned.

While quoting from State papers I am reminded of the ease with which they can now be seen, in comparison with the difficulty in Sir Kenelm Digby's time, by a letter among them, written by Sir Kenelm to Coke, asking him to procure the king's warrant to permit a certain Dr. Dorislaus to look at and use such papers of State as might help him in writing a story that he had in hand ; for there seems to have been considerable delay in obtaining it.§

We find Sir Kenelm ‖ writing about the impertinence of a captain whose head had been so turned by his appointment to the command of a ship that he asked Sir

---

* S. P. Dom. Charles I., vol. clxxiv., No. 29.
† Ib., No. 21.
‡ Ib., vol. clxxvii., No. 13.
§ Ib., vol. ccxxii., No. 11.
‖ Ib.

Kenelm to lend him money, and hinted that unless it were so lent he would complain of him to the king. Nicholas, to whom the letter was addressed, had now a high respect for Sir Kenelm's influence, and in a letter to Pennington told him * that Coke was in effect sole secretary, and that Sir Kenelm Digby had more power with him than any one else. In another letter † to the same correspondent, he expresses a suspicion that Sir Kenelm's friends are intriguing to get him made an Admiral of the Navy.

Sir Kenelm does not appear to have been universally popular among those under his command. A shipbuilder named Goddard writes to Coke,‡ complaining bitterly of his treatment by Sir Kenelm, although, he says, he will not go quite so far as another builder, who said he would as soon build a ship in hell as in Deptford Yard. Yet Sir Kenelm felt no ill-will towards the man in question ; for, in writing to Coke,§ he says that, in spite of queer humours, he (Goddard) is a very able man, and that a ship which he is building will prove a particularly good one.

At this time Sir Kenelm appears to have been living at Deptford ; for he tells Coke ‖ that he finds little to do there, except to please himself by looking over a few books —he cannot call it studying. It is a mere pretence for idleness. Yet naval matters evidently occupied his time and attention to a great extent ; for he goes into several details with regard to shipbuilding, victualling the navy, and the conduct of officials.

If Sir Kenelm was generally anxious for the advancement of his own family, he cannot be accused of actual nepotism ; for, in a letter to Coke,¶ while he describes one

---

* *S. P. Dom. Charles I.*, vol. ccxx., No. 44.

† *Ib.*, vol. ccxxi., No. 24.

‡ *Ib.*, vol. ccxxii., No. 57.

§ *Ib.*, vol. ccxxiii., No. 21.

‖ *Ib.*

¶ *Ib.*, vol. ccxxii., No. 22.

of his cousins, who wished to be made a lieutenant in the navy, as a discreet and well-tempered gentleman, he says of another relation that he cannot recommend him so highly, because, although he is courageous and honest, he has not brain enough for command.

On the other hand, he was ready to use his influence on behalf of friends. In a letter to Coke,* he asks for the appointment to some ship of Sir Beverley Newcome, a very great friend of the Earl of Dorset. The earl had expressed a great wish for the favour for this playmate of his childhood ; and it is the more remarkable that Sir Kenelm should have urged Coke to grant it, when we remember that this Earl of Dorset had been Sir Edward Sackville, his former rival for the hand of Venetia Stanley. Sackville had succeeded his brother in the title in the year 1624, and after Sir Kenelm's return from the Mediterranean, the two men appear to have made up their quarrel. A few months after Sir Kenelm landed, Dorset wrote † to Dorchester, saying that, owing to the illness of his eldest son, he was obliged to steal away from Court for a few days, and begging him to present Sir Kenelm Digby to the king in order that he may offer his thanks for a favour granted at the earl's request. And Aubrey tells us in his amusing, if not perhaps invariably veracious, *Letters*,‡ that " Once a yeare the Earle of Dorset invited her (lady Digby, his former flame) and Sir Kenelm to dinner, where the Earle would behold her with much passion and only kisse her hand ".

Dorset by letter and Sir Kenelm Digby in a conference were on one occasion mutually concerned and appa-

---

* *S. P. Dom. Charles I.*, vol. ccxxii., No. 37.

† *Ib.*, vol. clxviii., No. 99.

‡ *Letters by Eminent Persons*, vol. ii., Appendix, 323 *seq.* Aubrey represents the Earl of Dorset, with whom Venetia Stanley's name was coupled by the scandal-mongers of the period, to have been Richard Sackville. Elsewhere I have given my reasons for believing it to have been Edward.

rently officially in endeavouring to persuade Sir Henry Mervyn, the Admiral of the Narrow Seas, to part with his post, on condition of receiving his arrears of £10,000 * from the king. They had already offered him in vain £5000 for his arrears and £3000 for his appointment, which was exactly what it had cost him.

Sir Kenelm was also engaged in arranging for the supply of gunpowder. A contractor † begged the Lieutenant-General of Ordnance for a personal interview, because Sir Kenelm Digby had refused to present him to that official, unless he would make a lower tender than 8½d. per pound, at which price a rival contractor had already offered to undertake the entire supply.

Never, after his return from the Mediterranean, did Sir Kenelm go to sea as an officer; but in 1631 some of the Lords of the Admiralty were anxious that he should be commissioned, not again as a privateer, but as a captain or an admiral of His Majesty's Navy.

If the friends of Sir Kenelm always represented him as a great naval hero, others took a different view, as the following extract will show :— ‡

"When the same Sir Kenelm was provoked in the king's presence (upon occasion of the old business of Scanderoon) by the Venetian ambassador, who told the king it was very strange that His Majesty should slight so much his ancient amity with the most noble state of Europe, for the affections which he bare to a man (meaning Sir K.) whose father was a traitor, his wife a ———— and himself a pirate, altho' he made not the least reply (as long as the ambassador remained in England) to those great reproaches, yet after, when the quality of his enemy was changed (by his return) to that of a private person,

---

* *S. P. Dom. Charles I.*, vol. clxxiii., No. 6.

† *Ib.*, vol. clxxii., No. 23.

‡ *Crosby Records. A Cavalier's Note-book.* Notes of William Blundell of Crosby, Lancashire. Edited by the Rev. T. Ellison Gibson, pp. 152-3.

Sir Kenelm posted after him into Italy. There sending him a challenge to Venice (from some neighbouring state) he found the discreet Magnifico as silent in Italy as himself had been before in England, and so he returned home."

As Aubrey says that in " 163—," which some historians believe to have been one of the earliest years of the thirties, "tempore Car. I.," Sir Kenelm "received the Sacrement in the chapell at Whitehall, and professed the Protestant religion, which gave great scandall to the Roman Catholiques, but afterwards he looked back," this may be a fitting place to consider the disputed question when he became a Protestant. If Aubrey is correct, it may have been a year or two after his return from the Mediterranean.

The fact that he was then in the full tide of favour at court might make the period a likely one for his yielding to the temptation of still further ingratiating himself with the king by embracing the State religion. The already given evidence in his own writing in his *Private Memoirs* * that he was a Catholic when he was in Spain with Prince Charles, is the strongest of all in favour of the theory that he did not desert the faith of his father as a youth ; and, as the *Private Memoirs* were written in 1628 on his voyage, and he makes no mention of a change of religion in them, it may be that that change was not made till after his return, that is to say, some time after 1629, which would fit in with Aubrey's statement.

Another argument in favour of Sir Kenelm's having abjured the Catholic religion after he was fully grown up consists in some passages of Archbishop Laud's letter to him after he returned to the Catholic faith in 1636. In the letter to which it forms a reply, Sir Kenelm had apparently maintained that by birth he had been a Catholic

* *Priv. Mem.*, K. D., p. 172.

and ought still to be one, "unless clear and evident proof" should lead him to remain a Protestant.

" Truly, sir," said Laud, " I think this had been spoken with more advantage to you and your cause before your adhering to the Church of England, than now, for then the right of possession could not have been thought little. But now, since you deserted that Communion, either you did it upon clear and evident proof, or upon apparent only. If you did it upon clear and evident proof, why say you now no such can be found? If you did it but upon apparent and seeming proof (a semblance of very good reason, as yourself calls it), why did you then come off from that Communion, till your proof were clear and evident? And why may not that, which now seems clear and evident, be but apparent, as well as that, which then seemed clear unto you, be but semblance now?"

It has been argued that Laud could not reasonably have written in such a strain to a man of thirty-three, if his adherence to the Anglican Church, "upon clear and evident" proof, had taken place when he was only fifteen years old or less.* This view is taken by Mr. Bruce in his exceedingly able Preface to *The Voyage into the Mediter-ranean*.

Yet it must be admitted that the opposite is the more common opinion. Aubrey's "worthy friend, Anthoine à Wood, antiquarie of Oxford," † states that " he was sent to Gloucester Hall, after he had been trained up in the Protestant Religion ". This " after " is of great importance.

The *Biographia Britannica* ‡ says " it is certain that he renounced the errors of popery very young, and was care-fully bred in the Protestant Religion, chiefly, as there is good reason to believe, under the direction of Archbishop

---

* I was not in possession of so much evidence on this question, when I noticed the matter in my *Life of Archbishop Laud*, and treated it in a some-what different light.

† *Ath. Ox.*, vol. ii., p. 351.

‡ Ed. 1750, vol. iii., p. 1701.

Laud, then Dean of Gloucester". Dr. Campbell, in his
very valuable notes to the Kippis edition of the same work,[*]
supports this theory. Lodge [†] speaks of his having been
" bred at least under Protestant forms". Chalmers,[‡] in
his *Biographical Dictionary*, says much the same as the
Biographia Britannica on this question. Again, Sir Egerton
Brydges, in his edition of Collins' *Peerage of England*,
states that he was " trained up in the Protestant religion
under Archbishop Laud ".[§]

Of course several of these authorities may have copied
from each other; I only quote them to show that no other
opinion on the point appears to have been advanced in
their time. There is, however, this very important point
to be considered, that they do not appear to have been
familiar with Sir Kenelm's *Private Memoirs*,[||] which
contain the evidence already mentioned.

Even Sir Harris Nicholas, in his Introduction [¶] to those
Private Memoirs, which furnish the strongest evidence
adduced by Mr. Bruce in favour of his own opinion, never
seems to have taken, or even perceived the possibility of,
such a view. Sir Harris draws attention to this very
evidence, which consists of Sir Kenelm's personal testimony
that he was a Catholic as early as 1623, when he was in
Spain and twenty years old; but, at the same time, he
accepts the evidence of Lodge that he was "educated a
Protestant," and the inference he draws from these
apparently contradictory statements is that, although he

---

[*] Vol. v., p. 185.

[†] *Portraits*, ed. 1850, vol. v., p. 148.

[‡] Ed. 1813, vol. xi., p. 70.

[§] Sir Kenelm Digby must at least have committed a formal act of
apostasy when he went to Oxford, if Huber is correct in saying that, in the
reign of James I., " a literal subscription to the thirty-nine articles was made
a prerequisite for matriculation ". *English Universities*, Newman's translation.

[||] Harleian MS., No. 6758.

[¶] Pp. viii. and ix.

conformed to the practices of the Established Church of England, both when under Laud and when at Oxford, " it may fairly be doubted whether he was ever in reality of any other religion " than the Catholic, and he appears to consider the idea that he rejoined that Church when he was thirty-three erroneous.

It is possible that Sir Kenelm may not have practised the Catholic religion publicly or allowed the public to be aware that he practised, or even professed, it in private, until 1636 ; and it should be remembered that he lived at a period when there was some difference of opinion, not only among laymen, but also among ecclesiastics, as to the extent of public profession required from a Catholic. The times were, to say the least of it, exceedingly difficult, and there can be no doubt that there were Catholics who concealed their religion in a very questionable manner.

Panzani mentions some of these in his report of the condition of Catholics in England during the Vicariate of Dr. Smith, Bishop of Chalcedon, which began in 1625 ; and this condition may admit of Sir Kenelm's having been from about 1623 to 1636 a Catholic of the type he describes, which is the more likely since the greatest opponents of the lax Catholics, who took the oath of allegiance in its objectionable form and otherwise compromised their religion for their convenience, were the Jesuits; and Wood * tells us that the Jesuits " cared not " for Sir Kenelm, but " spoke spitefully " of him.

Another author † writes that he " declared himself, upon all occasions, an eager enemy to the Jesuits, who were not at all behind with him in resentment, but took all the care they could to lessen his character and to defame him ".

* *Ath. Ox.*, vol. ii., p. 351.

† *Biographia Brit.*, ed. 1750, vol. iii., p. 1712.

"Some* are Catholics in private only," says Panzani, "and for their selfish ends living outwardly in such a manner as not to be known for Catholics, and thus doing little benefit to their brethren in the faith. Among such are several persons of very high rank, who have all the greater fear on account of their position lest they shall lose the royal favour. Consequently, even if they keep a priest in their houses, they keep him so secretly that not even their own sons, much less their servants, are aware of it."

And then, after describing many very good and practical Catholics, he says : "Besides the above-mentioned Catholics there are Christians of another sort, who, although they detest in their hearts heresy and schism, yet through fear of losing their properties, offices or benefices, and through desire of advancing themselves at Court, live outwardly as heretics, frequenting Protestant churches, taking the oaths of supremacy and allegiance and speaking openly, when it serves their purpose, against Catholics. But inwardly they believe and live as Catholics."

Perhaps Sir Kenelm may have been one of these "Christians of another sort," calling himself a Catholic among the Spaniards at Madrid, and "frequenting Protestant churches" in London, "through desire of advancing himself at Court". And although he may have "detested heresy and schism" during the previous thirteen years in his heart, perhaps he only publicly declared himself a Catholic in 1636. Whichever of the theories advanced may be selected for approval, it is not without its difficulties. Certainly the necessity of taking the matriculation oath, as it then appears to have stood at Oxford, and just after he had left Oxford Sir Kenelm's request to "the Parson of Great Linford" to pray for him, are great obstacles to the theory that he did not

---

* I quote from *Annals of the Catholic Hierarchy*, by W. Maziere Brady, p. 83 *seq.*

become an Anglican until after his return from Spain with Prince Charles.

My own inclination is to the idea that Sir Kenelm had very little religion of any sort until 1636, and that he himself might have found it little less difficult to declare when he was a Protestant and when a Catholic before that date than do his biographers.

CHAPTER XXI.

DEATH IN THE HOUSE.

THE last chapter was closed with an inquiry into Sir Kenelm Digby's religion ; its successor shall be opened with a reference to his superstition. Soon after his return from his voyage to the Mediterranean, either in 1630 or 1631, he went with "one * who called himself Lord Both-well," to a certain John Evans, living in the Minories, and asked him to raise a spirit for them. This Evans had been an undergraduate, if not a graduate, at Oxford, had taken Anglican orders, and had held a curacy ; but, later on, he had turned his attention to astrology and necromancy, "having been well vers'd in the nature of Spirits". "He was the most perfect Saturnine Person that ever was beheld. He was of a middle stature, broad forehead, beetle-browed, thick-shouldered, flat-nos'd, full lips, down-look'd, of black curling stiff hair, and splay-footed." He "applied himself to the Invocation of the Angel Salmon, of the nature of Mars".

On Sir Kenelm asking him to raise a spirit for them, "he promised them so to do ; and when they were all in the body of the Circle which he had made, Evans upon a sudden, after some time of Invocation, was taken and carried into the Field near Battersea Causey close to the Thames. Next morning a Countryman going by to his labour, and espying a Man in black Cloaths, came unto him, awakened and ask'd him how he came there. Evans

* Wood's *Ath. Ox.*, vol. i., p. 579.

by this understood his own condition, inquired where he was, how far from London, and in what Parish, which when he understood, he told the Labourer he had been late at Battersea the night before, and by chance was left there by his Friends. The L. Bothwell, and Sir K. Digby, who went home without any harm, came next day to the House of Evans to know what was become of him; and just as they came into the House in the Afternoon, a Messenger came from Evans to his Wife to come to him at Battersea; which she did, and conveyed him home. This story being told by Evans to Will. Lilly, Lilly thereupon inquired upon what account the Spirits carried him away. To which Evans made answer, that *he did not at the time of his Invocation make any Suffumigation, at which the Spirits were vexed."*

It will be observed that owing to the absence of suffumigation, instead of the Rev. John Evans having kept his promise to Sir Kenelm to raise a spirit, a spirit raised the Rev. John Evans. The inquiry naturally presents itself—why did not this excellent clergyman come home to his wife, instead of sending for his wife to Battersea? The reply suggests itself that he may have taken unto himself other spirits, more material, and, in their own way, more potent than the first, in some tavern in Battersea; for " he was much addicted to Debauchery, and when in drink he would be very abusive and quarrelsome, so that he would seldom be without a black eye or one bruise or other ".

In his search for spirits, Sir Kenelm was not forgetful of his worldly interests; but several rumours of his approaching advancement were never fulfilled. We have already seen that some of the Lords of the Admiralty were anxious that he should be put in command of an English man-of-war in the regular navy; and after Lord Dorchester (Dudley Carleton) had died, on 15th February, 1632, it was rumoured that Sir Kenelm would succeed him

as Secretary of State.*   In the same year, Nicholas said
in a letter † to Pennington that Sir Kenelm was one of the
men spoken of as likely to be selected for the high office
of English Ambassador to France.

In 1632 died Sir Kenelm's great friend, Thomas Allen.
In his Introduction to the *Private Memoirs* ‡ Sir Harris
Nicholas says that some writers assert that Sir Kenelm
purchased Allen's library from him during his life, " though
he generously allowed him the use of them " ; but that,
" according to Kippis, he obtained them under a bequest
in Allen's will ".   He then quotes a letter from Sir
Kenelm § to Sir Robert Cotton, in which he speaks of Mr.
Allen's " friendly giving me his bookes and papers " ; and
requests Sir Robert " to advise him to settle them in a
direct and legal manner ".

And a codicil to Allen's will,‖ dated 26th Oct., 1630,
runs : " I give to Sir Kenelme Digbie Knight, my noble
friend, all my manuscripts, and what other of my bookes
he shall or may take a likinge unto," with a few exceptions.

The year after Allen's death,¶ Sir Kenelm presented
them to the Bodleian.   On the value of this addition to
that celebrated library it is needless that I should enlarge.

Mr. Macray makes Sir Kenelm's presentation to the
Bodleian Library a year later than Wood.   He says :—**

" In 1634 Sir K. Digby gave 238 MSS. uniformly
bound and stamped with his arms ; it was at Laud's instance, and through him as Chancellor of the University,

* Ellis's *Original Letters*, second series, vol. iii., p. 266, letter cclxxi.
Mr. John Pory to Sir Thomas Pickering.

† *S. P. Dom. Charles I.*, vol. ccxxii., No. 37.

‡ P. xlvi.

§ Cotton MSS. *Vespasianus*, f. xiii., f. 330.

‖ *Voyage into the Mediterranean*.   Additional Notes, p. 96.

¶ Wood's *Athen. Ox.*, vol. i., p. 575.

** *Annals of the Bodleian Library*, by the Rev. W. D. Macray.
Second ed., Oxford, 1890.

that the gift was made (see Wharton's *Remains*, ii., 73). Many of the volumes had previously belonged to Thomas Allen of Gloucester Hall, who bequeathed them to Digby. Two additional MSS., which formerly belonged to Digby, were purchased in 1825. The MSS. all contained in Digby's hand the motto, 'Vindicate tibi,' except one which has 'Vacate et Videte'."

There seems to have been at least one exception in Sir Kenelm's gift to the Bodleian Library of the books bequeathed to him by Thomas Allen ; for among the Ashmolean MSS.* is a curious folio volume, written in a secretarial hand and adorned with a rubric. A former owner has written in it: " This booke was given mee by Sir Kenelme Digby: it was written by Dr John Dee and vpon ye death of Mr. Allen of Oxford came to Sr K. D. hands, and he gave it to me. 1635 Fin. Jo. Bookery ".

Of the domestic life of Sir Kenelm Digby after his return from the Mediterranean little is recorded. It was but short, lasting, in fact, only about four years. History is silent on the question whether Lady Digby was popular at Court, nor does it even tell us whether she was received there.

Certainly Sir Kenelm was in great favour at this time. His good looks, his great size, his prodigious strength,† his smart attire, his position as Gentleman of the Bedchamber to the king, his office as a Commissioner of the Admiralty, the celebrity which he had obtained as "the hero of Scanderoon" and other exploits in the Mediterranean, and last, but not least, the additional wealth which he had secured by prizes taken during his voyage, combined to

---

* No. 1789.

† " He was a man," says Aubrey, "of extraordinary strength. I remember one at Shirbourne (relating to the Earl of Bristoll) protested to us, that as he, being a middling man, being sett in a chaire, Sir Kenelm Digby took up him, chaire and all, with one arme." Aubrey's *Letters*, vol. ii., Appendix.

exalt his position as a courtier, a man of fashion, and a public character.

But did Venetia share his honours? We do not know. At the Court of James I. or Charles II. the scandals with which her name, justly or unjustly, was connected might have been rather a recommendation than otherwise; but at that of Charles I. it was somewhat different.

It is just possible that, in addition to her too great celebrity as a girl, she had the even greater fault, from a courtier's point of view, of being a little dull, great as were the charms of her manner, grace, and beauty. That she was sometimes spoken of as stupid may be inferred from Feltham's lines :—*

> Yet there are those, striving to salve their own
> Deep want of skill, have in a fury thrown
> Scandal on her, and say she wanted Brain.†
> Botchers of Nature! your Eternal Stain
> This judgment is, etc.

Sir Kenelm, who was a dabbler in science, and medicines and nostrums—

> ‡ Hee, that all med'cines can exactly make,
> And freely give them,

as Townshend calls him—was fond of experimenting upon his wife. He "was so enamoured of her beauty," says Pennant,§ "that he was said to have attempted to exalt her charms, and preserve her health, by a variety of whimsical experiments. Amongst others, that of feeding her

---

* Feltham's *Lusoria*, No. xiv.

† It is but fair to say that this may refer to the report that, after her death, "when her head was opened there was found but little brain". Lodge's *Portraits*, ed. 1850, vol. v., p. 156. On the other hand, the fact of the quantity being small might have escaped notice if she had not been generally considered a stupid, if a very beautiful, woman.

‡ Aurelian Townshend on Sir K. Digby in his *Elegy in Remembrance of the Lady Venetia Digby.*

§ *Journey from Chester to London*, p. 452.

with capons fed with the flesh of vipers ['spiteful women' however, according to Aubrey,* said she had 'a viper-husband who was jealous of her'], and that to improve her complexion he was perpetually inventing new cosmetics."

When her health began to fail he tried to restore it with snail soup. "The Pomatum,† or large edible snail, which abounds in the spring months in many watery places and amongst woods, is found in abundance near Gayhurst (Gothurst). A coppice on the banks of Ouse abounds with them; and they are said to have been brought from France by Sir Kenelm Digby to be used by Lady Venetia as a restorative in consumption." Mr. Carlile, the present occupant of Gayhurst, tells me that these edible snails still exist there in considerable quantities.

The knowledge that his wife was a victim of consumption must have embittered the life of Sir Kenelm early in 1633. Unfortunately, in this particular year that trying month April "was most extreme wet, and cold, and windy," ‡ and, therefore, very trying to a person with delicate lungs. The court was on the point of starting for Scotland, and, in its absence, Sir Kenelm no doubt expected to enjoy a quiet time with his wife. Although delicate, she does not appear to have been then considered in a dangerous condition, and her husband might reasonably hope to do something towards improving her health, now that he would have more leisure to devote to her care and her entertainment.

He was still busy, however, with his Admiralty work, and on the 28th April § he wrote to Nicholas recommending for the vacant post of gunner to the *Dreadnought* a man who had served in his own fleet in the Mediterranean,

* Aubrey's *Letters*, vol. ii., Appendix.
† *Hist. and Antiq. of Bucks*, Lipscombe, vol. iv., p. 142.
‡ Laud's *Diary*, April, anno 1633.
§ *S. P. Dom. Charles I.*, vol. ccxxxvii., No. 56.

and had been two or three times to the East Indies. Little was he aware, as he attended to these and other naval matters, of the crushing blow which was about to fall upon him.

On the 1st May, Venetia, Lady Digby, was found dead in her bed, leaning her head on her hand.* So sudden was her end that it was feared at first that she had been poisoned, and a *post-mortem* examination was made of her body.

She had died in her thirty-third year. Sir Kenelm was only in his thirtieth. It was early for an end to be put to their brilliant prospects of happiness. There can be no doubt as to the sincerity of Sir Kenelm's grief. His whole manner was changed, and he threw off, once and for ever, the gay and smart cavalier garments, for which he had been so remarkable.

He tried to express his sorrow in the following morbid lines :—†

> Buried in the shades of horrid night
> My vexed soul doth groan, exiled from light.
> > And ghastly dreams
> > Are now the sad themes
> That my frighted fancy feeds itself withal.
>
> And to add afflictions with new paine
> Despairing thoughts possess my restless brain,
> > Persuading me
> > That I ne'er shall see
> Her that only can my past blest hours recall.
>
> Then as the damned tormented souls in hell
> Enraged 'gainst God with horror swell,
> > I now grown desperate
> > Curse my fate
> > And pray
> > All day
> To lose the life I hate.

---

* Collins' *Peerages*, vol. v., p. 358.
† *Poems from Sir K. Digby's Papers*, Rox. Club, pp. 7, 8, 9.

Like to the pale planet that doth reign
Queen of the darkness; if the dusky train
      Of earth's black robe
      Reach up to her globe
All the light and beauty that she had is gone;
      Forced sad
Right so by this constrained absence
My soul's eclipsed and hath now lost all sense
      Of ease or joy
      And nought but annoy
With impatience and despair do make me groan;
Yet in a harder state by much I live;
For unto her few minutes give
New beams to make her bright.
      But my night
      I fear
      Will ne'er
      Let me again see light.

Nor doth it avail me now to strive
With help or other pleasing thoughts to drive
      From me this one
      Which sure will alone
Dissolve me and turn me into earth again :
For as heretofore, to help men sought
The eclipsed moon, whom they in labour thought
      With strange noises
      And broken voices
When they did but beat the flitting air in vain.
So now all entertainments are to me
But discords void of harmony;
Since absence spoils that part
      Whose sweet art
      Kept best
      The rest
      In consort with my heart.

And I see those books are false which teach
That absence makes between two souls no breach
      When they with love
      To each other move

And that they (though distant) may meet, kiss and play,
For our body doth so clog our mind
That here no means of working it can find
'   On things absent
                Or judging present
Till the corp'ral senses first do lead the way.

Therefore until my soul with freedom may
Meet thine within her house of clay
                Nought else shall satisfy
                But still I
                Alone
                Will groan
                This doleful elegy.

He had his wife's body buried under the "east end of
the south aisle of Christ Church, within Newgate,"* which
he probably selected because it was one of the nearest
churches to a house which he was then building, or about
to build. He laid her in a brick vault, over which, says
Aubrey,† " were three steps of black marble, with four inscriptions in copper gilt affixed to it. Upon this altar was
her bust of copper gilt, all which, unless the vault, which
was only opened a little by the fall," was afterwards
" utterly destroyed by the great conflagration ".

One of these inscriptions ran :—‡

Mem. Sacrum.

Venetiæ.

Edwardi Stanlèy Equitis Honoratiss. Ord.
Balnei (Filii Thomœ, Edwardi comitis Derbiœ
Filii) Filiœ ac cohaeredi, ex Luciâ Thomœ
Comitis Northumbriæ Filiâ et Cohaerede,

* Collins' *Peerage*, vol. v., p. 355.
† I am quoting from the Introduction to the *Priv. Mem.*, p. 50.
‡ *Antiquarian Repertory.*

Posuit
Kenelmus Digby Eques Auratus
Cui quatuor Peperit Filios
Kenelmum Nat. VI. Oct. MDCXXV.
Joannem Nat. XXIX. Decemb MDCXXVII.
Everardum (in cunis Mortum) Nat. XII Jan.
MDCXXIX.
Georgium Nat. XVII, Jan. MDCXXXII.
Nata est Decemb. XIX, M.D.C.
Denata Maii l, MDCXXXIII.
Quin lex eadem monet omnes
Gemitum dare sorte sub una
Cognataque funera nobis
Aliena in morte dolere.

In this inscription, or perhaps in this copy of it, there seems to be a mistake; for it gives the birth of Everard as 12th January, 1629, or about three weeks before Sir Kenelm's return from his voyage to the Mediterranean, when he had then been more than a year at sea, which renders it impossible. Another of the inscriptions was :—*

Insig. Praeclariss. Dominœ D. Venetiæ Digby è
Familia Stanleyorum, Com. Darbiœ. ex parte
Patris, et Perciorum, Com. Northumbriœ,
Materno jure, aliisque quamplurimis Christian.
Orbis Principibus Griundœ.

Of the two others I can find no trace.

In connection with her burial Ben Jonson wrote the following very gruesome lines. Their horrible false sentiment would give pain to most husbands under similar conditions in these days ; but they do not appear to have annoyed Sir Kenelm Digby :—†

---

* Collins' *Peerage*, vol. v., p. 356.

† *Works of Ben Jonson*, by W. Gifford, edited by F. Cunningham.

A FRAGMENT OF ONE OF THE LOST QUATERNIONS
OF EUPHEME.

You worms (my rivals), while she was alive,
How many thousands were there that did strive
To have your freedom ?   For their sakes forbear
Unseemly holes in her soft skin to wear ;
But, if you must (as what worm can abstain ?)
Taste of her tender body, yet refrain,
With your disorded eatings, to deface her,
And feed yourselves so as you most may grace her.
First, through yon ear-tips see you work a pair
Of holes, which as the moist enclosed air
Turns into water, may the cold drops take
And in her ears a pair of jewels make.
That done, upon her bosom make your feast,
Where, on a cross, carve Jesus in her breast.
Have you not yet enough of that soft skin,
The touch of which in time past might have bin
Enough to ransome many a thousand soul
Captived to love ?   Then hence your bodies roll
A little higher ; when I would you have
This epitaph upon her forehead grave ;
Living, she was fair, young, and full of wit :
Dead, all her faults are in her forehead writ.

It is uncertain in what house Lady Digby died. Aubrey
says * that " the faire houses in Holbourne, between King
Street and Southampton Street (which brake off the continuance of them) were built about 1633, by Sir Kenelm " ;
but whether they were finished so soon as the May of that
year, and whether Sir Kenelm had taken up his residence
in one of them before his wife died, is doubtful.   The pro-
babilities would certainly point the other way.

After his wife's death Sir Kenelm never again shaved,
and allowed a long unkempt beard to take the place of his
former dainty and curled moustache.   He substituted a
perfectly plain white collar for the rich lace which he

* *Letters*, vol. ii., Appendix.

Sir Kenelm Digby;
in the Costume which he affected after the death of his Wife;
from a painting by Cornelius Janssen in the possession of the Author.

formerly wore from his neck to his shoulders; he dressed himself in simple black garments without any kind of trimming or ornament, and, when he went out, he * "wore a long mourning cloake" and "a high cornered hatt," making himself look, says Aubrey, "like a hermite".

Turning his back on society he retired into Gresham College, which had been founded about fifty years earlier in a house in Bishopsgate Street, formerly the residence of Sir Thomas Gresham, a well-known merchant of the days of Queen Elizabeth. There he "diverted himself with his chymestry, and the professor's good conversation".†

In the midst of his grief Sir Kenelm had other matters to distract his attention; for, a few days before his wife's death, a boy named Henry Sawyer had gone to his mother's next neighbour, Sir Thomas Tyringham,‡ and reported that about eight weeks earlier, when he was with his father catching moles in the grounds at Gothurst, his father had told him that, when the king should go to Scotland on the 5th May, the Papists were going to rise against the Protestants, and that, near as it was, "men should go over their shoe-tops in blood before Whitsuntide". His father had strictly forbidden him to say anything about it; but he repeated the story to a tailor and a labourer, both of whom gave evidence. §

Two days after Venetia, Lady Digby's, death, the tailor in question gave further evidence,‖ and stated that the boy had said that a load of armour had been received by the Dowager Lady Digby at Gothurst—Gothurst, which had been one of the meeting places of the conspirators in the Gunpowder Plot—and that it had been sent to her

* Aubrey's *Letters*, vol. ii., Appendix.

† *Ib.*

‡ *S. P. Dom. Charles I.*, vol. ccxxxvii., No. 27.

§ *Ib.*, Nos. 29 and 30.

‖ *Ib.*, vol. ccxxxix., Nos. 61-3.

from London by "Sir Kellam Digby". A week later,* a
clergyman, the Rev. John Whalley, Rector of Cosgrave, deposed that he had been told by a man, who had been told
by the boy, that gunpowder had been taken to Gothurst
as well as arms; and so the story gathered strength.
Sir Robert Banastre, or Banister, sent the information to
Secretary Windebank; and in the first agony of his
bereavement Sir Kenelm became the subject of a very
ugly rumour.

Sir Thomas Tyringham's behaviour may not have been
unneighbourly; for Lady Digby herself, on hearing of the
matter, appears to have been most anxious to have it
thoroughly sifted immediately, and she took care to have
the boy † found and formally examined as soon as possible.
It may be that no credence was ever given to the story in
high quarters. The mole-catcher, the father of the boy,
as well as a man named Johnson, who, he said, had told
him of the projected rising, were both arrested and imprisoned in the Fleet, and the last we hear of them, or
indeed of the affair itself, is in a petition ‡ which these two
men wrote from that prison. In this document Johnson
says that the ostler at the Angel Inn at Stilton had said
that he had heard a Scotchman say: "Our king was now
to go into Scotland, but if they had him there they would
keep him, and that they should not have him back again
unless they won him with the sword"; to which Johnson
had replied: "Then there would be much hurly-burly, and
many a fatherless child". This Johnson had repeated to
the mole-catcher; the mole-catcher had misunderstood
the story and had exaggerated it to his boy; the boy had
misunderstood it and had exaggerated it to the tailor and
others; the tailor and others had misunderstood it and

---

* S. P. Dom. Charles I., vol. ccxxxvii., Nos. 61-2.

† Ib., vol. ccxxxvii., No. 42.

‡ Ib., vol. ccxxxix., No. 85.

had exaggerated it still further, until it came to the ears of the parson, and the parson—well, I suppose that, to use the words of Hood :—

> The parson told the sexton,
> And the sexton toll'd the bell.

CHAPTER XXII

EPITAPHS.

DURING the period immediately following Sir Kenelm's bereavement, poets vied with each other in composing elegies to the memory of the wife that he had lost. The best known of these are Ben Jonson's. All Jonson's poems on Lady Digby, with the exception of some that are altogether missing, are published under the title of *Eupheme*, and are well known; so it is needless that I should quote the elegy at length; but, for the benefit of those who may not be acquainted with, or may not care to acquaint themselves with, the poem in question, I will give a few extracts from it :—*

Elegy on My Muse,
The Truly Honoured Lady,
The Lady Venetia Digby,
Who living, gave me leave to call Her so.
Being her ΑΠΟΘΕΩΣΙΣ, or, Relation to the Saints,†
" Sera quidem tanto struitur medicina dolore ".
'Twere time that I died too, now she is dead
Who was my Muse, and life of all I did,
The spirit that I wrote with, and conceived :
All that was good or great with me, she weaved,

* *Works of Ben Jonson*, by Wm. Gifford, edited by F. Cunningham.

† The editor says in a footnote : The " *Apothesis* abounds in scriptural allusions, which I have left to the reader, as well as the numerous passages which Milton has adopted from it, and which his editors have, as usual, overlooked, while running after Dante and Thomas Aquinas". Well may it be " left to the reader " to consider the value of this note !

And set it forth ; the rest were cobwebs fine,
Spun out in name of some of the old Nine,
To hang a window, or make dark the room,
Till swept away, they were cancelled with a broom !
Nothing that could remain, or yet can stir
A sorrow in me fit to wait on her !
O ! Had I seen her laid out a fair corse,
By death, on earth I should have had remorse
On Nature for her ; who did let her lie,
And saw that portion of herself to die,
Sleepy or stupid Nature, couldst thou part
With such a rarity, and not rouse art,
With all her aids, to save her from the seize
Of Vulture Death, and those relentless cleis ? *

And presently he exclaims :—

Thou hast no more blows, Fate, to drive at one ;
What's left a poet, when his Muse is gone ?

Then he complains of his consequent loss of power,
and confesses that he murmurs against God for having
taken "her blessed soul hence"; but he checks himself,
and says, in a more resigned spirit :—

Dare I profane so irreligious be,
To greet or grieve her soft Euthanasy !
So sweetly taken to the courts of bliss,
As spirits had taken her spirit in a kiss.

He also in a long harangue upon the happiness of
heaven declares that he cannot grudge the object of his
admiration

That great eternal holiday of rest
To body and soul, where love is all the guest !
And the whole banquet is full sight of God,
Of joy the circle and whole period !
All other gladness with the thought is barred ;
Hope hath her end, and Faith hath her reward !

* Perhaps "claws".

By-and-by comes an extraordinary passage, in which Ben Jonson appears to imply that her noble ancestry gave her some sort of right to the company of saints and archangels in heaven. " God," says he,

> Knows what work he hath done, to call this guest
> Out of her noble body to his feast :
> And give her place according to her blood
> Amongst her peers, those princes of all good !
> Saints, Martyrs, Prophets, with those Hierarchies.
> Angels, Archangels, Principalities,
> The Dominations, Virtues and the Powers,
> The Throne, the Cherube, and Seraphic bowers,
> That, planted round, there sing before the Lamb
> A new song to his praise, the great I AM.

After going on much in the same strain for a good many more lines, he appeals to her husband not to mourn, but to look forward to meeting her in heaven :—

> And will you, worthy son, sir, knowing this,
> Put black and mourning on ? and say you miss
> A wife, a friend, a lady, or a love ;
> Whom her Redeemer honoured hath above
> Her fellows, with the oil of gladness, bright
> In heaven's empire, and with a robe of light ?
> Thither you hope to come ; and there to find
> That pure, that precious, and exalted mind
> You once enjoyed : a short space severs ye,
> Compared unto that long eternity,
> That shall rejoin ye.

The remainder of the poem is principally theological ; it describes Venetia mentally reviewing the whole scheme of man's salvation, in her last moments, and then ends with :—

> In this sweet extasy she was wrapt hence,
> Who reads, will pardon my intelligence,
> That thus have ventured these true strains upon,
> To publish her a saint, MY MUSE IS GONE !

The next elegy to be noticed I will give in full. It is by Thomas Randolph, whom Ben Jonson used to call his son. He writes as if he had personally known Venetia, Lady Digby. The first nineteen lines I have transcribed from a fragment of a copy made in Sir Kenelm's own handwriting, which I found among my own Digby papers; the remainder is from my cousin, the late Henry Bright's published volume of Sir Kenelm Digby's *Poems and Papers*. Randolph, who was a fellow of Trinity College, Cambridge, died at the age of thirty, surviving the subject of his elegy by only a couple of years.

AN ELEGY UPON THE LADY VENETIA DIGBY.

Death! Who'ld not change prerogatives with thee,
That doth such rapes, yet mayest not questioned bee
Here cease thy wanton lust, be satisfied,
Hope not a Second, and so faire a Bride.
Where was her Mars whose valiant arms did hold
This Venus once, that thou durst be so bold
By thy too nimble theft, I know 'twas fear,
Lest he should come and might have rescu'd her.
Monster, confess, didst thou not Blushing stand,
And thy pale cheek turne red to touch her Hand?
Did she not lightning-like stick suddaine heat
Through thy cold limbs, and thaw thy Frost to sweat
Well, since tho hast her, use her gently, Death,
And in requitall of such pretious Breath
Watch Sentinell to guard her, doe not see
The Worms thy rivals, for the gods will bee.
Remember Paris, for whose pettier sin,
The Trogian Gates let the stout Grecians in,
So when time ceases (Whose unthrifty hand
Hath now almost consum'd his stock of sand)
Myriads of Angels shall in armies come
And fetch (proud rauisher) their Helen home
And to revenge this rape thy other store
Thou shalt resigne too, and shalt steale no more,
Till then, fayre ladyes (for ye now are fayre)
But till her death, I fear'd your inste desparye
Fetch all the spices that Arabia yields;

Distill the choycest flowers of all the fields
And when in one their best perfections meete
Embalm her corse, that it may make them sweete
And for an Epitaph upon her stone ;
I can not write, but I will weepe her one.

EPITAPH.

Beauty itselfe Lyes here, in whom alone
Each part enioy'd the same perfection
In some the eyes we prayse ; in some the hayre
In this the lippes in her the cheeks are fayre
That Nymphs fine feete, her hands we beauteous call
But in this forme we prayse no parte but all
The ages paste haue many beautyes showne
And I as many in our age have knownne
But in the age to come I looke for none,
Nature despairs, because her pattern's gone.

Tho. Randolph.

Among my own Digby papers is a long elegy by
Aurelian Townshend, but in Sir Kenelm Digby's own handwriting.

" Philip,* Earle of Pembroke and Montgomery, in
some MS. notes, etc.," " says that Aurelian Townshend
was a poor poet living in Barbican, near the Earl of Bridge-
water's ". One of his daughters married George Kirke,
groom of the bedchamber to Charles I., of whom we have
heard before. I will only quote portions of it :—

AN ELEGY IN REMEMBRANCE OF THE LADY VENETIA DIGBY.

What travellors, of matchless Venice say,
Is true of thee, admir'd Venetia ;
He that ne'er saw thee wants beleefe to reach
Halfe those perfections thy first sight would teach ;
Imagination can no shape create,
Aiery enough thy forme to imitate ;
Nor beddes of Roses, Damask, redde and white ;
Render like thee a sweetness to the sight.

* Warner's Notes to *Poems from K. D.'s Papers.*

An Elegy
In remembrance of the
Venetia Digby

AUTOGRAPH OF SIR KENELM DIGBY.

P

He pays a very high tribute to her influence on poets :—

> Best in every place,
> Thou wert not borne as other women be
> To neede the helps of heightening Poesie,
> But to make poets.

This leads him to notice how Ben Jonson—though he does not mention his name—reached the climax of his power in describing Venetia's beauties :—

> He sate and drew thy beauties by the life ;
> Visible Angell both as Mayde and Wife ;
> In wch estate thou did'st so little stay,
> Thy noone and morning made but halfe a day ;
> Or halfe a yeare ; or halfe of such an Age,
> As thy complexion sweetly did presage
> An houre before those cheerful beams were sett
> Made all men losers to pay Nature's debt;
> And him the greatest that had most to do ;
> Thy friend, companion, and co-partner too;
> Whose head, since hanging on his pensive brest,
> Makes him looke iust like one had been possest
> Of the whole worlde, and now hath lost it all.

Like Jonson, he tries to comfort the husband whom she has left to mourn her :—

> I that delight most in unusuall wayes,
> Seeke to assuage his sorrow wth thy prayse;
> Which, if att first it swell him up wth griefe,
> At last may draw, and minister reliefe,
> Or att the least attempting it, expresse
> For an old debt, and friendly thankfulness.
> I am no Herald ! So yee can expect
> From me no crests, or scutcheons that reflect ;
> With brave memorialls, on her great Allyes ;
> Out of my reach, that tree would quickly ryse ;
> I onely strive to doe her fame some right,
> And walk her mourner in this Black and White.
>
>   Aurelian Townshend.

Endorsed : " Mr. Townshend verses :—

Vsque
    Sequetur amor. Prop.
Sequor, et quo ducitis. Virg.
vertitur ad solem. Ovid."

Another minor poet sang her elegy in " Funebre Venantianum,* on the Lady Venetia Digby, found dead in her bed, leaning her head on her hand," of which, perhaps, the following may be the best lines :—

                  And this was it
Which made Death mannerly, and strive to fit
Himself with reverence to her ; that now
He came not like a Tyrant, on whose brow
A pompous terror hung ; but in a strain
Lovely and calm, as in the June serene,
That now, who most abhor him can but say,
Gently he did imbrace her into Clay.

In an earlier chapter I quoted a portion of this poem as a testimony to Venetia's character.

There is another elegy from which, I think, it will be sufficient that I should give extracts. It was written by a relative, William Habington or Abington, and it is part of a poem addressed to "Castara," that is to say, his own wife, Lucia, daughter of William, Lord Powis. He was a loyalist and a Catholic. His father was sentenced to death for concealing in his house Father Garnet and Father Alcerne ; † but was reprieved and pardoned at the intercession of his brother-in-law, Lord Mounteagle. The poet's mother, Mary, sister of Lord Mounteagle,‡ was in fact the real author of the celebrated warning letter which Lord Mounteagle received the day before the meeting of Parliament, when the Gunpowder Plot was so nearly successful ;

* Feltham's Lusoria, No. xiv.
† Preface to Castara, pp. 2, 3.
‡ Ib., p. 3.

and, through her,* William Habington was related to Lady
Venetia Digby :—

> Castara, weepe not, tho' her tombe appeare
> Sometime thy grief to answer with a teare :
> The marble will but wanton with thy woe,
> Death is the sea, and we like rivers flow
> To lose ourselves in the insatiate maine,
> Whence rivers may, she ne're returne againe.
> Nor grieve this cristall stream so soon did fall
> Into the ocean ; since shee perfum'd all
> The banks she past, so that each neighbour field
> Did sweete flowers cherish, by her watering yeeld.

From her illustrious ancestry he draws a gloomy moral
very different from that of Ben Jonson, who, as we have
seen, almost implied that her noble terrestrial birth gave
her a claim to a place among the archangels :—

> Come you, who speake your titles.   Reade in this
> Pale booke, how vaine a boast your greatness is ;
> What's honour but a hatchment ?   What is here
> Of Percy † left, and Stanley, names most deare
> To vertue ! but a cresent turn'd to the wane ‡
> An eagle groaning o'er an infant slain ? §
> Or what avails her, that she once were led,
> A glorious bride, to valiant Digbie's bed,
> Since death has them divorc'd ? if then alive
> There are, who these sad obsequies survive,
> And vaunt a proud descent, they onely be
> Loud heralds to set forth her pedigree.

Like most of the other poets who sang of her death, he
has a word to say as to its apparent gentleness and ease:—

* Preface to *Castara*, p. 194.
† Lady Venetia Digby was daughter of Sir E. Stanley and his wife,
Lady Lucy Percy.
‡ The crescent was the badge of the Percies, Earls of Northumberland.
§ An eagle, with wings expanded, preying upon an infant in a cradle,
was the crest of the Stanleys, Earls of Derby.

Come likewise, my Castaara, and behold
What blessings ancient prophesie foretold
Bestowed on her in death. She past away
So sweetly from the world, as if her clay
Laid onely down to slumber. Then forbeare
To let on her blest ashes fall a teare.
But if th' art too much woman, softly weepe,
Lest griefe disturbe the silence of her sleepe.

This poet was such a good Catholic and so upright and honourable a man that his panegyric of Venetia Digby is stronger evidence in her favour than that of any other.

In the first year of his widowhood, Sir Kenelm did not neglect his duties at the Admiralty.

Little more than four months after his wife's death he wrote a letter to Nicholas, now in the State Paper Office,* concerning the appointments of a ship's carpenter and a gunner.

As a widower, for a time he turned his back on the gaieties of the Court, and consoled himself with the society of a few friends. One of these was Lucius Cary, who had lately inherited the title of Viscount Falkland.† Great Tew, his place in Oxfordshire, was the resort of scholars and divines, wits, poets, and men of science, and to such as these the house was always open. Here Sir Kenelm would meet his friend Ben Jonson, as well as Waller, Selden, Hobbes, Carew, Suckling, and Walter Montague.

Two years after his wife's death, Sir Kenelm went to Paris, and, while there, he seems to have felt an inclination to return to a more active life; for he wrote to Winde-bank,‡ informing him that he intended to remain some time in Paris and that he should be happy to do him any service there. A year later he wrote to Windebank §

---

* S. P. Dom. Charles I., vol. ccxvi., No. 32.
† Gardiner's Hist. Eng., vol. viii., p. 256.
‡ S. P. Dom. Charles I., vol. ccxcviii., No. 66.
§ Cal. Sta. Pa. Dom., 1636-7, p. 168.

again, saying that he had had a license from King Charles to go abroad for three years ; but that the greatest part of the time had run out before he started ; and he requested the Secretary to procure him foreign leave for another term of three years.

While in Paris, Sir Kenelm gave his mind much to religious study, considering the rival claims of the Catholic and the Anglican Churches,* and omitting "no Industry, either of conversing with Learned Men, or of reading the best authors, to beget in " him "a right Intelligence of this Subject " ; and while there he publicly declared himself to be a Catholic.

At or about the period at which Digby announced to the world that he was a Catholic, the already quoted Panzani, an oratorian, who had been sent from Rome, primarily, to settle some dispute between the regulars and seculars in this country, secondarily, to endeavour to obtain some alleviation of the persecution of English Catholics, and lastly, to ascertain whether there was any hope of a return of the English, as a body, to the Catholic Church, was discussing with Sir Kenelm's friend, Winde-bank—who, by the way, eventually became a Catholic—and with the Anglican Bishop, Montague,† the question of reunion. It is likely enough that Sir Kenelm may have heard something of this, and also of a promise obtained by Panzani from King Charles that the English Catholics should be relieved from the annoyance of domiciliary visits from pursuivants. If so, it may have emboldened him in his determination to proclaim his own submission to the Pope, especially if the news reached him that Panzani had written to Rome, reporting Catholic doctrines to be increasing in favour at the Court of St. James's.

---

* Laud's letter to Sir Kenelm Digby, Wharton's *History, etc., of Laud*, p. 611.

† *Memoirs of Gregonio Panzani*, by J. Berington, pp. 229, 237.

Immediately * before Sir Kenelm declared himself a
Catholic, it was announced that in a short time Panzani
would return to Rome to be succeeded by Con, a Scotchman, who was to come to England with some splendour,
to represent the Pope at Somerset House.   As is well
known, Con did come to England, and, as Clarendon
states, he " resided at London in great part," † " Publickly
visited the court, and was caress'd by the Ladies of
Honour who inclined to that Profession," *i.e.*, the Catholic
Faith.   Even King Charles himself, says Mr. Gardiner, ‡
" was quite satisfied to find in Con a well-informed and
respectful man, ready to discuss politics or theology without acrimony by the hour, and to flatter him with assurances of the loyalty of his Catholic subjects without forgetting to point to the sad contrast exhibited by the stiff-
necked and contemptuous Puritans ".

I do not go so far as to say that Kenelm Digby deliberately waited for a safe opportunity to declare himself
a Catholic, but human nature is human nature, and Sir
Kenelm was essentially human ; he was no great saint, he
was naturally of a diplomatic disposition, he was a courtier,
and he had what is called " a keen eye to the main
chance ".

His allegiance to the Catholic Church made no break
in his friendships with his old tutor, Archbishop Laud.
He bore witness in Laud's favour when Laud was a prisoner
in the Tower, and after his death he wrote to the Keeper
of the Oxford University Archives : " As I was one day
waiting on the late king, my master, I told him of a collection of choice Arabic manuscripts I was sending after my
Latin ones to the University.   My Lord of Canterbury
(that was present) wished they might go along with a

* Gardiner's *Hist. Eng.*, vol. iii., p. 136.
† *History of the Rebellion*, vol. l., p. 149.
‡ *Hist. Eng.*, vol. viii., p. 236.

parcel that he was sending to St. John's College, where-upon I sent them to his Grace," etc. " The troubles of the times soon followed my sending these trunks of books to Lambeth House," etc. This showed * that he and Laud were still on a friendly footing.

Laud himself recounts Sir Kenelm's good offices in his favour.† He wrote in the Tower: " My Servant, Mr. Edward Leuthrop, came to me and told me that the day before he met with *K. Digbye*". And then he went on to say: " Before he took his journey "—he was going to France—" he was to come before a *Committee*, and there (he said) he had been. It seems it was some Committee about my business, for he told Mr. Leuthrop, and wished him to tell me, that the Committee took special notice of his Acquaintance with me, and Examined him strictly concerning me and my Religion, whether he did not know that I was offer'd to make a Cardinal, and many other such like things. That he answer'd them, That he knew nothing of any Cardinalship offer'd to me. And for my Religion he had Reason to think I was truly and really as I professed myself; for I had laboured with him against his return to the Church of Rome. But he farther sent me word that their Malice was great against me, though he saw plainly they were like Men that groped in the dark, and were to seek what to lay to my Charge."

In the first fervour of his revived Catholicism, Sir Kenelm wrote a book entitled *A Conference with a Lady about the Choice of a Religion*, which was published in Paris a year or two later. Among my own papers which formerly belonged to Sir Kenelm Digby is a manuscript in an unknown hand of this very book, but addressed to a man instead of to a lady. Possibly Sir Kenelm may have had it written out in this form, with the intention of

* Aubrey's *Letters*, No. 1.
† *History of the Troubles and Tryal of the Most Rev. Father in God and Blessed Martyr William Laud, etc.*, Wharton, 1795, p. 209.

sending it to a male friend. Part of the manuscript is missing, and, on the back of one page of it, is a memorandum about some "verses upon the Lady Venetia Digby," in Sir Kenelm's own handwriting.

An incident relating to Sir Kenelm's adhesion to the Catholic religion is noticed by Lipscombe,* who states that the advowson of the living of Gothurst was granted to Sir Richard Farmer, who was made patron of the living during Mr. Digby's life, the latter being a Roman Catholic.

When he had been about a year in Paris, Sir Kenelm seems to have had his children sent out to him, or at any rate to have had them sent abroad, so as to ensure their receiving a Catholic education ; for, with the date of 7th August, 1637, there is a State Paper † granting a license to travel for "Kenelm and John Digby, sons of Sir Kenelm Digby, with three servants and £50 in money for three years". Licenses for foreign travel appear to have been often made out for that length of time; and, of course, those who wished to remain longer had to apply periodically for their renewal.

* *Hist. and Antiq. of Bucks*, vol. iv., p. 162.

† *Cal. Sta. Pa. Dom.*, 1637, p. 359.

CHAPTER XXIII

RETURN TO ENGLAND.

AMONG Sir Kenelm's correspondents when at Paris was Lord Conway, who was soon afterwards to meet with defeat when in command of the king's troops at Newcastle. This unfortunate soldier seemed always fated to fight under disadvantages. When in the Isle of Rhé, he wrote : [*] " The army grows every day weaker, our victuals waste, our purses are empty, ammunition consumes, winter grows, our enemies increase in number and power; we hear nothing from England ". And thirteen years later he was campaigning in as bad a plight ; for he wrote from the army in the north that his soldiers [†] " to the uttermost of their power never kept any law either of God or the king ". Perhaps literature may have been more to his taste than warfare, and we find letters from Sir Kenelm Digby to him recommending a Monsieur Cottard,[‡] " whose brother is the chief bookseller in Paris for curious books, and has correspondence in Italy, Germany, Spain, and everywhere ". Therefore, if Lord Conway should require any literary curiosities, he " would fit him withal, better than any man Sir Kenelm knows ".

Later in the same month [§] Sir Kenelm wrote to Lord Conway that " Mr. Selden's book has been sent there, and

---

[*] *S. P. Dom. Charles I.*, vol. lxxviii., No. 71.
[†] *Ib.*, vol. cccliv., Nos. 30, 38.
[‡] *Cal. Sta. Pa.*, 1636-7, p. 345.
[§] *Ib.*, p. 378.

is much esteemed". "He is promised *La Conqueste du sang real* for Lord Conway, and the *Legend of Sir Tristram*, and can procure him an entire collection of all the books known here of that kind, and in particular a curious *Amadis*, twelve vols. Requests he will let him know what he wants, and in what bindings. England is happy in producing persons who do actions which after ages take for romances ; witness King Arthur and Cadwallader of ancient time, and the valliant and ingenious peer, the Lord Wimbledon, whose epistle exceeds anything ever done by so victorious a general governor of towns." In a third letter * he says to Lord Conway, " I will obey your commands for books and Burgundy wine ".

While in Paris Sir Kenelm interested himself in a recent convert to the Catholic Church—Lady Purbeck. She had not always lived in the odour of sanctity. Some ten years earlier she had been convicted before the High Commission in London of adultery, and had been ordered to do penance, bare-footed, in a white sheet, in the church of the Savoy. Instead of obeying, she escaped, disguised in male attire,† and joined her paramour at his country house in Shropshire.‡ Sometime afterwards she and her friend ventured to London, where Laud " had the good hap to apprehend " them both, and imprisoned one in the Gate-house and the other in the Fleet. Some one, however, says Laud, " with Mony corrupted the Turn-Key of the Prison " " and conveyed the lady forth, after that into France in man's apparel ".

In Paris, or at least in France, she became a Catholic, and there Sir Kenelm Digby championed her cause. In one of his letters § to Lord Conway (31st January, 1637) he,

---

* *Cal. Sta. Pa.*, 1636-7, p. 332.
† Lingard's *Hist.*, vol. vii., chap. v.
‡ Wharton's *Laud*, p. 146.
§ *Cal. Sta. Pa.*, 1636-7, p. 378.

"runs out into great praises of Lady Purbeck. The genius that governs that family was asleep when he gave her a double portion of noble endowments and left her poor uncle so naked and unfurnished. Is it not a shame for Lord Conway and the other peers about the king to let so brave a lady live in distress and banishment?"

A Mr. E. R. wrote to Sir R. Puckering:* "The last week we had certain news that the Lady Purbeck was declared a papist". Then he said that she had persuaded the King and Queen of France and Cardinal Richelieu to beg King Charles to pardon and allow her to return in peace to England, and that the French ambassador at St. James's was "very zealous in the business". And presently he went on to say: "It is said she is altogether advised by Sir Kenelm Digby, who indeed hath written over letters to some of his noble friends of the privy council, wherein he hath set down what a convert this lady is become, so superlatively virtuous and sanctimonious, as the like hath rarely been either in men or women; and therefore he does most humbly desire their lordships to farther this lady's peace, and that she may return unto England, for otherwise she does resolve to put herself into some monastery. I hear his Majesty does utterly dislike that the lady is so much directed by Sir Kenelm Digby, and that she fares nothing better for it."

Richelieu in reality had been greatly incensed at an attempt made by Lord Scudamore, the English ambassador in Paris, to get a writ† of the King of England's served upon Lady Purbeck in the streets of that city, and had sent a guard of fifty archers to protect her.

In foretelling that, in default of pardon from King Charles, Lady Purbeck would "put herself into some" convent, Sir Kenelm Digby did not write without reason,

* I quote from D'Israeli's *Court and Times of Charles I.*, vol. ii., p. 242.
† S. P. Dom. Charles I., vol. cccxiii., No. 58.

for this was exactly what she did,* although her conventual life was of very short duration.   She appears to have gone to a convent as a visitor and not as a postulant or novice, and she refused to conform to the regulations of the establishment.†   Having left the convent she lived for some time in great wretchedness in Paris, but she eventually returned to England, died in the year 1645, and was buried at St. Mary's Church, Oxford.‡

Another convert friend of Sir Kenelm's had declared himself a Catholic about a year before Digby himself took this step.   This was Walter Montague, the second son of the Earl of Manchester, and, like Sir Kenelm, a court favourite.   "The witty and accomplished favourite of the Queen,"§ he is called by Mr. Gardiner.   Perhaps for the same reasons which affected Sir Kenelm, he kept away from England for some time after the declaration of his change of faith.   Soon after his return the conversion of Lady Newport was announced.   Walter Montague was believed to have been instrumental in it by her husband, who enlisted the services of Archbishop Laud against him. Laud denounced him in the council and requested the king to banish him from the court.   Con, having been informed of this, urged the queen to espouse his cause.

On hearing about Laud's action in the matter she spoke to the king of what she termed his violence.   Laud, himself, in his diary, ‖ says : " The queen was acquainted with all I said that night, and highly displeased with me," and so continues : " A couple of months later," he says, " I had speech with the queen a good space, and about the business of Mr. Montague, but we parted fair ".

The news of these frictions concerning converts to the

* Scudamore to Coke, 25th March, *S. P. France.*

† Gardiner's *Hist. Eng.,* vol. viii., p. 146.

‡ Burke's *Dormant and Extinct Peerages,* p. 559.

§ *History,* vol. viii., p. 138.

‖ P. 55.

Catholic Church may have made Sir Kenelm Digby, who had remained longer abroad than Montague, consider it prudent to delay his return to England a little longer.

While he was in France, Sir Kenelm lost his friend Ben Jonson, who died in the year 1637. He wrote about Jonson's death to the Dean of Christ Church, Dr. Duppa, tutor to the Prince of Wales, who was collecting materials for a book which afterwards appeared under the title of *Johnsonius Virbius*. He tells * him that his doing so " is an office well beseeming that excellent piety that all men know " him by, adding : " I believe if care for earthly things touch souls happily departed that these compositions delivered to the world by your hand will be more grateful obsequies to his great ghost than any other that could have been performed at his tomb ; for no Court's decree can better establish a lawful claimer in the secure possession of his right than this will him of his laurel, which, when he lived, he wore so high above all men's reach as none could touch, much less shake from off his revered head ". Further on he enlarges on " the great value and esteem I have of this brave man, the honour of his age, and he that set a period to the perfection of our language ". And then he refers to the MS. poems by Jonson in his own possession, most of which I have already noticed, promising to make " the world " a sharer with him " in those excellent pieces, alas ! that many of them are but pieces, which he hath left behind him, and that I keep religiously by me to that end ".

In the same year a correspondent of Windebank wrote to him : † " Sir Kenelm Digby and Mr. Porter are reported to be at the conference at Brussels, where the jealousy of Bavaria must be guarded against ".

Porter's wife, by the way, was a sister of the then recent

* Introduction to *Priv. Mem.*, K. D., p. liii.
† *Calendar of the Clarendon State Papers*, vol. i., p. 148 (1044).

convert, Lady Newport, and was herself a convert.   Mr.
Gardiner calls her * " the soul of the proselytising movement " in England.

Meanwhile much was going on in Great Britain.   There
had been riots in Scotland at the attempt to enforce the
introduction of the Liturgy, and preparations were being
made for war between that country and England.   Cardinal Richelieu, too, was beginning to meddle in the dispute, and had sent D'Estrades to England.

The English Government were exceedingly suspicious
of the feeling in Paris with regard to the disloyalty in
Scotland, and the question of its suppression by force.   In
June, 1638, Robert, Earl of Leicester, who had been sent
to Paris officially, wrote to Secretary Coke that Lord
Scudamore, the English ambassador, had summoned
before him a Scotchman named Brisbain, who had been
accused by Sir Kenelm Digby of saying that there were
50,000 " Men in Armes " in Scotland, and " in England
25,000 to join with them, if occasion should require," and
that money would be forthcoming to support them.
Brisbain denied that he had said anything of the sort, and
complained to Leicester.   Leicester then, in the character
of an envoy from the English Government,† summoned
Sir Kenelm, and, in the presence of Brisbain, asked
whether he would bring the same charge against him
there and then which he had brought against him before
Lord Scudamore.   Sir Kenelm Digby answered : " If Mr.
Brisbain be aggreeved for anything that I have done he
may follow me into England where I am now going and
seeke such reparation there as he shall think fit " ; but he
said that he had had official orders to act as he had done,
and he refused to enter upon the matter in the presence of
Leicester.

* *Hist. Eng.*, vol. viii., p. 238.

† Scudamore was English ambassador in Paris.   Leicester was ambassador extraordinary.   Gardiner's *Hist. Eng.*, vol. viii., pp. 145 and 161.

Leicester replied, "Well, Sir Kenelm Digby, since you are so reserved concerning others, give me leave to ask you a question which concerns yourself, and hath some Resemblance to the other"; and then he inquired whether Sir Kenelm himself had not stated that "the Scotts were in Armes," and that men were being raised. "No, said Sir Ken. Digby, I have never said any such thing."

Leicester replied, "Father Talbot, a great and familiar Acquaintance of yours," told me "that you said thus to him in your chamber, and offered to show him the letters which lay upon your table, wherein you had lately received that Advertisement". This Sir Kenelm Digby denied "flatly". Sir Kenelm seems to have had reasons, as well as good authority, for his proceedings in this matter; for in a letter to Archbishop Laud, a few days later, Leicester wrote,* "And now having discharg'd myself of that which I thought my duty required of me, I will give your Grace no further trouble concerning Sir K. Digby unless I be commanded," etc, from which it may be inferred that he had received a hint to mind his own business.

As we have seen, Sir Kenelm said to Leicester that he was on the point of starting for England. He had an important object in going there.

The question had arisen whether the English Catholics would remain neutral; or, if not, which side they would join. Walter Montague and Sir Kenelm Digby, though both Catholics, were ardent courtiers and devoted to their king and queen; and they agreed together to do all in their power to induce the English Catholics to support the Crown, and they remained awaiting their opportunity of doing so.

Here was an admirable occasion for Sir Kenelm to return to his native country, not only free from all danger of banishment from court and disgrace on account of his

* *Sydney State Papers,* vol. ii., p. 557.

allegiance to the Catholic Church, his friendship with such men as Montague and his late espousal of the cause of Lady Purbeck, but in high favour as the champion of royalty among his somewhat distrusted co-religionists. In short, he came back to England in the character of a useful tool in the hands of the king.

Soon after his return, his mother was seriously ill, and he went to visit her, probably at Gothurst; for he writes to Lord Conway :—*

"I have been in the country upon the occasion of the dangerous sickness of my mother, but now she is well recovered. The King and Queen will be in London on Thursday to assist at the Duke's marriage; but I believe there will not be so great flocking of the people to it as was this last week to accompany Mr. Prynne and Mr. Bastwick's pilgrimage to their stations in the country." Prynne and Bastwick, after standing in the pillory, had been sent to different prisons in the country; and when they left London there was such a popular demonstration in their favour that their journey partook more of the character of a triumphal progress than of a disgraceful journey to jail. Of their severe treatment in the pillory, Sir Kenelm goes on to say in the same letter: "The Puritans keep the bloody sponges and handkerchiefs that did the hangman service in the cutting off their ears. You may see how nature leads men to respect relics of martyrs."

His mention of relics reminds me of one of his habits which may be worth recording. Burnet states † that "when the executors were looking out for writings to make out the title of estates they were to sell, they were directed by an old servant to a cupboard that was very artificially hid, in which some papers lay that she had observed Sir Kenelm

---

* *Cal. Sta. Pa. Dom.*, 1637, p. 332.

† Bishop Burnet's *History of his Own Times*, 1724, vol. l., p. 11.

was oft reading. They looking into it found a velvet bag within which were two other silk bags (so carefully were these relics kept). And there was within these a collection of all the letters that Sir Everard writ during his imprisonment."

Archbishop Laud summoned the Clergy of the Established Church to assist with subsidies the English army,* which was being prepared for the war against the Scots. Meanwhile the queen called upon the English Catholics to show their loyalty by subscribing to a fund for the same purpose.

Accordingly she wrote a letter † beginning : " We have so good a belief in the Loyalty and affection of his Majesty's Catholic Subjects, as we doubt not but upon this occasion," etc., " they will express themselves so affected, as we have always represented them to his Majesty". She tells them that she believes " it became us, who have been so often interested in the solicitation of their Benefits, to show ourselves now in the persuasion of their gratitudes ". She trusts that they will " assist and serve his Majesty by some considerable sum of money freely and cheerfully presented ". Copies of her letter are to be distributed in every country.

Sir Kenelm Digby, always a favourite with the queen, was summoned by her to assist in this matter, and he went to her and offered her his best services, and then began an increase in their intimacy and friendship which lasted with life. It soon became evident to the king, as well as to the queen, that Sir Kenelm's recent conversion to, or declaration of, Catholicism, was about to prove of material practical service to the Royalist cause.‡ In conjunction with his friend, Walter Montague, he wrote the following letter :—

* *Cyprianus Anglicanus*, p. 357.

† Rushworth's *Collections*, vol. ii., p. 820.

‡ See *Athen. Oxon.*, vol. ii., p. 251 ; *Biograph. Britan.*, vol. iii., p. 1704, and *Whitelock's Memorials*, p. 32.

" Sir Kenelm Digby, and Mr. Montague's Letter, concerning the contribution against the Scots, by the King's subjects of the Romish Religion.

" *April.*

" It is sufficiently already known to every one, the extraordinary graces and Protections we owe the Queen's Majesty, to whose favourable Intercession we must ascribe the happy moderation we live under ; so as we doubt not but an occasion of the expression of our gratitudes will joyfully be embraced by every Body, which the present estate of His Majesty's Affairs doth now offer us. We have already by our former letters endeavoured to prepare you to a cheerful Assistance of his Majesty, on his declared journey to the Northern parts, for the securing of his Kingdom, and such other Purposes as his Roial Wisdom shall resolve of ; that so you may really demonstrate your selves as good Subjects as God and Nature requires of you. Now her Majesty hath bin graciously pleased to recommend unto us the Expressions of our duties and zeal to his Majesty's service by some considerable gift from the Catholicks, and to remove all scruples (that even well affected Persons may meet with) she undertakes to secure us and all that shall employ themselves in this Business from any inconvenience that may be suspected, by their or our forwardness and declaration in this kind ; it will easily appear to everybody how much it imports us, in our sense of his Majesty's Desires, to press every Body to strain himself, even to his best Abilities, in this proposition, since by it we shall certainly preserve her graciousness to us, and give good characters of our devotion to the King and State ; of whose benignity we have all reason to give Testimonies, and to endeavour to produce Arguments for the prosecution and increase of it.

" Now for the best expedition of this Business (which is the circumstance that importeth in it) we have thought fit to recommend it to your nominations of such Persons as

shall in your opinion be agreed, for the ablest and best disposed in every several county, not only to sollicit, but to
collect such voluntary contributions, as every Bodies Conscience and Duty shall proffer.   And we shall desire you
to give us an account of that acceptation it receives from
Friends, which we cannot but expect very successful, and
answerable to the forwardness we meet with here about
London, for which we shall offer up our Prayer to God.

> " Wal. Mountague.
> " Ke. Digby."

The Catholics agreed to contribute £10,000 at once,
and an equal subsidy three months later.   Sir Kenelm
Digby, therefore, was in high favour at court.

An event occurred in 1638 which may have half amused,
half embarrassed Sir Kenelm Digby. This was the arrival in
England of his former devoted admirer, the queen's mother,
Marie de Medici.   Eighteen years may have sufficiently
cooled Marie de Medici's affections to enable her also to
look back upon the adventure as a ludicrous piece of folly ;
yet to meet her old love, as she can scarcely have failed to
have met him, when he was so much at her daughter's
palace, must have had the effect of making her feel somewhat uncomfortable.

Sir Kenelm, whatever his shortcomings, was never
wanting in tact or courtesy ; be matters as bad as they
might, he always tried to make the best of them ; and he
had ever an eye to his own interests ; it is probable, therefore, that he behaved towards the ancient queen as an old
and humble servant and thereby gained a further step in
her royal daughter's good graces.   As we shall see by-and-
by, too, Marie de Medici herself appears to have been
able to render him a signal service a little later.

CHAPTER XXIV

THEOLOGY, ASTROLOGY AND DUELLING.

IN addition to summoning his fellow Catholics to help the army with voluntary contributions, Sir Kenelm was employed by the English Government in another way. Pirates from Algiers and Tunis were seizing British merchant vessels in the Mediterranean, and Digby's experiences in that sea were thought calculated to make his advice valuable in providing a remedy; therefore,* "Sir Kenelm Digby and others" were appointed to inquire into the affair and to report thereon.

The advice tendered by Sir Kenelm and his co-adjutors was that "a strong fleet" should be sent "right down to Alexandria, when the Turks' ships were there laden, and to make prize of all men and goods; and to afterwards range the coast of Barbary, and among the villages, and make prisoners of all men and goods; and then return to Algiers and Tunis and there exchange the prisoners taken, and so redeem the English captives. If they refuse to exchange, then go over to Majorca, Sardinia and Spain, and to sell the Turks for money."

Excellent advice, no doubt; but, considering the obstacles encountered at that period in raising ship-money for use even in home waters, to say nothing of the expenses of the impending war with Scotland, it was somewhat difficult to carry out.

Like many men of modern days, who have lately de-

* *Cal. Sta. P. Dom.*, 1637-8, p. 192.

clared their adhesion to the Catholic Church, Sir Kenelm
Digby was drawn into a correspondence upon the subject
with a relation, shortly after his return to England. This
relative was Lord George Digby, the eldest son of Sir
Kenelm's great patron, the Earl of Bristol. Their correspondence was published a few years afterwards in a little
book of 132 pages, of which Lord George wrote 120 and
Sir Kenelm the remaining dozen.*

Into the theology of this controversy I do not intend
to enter; but I may observe that the courtesy exhibited
in it contrasts very favourably with the tone of most religious correspondences. Lord George begins one of his
letters:† "My Noblest Cousin and best friend, I beg your
pardon for making you so slow a return of my humble
thanks for your excellent Letter of the 26th of December;
and I should have needed your pardon much more, if your
favours in it had been lesser. The excesse of them in such
variety of obligations justifies me in the leasure I take to
taste and enjoy each endearing circumstance apart; weighing and comparing with one another the severall delights
I ough you, whilst everywhere I finde my self either
courted by him I love most, or applauded by him I emulate
most, or instructed by the person whose abilities I admire
most; and all this by you my dear Cousin, the prime
object of my noblest affections."

In his final letter Lord George accounts for their differ-
ences of opinion on religious questions on the ground that
"conformity and uniteness of minde are rarely flowing
from contrary Educations, as the same River from opposite springs," and he ends by assuring his theological
opponent that "it is impossible without an intire con-

---

* "*Letters between the Lord George Digby and Sir Kenelm Digby Kt.
Concerning Religion.* London. Printed for Humphrey Moseley and are
to be sold at his shop at the sign of the Prince's Arms in St. Paul's Church-
yard, 1651."

† P. 23.

currence of all the forces of sympathy, for any man to reverence, admire and love another, with that Ardour as I love
you, dearest Cousin, and which you cannot but own in
your most faithful and most Affectionate Servant, G. D.".
In one letter he apologises for the " rude and indigested
reflections" which he sends, complaining, that some of
them had been written down as " an after-supper's work,
and after coming home from vain entertainment with some
impertinent she-wits that most tyrannically seized upon "
him.

In no part of his letters does Lord George admit himself worsted in argument ; yet he afterwards became a
Catholic, whether owing to his cousin's letters or not is
very doubtful. Walpole says of him :* " He wrote against
popery and embraced it. He was a zealous officer of the
court, and a sacrifice for it ; was conscientiously converted
in the midst of his conversion of Lord Strafford, and was
most unconscientiously a persecutor of Lord Clarendon.
With romantic bravery he was always an unsuccessful
commander. He spoke for the Test Act, though a Roman
Catholic ; and addicted himself to astrology, on the birthday of true philosophy." Lord Clarendon says† that he
had to resign the signet owing to his change of religion.

George, Earl of Bristol, was not the only " Roman
Catholic " who " addicted himself to astrology, on the birthday of true philosophy ".

Almost at the very time of his correspondence about
the Catholic Church with his cousin Sir Kenelm Digby
was interesting himself in the astrology which was forbidden by that Church.

Beneath the Horoscope‡ given in the illustration is
written :—

---

* I quote from Burke's *Dormant and Extinct Peerages*, p. 171.

† *Hist. Reb.*, vol. iii., part ii., p. 741.

‡ Ashmole MS., 243, fol. 124 (art. 27): " At the end of Naibode's Com-
ment upon Ptolemy MS. in St. John's Colledge in Oxford ".

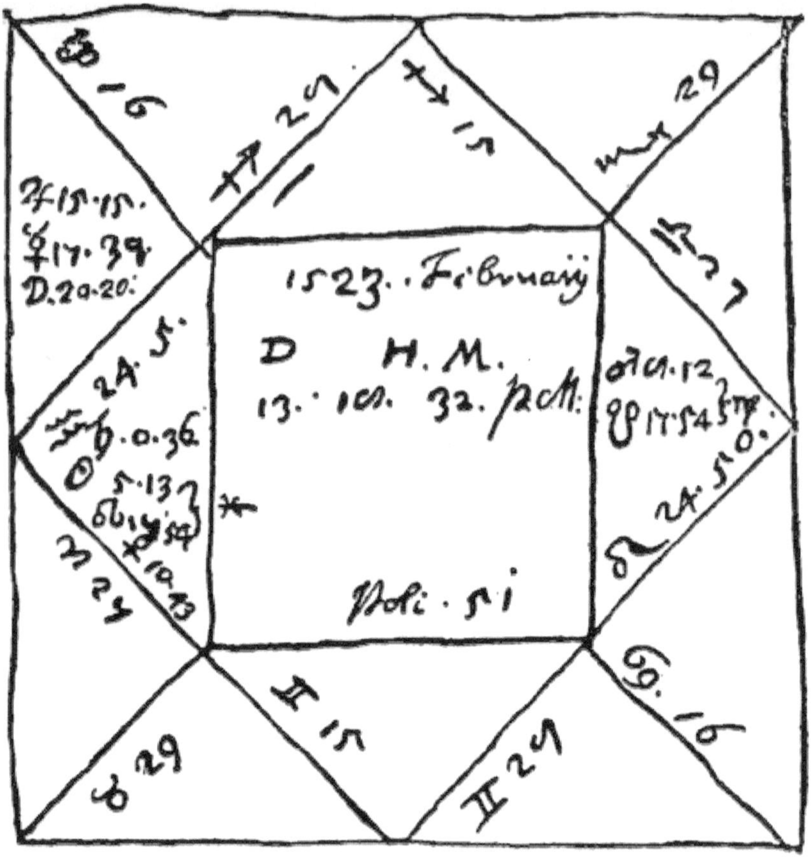

♋ -6

♃ 15·15.
♂ 17·39
☊ 20·20:

♐ 29
↑

↓ 15

♈ 29

♉ 7

24·5·

♏ 0·36
☉ 5·13
☿ 19·50

1523 · February

D   H. M.
13· 10· 32 pcM:

♂ 19·12
♄ 17·54 ½ᵐ
24·50·

♑ 10·43

♐ 29

Poli · 51

♉ 29

♊ 15

♊ 29

♋ 16

" Hac est genesis Valentini Naibodœ Erphordiensis huius operis author qui inventus fuit Patavij in proprio domo Ense transfixus post tridium, Et ignoratur an a se vel ab alio Credibile tamen est ipsum sibimet mortem attulisse. Quiæ h^{us} est dominus horoscopi and 8me and ♀ altera 8^a domina cadens in v^e .

" After this the following lettre is fixed to the Booke :—
   " Sir,
               " At the end of y^t MS. booke which I presumed to present the other day vnto my Lordes grace (which was Vallentine Naibodes Comentary vpon Ptolomies Quadripartite) you will finde the Authors Natiuity, and the story of his death. Vpon which happened a very remarkeable thing, that I will make bold here to tell you. The person y^t had the Booke at Paris (which was ye only copy of that worke in the World) hearing that Mr. Wells of Deptford was a great astrologer, transcribed y^t natuivity, without expressing whose it was nor what had hapned to him and by a frend of his that travelled into England desired to vnderstand Mr. Wells his opinion concerning the manor and tyme of y^t persons death, whose natuivity was shewed him conceiving that if there were any truth in the art, it would apper by the judgment of so able a man and vpon so notable an accident as soone as it was shewed to Mr. Wells he pronounced Confidently that the owner of that scheame did assuredly kill himselfe with his owne Sword, and taking a little tyme to determine of the tyme, he at hom made ye direccions of the Significators, and then aver'd as confidently that it was at such a tyme of his age as agreed punctually with the Story, and all this he did without so much as suspecting whose Geniture it was, or having any hint what had befallen him, which being an observable thing, I thought it not amiss to acquaint you with it, and so crauing pardon for thus holding you, I rest,
                              " Your humble servant,
                                        " Kenelme Digby.
   " This 17th July, 1640.

" To my honoured and worthy frend Doctor Barkeham at Lambeth :—

"Valentinus Nabodus Erphordiensis, mathoseos professor doctissimus in Academia Colonenti natus anno 1523 13th Feb. H. 18 M. 32 Mercurium habuit iunctum lunæ in domo 12 Sic refert Sixtus orb Hemminga. Astrol. ref. p. 280."

When the Short Parliament had been summoned, the Catholics had good cause for apprehension ; nor without cause did the queen fear that parliament would ask for a renewal of their persecution.

In January, 1640, the House of Commons summoned Sir Kenelm Digby to appear before it,* and he was there asked to state upon what grounds, upon what terms, and to what extent he had instituted a collection of money among the king's Catholic subjects on behalf of the army. †

The answer which he returned was to this purpose : " That he did consider before whom he did appear, and in whose presence he spake, the gravest and wisest Assembly in the whole world, whose majesty is so great, that it might well disorder his thoughts, and impede his expressions. That he was suddenly surprised with unexpected questions ; and apprehended there might be some dislike in that honourable House, of that which once he did conceive was an act of service and merit. But since he is askt of things apart, he shall humbly represent what he can remember upon this occasion, and what may be satisfactory to the House. So he related the beginning of the business, and took along the series as it went from step to step."

He then told them the story without, so far as is known, concealing anything. The queen had been " pleased to recommend to those who were Catholics of this kingdom, to show themselves as forward as others were in serving the King ; and to each Catholick to speak to his acquaintance

---

* *Biog. Brit.*, vol. iii., p. 1705.
† Rushworth, vol. ii., p. 1327.

to do the like. I was one of those Her Majesty spake unto." Meetings to arrange about the matter were held at the house of "Seigneur *Con*, who was resident here from the Pope, I conceive to attend the queen". The chief motive which induced him to be active in the matter was "that his Majestie's Grace and Goodness had been much extended to Catholics, considering how sharp and penal the laws were against them". "There were at the meetings several times Sir *John Winter* the queen's secretary, Sir *Basil Brookes*, Mr. *Mountague*, and one Mr. *Foster*, who was a person Seigneur *Con* had particular confidence in." Sir Kenelm very truly said in conclusion that "he had dealt clearly and candidly with the parliament, and declared as much as he knew of this business"—more indeed than one would suppose the queen and his friends to have wished revealed.

Two days afterwards he was again called before the House of Commons and asked on what footing Con had come to England and what interest he had in this country. "How his acquaintance came to be so great in the Nation" Sir Kenelm "could not tell; but sure he was that his interest was greater than any interest Sir *Kenelme Digby* had to advance the business". This time he seemed to feel that he was being unfairly cross-questioned, or "heckled," as it is now called. Concerning Con's exact authority and position he neither knew nor wanted to know a great deal.

"He was willing to keep himself ignorant as much as he might of many things, having much less acquaintance with Catholicks than is imagined he had."

His candour did not appear to satisfy the House of Commons, for it shortly afterwards sent an address to His Majesty, praying him to remove all Papists from the Court, and especially from his own presence,* particularly naming Sir Kenelm Digby and Walter Montague.

* Introduction to *Priv. Mem.*, p. lxii.

Whether at Charles's own request, or voluntarily in order so save him from embarrassment, Sir Kenelm seems to have forthwith gone to France.* All we know of his sojourn there is contained in a tract " printed at London for T. B., 1641," and entitled *Sir Kenelm Digby's Honour Maintained*.†

In this he is represented as miserable in being separated from the king whom he so dearly loved, and as " oftentimes " crying out : " Woe is me, because it is unlawful for me to see my master ". He lived near the French Court, where he was very well received, and among his many invitations was one from a Count or Baron Mont de Ros, who asked him to dine with him. " Very merry they all were for a certain space." " At length they fell to drinking of healths to certain Kings, as to the King of France, the King of Spain, the King of Portugal, and divers others ; but in the conclusion," the host " peremptorily began a health to the arrantest coward in the world, directing the cup unto Sir Kenelm," who asked who that coward might be. Mont de Ros replied that when Sir Kenelm had drunk the toast he would tell him. So soon as Sir Kenelm had done so, his host said : " I meant your King of England ". On hearing this, Sir Kenelm " seemed very distracted," but he said nothing until he was about to take his leave, when he courteously invited his host to do him the honour of dining with him on the following day, and Mont de Ros " promised him, upon his honour, that he would ". On the morrow, Sir Kenelm had a grand dinner prepared at his " lodging," and, when his guests arrived, he showed no signs of remembering " the former day's discontent, but was very frolic and merry ". The entertainment was passing off brilliantly when, " in the midst of the dinner-time," Sir

* Introduction to *Priv. Mem.*, p. lxii. and *seq*.

† The entire tract will be found in pages lvii. lxi. of the Introduction to the *Priv. Mem.*

Kenelm " desired them all to be bare, for he would begin
a health to the bravest king in the world ". Mont de
Ros inquired whom he meant. Sir Kenelm told him that
as soon as he had drunk the toast he should hear. The
cups being drained, Sir Kenelm exclaimed : " It is the
health of the bravest king in the world, which is the King
of England, my royal Master, for, although my body be
banished from him, yet is my heart loyally linked ".
Hereupon Mont de Ros began to laugh, and repeated
his former opinion that he was " the arrantest coward in
the world ". Sir Kenelm was now " thoroughly moved in
the behalf of " his " Sovereign King Charles," and, leaning
towards Mont de Ros, he whispered in his ear that he had
twice " reviled the best king in the world " in the hearing
of " one of his faithful subjects," adding, " I require a single
combat of you, where either you shall pay your life for
your sauciness, or I will sacrifice mine in the behalf of my
king ". Mont de Ros gave his consent in an undertone ;
but no further notice was taken of the matter during
dinner, which proceeded gaily, as if nothing unusual had
happened.

When the entertainment was over, the two antagonists
rose from the table " and privately went out together,"
unaccompanied, it would seem, by seconds, whose presence
was not considered imperative in France, or indeed in
other countries, during the seventeenth century.* Having
proceeded to a field, " off they plucked their doublets, and
out they drew their " swords. Having saluted and taken
their ground, the two duellists crossed swords. No result
followed the first " bout ". In the second, each attack was
well guarded, and neither combatant could reach his adver-

---

* *The History of Duelling*, by J. G. Millingen, 1841, p. 113. Less
than a hundred years ago, the author's great-grandfather declared that if he
ever fought a duel, he would not put a friend in the unpleasant position of a
second. In 1799 he challenged a man, went into the field unaccompanied
by a second, and was killed.

sary with his point.   A third was fought without either side getting an advantage ; the Englishman and the Frenchman were evidently very evenly matched.   A fourth time they engaged each other, and suddenly Sir Kenelm's weapon flashed past his enemy's guard, plunged into his breast, until the point came out through his neck.

Although his fallen foe and late guest was lying on the ground, covered with blood from a ghastly wound, without a second or a surgeon to attend to him, Sir Kenelm had to think of his own safety ; for, to say nothing of dangers from Mont de Ros's friends or retainers, duelling was then punishable with death, and efforts were being made to put a stop to it by the aid of the law.   Only a few years earlier, Bouterville * had been executed on the Place de Greve, for fighting a duel with the Marquis de Beuvron, although the result had not been fatal.   It was very necessary, therefore, for Sir Kenelm to take care of himself.   He adopted very bold, very decisive, and, as it turned out, very prudent measures.   He went straight to the French Court, straight to the French King, told him the whole story, and begged his protection.   Louis XIII. said the proudest nobleman in France should never dare to revile his brother, the King of England, and he ordered a guard to protect Sir Kenelm Digby to the Flemish frontier.

The tract, in honour of the event, ends :—

> Now I conclude, commanding fame to show
> Brave Digby's worthy deed, that all may know
> He loved his King ; may all as loyal prove,
> And like this Digby to their King show love.

* *The History of Duelling*, by J. G. Millingen, 1841, p. 149 *seq*.   This was in 1626.   The Bishop of Nantes, who was present at the execution, observing the care with which the condemned man was twirling his moustaches, said : "Oh, my son, you must no longer dwell on worldly matters ! Do you still think of life?"   "I only think of my mustaches," replied Bouterville.   His moustaches were said to be the finest in France.   In the reign of Henry IV. of France (1589-1607), 4000 men are said to have been killed in single combat and 14,000 pardons to have been granted for duelling. *Ib.*, p. 122.

No doubt the report of the duel reached King Charles, who could not well do otherwise than recall his champion to England.

When Sir Kenelm had returned to his own country, he found the position of the king and queen becoming more difficult and precarious from day to day. Insulting placards were posted in the streets calling upon the mob to make a raid on the apartments of the queen's mother at St. James's, to pull down the queen's chapel, and to drive away her priests. A large number of Catholic books, which had been seized, were publicly burned. Worst of all, the apartments of Sir Kenelm's great friend, Queen Henrietta Maria, were regarded by the people as the centre of the worst intrigues against their rights, and those who chiefly frequented them as the most dangerous traitors to their nation.

Sir Kenelm Digby had been dismissed from the court and country, and now he was back again, going in and out of the queen's palace as he pleased. Selden said:* "I can compare him to nothing but to a great fish that we catch and let go again; but still he will come to the bait; at last therefore we put him into some great pond for store".

* *Table Talk*, No. lix., p. 82.

R

CHAPTER XXV.

A PRISONER.

To use a very mild term, Sir Kenelm was of an exceedingly diplomatic disposition. I do not say that he was a skilful diplomatist. He mixed fearlessly, freely and on a more or less friendly footing with men of all shades of opinion on religious, political, and other vexed questions ; yet, with all his astuteness and tact, the difficulties of the latter part of the reign of Charles I. were a little too great for him. In May, 1641, a committee of six members of Parliament was appointed to summon Sir Kenelm and others before them and to offer them the Oaths of Allegiance and Supremacy.* A month later an order was made that Sir Kenelm should attend the Committee for Recusants Convict.† He was shortly afterwards committed to Winchester House.

On some very ancient Roman foundations‡ Bishop Giffard had built this palace for himself about 1107. The principal frontage is supposed to have been towards the River Thames, while on the south side was a beautiful garden with statues and fountains and a park. It had been the residence of William of Wykeham, of Stephen Gardiner, of Cardinal Beaufort, and, shortly before the time of which I am writing, of Bishop Andrewes. After all this glory as an episcopal palace it was converted into a prison

* *Commons Journals*, 11, 158.
† *Ib.*, 11, 182.
‡ Rendle's *Old Southwark*, p. 204 *seq.*

"for the royalists"* by order of the Parliament, just about, or immediately before, the date of Sir Kenelm Digby's committal. Some years later the place became neglected, surrounded by houses of a low class, and "pestilential"; but, at the time of Sir Kenelm's incarceration, Winchester House had probably suffered little change, beyond dismantlement, since it had been a bishop's palace, and there is no reason for supposing that Sir Kenelm was otherwise than comfortably lodged there.

It is stated in the *Biographia Britannica* † that he "was treated with great respect, was visited by men of all parties, and some amongst them of the first distinction". "Which," says a marginal note, "created great jealousies." One thing must have considerably annoyed Sir Kenelm at Winchester House, especially in his new character of a zealous Catholic. "The Parliament," says Rendle,‡ "were not unmindful of the prisoners, so they ordered some orthodox and godly minister, well affected to the King and Parliament, to preach to them."

To a man of literary and scientific tastes a very qualified imprisonment would be less wearisome than to others, and Sir Kenelm not only interested himself in his books but also in experiments in glass-making. What opportunities and conveniences he may have had for carrying them out it is impossible to learn, but Southwark has long been famous for glass manufactures, and Sir Kenelm may have been allowed to call in some workmen from a neighbouring factory, which, as will be shown in the following extract from *The Antiquary*,§ existed there :—

"A patent for glass bottles, granted to John Colnett in 1661 (not included in the Official Blue Books), was revoked (*Hist. MSS., Comm., Rept. VII.*, p. 164) on the

* Brayley and Britton's *Hist. of Surrey*, vol. v., p. 349, footnote.
† Vol. iii., p. 1705.
‡ Rendle's *Old Southwark*, p. 222.
§ *The Antiquary*, No. 65, new series, p. 135.

ground that the invention had been made many years previously by Sir Kenelm Digby, and that Colnett and others
had worked under his instruction. The connection of
Digby with the green glass trade is a curious fact which
has been overlooked by his biographers. The invention
appears to have consisted in the manufacture of bottles of
standard sizes, and the period of the invention may be
attributed to the date of Digby's confinement at Winchester
House, Southwark, where, as previously shown, a green
glass factory existed in 1612." *

Although the use of glass for making bottles was
known to the Romans at least as early as the year 79,
since they have been found among the ruins of Pompeii,
they do not appear to have come into use in England until
about 1558.†

It was in his prison at Winchester House that Sir
Kenelm wrote his "*Observations upon Religio Medici occasionally written by* Sir Kenelme Digby Knt".‡

In the form of a letter to Edward, Earl of Dorset, Sir
Kenelm "digested these observations during the night between 22nd and 23rd December, 1642".§ "In this work,"
says Dr. Johnson in his *Life of Browne*, "though mingled
with some positions fabulous and uncertain, there are acute
remarks, just censures, and profound speculations; yet its
principal claim to admiration is, that it was written in
twenty-four hours of which part was spent in procuring
Browne's book and part in reading it."

* See also *Notes and Queries*, 27th July, 1895. "In or before 1662 a
certain John Colnett obtained a patent for glass bottles and procured a bill
confirming the patent, which was bad for want of novelty," etc. "A petition against the Bill was filed by John Vinion and Robert Ward on behalf
of the London glass trade," because "Colnett was not the inventor. The
Attorney-General reported in favour of the petitioners, and stated that 'Sir
Kenelm Digby first invented glass bottles nearly thirty years since, and
employed Colnett and others to make them for him '."

† Haydn's *Dic. of Dates.*

‡ *Biog. Brit.*, vol. iii., p. 1706, Note G. III.

§ Chalmers' *Biog. Dict.*, vol. xi., p. 73, footnote.

While at Winchester House Sir Kenelm also wrote his *Observations on the twenty-second stanza in the ninth canto of the second book of Spencer's " Faerie Queen,"* * in a letter to his friend Sir Edward Stradling, who had accompanied him in his expedition to the Mediterranean.

Aubrey † states that while "a prisoner for the King at Winchester House," Sir Kenelm "practised chymistry, and wrote a booke of Bodies and Soule".‡ Very likely he may have done so ; but the dedication to his son, Kenelm, with which it opens, is dated "*Paris* the last of August 1644". In this bulky treatise, 429 pages are devoted to the body and 144 to the soul. The volume forms the most preten-tious of the author's books, although, to his biographers, his *Private Memoirs* and his *Voyage to the Mediterranean* are infinitely more interesting. *The Nature of Bodies* is full of curiosities. Only a few examples can be given here.

"The first most general operation of the sunne is the making and raising of atomes."§ "The light rebounding from the earth with atomes, causeth two streams in the aire ; the one ascending, the other descending ; and both of them in perpendicular line."║ Now the descending atoms are the most "dense," and the ascending atoms are "more rarified," hence it follows that the reason why an object "placed at liberty in the open aire" falls to the ground is because "if you compare the impressions that the denser atomes make" upon the body, "with those that proceed from the rare ones, it is evident that the dense ones must be the more powerfull ; and therefore will assuredly de-

---

* Chalmers' *Biog. Dict.*, vol. xi., p. 73, note 4.

† *Letters written by Eminent Persons*, vol. ii., Appendix.

‡ "*Two Treatises : In the one of which The Nature of Bodies, In the other The Nature of Man's Soul is looked into In way of Discovery of the Immortality of Reasonable Soules*, London MDCLXV." The first edition was published in Paris in 1644.

§ P. 94. ║ P. 96.

termine the motion of the body in the aire, that way they go, which is downwards ".*

Why does the heart beat? †   " And what can that be else, but heat or spirits imprisoned in a tough viscous bloud ; which it cannot so presently break through to get out : and yet can strive within it and lift it up?"   " This virtue of moving is in every part of the heart, as you will plainly see if you cut into several pieces a heart, that conserveth its motion long after it is out of the animal's belly : for every piece will move."

"Mounsier des Cartes" taught that sensations are carried to the brain by the nerves ; but Sir Kenelm, while partially agreeing with him, preferred to "goe the more common way " ; and believed that sensations were conveyed to the brain by "the spirits ".   These " spirits" were " the watery and the oyly parts " of the body.

Poultry fanciers may be interested to learn that Sir Kenelm had been initiated into the mysteries of an incubator.   " Sir John Heydon," he tells us, " the Lieutenant of his Majesties Ordnance (that generous and knowing gentleman, and consummate souldier both in theory and practise), was the first that instructed me how to do this, by means of a furnace so made as to imitate the warmth of a sitting hen.   In which you lay several eggs to hatch : and by breaking them at several ages, you may distinctly observe every hourly mutation in them, if you please."

On the philosophical treatise on *The Soul*, I am very ill-qualified to give an opinion ; I therefore asked a very able critic of such matters to read the book and report on it.   He writes that it is of some interest because it dated before the philosophical speculations of Hobbes, Cudworth, Locke and Berkeley, but that it is of little intrinsic value.

---

* The principles of gravitation had been demonstrated by Galileo about eight or nine years before this was written ; but Newton's famous apple did not fall until about a quarter of a century later.

† P. 294.

That which is true in it is not new, and that which is new
in it is not true. Digby's explanations of simple apprehension, judgment and reasoning are, for the most part, little
more than the ordinary Aristotelian doctrine expressed in
somewhat inflated language ; and his whole system may
be said to be rather Aristotelian than Cartesian. Ex-
aggeration and want of precision are two of the chief faults
of his work : a failure to work out systematically the consequences of his own principles is its chief weakness. Both
the mental tone and the literary style are exceedingly
bombastic, and the author writes contemptuously of things
which he does not seem to understand. Such, at least, is
the drift of my friend's criticism of the book, and it is the
criticism of a very learned man.

Another of Sir Kenelm's books, *The Closet of the
Eminently Learned Sir Kenelme Digby, Knt., Opened*, has
already been noticed at some length in an earlier chapter.
It was not published until four years after his death.
This work practically consists of Sir Kenelm's private
receipt book. I must resist the temptation to describe
more of the curious and uninviting messes which it recommends ; and there is no need that I should notice the book
further, especially as its preface informs us that "there
needs no Rhetoricating Floscules to set it off".

A book of a very different nature was compiled by Sir
Kenelm, or compiled at his orders. The author of the
Biographia Britannica * calls it "that noble manuscript
which Sir Kenelme caused to be collected at the expense
of a thousand pounds, as well out of private memorials,
as from publick histories and records in the Tower, and
elsewhere, relating to the Digby family in all its branches".
Aubrey describes † this book as being "as big as the
biggest Church Bible that ever I sawe, and the richest

---

* Vol. iii., p. 1713.
† *Letters*, vol. ii., Appendix.

bound, bossed with silver, engraven with scutchions and crest ". At what date this book was written there is no evidence, nor am I able to say where it is at present; but in 1794 it was in the possession of Mr. W. Williams of Penbeddw in North Wales.*

It must have been far from consoling to Sir Kenelm, in his imprisonment, to hear that the persecutions of the Catholics were taking the violent form of martyrdom of priests for their religion. Soon after he had been incarcerated at Winchester House, a priest, an old man of seventy-six, was hanged and quartered at Tyburn.† As his imprisonment progressed, things looked worse and worse for Royalists as well as Catholics. Strafford was executed, Laud was in the Tower. Sir Kenelm had not been very long a prisoner when the flight of his great patroness and friend, Queen Henrietta Maria, to the Continent, warned him that, if he were set free, he would be unsafe except in exile. His own family, too, was getting into ill repute with the Parliament. A letter‡ from his cousin and intimate friend, Lord George Digby, written from Middleburg, whither he had fled, and addressed to the queen, had unfortunately fallen into the hands of Prynne, who took it to the House of Commons where the seal was broken and the letter read. In the course of it Lord George had written: "I shall remain in the privatest way I can till I receive instructions how to serve the King and your Majesty in these parts, if the King betake himself to a safe place where he may avow and protect his servants from rage and violence," etc. A few days later Lord George was impeached for high treason. In the face of his impeachment he returned to England some months afterwards to bring the king news of the queen. After re-embarking to return to the Con-

---

* Introduction to *Priv. Mem.* p. lxxxi.
† Gardiner's *Hist. Eng.*, vol. ix., p. 411.
‡ *Ib.*, vol. x., p. 167.

tinent he was captured and taken to Hull, but he managed to escape. His proceedings, however, helped to make the name of Digby as odious to the Parliament as it had been to Buckingham.

After having been for about two years a prisoner, Sir Kenelm Digby was rescued through the influence of a powerful friend. The queen-mother of France wrote to the English Parliament begging that he might be set free. At first sight it might appear an unlikely petition to be granted; but probably the Government did not know what to do with Sir Kenelm, found him an expensive encumbrance, and was glad of an excuse to get rid of him. He had so many friends, too, among men of all parties, that some few of the Parliamentary party may have urged his release; and he may have been regarded rather as an eccentric philosopher than as a dangerous politician. The following was the reply of the Parliament to the Queen of France :—*

" Madam,

" The two Houses of Parliament having been informed by the Sieur de Gressy of the desire your Majesty has, that we should set at liberty Sir Kenelme Digby; we are commanded to make known to your Majesty that although the religion, the past behaviour, and the abilities of this gentleman, might give just umbrage of his practising to the prejudice of the constitutions of this realm; nevertheless, having so great regard to the recommendation of your Majesty, they have ordered him to be discharged, and have authorised us farther to assure your Majesty, of their being always ready to testify to you," etc., etc.

The terms on which Digby was set at liberty were thus written out and also subscribed by his own hand :—

* *Walteri Hemingford Chronicon.*, p. 581.   *Biog. Brit.*, vol. iii., p. 1706.

"Whereas upon the mediation of her Majesty the Queen of France it hath pleased both Houses of Parliament to permit me to go into that kingdom, in humble acknowledgement of their favour therein, and to preserve and confirm a good opinion of my zeal and honest intentions to the honour and service of my country, I do here, upon the faith of a Christian, and the word of a gentleman, protest and promise, that I will, neither directly nor indirectly, negotiate, promote, consent unto, or conceal, any practise or design, prejudicial to the honour or the safety of the Parliament. And, in witness of my reality herein, I have hereunto subscribed my name this 3rd day of August, 1643.

"Kenelme Digby."

Sir Harris Nicholas thought that the Queen of France, who interceded with the English Parliament on behalf of Sir Kenelm Digby, was Marie de Medici.* "He was released," says he, "at the intercession of the queen-mother of France, the lady whom in his *Memoir* he represents to have been enamoured of him about twenty years before, but whose advances he declined. Whether it was to the passion there imputed to her, or to the high favour in which he stood with the Queen of England, her daughter, or to both these causes, that he was indebted for the favour is uncertain; but the House returned a respectful answer to her Majesty, and he was released," etc.

Sir Harris may have been right; but the queen-regent of France, at the time of Sir Kenelm's release, was Anne of Austria; the English Parliament had obliged Marie de Medici † to leave England in 1641, and she died abroad in great misery and want in 1642,‡ at least seven months before Sir Kenelm's release; and the *Biographia Britan-*

---

* Introduction to *Priv. Mem.*, K. D., p. lxiii.

† She is said "to have died in a hayloft," at Cologne, "almost without the common necessaries of life". Beeton's *Ency.*, vol. ii., p. 279.

‡ Bush's *Queens of France*, vol. iii., pp. 102, 103.

nica * speaks of his going to France to thank the queen, who could have been none other than Anne of Austria, for obtaining it for him. Nevertheless it is likely enough that it may have been a letter from Marie de Medici which in the first instance induced the Parliament to consider the question of setting him at liberty.

Before leaving England, Sir Kenelm was required to appear before a Commissioner to answer some interrogations respecting Archbishop Laud, as has been explained in an earlier chapter.

On reaching France, according to the authority above quoted, he hastened to the Court, in order to return thanks to the queen-mother for the liberty which she had obtained for him ; and his appearance there † " was highly acceptable to many of the learned in that kingdom, who had a very high opinion of his abilities, and were charmed with the life and freedom of his conversation, which is on all hands allowed to have been very agreeable, notwithstanding that spirit of envy which pursued him living, and which has not ceased to persecute his memory since his death ".

He took up his residence in Paris the very year that Louis XIV. ascended the throne. It was most likely soon after his arrival in France that he made the acquaintance of a much more celebrated philosopher than himself, namely, Des Cartes. Their first meeting was at Des Cartes' home in Holland, whither Sir Kenelm had gone for the express purpose of visiting him. On this occasion he ‡ told the great philosopher that speculative theories were more or less unprofitable, and that it were better that one who understood the human body, so well as Des Cartes, should study to prolong its existence, than that he should expend his energies on the barren speculations of

---

* *Biog. Brit.*, vol. iii., p. 1706.

† *Ib.*

‡ Des Maizeaux's *Life of M. St. Evcremond*, p. 41. *Biog. Brit.*, vol. iii., p. 1707.

philosophy. " Des Cartes assured him that he had
already considered that matter, and that to render a man
immortal was what he would not venture to promise, but
that he was very sure it was possible to lengthen out his
life to the period of the Patriarchs."

Many people believed Des Cartes to be in possession of
this secret ; so much so that, when one of his disciples
heard of his death, he refused to believe that it had taken place.

The publication in Paris of Digby's treatise on *The
Nature of Bodies* and *The Nature of the Soul* greatly
increased his celebrity in that city ; but a year later a
reply appeared in England * from the pen of Alexander
Ross, entitled *The Philosophical Touchstone,* in which it was
professed that Sir Kenelm's " erroneous Paradoxes " were
" refuted ". A Bavarian, named Chrisostom Ezzenfield,
also attacked him, some time later, under a feigned name,
in a little treatise called *Triumphans Anima.* It was
probably while in France that Sir Kenelm wrote, or suggested the matter to White for, *Five Books of Peripatetic
Institutions,* with a Theological Appendix concerning the
origin of the world.†

Meanwhile constant bad news was coming from England
to Sir Kenelm. His old friend and tutor, Archbishop Laud,
was executed early in 1645, and an ordinance was passed
which was likely to affect his own finances to a very serious
extent. By this instrument ‡ two-thirds of the estate, both
real and personal, of every Catholic, was to be seized and
sold for the benefit of the nation.

The war in England brought personal bereavement to
Sir Kenelm, as his own brother, Sir John Digby, a Major-
General in the King's Army, was mortally wounded in a
skirmish in Somersetshire and died soon afterwards.

---

* Yes, Mr. Reviewer, in those days the only method of criticising a
book was to write another in reply.

† Lodge's *Portraits,* vol. v., p. 152.

‡ Lingard, *Hist. Eng.,* vol. viii., chap. i.

Notwithstanding his written promises to the Parliament " on the faith of a Christian and the word of a gentleman " not to " negotiate " anything " prejudicial to the honour of " the Parliament, Sir Kenelm seems to have conducted some negotiations with Rome, with a view to " driving the Scots and the Parliamentarians out of Ireland ". An Italian * transcript of these is endorsed by Hyde " *The Pope's Promises*, by Sir Ke. Digby, November, 1646 ". This document includes a long list of provisions, on either side, and it had been transmitted by Cardinal Panfilio from Rome to Monsignor Rinuccini, the Papal Nuncio in Ireland. All penal laws against Catholics were to be revoked ; all their disabilities were to be removed, the chief offices were to be placed in their hands ; the King's forces were to join the Irish " in driving the Scots and Parliamentarians out of Ireland, and the existing oaths of supremacy and allegiance were to be revoked. In return, the Pope was to pay 100,000 crowns to the Queen of England."

Sir Kenelm had been sent to Rome, as the envoy of the Queen of England, to conduct these negotiations, and he appears to have stayed there some time ; for there is evidence of his having been there a year later than the date above mentioned.

There had been an insurrection at Naples, and in 1647 the second Henri, Duke of Guise, conspired against the powerful Cardinal Richelieu, and put himself at the head of the revolted Neapolitans. In a " Letter of Intelligence," † dated from Rome, 18th November, 1647, there is a " Detailed account of affairs at Naples. . . . The Duke of Guise invited to be King. Details of his expedition, the design of which is due to Sir Kenelm Digby." Why Sir Kenelm should have meddled in the

---

* *Clarendon State Papers*, vol. ii., p. 298.
† *Calendar of the Clarendon State Papers*, vol. i., p. 400.

matter, or why his advice should have been taken in it, it
is difficult to conceive.   The same paper, however, states,
further on, that " Sir Kenelm Digby has taken leave of the
Pope : he has done more honour to the English nation
here than ever man did ".

It must be admitted, however, that there is another
side to the story.   Aubrey * says that during the first part
of his stay in Rome Sir Kenelm " was mightily admired ;
but after some time he grew high, and hectored at His
Holiness, and gave him the lye.   The Pope † sayd he was
mad."   And Wood says something much worse : ‡
" Huffing his Holiness, he was in a manner neglected, and
especially for this Reason, that having made a Collection
of Money for the afflicted Catholics in England (he)
was found to be no faithful steward in the matter ".   How
far this was true, or what it exactly means, it is impossible
to determine.   Nothing else anywhere related of him
makes it at all likely that he could have been guilty of
embezzlement ; but that he may have raised funds to help
the king in his war against the Parliament, under the
name of making a collection for the distressed Catholics
of England, persuading himself that it would be to their
interest to crush the Puritan party, is not unlikely ; and,
if this was what he did, the Pope may not have considered
him a very " faithful steward," in using for the Protestant
English king money that had been contributed to the
distressed English Catholics.

While he was in Italy, he visited the courts § of several
other princes besides the Pope, and " at each of them he
was treated with great respect, as well on account of his
personal qualifications, as the esteem those princes had

* *Letters*, vol. ii., Appendix.

† Innocent X.

‡ *Ath. Ox.*, vol. ii., p. 352.

§ *Biog. Brit.*, vol. iii., p. 1709.

of the queen, his mistress ".* " Of one of the Princes "
it is reported that, having no children, he was very
willing that his name should be perpetuated by a son of
" Sir Kenelm, whom he imagined the just measure of
perfection ".

In 1648 a very grievous sorrow befell Sir Kenelm
Digby. His eldest son, Kenelm, was killed when carrying
arms for King Charles at St. Neots, a town on the very
river which flowed past his own home at Gothurst. Lord
Holland with about 100 horse had been retreating before
Colonel Rich, and they were wandering about " without
purpose or design,"† when they were " beset in an Inn at
St. Neots in Huntingdonshire, by those few Horse who
pursued him, being joy'nd with some troops of Colonel
Scroop ".

" The Earl delivered himself without resistance ; yet
at the same time *Dalbeer*‡ and *Kenelm Digby*, the eldest
son of Sir Kenelm, were killed upon the place ; whether
out of former grudges, or that they offer'd to defend themselves, was not known." Kenelm's death must have been
the more distressing to his father because the latter was
not on good terms with his son John. Aubrey says § that
there was " great falling out betweene " Sir Kenelm and his
" son John ".

In the same year that his eldest son was killed, Sir
Kenelm contemplated returning to England. One, ‖
" Scout-master Watson," of whom we shall hear more by-
and-by, wrote from Paris in 1648 " to a brother Inde-

---

* Lloyd's *Loyal Sufferers*, p. 582.

† Clarendon's *Hist. Reb.*, book xi., p. 179.

‡ " A Dutchman of name and reputation and good experience in war."
He had been Commissary General of the Horse under Essex in the
Parliamentary Army; but he had left it, being disgusted with the " ill-
breeding and much preaching which prevailed in it ".

§ *Letters*, vol. ii., Appendix.

‖ *Calendar of Clarendon State Papers*, vol. i., p. 448.

pendent" in England : " Lord Say has undertaken to procure a pass for Sir Kenelm Digby to come to England ; and begs him to promote the motion when it comes before the House ". Are we to infer from this that Sir Kenelm, if negotiating with the Pope on the one hand, was gently feeling his way towards making terms with the Independents on the other? We shall see presently.

CHAPTER XXVI

NEGOTIATIONS WITH THE ENEMY.

KING CHARLES I., the master to whom Sir Kenelm Digby had ever professed himself devotedly attached, was shamefully beheaded on the 30th of January, 1649. Sir Kenelm was then in France, the country in which he had killed a nobleman, in a duel, for speaking slightingly of that very king ; and he was in the service of that king's widowed queen, having been appointed her Chancellor. Surely, if any man were a Staunch Cavalier and an unyielding foe to the Roundheads, it should have been Sir Kenelm Digby !

I am afraid so much as this cannot truthfully be said. His dearly beloved master had been dead but a very short time, when he began to consider whether some terms for the saving of his own estate and those of other English Catholics might be made with his master's chief murderer.

Sir Kenelm and some of his friends, if they did not exactly say : " *Le roi* (Charles I.) *est mort, vive le roi* (Cromwell)," at any rate seem to have made up their minds to attempt a compact with the new Government ; nor were their designs unknown to others. This was so explained at some length in a letter * from Lord Byron to the Marquess of Ormonde dated Caen, 1st March, 1649.

Byron said that he had obtained his information through the bearer of his letter, " Major Jamot, who, though a Roman Catholic, yet herein so much detests their ways,

---

* *Ormonde Letters*, by Thos. Carte, ed. 1739, vol. i., p. 216.

that truly I believe it will alter his opinion. The business is chiefly this : Sir Kenelm Digby, with some other Romanists, accompanied by one Watson, an Independent "—we heard of him at the end of the last chapter— "who bought them passes from Fairfax, is gone for England to join the interests of all the English Papists with the bloody party that murdered the King, in the opposition and extirpation of monarchical government, or if that government be thought fit, yet that it shall be by election, and not by succession as formerly provided ; that a free exercise of the Romish religion be granted, and of all other religions whatsoever, excepting that which was established by law in the church of England ".

Byron believed that " this devilish design " would " have an evil influence on Ireland," and he had heard that " Poyntz (my Lord Worcester's devil) " was " a prime actor in it ". He also suspected " Walsingham, whom your Excellency knows for a pragmatical knave," to be " employed by Sir K. Digby, though pretending some other business ". Lord Byron added that, when he had been " in England, something to this purpose was propounded by the Independent party to the Recusants ".

On 3rd March, Nicholas wrote * to Ormonde from Caen, enclosing a letter which he had received from a Catholic doctor of the name of Winsted, living at Rouen, dated 7th February. The portion of this letter referring to Sir Kenelm ran as follows :—†

" Tuesday last arrived here Sir Kenelme Digby from Paris, with divers young gentlemen in his company, only there was a wry-necked fellow amongst them which Sir Kenelme commended to my acquaintance and care as being, he said, in a consumption, and for that cure had changed the air and come into France, but was now going into England with an intention to return within sixteen or twenty

* *Ormonde Letters*, by Thos. Carte, ed. 1739, vol. i., p. 219.
† *Ib.*, p. 220.

days, and then would stay here, or go into Languedoc for his health. Feeling his hand and pulse I assured him he was in no consumption nor never had been. Afterwards I perceived that this was but a pretence, and that he was an agent for that accursed crew, his name Watson, Scout-master to the rebels."

Here we have Watson again, and be it observed that that faithful cavalier and courtier, Sir Kenelm, had gone to Rouen in this queer company within a week of the murder of his beloved master.

" I spake freely my mind of the murther," continued the doctor, and the " judgment that was made here by the French ; his answer [Sir Kenelm's] was, that the French abhorred the fact in general. I spared no curses, for I assure myself it is no sin to curse the enemies of God and my King. I asked Sir Kenelm Digby why he would go now into England considering the abomination of that country ; his answer was, that he had not any means to subsist longer, and if he went not now he must starve. I answered it was the better choice to die, if he remembered the obligation that he owed to the Queen-Regent of France,* who took him from those who would have destroyed him. He answered that the Queen-Regent knew of his going, and that he had the King of France's pass, and would return again suddenly." And presently the writer stated that Sir Kenelm Digby was employed as agent in a plot " to treat with those horrid rebels, the Independents of England," for " the subversion of hereditary monarchy there, and to make it elective, and to establish Popery there, and to give tolera-tion to all manner of religions except that of the Church of England ".

In enclosing this letter, Nicholas told Ormonde that he was " jealous that Walsingham, who is lately gone hence for Ireland, is sent to acquaint the Catholics in that king-

---

* This again favours the theory that it was Anne of Austria and not Marie de Medici who obtained Sir Kenelm's release.

dom with the design, and to feel how they like it ; for he did here speak much against the Papists endeavouring to join with the rebels in England, and seemed to be very sorry that Sir Kenelme Digby had a hand in it, which is like other of his small politics ".

On 3rd May Nicholas again wrote to Ormonde :—*

" I hear Sir Kenelme Digby, having been long at Dieppe for intelligence upon a design I formerly advertised your excellency, is now resolved rather to go for Ireland, where he hopes to do much for the Catholic cause, there being others in England sufficient without him to effect the same there ". And he adds that " the Pope's Nuncio and Worcester are laying their heads together at Rouen ".

A reader of the letters here quoted may feel inclined to say : This plot which manifested itself, according to your authorities, within a few days of King Charles's death, must have been hatching for some time before it. Certainly, this was the case ; though there is no reason for supposing Sir Kenelm to have joined in it until after the death of his royal master. There had been great dissatisfaction among the English Catholics at the conduct of the king. In spite of the large sum collected for his army by Sir Kenelm Digby and Montague among the Catholics of England, Charles had allowed them to be persecuted, in order to please the parliamentary party. In the discontented condition of the Catholics, the Independents perceived their opportunity, as the following statements of a contemporary Royalist will explain :—†

" The king had offended the Papists in the last Treaty, by granting so much to the parliament for their suppression. The Independents perceiving it, and willing to joyn with any interest to make good their designe, it was proposed at the Councill," etc., " *that the Papists do raise and pay*

* *Ormonde Letters*, by Thos. Carte, ed. 1739, vol. i., p. 272.

† *The History of Independency*. " Printed in the yeare 1648." By Walker, part ii., p. 150.

about 10,000 *additional Forces for this Army, in recompense whereof, all penall Lawes concerning them to be repealed, all Taxes and Contributions taken off, and they to have the protection of this Parliament and Army*". And, after saying that " Owen Roe Oneale, that commanded the bloody party of Massacring Irish," "O'Really, the Pope's Irish Nuncio," and Sir John Wynter were enlisted into the plot, the writer added that " to the regret of the country, *Sir Kenelme Digby* had a Pass to come into England, and came ". " Wherefore," he asked, were " *Sir John Winter* and *Sir Kenelme Digby* sent for over . . . but to drive on treaties of Association of this nature? insomuch that long since it was whispered among *Cromwell's* party in *England* (to uphold their spirits) *that upon his shewing himselfe in armes in Ireland, Ormonds Catholique Irish party would all forsake him and go over to O'Neale, who maintained the Pope's interest in that kingdome*".

A secular priest, named Thomas White,* a very intimate friend of Sir Kenelm Digby, published a work entitled *The Grounds of Obedience and Government*, in which he upheld the theory that, by the misconduct of the civil magistrate, the people were released from obedience, but that when once a ruler is deposed, equally when unjustly as when justly, it may be advisable and right to acquiesce in his removal, instead of attempting his restoration. Judging from the great intimacy which existed between this author †️ and Sir Kenelm Digby, coupled with the actions of the latter, it seems likely that Sir Kenelm may have agreed with the theories expressed in this book.

---

* Lingard's *Hist. Eng.*, vol. viii., chap. iv.

† Thomas White was the son of Richard White of Hutton, by Mary, daughter of Edmund Plowden, a great lawyer of the reign of Elizabeth. " Hobbes," says Wood, " had a great Respect for him . . . and would often visit him." They " seldom parted in cool blood: for they would wrangle, squabble and scold about philosophical matters like young sophisters, though either of them was eighty years of age ". White died at the age of ninety-four in 1676. See *Ath. Ox.*, vol. ii., p. 665.

Father White acted as a sort of Boswell to Sir Kenelm Digby, and for a considerable time lived in his house.* He wrote a Latin book, the title of which, translated into English, is *Institution of the Peripatetic Philosophy, according to the Hypothesis of the great and celebrated Philosopher Sir Kenelme Digby.* This book was put on the " Index Expurgatorius " at Rome, which was no great compliment to Sir Kenelm's orthodoxy from a Catholic point of view. Father White also wrote two other Latin books, *A Theological Question, in what Manner according to the Principles of Sir Kenelme Digby's Peripatetic Philosophy, or according to Reason, abstracting, as much as the Subject will admit, from Authority, the Freedom of a Man's Will, is to be explained and reconciled with Efficacious Grace,* and also *Institutions of Divinity, built upon the Foundations laid down in Sir K. Digby's Peripatetic Philosophy.* Father White wrote several other works, of which three received notice at Rome by being placed on the " Index ". Curiously enough one of them was publicly censured by a very different authority, the Puritanical English House of Commons.

A student of Sir Kenelm's life should not be too hasty in condemning him for temporising with his master's enemies. It is just possible that his conduct in that affair may have been more justified than is commonly supposed ; for Sir Harris Nicholas says : † " All his biographers admit that he was well received at Court [the Court of Charles II. after the Restoration], notwithstanding his conduct towards Cromwell was far from being a secret, a fact which powerfully supports the opinion that his real designs were not so inimical to the monarchical interest as has been supposed ". I shall have occasion later to show that at least one of his contemporaries doubted his warm reception at Court ; but, on the whole, evidence is in favour of Sir Harris's statement.

* *Biog. Brit.,* editn. Kippis, vol. v., p. 198.
† Introduction to *Priv. Mem.,* K. D., pp. lxxiv.-v.

If Sir Kenelm thought it right to attempt to make terms with the murderers of his much-loved monarch, how, it may be asked, could he at the same time justify his tenure of an office in the household of that monarch's widowed queen?

To what extent, if at all, he took his royal mistress into his confidence is doubtful, but, considering that his negotiations with Cromwell and the Independents became well known, it is remarkable that Henrietta Maria never dismissed him from her service. This looks as if she must have thought his conduct, at the very least, pardonable. To some extent, like Sir Kenelm Digby, she had given up hope of a restoration. When, in the autumn of 1649, her son, afterwards Charles II., announced his intention of going to Scotland or Ireland to attempt to recover his throne, she strongly opposed it ; * when Sir Edward Hyde proposed to go to Spain to beg for help against the English regicides, she declared that it would be waste of time ; † when she found that, in spite of her remonstrances, her son persisted in his design of venturing into his lost dominions, she begged Lord Jermyn to dissuade him from doing so, and to represent the dangers which would await him in the three kingdoms. It may be, therefore, that she believed the position to be quite hopeless ; and thought it would be better for the Catholics to come to some terms with the revolutionists ; although she may not have realised that those terms would include the subversion of hereditary monarchy.

Lord Holles published a pamphlet ‡ addressed to Cromwell in which he wrote : " Your private negotiations with the Pope, and your promises that, as soon as you can establish your own greatness, you will protect the Catho-

* Strickland's *Queens of England*, vol. viii., pp. 188-190.
† *Life of Clarendon*, vol. i., p. 262.
‡ *A Letter from a True and Lawful Member of Parliament*, etc., London, 1656, p. 58. *Biog. Brit.*, vol. iii., p. 1710.

licks, and the insinuations that you will countenance them much farther, are sufficiently known and understood, and of their dependance upon, and devotion to, you, there needs no evidence beyond the book lately written by Mr. White [the work referred to above], a Romish priest, and delivered to your favourite Sir Kenelme Digby," etc.

Prynne again says* of Cromwell "that Sir Kenelme Digby was his particular favourite, and lodged him at Whitehall". Prynne is not a very trustworthy authority; but he may have told the truth in this instance.

In the Council of State,† 17th August, 1649, an inquiry was made concerning Sir Kenelm's having left the kingdom and returned, and an order was made to send for him and examine him. On the 30th of the same month‡ an order was made in the Council " To report to the House that Sir Kenelm Digby, a dangerous man, is now in England without leave, and to desire their pleasure concerning him ". Evidently all the parliamentary party were not so well disposed towards Sir Kenelm as was Oliver Cromwell. The next day there was an "Order in Parliament §—on Col. Purefoy's report from the Council of State, that Sir Jno. Winter, Sir Kenelm Digby, and Sir Walter Montague are here without leave, and being conceived dangerous persons, they desire the House to declare their pleasure concerning them ".

Lingard states‖ that the authorities perceived the dangers of the proposed compact with the Catholics, "and after some time, to blind perhaps the eyes of the people, severe votes were passed against [Sir Kenelm]

---

* *True and Perfect Narrative*, etc., London, 1659, p. 57. *Biog. Brit.*, vol. iii., p. 1710.

† *S. P. Dom.*, 1649, vol. ii., No. 80.

‡ *Ib.*, No. 91.

§ *Cal. Sta. Pa. Dom.*, 1649, p. 295.

‖ *Hist. Eng.*, vol. viii., chap. iv.

Digby, Montague, and Winter, and orders were given for the apprehension of priests and Jesuits ".

Although again exiled, Sir Kenelm appears still to have had hopes that the negotiations would be reopened. At any rate, about ten weeks later, he was at Calais, expecting to return to England, as the following characteristic letter, probably to his friend Lord Conway, will show :—

" Now * that the Protestant Church is grown invisible again, I cannot hear with patience of imputative righteousness. Pray allow me to believe not your justice but your mercy to me, and to profess myself your most obliged. Those innocent recreations you mention, of tabors and pipes, and dancing ladies, and convenient country houses, shady walks and close arbours, make me sigh to be again a spectator of them, and to be again in little England, where time slides more gently away than in any part of the world. *Quando sia mai, ch'a rivederti io torni?* Instead of your smiling English sky [our ' smiling English sky ' in November is surely a very liberal poetical license !] I am here weatherbeaten with winter storms ; for your smooth well-natured ladies, we see nothing but rough-hided, savage sea-calves ; for your delicious wine and curious fruit, our diet is red puddle beer—made of brackish water, and wood-dried malt—the flesh of seals, porpoises, etc., dressed with whale oil, and our bread is made of tainted rye, fished out of wrecked Holland hulks cast away upon these sands." " Send your letter for me to my servant John Lee, at Gresham College, or to the post house, directed, ' A Monsieur le Chevalier Digby, a Calais '; it will find me, if no curious overseer of the packets at the post break it open for the superscription's sake. But I hope I am now thought so innocent that neither my commerce will be suspected, nor my person interdicted. I desire liberty of return, for no one thing in the world than to have the comfort of waiting continually upon you."

* S. P. *Dom.*, vol. iii., No. 55, 1649, 6th November.

For the next few years Sir Kenelm was unable to meddle in English politics, and he remained abroad, watching events, and nominally, if not actually, Chancellor to Queen Henrietta Maria. It is not unlikely that he may have considered his advances to the parliamentary party fully justified when he heard that Charles II. had signed a treaty, binding himself* "never to permit the free exercise of the Catholic religion in Ireland". Meanwhile the future king of England's attempts to reconquer his father's kingdom were very unsuccessful, and in 1651, having met with the defeat which his mother had foretold, Charles fled from England and returned to France.

In 1653 Cromwell dissolved the parliament and was proclaimed Protector.

On 16th January, 1654, Hyde † wrote to Clement, that "as soon as assurance came of Cromwell assuming the sole power, Sir Kenelm Digby went privately from Paris to England ; it is generally believed that he long held correspondence with Cromwell, and " had "done him good offices in Paris, but Hyde is unwilling to think it possible". I may mention, in passing, that it was in this same year, 1654, that Sir Kenelm's English translation, *A Treatise of Adhering to God*, from the Latin of Albertus Magnus, was published.‡

It is pretty certain that Sir Kenelm Digby was well received by Cromwell, who was greatly taken with him, and his stay in England must have been of considerable length ; for, in November, 1654, he wrote a letter from his own home at Gothurst. This letter may be worth notice as showing that his political intrigues did not make him forgetful of "letters". §   It was written to Dr. Gerard Langbaine, Provost of Queen's College and Keeper of

---

* Lingard, viii., chap. iv.
† *Calendar of Clarendon S. P.*, vol. ii., p. 302.
‡ Chalmers' *Biographical Dic.*, vols. xi.-xii., p. 76.
§ Aubrey's *Letters*, vol. i., p. 1 *seq.*

the University Archives ; and it concerned his donation of manuscripts to the Bodleian Library. He stated that he had already expressed his wishes, " one main one whereof was, that whensoever a deserving person desired to make use of any of the books I gave (especially for printing them), they to whom the care of the library was committed might pleasure him by the loan thereof : such person giving them satisfaction for the restitution of the book in due time ".

In 1656 Sir Kenelm returned to Paris ; and, soon after reaching it, he wrote the following letter, which leaves no kind of doubt as to his friendly relations with Oliver Cromwell :—

" Sir Kenelm Digby * to Secretary Thurloe.

" Paris, Mar. 18, 1656.

" Right Honourable,

" The French Ambassador taking leave of me yesterday told me, that his Secretary at London had, among other things, written to him, that Sir Robert Welsh had spoken something to your Honour much to my prejudice, and that since some letter of a Lady to me had been intercepted, the contents whereof did in some sort make good what he had spoken, I believe your Honour hath so good information what this woful knight is, that if there was nothing but the venom that his malicious tongue can spit, I should not think it needful to trouble myself, much less your Honour's more serious occasions, with taking notice of it. But since he hath contrived, as I verily believe, some better name than his own, to seem to justify what would have no credence from him, I may not sit down without beseeching your Honour to search the matter to the bottom, and to drive it to the utmost. I look upon this as a contriving of his, because forging of

* *Biog. Brit.*, vol. iii., pp. 1710-11.

letters, and doing treacheries of this kind, hath been his
ordinary course, and because I am confident that nobody
in the world, who hath so much familiarity with me as
to write to me, but knoweth me so well, as to be sure that
whatsoever may be disliked by my Lord Protector and the
Council of State, must be detested by me. My obligations to his Highness are so great, that it would be a crime
in me to behave myself so negligently as to give any
cause for the least suspicion, or to do anything that might
require an excuse or apology. I make it my business
everywhere, to have all the world take notice how highly
I esteem myself obliged to his Highness, and how
passionate I am for his service, and for his honour, and
interests, even to the exposing my life for them.* If
your Honour cannot readily find out the bottom of this
villainy plotted against me upon notice of so much, I will
take post the next day to return to London (though it
may be much to the prejudice of my domestick affairs,
in my broken estate, because my debts are not yet
quieted) and I doubt not but I shall soon make discovery
of some wicked treachery intended against me; for this
wretched creature hath as much malice to me as he is
capable of, first, as being an Irish Papist (whose whole
tribe have an implacable animosity against me), and next,
because I have heretofore shamed him, and have broken
some cheating designs of his by making publick some of
his infamous villainies, for which he never durst make
any expostulation with me. I humbly crave pardon with
your Honour for suffering myself to be thus far transported.
My excuse is, that I should think my heart were not an
honest one, if the blood about it were not warmed with
any the least imputation upon my respects and duty to
his Highness, to whom I owe so much. I humbly crave

* He had already fought one duel for the honour of Charles I. He
now seems to have been ready to fight one for that of Cromwell.

a line or two from your Honour, that I may either resolve to return presently home, or remain satisfied by your having discovered the villainy attempted against me, which, with all humility, expecting, I rest,

> " Your Honour's Most Humble
>
> " and Most Obedient servant," etc.

I am indebted to the courtesy and kindness of Professor Gardiner for the following information respecting Sir Kenelm Digby's negotiations with the Protector : " What the entries in Bordeaux's despatches show is that Sir Kenelm in the spring of 1654, when Cromwell was almost making up his mind in favour of the Spanish Alliance, was urging the claims of France with the Protector, and at one time elicited from Cromwell an asseveration that he wished well to France. The question of Cromwell's position in those days is one of exceeding difficulty."

Professor Gardiner quoted letters written by Bordeaux, stating that he had been informed by Sir Kenelm Digby that, from a conversation with Cromwell, he understood the Protector's sentiments to be friendly to France, and that the extensive naval preparations which he was then making had not been undertaken with any hostile intentions towards that country. This is very important, as it makes it possible that Sir Kenelm's notorious negotiations and intimacy with Cromwell may have been very much more on behalf of the French Government than of the English Catholics, which would place his conduct in a different light.

CHAPTER XXVII

OLIVER CROMWELL.

BEFORE he left England Sir Kenelm had found time to interest himself in science. Samuel Hartlib, the agriculturist, in a letter to Boyle,* writes (8th May, 1654) : " A great abbot in *France*, intimately corresponding with *Sir K. Digby*, is said to have other furnaces than any of *Glauber's*, which will be erected, ere long, amongst ourselves, to prosecute really philosophical studies ". Further on he said : " I suppose you have heard how that Sir *Kenelm* is in very good favour with the lord protector ; his sequestration is taken off, and as soon as he hath gotten his lands into his own possession (which will be suddenly) he speaks of engaging six or seven hundred pounds for his own part in the foresaid laboratory, besides some other friends, which he can procure ". And again : " Sir *Kenelm* commends hugely the medicine of the *virga aurea*, which *Barcleius* in his *Euphormio* hath so remarkably discovered to the world," etc.

In another letter † (15th May, 1654) Hartlib writes : " Sr *K. D.*, of whom I have written so largely in my last, being yesterday morning with me at my own house, and pressing most earnestly the accepting of his generous offers towards my son (for a plentiful provision of himself and family for two years, with the furnishing of a complete laboratory)," etc. When, however, Hartlib told this to a friend and consulted him upon the matter, he replied : " *Timeo Danaos sua dona ferentes* ". " For whether his

* *Boyle's Works*, vol. v., p. 263. ‡ *Ib.*, p. 265.

estate will suffer him to contribute little or much for the carrying on of all our physical and chemical affairs and designs, he alone is to be entrusted with a full and entire communication of them." That is to say, Sir Kenelm was to have the exclusive advantage of all the discoveries. "He said, indeed, that Sir K. was as gallant a gentleman as ever he met withal, but yet he could discern rather gallantry than goodness in the frame of his spirit, and of all his actions." He further proves Sir Kenelm's interest in men of science by stating that he had "specially recommended unto" him a Captain Sanderson, "a very pretty gentleman, full of good arts and contrivances," whose "main design" was "by a new experiment or ferment to make as much saltpetre as you please out of salt or sea-water".

To return to the matter of what Hartlib terms Sir Kenelm's "good favour with the lord protector," it has been so much the custom to represent Oliver Cromwell as above all things a man of narrow, sectarian pietism, that his position towards Catholics has been to some extent misunderstood. What religion Cromwell had was of the broadest description. Himself an Independent, he allowed the Presbyterians, Manton, Baxter and Calamy, to pray, preach, or advise, at his Court and his State functions. He received and held intimate intercourse with several Episcopalian bishops ; he gave a pension to John Biddle, the father of English Unitarianism ; he selected certain men of very latitudinarian views as his chaplains ; he even favoured a plan for giving an asylum to Jews in this country ; and, hateful as the religion of Catholics was to him, he was accused by Prynne of suspending " penal laws against Romish priests," and " of protecting several of them under his hand and seal ".*

Paxton Hood in his life of Cromwell, after giving in-

* *Oliver Cromwell*, by William Hazlitt, pp. 316-317.

stances of his toleration in religious matters, says : * " Even Sir Kenelm Digby, Royalist as he was, found himself at the Protector's table, who, no doubt, enjoyed the mystical wanderings of his mind, and certainly did honour to his literary merits ".

Shortly after writing the letter to Thurloe quoted in the last chapter, Sir Kenelm left Paris and went to Toulouse, if we may judge from the fact that a letter † was addressed to him there about three months later.

Besides his schemes for concluding a give-and-take treaty between the Catholics and Cromwell, Sir Kenelm had a purely personal object to negotiate, if possible, with the Protector's Government. This was the repayment of the money which he had spent in redeeming captives when at Algiers, as appears by a State Paper ‡ to be noticed by-and-by.

Although Sir Kenelm remained Chancellor to Queen Henrietta Maria, there are few records of his having been in her company during the years in which he was attempting to negotiate with her late husband's enemies. So early as 1650 she sent another emissary to Rome to endeavour to enlist the interests of the Holy Father on behalf of her son.§ On the 24th of June, Robert Meynell wrote from Rome to Cottington and Hyde that " Daniel O'Delly, an Irish Dominican, has come to Rome with a commission from the Queen to treat with the Pope : he was formerly at Lisbon, where he did many good offices for the late King; was with the present King at Jersey, and came from him extremely satisfied. Meynell has given him an account of Sir Kenelm Digby's proceedings at Rome, that he may avoid the rocks Sir Kenelm has touched upon."

* *Oliver Cromwell*, by P. Hood, p. 300.

† *Biog. Brit.*, vol. iii., p. 1711, footnote N.

‡ *S. P. Dom. Charles II.*, vol. xlv., No. 19.

§ *Calendar of the Clarendon State Papers*, vol. ii., p. 66.

And then he adds that "there is small hope of effecting anything at Rome, as the Queen's authority is much on the wane there".

If it be just possible that Queen Henrietta Maria may have connived at Sir Kenelm's overtures to the Independents and the Parliament, it is more likely that the queen-mother of France may have given them some encouragement. As we have seen, she may have assisted in obtaining his release from Winchester House, and he was evidently a favourite of hers. In 1657, after Sir Kenelm had returned to Paris, he took a letter from Cardinal Mazarin to Lockhart in Paris, making a humble suit to Cromwell's Government on behalf of his friend Montague,* "and the Queen of France sent to the same purpose". Perhaps her own troubles with *La Fronde* had made her respect the power of insurrectionists in other countries. But a personal motive may have been more potent in inducing her to keep her English friends on good terms with Cromwell. She was anxious for the support of England against her enemies, and the strangest of Cardinals was exercising his diplomatic powers to that end.

Sir Kenelm seems to have continued to be more or less of a correspondent with Cromwell, and to have been on good terms with Cardinal Mazarin ; for in September or October, 1657, Sir Robert Walsh, on being liberated from the Bastille,† "offered his service to Cromwell, to whom, however, Sir Kenelm Digby and Cardinal Mazarin wrote 'very invectively' against him ".

According to Lodge,‡ for the next two or three years Sir Kenelm "travelled through France and Germany, fixing his residence occasionally for long intervals in different cities, and collecting and bestowing treasure in every branch of science ". It was during this period that he was called,

---

* *Calendar of the Clarendon State Papers*, vol. ii., p. 390.
† *Ib.*, p. 356.
‡ *Portraits*, vol. v., p. 154.

by Dr. Stubbes, "The Pliny of our Age for lying,"* for
having sent to a friend in England a story which he had
received from Mr. Fitton, Librarian to the Grand Duke of
Florence.   It was to the effect that " a city in *Barbary*
under the King of Tripoly " † was turned into stone in a very
few hours by a petrifying vapour that fell upon the place,
that is, Men, Beasts, Trees, Houses, Utensils, etc., everything remaining in the same posture, as "Children at their
Mothers' Breasts," etc.   This "strange accident, being
look'd upon as the great wonder of the world," says Wood,
" was put into the common newsbook of that time called
Mercurius Politicus".   A footnote in the *Biographia
Britannica* ‡ defends Sir Kenelm on the ground that so late
as 1713, a paper was read before the Royal Society by Mr.
Baker, the English Consul at Tripoli, who stated that " about
forty days' journey S.E. from Tripoli, and about seven
days' journey from the nearest sea-coast, there is a place
called Ongila, in which there are found the bodies of men,
women, and children, beasts and plants, all petrified of a
hard stone like marble ".

If less severe upon him than Stubbes, Robert Boyle,§ a
man like Sir Kenelm himself, of good family, who devoted
himself to philosophy, chemistry, and theology, and
became one of the first members of the Royal Society,
does not seem to have held his brother philosopher's
opinions in very high esteem.   In a letter ‖ about the
penetrability of glass, he writes : "As for the authority of
Sir *K. Digby*, I am glad my censurer has so much deference
for it, since that famous knight relates, that he had made
quicksilver pass in small drops through glass itself ; which,
if true, will quite destroy *P. Cherubius'* denial of the porosity

* *Animadversions upon Glanville's Plus Ultra*, p. 161.
† *Ath. Ox.*, vol. ii., p. 351.
‡ Vol. iii., p. 1711.
§ He was the seventh son of the first Earl of Cork.
‖ *Boyle's Works*, vol. v., p. 233.

of glass; but, for a reason I have elsewhere declared, I will lay no weight on this," etc.

In 1658 Sir Kenelm's attempted negotiations with Oliver Cromwell were brought to an end by the death of the Protector. Then followed the short Protectorate of his son Richard, and I can find no record of any attempt on the part of Sir Kenelm to enter into relations with Cromwell's son and successor.

He spent some time at Montpelier in the south of France, where there was at that time a literary coterie, and it was there that he read his celebrated paper upon the Sympathetic Powder, referred to in an early chapter. He may have found congenial companions among the professors of the university, and the views which the neighbourhood of Montpelier commands of the Mediterranean, the Pyrenees, and the Cevennes would render it a delightful temporary residence to a man of his tastes. But he went there also for another reason. His health was beginning to fail. Although not yet an old man—he was fifty-four—he was the victim of an incurable disease,* and in those days the climate of Montpelier was strongly recommended to invalids.

About the time of the death of Oliver Cromwell, Sir Kenelm was in Germany. Algernon Sydney wrote to Leicester † from Frankfort-upon-Main : " I was yesterday informed by some persons of quality, that Sir *Kenelme Digby* had bin heare for many months, and went hence about a Yeare since. He went under the name of Earle *Digby*, Admirall of the *British* seas, and Chancellor to the Queene of *England*, beaten out of his Country with the rest of the King's Party, of which he had bin. He caused his Book *de Corporibus* or *de Immortalitate animae*, and some others, to be heare printed, and pretended to be the first

---

* Calculus.

† *Sydney State Papers*, vol. ii., p. 698. Some writers discredit the following evidence, but it ought to be given for what it is worth.

inventor of the Sympatheticall Powder, and magneticke
Cures of Wounds and Diseases. When he went from that
Towne, he tooke upon him another Personage, and passing
through Places in Alliance with *Sweden*, pretended to be
an Ambassador of that Crowne into *England*, and was
believed, untill one of the Counts of *Lionhead*, a Man of
one of the principall Familyes in *Sweden*, whoe lyes now
in this House, and told me the Story, did rectify the
Mistake, informing them that the King of *Sweden* did use
neither to imploy Strangers nor Papists in Embassyes."

At the date of the restoration of Charles II., Sir Kenelm
had returned to Paris, where he appears to have entirely
abandoned political, diplomatic, and even Court life, and
to have devoted his whole attention to literature and
science. In a letter dated "Paris, Mar. 20, 1660,"
Oldenburgh, afterwards Secretary to the Royal Society,
wrote to Boyle * that he met Sir Kenelm "at the house of
a Chemist, where the question was agitated about the
dissolvent of gold, whether the universal spirit of the world,
in its undetermined nature, or, as it is specified, and contracted to a mineral, be the menstruum of that noble metal?"
Sir Kenelm did not "determine the question"; but, in the
course of his conversation on the subject, he made some
statements which "did ravish the hearers to admiration".
One was that when the lead which had covered the roof of
a royal palace in England "for five or six ages" was sold,
three-fourths of it was found to be silver; another was that,
"at a place called Arcueil" in France, there was "a fixed
salt," "which salt being for some time exposed to the
sun beams, became saltpetre, then vitriol, then lead, tin,
copper, silver, and, at the end of fourteen months, gold;
which he assured to have experienced himself, and another
able Naturalist besides him".

Private as had been his life of late, Sir Kenelm had

* *Boyle's Works*, vol. v., p. 302.

not given up all idea or hope of obtaining some employment under the Government of Charles II. ; for, in July,
1660, he wrote * to Secretary Nicholas that the queen had
promised him leave to return to England very shortly, and
that he would then explain to him his claim to the office of
" Ballastage " throughout England, an appointment which
had never yet been held by any one.

In 1661 Sir Kenelm returned to England, where he
seems to have established himself at his London home,
"the last fair house westward in the North portico of
Covent Garden ".†

Besides a wish to be in his native land, Sir Kenelm had
a desire to obtain repayment of the sums which he had
expended in redeeming captives at Algiers during his
voyage to the Mediterranean, some thirty-three years
earlier. On the 6th of December, 1661, a warrant was
issued, says Mrs. Everett Green in her summary of a
State Paper,‡ " for a grant to Sir Kenelm (Digby) of bonds
for £12,000, £2000, and £300, entered into by John
Langley and Wm. Williams, with the late pretended
powers, for disposal of certain sums entrusted to them for
redemption of captives from Algiers, Sir Kenelm having
expended £1650 in 1628 in redeeming captives from
Algiers at his own cost ".

Very possibly this may be correct ; but I confess that
the State Paper in question § seems to me difficult to
interpret as to the exact sum to be paid to Sir Kenelm.
This, however, it makes clear, that, in the days of "the
then pretended Oliver Lord Protector," the men mentioned
" did become bond," in a "penall sume " to repay Sir
Kenelm his losses ; because, in the year 1628, he had
redeemed "all the captives being then in slavery in

---

* S. P. Dom. Charles II., vol. vi., No. 208.

† Aubrey's Letters.

‡ Cal. Sta. Pap., 1661-2, p. 170.

§ S. P. Dom. Charles II., vol. xlv., No. 19.

Algiers amounting unto the sume of 1650*l.*, which said sume he then burrowed att interest for the effecting so good and charitable a worke and hath ever since paid interest for the same and as yett hath had noe repayment or satisfaction of the same or any part thereof out of any dutyes imposed or raised to that purpose in any of the times of the late Usurper's or any otherwaies as hath appeared unto us by the certificate from our attorney generall," etc.   It will be observed that nothing is said of all the years in which Charles II.'s sainted father had neglected to give Sir Kenelm "repayment or satisfaction ".

Soon after his return to England, Sir Kenelm became interested in a scheme which was much to his taste, namely, the founding of the Royal Society.   Although that society was not incorporated until 1663, it appears to have been in course of formation for some time previously, and many informal meetings of the future members were probably held before its regular institution.   According to Wood,* Sir Kenelm's *Discourse Concerning the Vegetation of Plants* was "spoken on the 23rd of Jan., 1660, in a large meeting of the *Royal Society* in *Gresham* Coll.".   This "discourse" was published in London in October, 1661.   When the Royal Society was regularly established, Sir Kenelm was appointed a member of its council,† and "as long as his health would permit, he attended the meetings," ‡ and "gave his assistance towards the improvements that were then made in useful knowledge ".

For the remainder of his life as it would seem, he almost completely dropped out of court and political circles, and fell to frequenting men of learning.   At his house in Covent Garden he endeavoured to establish a literary *salon* after the fashion already prevailing in France,

---

* *Ath. Ox.*, vol. ii., p. 353.
† Chalmers' *Biog. Dict.*, vol. xi., p. 76.
‡ *Biog. Brit.*, vol. iii., p. 1712.

and it became a *rendezvous* of mathematicians, chemists, philosophers, and authors.*

It is curious that, when he had made letters almost his sole employment, and was living chiefly among literary men, he should not have sent for his valuable library from France, whither it had been transported at the first outbreak of the troubles preceding the rebellion. He chose, however, to leave it where it was, with the result that, at his death, it became the property of the Crown of France,† "according to that branch of the prerogative which the French stile *Droit d'Aubain*". It was afterwards sold (and it is very probable below its real value) "for ten thousand crowns".

In 1663 Sir Kenelm's son, John, together with his relative, the Earl of Bristol, was indicted ‡ at the Old Bailey, for recusancy. Perhaps it may have been in consequence of this indictment that he determined to go abroad for a time. Some seven months later (in April, 1664) he was given a "Pass § to go, with his wife, servants and sixteen horses, into France".

Although details on the subject are exceedingly meagre, it may be that Sir Kenelm's withdrawal from Court life was not altogether of his own choosing ; for in January, 1664, Clifford ‖ wrote from Ugbrooke to Williamson, stating that he had heard that Sir Kenelm Digby had been forbidden to appear at Court, and begging to know the reason. Considering the overtures which he had made to Cromwell and the Roundheads, almost as soon as the breath was out of his dear king's body, one would be more inclined to wish "to know the reason" why he ever was allowed to "appear" at all at the Court of Charles II.

---

* See Appendix F.
† *Biog. Brit.*, vol. iii., p. 1713.
‡ *S. P. Dom. Charles II.*, vol. lxxx., No. 9.
§ *Ib.*, vol. xcvi., No. 53.
‖ *Ib.*, vol. xc., No. 36.

He continued to hold the office of chancellor to Queen Henrietta Maria to the end. To what extent he had any management of her affairs I cannot find out. Her lord chamberlain, the Earl of St. Albans, to whom scandal-mongers declared she was secretly married, is said to have had the control of her revenues.* Most of her dower lands had been divided among the regicides; but at the restoration the parliament granted her £30,000 a year in compensation, and to this her son, the king, added a like income as a pension from the exchequer.†

A State Paper of July, 1664,‡ consists of an "Indenture between Queen Henrietta Maria and Henry, Earl of St. Albans, her chamberlain, Sir Kenelm Digby, her chancellor, and others, her trustees, on the one part, and Sir Cyril Wych of London, on the other, whereby the queen and her trustees grant to the latter and to Hen. Gay of Westminster all reliefs due or to be due to her Majesty from her jointure bonds, for twenty-one years, on rental of £6 13s. 4d.".§

In 1664 the health of Henrietta Maria was visibly failing, but that of her chancellor was in an even worse condition. Frequent attacks of his very distressing malady reduced "him to a state of extreme weakness".‖

In January, 1665, he intended to go to Paris, either to see old friends there, to fetch his books, or to endeavour to obtain some relief from his bodily sufferings; but he became too ill to undertake the journey, and he was soon a complete invalid. After some months of great pain he was seized with a violent paroxysm on the 11th of June, 1665, and his

* Strickland's *Lives of the Queens of England*, vol. viii., p. 234.
† *Ib.*
‡ *S. P. Dom. Charles II.*, vol. c., No. 92.
§ *Cal. Sta. Pa. Dom.*, 1663-4, p. 648.
‖ Lodge's *Portraits*, vol. v., p. 157.

varied and eccentric life was brought to a close at the age
of sixty-two.*

His body was laid in the gorgeous sepulchre prepared
for it, beside that of his wife, and his epitaph was written
by Ferrar :—

> Under this tomb the matchless Digby lies,
> Digby the great, the valiant, and the wise;
> This age's wonder for his noble parts,
> Skilled in six tongues and learned in all the arts.
> Born on the day he died, the eleventh of June,
> And that day bravely fought at Scanderoon.
> It's rare that one and the same day should be
> His day of birth, of death, of victory !

* " What by reason of the civil wars, and his generous mind, he contracted great debts ; and, I know not how, there being a great falling out
between him and his then only son, John, he settled his estate upon Corn-
walleys, a subtle solicitor "—evidently as trustee—" and also a member of
the House of Commons, who did put Mr. John Digby to much charge in
law ". Aubrey's *Letters*, vol. ii., Appendix. John Digby, says Lodge
(*Portraits*, vol. v., p. 157), " certainly inherited, though under many disadvantages and vexations, the most part of his father's estates. In him the
male line of his branch of the Digbies became extinct, for he had by his
wife, Margaret, daughter of Sir Edward Longueville, of Wolverton, in
Bucks "—Wolverton was but five miles from Gothurst—" two daughters
only, Margaret Maria, married to Sir John Conway, of Bodey [Bodryddan],
in Flintshire, and Charlotte Theophila, to Richard Mostyn, of Penbeddw,
in the same county ". The issue of the younger of them is now extinct ;
but the elder (Lady Conway) left one son and one daughter, who became
the ancestors of all the descendants of Sir Kenelm Digby now living. The
son left a sole heiress, who married Sir John Glynne ; the daughter married
Sir Thomas Longueville.

CHAPTER XXVIII.

EPILOGUE.

AFTER recording the death of Sir Kenelm Digby, ought his biographer to claim that thereby the world lost a philosopher, a politician, a diplomatist, and a theologian, who acted on the motto which he had inscribed on one of his portraits :* " *Saber morir la mayor hazana* " [" To know how to die is the greater achievement "], or should he exclaim in the words of the dying actor : " Drop the curtain, the farce is ended " ? The answer to this question requires some consideration ; nor do I think that it is necessary to accept either of these alternatives.

The chief difficulty in forming a correct judgment of the character of Sir Kenelm Digby lies in the unsatisfactory nature of a great deal of the evidence concerning him. He was enough of a celebrity to be much talked about and much written about ; he was not sufficiently celebrated to be the subject of records giving a deep insight into his actions or his motives. His charming manners on the one hand, and his affectation on the other, had the effect of gaining him many ardent admirers and also many bitter enemies, and the exaggerated testimonies due to both impressions must be accepted with reserve. Again, one of the most often-quoted authorities on his life and character, John Aubrey, was a garrulous, gossiping, scandalmonger-

* See right hand upper corner of the illustration giving portrait of Sir K. D. in later life.

ing sort of witness, whose evidence must only be taken *cum grano salis.* Then, with regard to Sir Kenelm himself, without going so far as to say with Dr. Stubbes that " he was the Pliny of" his " Age for lying," I cannot deny that there is a great deal in his *Private Memoirs,* especially in the so-called "Castrations," which has a very decided air of fiction, if not of deliberate untruth. Yet it is only fair to remember that these memoirs were ostensibly written for the amusement of his wife. Even the names are unreal, and, although the story is mainly that of himself and Lady Digby, he may possibly have told her that he had worked it up into a romance in which he gave himself license to imagine what might conceivably have happened under similar circumstances, rather than that he had accurately set down incidents as they actually occurred. A critic may object that I, holding this opinion, ought not to have made a free and unconditional use of these *Memoirs.* My reply shall be that I have not said that I do hold such an opinion ; all I have said is that it may be tenable, and, on the whole, it appeared to me best to use the *Memoirs* as they stood, and to leave my readers to judge of their veracity for themselves.

The preceding pages have testified to Sir Kenelm's brilliancy and celebrity ; but they have not established him as either a notable leader of men or a very profound and original thinker. Even some of his contemporaries who admitted that "he had so graceful elevation and noble Address, that had he been dropt out of the Clouds in any part of the World he would have made himself respected," qualified these praises by adding, "but then he must not have stayed there above six weeks ".*

---

* *Ath. Ox.*, vol. ii., p. 351. The word "not" is omitted in the original, obviously by mistake. The sentence makes no sense without it, and it has been quoted elsewhere (*Biog. Brit.*, vol. iii., p. 170, footnote) with the word inserted as I have put it.

He was much more remarkable for versatility than for thoroughness. He played many parts, and, with all his dignity, solemnity, and bombast, it may be doubted whether he took himself very seriously. To him, the world would appear to have been a stage, and all the men (himself included) and women merely players. Sometimes he played the sage philosopher, at others the gay courtier, at one time the pious theologian, at another the un-scrupulous libertine; and he could with equal ease act the part of the healing physician, or the murderous duellist, the astute modern diplomatist, or the almost obsolete astrologer, the coolly calculating man of science, or the superstitious dupe of the spiritualistic medium. As easily as a versatile actor, again, he could throw off one dress and put on another in the same piece. Once he wrote of Charles I. that he did " not only dedicate his ordinary attendance to him, but also his heart and all the faculties of his soul ". Once, also, he wrote concerning King Charles's chief murderer, Oliver Cromwell, " I should think my heart were not an honest one if the blood about it were not warmed with any the least imputation upon my respects and duty to his highness ".

He lived at a time when great philosophers and men of science were beginning to make a succession of dis-coveries of enormous importance; he also lived at a time when a school arose—he may almost be said to have founded it—of men who made philosophy and science their hobbies and playthings, and, by-and-by, put literature and art to the same purpose. It is needless that I should point out how this school has thriven and increased and multiplied since his days; but it may be worth while to observe that Sir Kenelm Digby had much in common with many non-professional dabblers in great subjects in our own time. He was of a good family, of ample private means, and high social standing; he had a tutor who became a bishop, he was an Oxford man, he travelled, he held office, he was an author, he was a member (indeed, he was one of the founders) of a learned society, he read papers before assemblages of savants, he bought expensive books, he tried experiments, he made religion a pastime, he was proud to number literary and scientific lions, as well as his social equals and superiors, among his intimate acquaintances and friends. There are men now of whom much the same might be said, and this it is which makes me hope that a study of the life of Sir Kenelm Digby may not be considered inopportune.

The personage—for he was essentially a personage—to whom I have introduced my readers, was very distinguished ; yet it can scarcely be said that he was extraordinarily eminent : and it can only just be said that he was an historical character ; but he who knows none but great historical characters, knows little of history, and, if it be a truism that, in order to acquire a thorough knowledge of a particular period, it is as necessary to become familiar with the habits and surroundings of its peasants as of its monarchs, it is almost as true, if less of a truism, that to the same end it is well to acquaint oneself not only with its politicians but also with its prigs.

In my early studies of Sir Kenelm Digby's life, I was at one time inclined to believe in him as a great man, at another to consider him a charlatan : a further acquaintance made me disinclined to consider him either. In the course of my work I have quoted many different opinions of his character, and it may be reasonably expected that, before finishing it, I should give my own.* Of my esti-

* The following opinion was given me by Mr. W. H. Pollock, who, after revising more than 500 articles of mine as editor of *The Saturday Review*, extended his good nature by undertaking the revision of this book : " Sir Kenelm Digby *did* go from one side to the other in religion, love, loyalty and politics. Yes—but nobody thought the worse of him for that. It was the habit of the age—an age in which nobody ought to have lived. Sir Kenelm topped the others in that, despite the age's dishonourable tendencies, he wore and kept the robes and trappings of a gentleman of honour."

mate of that character, however, I think enough will have
been inferred from what I have written in describing the
various incidents of his life, and it only remains for me to
say of it that it appears to have been prominently distinguished for one feature above all others—his amateur-
ishness. He had most of the faults and the failings and
the weaknesses of amateurs ; but at the same time he was
gifted and brilliant, as an amateur, to a very high degree ;
he was certainly the leading amateur of his period ; he
was, perhaps, the arch-amateur of all history.

It must not be supposed that, in saying this, I am
decrying the subject of my biography ; that, after
endeavouring to represent him as a hero, I have ended in
exposing him as a failure ; or that, after writing with impatience the history of a would-be philosopher, I have
finally repudiated him as "a mere amateur ". On the contrary, I submit that he occupied, not only a high position,
but a useful one. He taught by his example that philosophy, physical science and literature, far from being only
suited to professional men of the middle classes, were so
exalted that nobody was too aristocratic to engage in
them ; that they could still further ennoble the noblest ;
and that they themselves would ever be infinitely more
magnificent than their most princely votaries or students.
He proved, in his own person, that they could form the
leading interests of life to a man distinguished for his
courtly and martial bearing, for his good looks, for his
hospitality, for his brilliant conversation ; that they could
serve for the recreation of the official or the politician, for
the consolation of the widower or the prisoner, for a refuge
in disgrace or in exile ; and, perhaps best of all, that they
could supply a form of labour which should prove a refresh-
ment and a repose.

Men of intellect, with affluent circumstances and high
social position, might learn from observing Sir Kenelm
Digby the important lesson, that it was their duty rather

to graduate in several great subjects than to concentrate their energies in attaining the highest honours in any one of them, to advance the cause of learning by benefactions carefully and judiciously bestowed, to encourage the hardworking slaves of science with an intelligent, appreciative and friendly interest in their labours, and by giving them to understand that, in the exalted regions of intellectual development, they were regarded as superiors by men of the most distinguished parentage and the most ancient lineage.

For these reasons, whether the life of Sir Kenelm Digby was ill spent or well spent, so far as others were concerned it certainly was not altogether wasted.

APPENDICES.

APPENDIX A.

CHAPTER III.

ACCORDING to the *Encyclopædia Britannica* (8th ed.) wolves have been "almost extinct" in England since the end of the thirteenth century. Beeton's *Encyclopædia* dates their extinction two centuries later. It is possible that a few rare specimens may have existed, here and there, early in the seventeenth century. I take Sir Kenelm's statement as I find it. The last wolf in Scotland is said to have been killed in 1680, and in Ireland in 1710. So lately as 1891, as many as 404 wolves were killed in France, says Hadyn's *Dictionary of Dates*.

APPENDIX B.

CHAPTER III.

FROM *Poems from Sir Kenelm Digby's Papers in the Possession of Henry A. Bright, Roxburghe Club, London: Nichols & Sons,* 1877.

Note by Mr. Warner in the Appendix, page 49 :—

In the very curious *Private Memoirs* of Sir Kenelm Digby, alluded to by Mr. Bright in his Introduction, most conspicuous of the characters left unidentified by the editor is Mardontius. As to his part of the story, without entering into particulars, it is enough to say that, when Theagenes (K. D.) was abroad and had been reported dead, Stelliana (Venetia) became so intimate

U   (301)

with him as to provoke serious scandal ; that finding "she had inconsiderately brought herself so much upon the stage and submitted herself to the world's censure," for his sake, she consented to marry him ; and that she allowed him to have her portrait, which he afterwards "used to shew as a glorious trophy of her conquered affections". It is through this portrait that I am now, as I believe, enabled to identify Mardontius and to clear up a difficulty in Aubrey's well-known account of Venetia. That Stelliana attached a special importance to the picture is seen later on in the *Memoirs*, where we are told that, when Theagenes returned and was eager to renew his engagement, she refused to become his wife as long as it remained in the hands of his rival ; that Theagenes, therefore, unable to recover it in any other way, was obliged to challenge him ; and that finally Mardontius, refusing to fight in such a cause, gave it up on the field, together with a declaration withdrawing all imputations on the lady's character. Now in the Public Record Office (*Sta. Pa. Dom. James I.*, vol. clxxx., No. 13) there is the following letter, endorsed : " Richard, Erle Dorsett, his lrė to my lady Killigrew abt Mrs. Stanley's picture " :—

" Madame, I would most unwillingly lay a violation of this commandment, Thou shalt not steale, upon my brother ; yet Mrs. Stanley tells me I have not her picture, wche he tooke long since from her, but a coppy of it ; and the originall remaynes with you. To confirme this she assures me he shewed it her not long since. As at first I could not believe he would take it, conceale it, deny it as he did, so this latter fiction seemes rather a vision or a dreame then a reale thinge. Let your goodness be pleased to dissolve this riddle and to cover over with the ashes of your judgment those lively quicke imbers of an iniure so raked upp as it was forgotten till his indiscretion (wche is a word of the least weight I can lay uppon it) hath blowen and kindeled them agayne. So shall you doe a noble parte of justice, and gaine one that while he lives will be ambitious to

                           " Serve you truly,
                              " Ri. Dorset."

Comparing this with the *Private Memoirs*, there can, I think, be as little doubt that Sir Edward Sackville, Dorset's only brother

and successor, is Mardontius, as that "Mrs. Stanley" is Venetia.
But this is not all.   In his interesting notice of Venetia, Aubrey
says plainly that, before she became Digby's wife, she had been
the mistress of the writer of this letter, Richard Sackville, Earl of
Dorset ; to which he adds, that, after her marriage, "once a
yeare, the Earle of Dorset invited her and Sir Kenelme to
dinner, when the Earle would behold her with much passion and
only kisse her hand".   To the latter statement Sir Harris Nicholas
(in his Introduction to the *Private Memoirs*) replies that it is
pure imagination, as Dorset was dead before her marriage took
place ; and the answer is apparently so conclusive as to throw
discredit on Aubrey's whole story.   If, however, Edward Sackville is Mardontius, the explanation is simple enough ; for it at
once becomes evident that Aubrey has confounded Richard,
Earl of Dorset, who died in 1624, with his brother, who succeeded
him and held the title till 1652.   We have only, therefore, to
correct this mistake, and we see that in point of fact he merely
puts into definite shape what Digby admits was a common report
as to the relations between Mardontius and Stelliana of the
Memoirs.   At the same time, of course, the ingenious, if not convincing, defence Digby there offers of his heroine's conduct now
holds equally good against Aubrey's charges.

APPENDIX C.

CHAPTER V.

I ADMIT that here, as well as in one or two other places, I have
made omissions which considerably lower the colouring of the
narrative, and have the effect of slightly altering its character.   In
pleading guilty to this offence, my excuse must be that I wished
to render my story readable for ladies, and if I have left out, or
modified, certain incidents, I have not substituted fiction for fact,
by inserting others in their places.

APPENDIX D.

I HAVE found it necessary to curtail considerably the details given
by Sir Kenelm Digby of this incident.   Moreover, it is not at all

impossible that his own account of it may be somewhat exaggerated.

APPENDIX E.

THE following is from a list of the works of Sir Kenelm Digby given by Wood (*Athenae Oxoniensis*, vol. ii., pp. 352-3), but some of these, as Chalmers says (*Biographical Dictionary*, vol. xi., p. 79), were probably "published after his decease by one Hartman, who was his operator, and who put his name in the title-page, with a view of recommending compositions very unworthy of him to the public".

Letter giving an account of the Fight with the Venetians in the Bay of Scanderoon.

Conference with a Lady about choice of Religion. Paris, 1638. London, 1654.

Observations upon Religio Medici. London, 1643-44.

Treatise of the Nature of Bodies. Paris, 1644. London, 1658.

Treatise of the Nature of Man's Soul. Paris, 1644. London, 1645, 1658 and 1669.

Observations on the 22nd Stanza in the ninth Canto of Spenser's " Faerie Queen ". London, 1644.

Institutionum peripateticarum libri quinque cum appendice Theologica de origine mundi. Paris, 1651. English translation by Thos. White. London, 1656.

Letters to Lord George Digby concerning Religion. London, 1651.

Of the Cure of Wounds by the Powder of Sympathy. London, 1658, 1660, 1669.

Discourse concerning the Vegetation of Plants. London, 1661, 1669. Amsterdam (in Latin), 1663.

Choice and experimental Receipts in Physic and Chirurgery.

Cordial and distilled Waters and Spirits, Perfumes and other Curiosities. This and the above were published by Hartman, " some time Steward to Sir Kenelme the Collector ". London, 1668. Paris (in Latin), 1677.

His Closet Opened. London, 1669, 1677.

Excellent Directions for Cookery.   London, 1669, 1677.

Choice Collection of rare Chymical Secrets and Experiments in Philosophy. As also of rare and unheard of Medicines, Menstruums and Alkahests, with the true secret of volatising the Salt of Tarter. London, 1682.

Letter to Dr. Sam. Turner concerning the Church and the Revenues thereof.   London, 1646-7.   This is doubted by Wood.

A Treatise of Adhering to God.   London, 1644.

INDEX OF PROPER NAMES.

N.B.—*n* only = note.

U*

www.ingramcontent.com/pod-product-compliance
Lightning Source LLC
Chambersburg PA
CBHW020942030726
47496CB00005B/1320